HILL OF GRACE

Stephen Orr works as a high school teacher in Adelaide's northern suburbs. His first novel, *Attempts to Draw Jesus*, was the runner-up in the 2000 Vogel/*Australian* award. Stephen conducts writing workshops with school groups and was the judge of the 2003 *Advertiser* Young Writers' Award.

HILL OF GRACE

Stephen Orr

Wakefield Press

Wakefield Press
1 The Parade West
Kent Town
South Australia 5067
www.wakefieldpress.com.au

First published 2004

Cover designed by Liz Nicholson, designBITE
Text designed and typeset by Ryan Paine, Wakefield Press
Printed and bound by Hyde Park Press

National Library of Australia
Cataloguing-in-publication entry

Orr, Stephen, 1967–   .
Hill of Grace.

ISBN 1 86254 648 7.

I. Title.

A823.4

Publication of this book was assisted by the
Commonwealth Government through the Australia
Council, its arts funding and advisory body.

My father believed that grace was like cinnamon sprinkled onto a freshly baked teacake. It was like icing sugar, or dandruff, settling on people's hands and faces. It was the love of God. As he always reminded us, grace was the potential for belief, for salvation (or so Luther had said). This is why William Miller ended up so angry. He could never understand why others couldn't see such a simple thing.

William Miller saw the world in black and white, when it was really a landscape full of yellow calendulas and a deep blue sky.

NM

PART

One

Chapter One

William Miller believed in the end of the world.

To him it was as real as the odour in Christ's sandals, or all the business of water into wine. It was as real as the saucepan constellation, or the taste of his wife Bluma's rhubarb crumble. It was as certain as a finely balanced algebraic equation or the week, or day, the autumn leaves turned on his vines.

William Miller had gone beyond wondering, guessing or suspecting. His study of the Bible had revealed clues and facts missed by others. They spoke of a time when Christ would return and walk confidently down Adelaide's seediest streets – through workplaces and pubs, backyards and grocery stores – gathering the faithful.

From the day William Miller began to believe, he knew it was all just a matter of waiting: singing hymns and worshipping, playing kegel and perfecting his merlot-shiraz blend. Giving and receiving love, these were important too. Bluma and Nathan, his son, were angels with frantically flapping wings, holding him under the shoulders, lifting him.

But none of this was as important as God, and his son, who *it was written*, was due to return any time.

William stood in front of his oldest shiraz vines, rolling a grape between his fingers. With only a slight pressure the skin split and grape-juice ran down his hand. Tasting it with his tongue he smiled and whispered, 'A few more weeks,' recognising the unmistakable iron of his soil and purity of his ground water.

He squinted and off, down Langmeil Road, saw a boy climbing a date palm like a monkey. The boy slipped and he held his breath. Beyond, in the near distance, he could see some fires on the Kaiserstuhl, the highest of the hills which enclosed the Barossa Valley, keeping them safe from the suburbs of Adelaide which had started creeping north like rampant lantana.

Throwing the grape into a carpet of yellow harlequin he turned and made his way towards the house. Stopping in front of Bluma's vegie patch he picked a dozen moths off the cabbages and pocketed a cucumber to eat after tea. 'No pesticides, ever,' he'd bragged to Bruno Hermann, one of his neighbours with a fetish for the perfect blutwurst. 'Impossible,' Bruno had replied, although William knew better.

If William were mostly right, it was because Bluma allowed him to be. Every few months she'd dust the cabbages and hide the container in the back of her cold cellar. She would mix curry, which he claimed he couldn't stand and wouldn't touch, into stews he'd describe longingly to strangers waiting to be served at Linke's butcher.

William detested luxuries, but Bluma lived a secret life of sorts, surviving on distractions put before them by the very devil himself. Sitting beside a neighbour's wireless, she'd close her eyes and slip into another world as Nat King Cole described love. Romantic love, that is, not the practical, toe-nails and all love she knew. Beyond Tanunda things were different, it seemed: men wore clothes with at least a faint whiff of style, bought books of poetry (which they read to their wives) and ate meat they hadn't slaughtered themselves.

Unlike Tanunda men.

Like her husband, William Miller, talking to himself in Barossa Deutsch, scraping a cow pat from the tread of his boots with a stick that kept snapping. William Miller, with his neatly trimmed chin whiskers and his electricity-free existence. Electricity meant bills and bills meant servitude and, worse, people reading your meter, keeping your details in a filing cabinet and counting you amongst the throng. Like the army of ants which covered every inch of his old myrtle, scurrying to and fro with no apparent purpose, driving to keep moving and working until the End arrived. The End: an apocalypse of atomic flashes and sulphur dioxide – a moment which William simulated with his shit-tipped stick, bashing the trunk until there was a complete frenzy. Ants minus the message of Revelations and Daniel.

This, he guessed, is what the End would be like – people loading their possessions into carts and car boots, driving away from the sun as it engulfed the sky, while he and Bluma knelt in a soft sea of gazania and prayed. The secrets of the seven scrolls revealed at last, as dressmakers and bakers screamed in the distance and Friesian cattle moaned inconsolably as their bodies burned.

Imagining all this was a daily joy for William, who sat in the swing he'd hung for Nathan (years ago, when he was a small boy) and listened as the bough of his myrtle creaked beneath his weight. He started to swing in ever-increasing arcs, smiling, pushing back his head and watching the world fly by in a blur of clouds and tree tops, birds (half sound, half movement) and the smoke of the Kaiserstuhl fires. This, to him, was the End. A blur of everything real becoming unreal, as body was transformed into spirit and the world into a new heaven of familiar things: an eternity of sauerkraut, God's reward for those who'd stayed faithful.

The list included all of the Millers, from Anthelm, his grand-father, who migrated from Posen in 1844, to his father Robert, who helped Anthelm build the family farm. Through to Nathan, William's own son, who would continue it on. Although there would be an End it was important the land was taken care of and farmed properly, the alternative being a heaven of weeds and Anglican idleness. The ironstone farm house William stood before was Anthelm's legacy to him, as were the vines. The weight on his shoulders was the weight of knowing, of needing to know more, and to convince others.

William walked past Bluma's herbs, touching the cross on his back door and entering. Bluma was still busy in her Schwarze Kuche, a medieval black kitchen in the form of a hearth of flagstones which she stood on to cook, feeding the smells and heat of sausage and corned beef into a giant chimney-cum-smoke-house. 'Ready?' she asked, washing the last of the pots in a sink as deep as it was wide.

'Not yet,' William replied, sitting down at the dining-table next to Nathan and casting an eye across his books.

'The Rasch's have started picking,' she continued, but William pointed out they were still on whites. 'When Henschke starts I'll start,' he said, spreading his fingers like a web above Nathan's algebra.

'How long?' she harped.

'Two, three weeks.'

But she knew she'd have him out long before that, considering he didn't have the bother of chardonnay or semillon, large produc-tion runs or interstate markets.

'The search for x,' William smiled, studying Nathan's book up closely. 'If x is addition, it has to jump to subtract.'

'I know,' Nathan replied.

'Here for instance, two step, which of the numbers is linked more closely to x?'

'William!' Bluma moaned, wiping hair from her eyes with her forearm. 'It's not the maths we studied.'

'It is.'

William knew Nathan understood, but he had the hankering to explain it anyway, in his words, words more fluid and under-standable than any maths teacher. Words which could make sense of Baume (to everyone except Bluma), the Cartesian plane and Corinthians. Words wrapped in a gentle poetry which made the complex simple, the unfathomable obvious. And in algebra, just as in Revelations, the clues were there for those who looked: $2x + 5$ equals 25. So, obviously, x equals ten, but what about more complex problems? Explained just as simply through observation – rules and patterns. What was hinted at in Matthew was repeated in Mark; what was suggested in John was explained in Daniel.

A thorough study of the whole was necessary for an under-standing of the parts.

William took the cucumber from his pocket and bit into it. Nathan kept scribbling as Bluma drained the sink. An example of her white-work hung below a half-cured ham: *Kinder, Kuche und Kirche*—which might have been enough for the old Lutherans, but didn't begin to explain her. The white thread on white cloth had grown grey and fat-stained over the years, filled with the steam and smoke of a thousand lamb shanks.

William opened his family Bible and flicked pages through his fingers. He smelt the mustiness of old paper and, as he did every time, admired the clumsy copperplate of his grand-dad inside the front cover: *I come to Klemzig in 1844 (24). I move to Tanunda in 1849 (29). I marry Marg. in 1868. Robert come from Lord in ad 1870.*

The saga continuing in William's father's hand, explaining how he'd married William's mother Brigid in 1898, delivering up the child Wilhelm Muller in 1901. *W. Muller, come from the gracious arms of the Lord Jesus* ... And William wondering again, as he did every time, if it wasn't time to change his name back and whether Anthelm and Robert would have been ashamed of what he'd done, considering they'd retained their names during the First World War.

Different thing all together, Bluma would console. Hitler's war had been longer, brewing in an atmosphere of anti-kraut hysteria that had its epicentre (again) in Adelaide. Just the same, it had been six years since it all ended, maybe it was time for William to return to Wilhelm, for Miller to restore the Muller honour.

The photos of Loveday Internment Camp were still in his mind, set out proudly on the front page of Adelaide's daily *Advertiser*. And although he'd narrowly avoided a visit, the headline was still clear in his mind: Who Can Tell A Nazi Spy? Taking him even further back to a stinking hot day in March 1918, when he watched his father almost come to blows with a train conductor who wouldn't accept his pass.

Bluma sat down opposite them and William looked at Nathan, who cleared his exercise books and maths text and bowed his head.

'Jesus Christ, Saviour,' William began, laying aside his half-eaten cucumber as they joined hands. 'Guide our devotion, as we're inspired by the words of your companion Matthew.'

As they did every night at this time, Nathan's thoughts drifted off across the school oval to assignations more Janet Leigh than Luther, to landscapes more Picasso than Barossa. And in remembering his odd, occasional romantic embrace (mostly imagined), he contemplated a world full of more fire and excitement than anything in the Bible. As his father's voice drifted into his ears it wasn't Jesus he described as much as the possibility of underwear; it wasn't the Gospels as much as a stray page of D.H. Lawrence. Not so much the tribes of Israel as tribes of atheistic Commie hordes over-running Asia.

If Bluma was not entirely with William, it was because she knew the Gospel of Matthew better than her very own brother. She sat with her head bowed, breathing shallow breaths of smoked meat and the riddle of seventy times seven.

William started reading. '"The Pharisees also came unto him . . ."' Droning on until the bells of Langmeil Lutheran tolled nine and he closed his gigantic Bible to mixed feelings of relief and immolation.

The next morning William and Nathan set off, as they did every Saturday, in search of papers and yeast. Passing by the dry stone walls near Seppelt's, William stopped to pick a bunch of belladonna lilies for Bluma. He sniffed them but there was nothing there, only the hot, pink flowers of a hundred Tanunda roadsides. Off in the distance the colour faded to the monotony of blue gums and sugar gums and the odd river red clinging desperately to life beside Jacob's dried-up creek.

Beyond the Kaiserstuhl the Flaxman Valley floated olive and treeless above the horizon. The High Eden Ridge stretched east towards Cambrai, taking with it endless grasslands which were destined for the vine. So far it was just a few Angus cows, and paddocks eaten clean by merino sheep and rabbits. Dams full of brown water spotted the landscape like crater holes. Granite outcrops erupted like pimples from far below the earth, making otherwise arable land unworkable.

As they passed the Langmeil Lutheran Church, William jumped up the few crumbling steps (another working-bee for him to organise) to the notice board. Tomorrow would be an easy day. Ian Doms was usher and Bruno Hermann, William's blutwurst neighbour, welcomer. William could sit back and enjoy listening to the pastor, Henry Hoffmann, a Tanunda treasure, whose sermons linked the Bible to the daily lives of his parishioners in ways William could only marvel at. The way in which Adelaide became Babylon, Rundle Street the temple of money-changers and the twin towns of Tanunda-Nuriootpa themselves, a new Jerusalem. The way in which Emperor Wilhelm Friedrich became Satan (not in so many words) and Sir Robert Menzies a glowing saint on a holy card, stepping out the red devils surging down from the North. Even Premier Playford got a mention, praised for speaking out against the Asiatic hordes who'd like nothing more than to re-populate the Barossa with gin stills and opium farms.

There were immigrants and there were immigrants. Some bringing the vine, others the rice paddy. The Greeks, maybe, could be tolerated, spreading their souvlaki song-lines down the already cast-over Hell that was Hindley Street. But hot on their heels would be the Serbs and Croats and Bulgarians with their body odour. Mandolins and the Commie manifesto in Tanunda's Goat Square. This was the miracle of Pastor Henry, warning them against foreigners. Amongst all this cultural baggage (although Hitler was never mentioned) Pastor Henry's thoughts were never more than a step away from Loveday Internment Camp.

William and Nathan passed Jenke's winery, the heavy smell of grape-must blowing over through canopies of coppiced carob. 'Too soon,' William whispered, watching workers in singlets unloading grapes.

'Maybe they ripened earlier,' Nathan offered.

William didn't answer, smoothing his chin whiskers and contemplating the A-bomb. One of the reasons he bought newspapers: to gather evidence of the End. Every Saturday, every local and national paper. Taking them home, spreading them out on his dining-table, scissors at the ready. Every time there was something about the Koreans or Russians, snip snip, laying them out on the table as Bluma took a pot of home-made glue and stuck them in his scrap-book, writing the date and source, wiping off the excess and smoothing them down. A Saturday ritual, sipping coffee and eating Streuselkuchen as Nathan sat in the corner with a book and just wondered.

William believed if he gathered enough evidence about the bomb and its keepers with their belief in evolution and the need to share capital, then others would see what he could see. Man as a product of apes? The forsaking of farms for factories. People who didn't make their own cheese or grow their own gherkins. It was all there, cross-referenced in an index: A-bomb, Automat, Barrymore, Chaplin, China, Communism, Durkheim, Einstein . . .

William and Nathan entered the Apex bakery, William with his papers, Nathan with his tennis racket. William smiled at Bruno's and Edna's grand-daughter, whose name he could never remember, and ordered honey cakes for his whole family. Nathan, not much younger than the girl, rolled his eyes for her benefit and started kicking the strings of the racket against his tennis shoes. 'Don't do that,' William scolded, reminding him how they couldn't afford a press.

'Have you heard, Mr Miller,' the girl began, smiling, baiting him, 'the British are going to test a bomb next year?'

William shook his head. 'In Australia?'

Nathan smiled. 'The Barossa?'

Lilli looked at William. 'Place up north. Middle of the desert. Maralinga.'

As she wrapped his honey cakes and put them in a bag beside a half pound of the bakery's yeast, William watched her fingers become the legs of a spider, crawling down from China towards South Australia, consuming everything and everyone in its path. 'The British are too quick to be with the Americans,' he observed, to which she replied, 'It took both of them to stop the Fascists.'

'*He* was the least of our concerns,' Miller continued.

She smiled one last time and gave him his change. 'We're all quick to change our tune.'

'Not me,' he trailed off, as he dropped the coins in his pocket and exited the shop.

William sat under a pencil pine and ate his cake as he watched Nathan lose again. Bluma had warned him to keep his comments to himself: Nathan had threatened to stop playing if William kept coaching him from the sidelines. 'Backhand, Nathan, both hands ... watch your footing!' A shop-keeper's son from Gawler demolished him in straight sets and they were soon walking home across paddocks overgrown with freesias and wood sorrel.

As they went, William's landscape smelt more of sulphur than must, was lit more by atomic flashes than the dusty summer light over the Pewsey Vale Peak. Nathan, meanwhile, had other thoughts on his mind: Lilli Fechner's green, translucent eyes, her Shirley Temple dimples and her uncanny ability to say something without saying it. Lilli, his hero, the only girl he knew who could publicly humiliate his father without him knowing.

William Miller passed along the creek which formed the bottom boundary of his property. Wild olive trees, their fruit only of interest to the crows, clung to the banks where floods had washed away the silt and exposed their roots. A white flowering iris crept down from a fallow paddock but mostly the creek was just rocks and the murky water they shared with the Seppelts.

Harlequin flowers ranged yellow to orange as they followed the path up toward the showground. Off amongst his carnations, Arthur Blessitt, the Miller's other neighbour, worked on his knees debudding stems as straight as a Cartesian plane. 'Coming?' William called, across a paddock Arthur had turned over to roses.

'Of course,' he replied, standing and shaking his head. 'Go on without me, I've finished the new pins.'

Arthur watched William continue on toward the showgrounds then made for his lean-to laundry to wash up. After cleaning his face and the back of his neck he grabbed a few bottles of home-brewed beer, his three new kegel pins and set off in a scurry along a path of wild oats William had laid flat.

Arthur had turned over his property, not entirely forsaking his vines, to cut flowers: lisianthus, carnations, wallflowers, calendulas and in summer, endless fields of sunflowers. Everybody thought he was loopy, although William knew he was making money packing them off to Adelaide twice a week. Department stores, florists and the odd fruit shop had come over to his way of thinking: where others had started making plastic azaleas, he would make a killing with the real thing.

Arthur was a confirmed bachelor, the only child of parents who'd smothered him with love then demanded he go out to find a bride. He'd brought a few girls home to meet them and they'd quickly sized them up, dismissing them as entirely inadequate. Arthur, who was more interested in his woodwork and flowers anyway, was happy to let a future of nagging and baby vomit pass him by.

He called after William but saw that his friend was caught up in the cries of a flock of sulphur-crested cockatoos come to feed on the soft female cones of a native pine.

William arrived at the Kegelbahn and put his jacket on the back of a chair. He deposited his few drinks and wurst and said to Julius Rechner, Nathan's history teacher at the Lutheran school, 'Arthur is on his way.'

The kegel club was a single-lane bowling alley built in the form of a long shed. Wives took it in turn to stand at the far end of the alley, re-setting the wooden pins and returning the balls down an angled gutter lined with white cotton. The men stood about in the shed proper, drinking, telling lies about their working weeks and wishing there was another kegel club for them to compete against.

But there wasn't. They only had each other, week after week, taking turns to tabulate the same pitiful scores on the same commandeered blackboard, courtesy of Julius.

'What sort of history are you teaching these kids?' William joked to Julius. 'Too much of the Austrian. Not enough of the Prussian.' Referring to Hitler, the upstart who'd been responsible for the demise of their social club and the Goethe Institute.

Arthur entered, dropping the new pins on the wooden floor. 'Let's look at these,' began Trevor Streim, president of the club, as he picked them up and ran his hands over the oak Arthur had sanded smooth.

'An exact copy,' Arthur smiled, putting down his beers and producing the original he'd used as a model.

'Good.' Trevor smiled, holding up a copy against the original. 'But how will they perform?'

'The same properties,' Arthur defended.

'Still,' Trevor half-sung, motioning for Rechner's son to run them up to the ladies.

'Oak develops a ripeness with age,' Arthur continued, trying to bring perspective, seeing how Trevor Streim was intent on stacking his pins up against others which had been used since the club opened in 1858.

Mrs Trevor Streim, the first and best matriarch of the Tanunda Kegelbahn, replaced three of the nine pins with Arthur's and stood back. The room fell quiet as Trevor took a ball and launched it down the lane. It was a strike, of course. As the pins tumbled Arthur pretended to listen but only Trevor could actually hear the dead lignin in the very heart of the pin. As they clattered and settled all eyes turned to the president. 'Close,' he said, 'but I can still tell the difference.'

Rubbish, Arthur thought, having spent endless hours choosing the right wood and turning it on a lathe in his workshop. 'You must have the ears of a bat,' he said, lifting his eyebrows – and for a moment everyone sensed an insurrection.

'It takes a Weidemann hand,' William said, to break the silence and lighten the mood, referring to Arthur Blessitt as Artur Weidemann, another of the valley's name-changers who wasn't yet comfortable changing back.

'Of course,' Trevor said, retreating. 'Only Arthur could make such a precise copy. Prosit, Arthur.'

And with this they all toasted Arthur, although Arthur himself was unhappy with his work being thought of as a copy, compared to its true status as *a thing unto itself*. In the same way his crucified Christs and scale-model Rx 93 steam were things unto themselves, representing the familiar but in a style which was distinctly Arthur's. This is what the Streims of the world couldn't understand. The carpet of wood-shavings and saw-dust on his workshop floor attested to this – the finely sharpened chisels and his grandfather's well-oiled lathe. Precise, razor-sharp pencil marks which were followed to the thousandth of an inch, his leather tool-belt and half moon bifocals – these were the signs of a true artisan.

Arthur and William walked home through the showgrounds, set up for Angus cattle the size of elephants and the dill cucumber championship which Trevor's wife regularly won. Passing through the Langmeil graveyard Arthur stopped to show William his grandfather's headstone, cracked neatly down the middle but refusing to yield. The vineleaf-entwined anchor still sung of Hessen and Posen, the town's founding father, August Kavel, and the promise of thirty-five bushels to the acre. As they made their way back along the familiar creek, William stopped to pick up a tin can he saw reflected in the moonlight. And said, 'This is the future, if we don't watch ourselves.'

On Saturday night, as the Seppelt date palms cast long shadows across the paddocks of West Tanunda, and the sun dipped and flattened itself against a horizon of stray eucalypts, William stood with his hands on his hips in his darkening kitchen as Bluma paced out their living space. 'Thirty by twenty-four, that's . . .'

William furrowed his brow. 'Seventy-two square . . . around eight yards.'

Bluma's eyes lit up. 'William, we could afford at least one room.'

'Bluma.'

'This floor's no good for my lungs.'

14

Bluma had read that patterned lino was out for thirty-seven shillings and sixpence a yard at the Big Store. Still, what was the point? William wouldn't have a bar of it. Just like the suits they were practically giving away at five-and-a-half shillings. Same story. She knew he was determined to go on wearing Robert's. 'This suit is so dated,' she'd argue, but in the same way he'd retained his chin whiskers, he would retain his dad's clothes. As long as they still fit and as long as the naphthalene did its job.

'I'm late,' he said, consulting Anthelm's fob-watch, slipping on his jacket and making for the door.

'At least consider it,' she pleaded, brushing him down as he left.

As the sun disappeared below the horizon the Langmeil bells rang out across the town, as they did from Gnadenberg and Strait Gate and every other church throughout the valley, reminding everyone that tomorrow was a day of worship.

William made his way between an avenue of candle pines which led up a hill to Langmeil. At the top, in front of the church's open oak doors, Joshua Heinz stood smiling, watching William's progress and sucking on a pipe.

'Evening,' William greeted him, crunching gravel and stepping over the crumbling steps. 'Is everyone here?'

'Just about,' Joshua replied. 'Apart from Carl Sobels, he sends his apology, apparently his daughter-in-law's in hospital.'

'Serious?'

'The voices again. She's soft, if you ask me.'

'Satan,' William smiled. 'What she needs is a good praying over.'

'Running over,' Joshua grinned at his old friend, tapping out the used tobacco.

Joshua lived in a three-roomed cottage with his wife and six children, all of whom slept in a single room with triple bunks which Sarah, his eldest, had pointed out, were no different from the ones in Auschwitz. He supported them by selling insurance, and at harvest, helping out with picking here and there. His Bible was just as well worn as William's, but he didn't share his friend's fixation with the promises of Revelations. I'm happy with an old-fashioned Jesus, he'd say to William. A Jesus who buys insurance and stops my milk from curdling.

While the Tanunda Liedertafel set up for Saturday night's rehearsal in the Langmeil vestry, the wives of the singers gathered in William's lino-less living-room, talking, drinking coffee and stuffing a quilt for Mary Hicks' daughter Ellen. It was an impromptu Federschleissen, a quilting-bee sustained by Bluma's finest rhubarb crumble. The feathers were replaced by a synthetic stuffing Bluma had ordered from a catalogue but not told William about. The coffee was instant – again, hidden in the cold cellar.

Back at Langmeil, William and Joshua sat among the small group, waiting for their conductor Harry Rasch. There were only three more Saturdays before Farm Day, their annual celebration of cucumbers and cows, work-wear, boots and demonstrator tractors.

As it generally always did, William's and Joshua's conversation drifted onto the North Koreans and the 38th Parallel, which could only lead to China and the bomb. William excitedly broke the news of Maralinga and Emu Plains, but Joshua already knew. 'I'm keeping a scrapbook,' William explained. 'I'm gathering documentary evidence.'

'Of what?' Joshua asked.

'Clues ... God speaks through the papers too, Joshua.'

Joshua Heinz thought about this and replied, 'Where is it written in the Bible, that this would be the time?'

William had to stop to think. 'Revelations.'

'Yes?'

But then realised he couldn't link it to the Bible, yet.

'The thing is,' Joshua continued, 'people have been looking for clues, and finding them, for two thousand years.'

William lit up, remembering a pasted article. 'What about Lake Eyre? First time it's flooded since white man.'

Joshua shrugged. 'William, there's always something going on: a bushfire, a flood ...'

William stared at the calluses on his hands and wondered whether he didn't have some work to do yet. 'I'll find it, and I'll show you,' he whispered.

'He's overdue,' Joshua agreed, consolingly, 'but if you're not careful people will laugh at you.'

'Who would?' Ron Rohwer asked, settling in behind them. Josh turned to him. 'Hello, Ron, we were just wondering –'

'When he's ready,' Ron smiled, moving his stare across to William. 'Wilhelm, you been reading the stars again?'

'Who'll be beside his throne?' William asked bluntly, refusing to have this conversation with Ron again.

'We all will. It's not helpful, Wilhelm.'

William stopped short, biting his tongue, shelving his lecture about Artaxerxes and the winepress of God's furious anger and his embryonic ideas about the 'prophetic period' as it related to Christ's ministry. Bluma had warned him off Ron Rohwer, seeing how Ron was an Elder at Langmeil, holding considerable sway within the congregation. Joshua was right, he had to have more than a few old clippings. He needed dates and facts as they were laid down in the Bible. Joshua was right also, of course, in saying many had mis-read the signs of their own time – describing the Egyptian village which, in 1912, stuffed and took to worshipping a dog that had been killed by a meteorite – but William had a gut feeling that *he* was right.

Harry Rasch arrived and produced his baton from a velvet-lined case. Soon they were set upon a song of praise which they would sing beside more gentle folk tunes.

Praise to the Lord, who doth prosper thy work and defend thee,
Surely his goodness and mercy shall attend thee . . .

As William used his ear to find harmony and fit his voice within the layers of song, all he could hear was the slightly flat bass of Rohwer in his ear, droning, threatening to upset the balance. He could imagine himself turning and shouting, 'Shut up!' but again could only hear Bluma warning him off.

Bluma stoked the fire of her black kitchen as the ladies' fingers darted over faultless seams the Big Store could only dream about.

'"Ponder anew, What the Almighty can do ..."' they sang, in harmonies less figured but just as lusty in their delivery.

Nathan Miller sat in the raised loft above the living-room which was his bedroom. He heard the women's melody but substituted his own words. '"Praise the Lord, the Almighty King of Pricks, under the table, with a dozen lopped dicks ..."'

Chapter Two

William stood in front of Langmeil with his hands behind his back, bobbing rhythmically to the song of a bar-tailed godwit in the candle pines. He read from the notice-board as the spirit of Kavel, Lutheran pioneer, drifted in fitful gusts from the cemetery.

> *Sunday School, 9.45, Herb Medlin and the older children will lead using the theme 'Ascension of Jesus' based on Acts 1: 6–11. Mrs Fox will provide the music.*

As they waited for the rostered usher, Ian Doms, to open the church doors, Bluma picked dead-heads off roses and Nathan sat on the steps crushing soursobs between his fingers. William looked at him – 'Nathan . . .' – and went on to survey a range of notices, from next week's quilting through to the sale of a washer with motorised wringer, near new, all offers over thirty pounds considered.

The bells started ringing and William, recognising Bruno's erratic style, knocked on the doors. 'Bruno, open up.' Ian arrived with his keys and started working on the cast-iron lock which hardly ever opened from the outside. 'Here, give me a go,' William demanded, but Ian was already halfway around to the back door.

The Millers stood before the locked doors silently as the bells stopped and William heard the voices of Bruno and Ian chatting. He fancied he could hear them laughing. 'Bruno, Ian,' William called, knocking even louder, but the laughing just started again. William shook his head and made his way around the back.

Bluma stepped towards the notices and admired a poster of

Victor Mature and Susan Heywood in *Demetrius and the Gladiators*. 'Unlike Pastor Henry,' she whispered to her son.

'It's a charity event,' he replied, glowing with visions of Christian-full lions parading before the Emperor with contented grins.

As the bells started again the Tanunda Lutheran faithful closed doors on warm cottages and made their way along streets of arum and belladonna lilies, under date palms heavy with fruit and past half-empty churches of every other denomination. William believed that the Catholic church, built in the 1890s, still stood for everything unreformed and unrefined, Father Pallhuber celebrating mass on behalf of dour, corpulent popes with a hankering for gold and choir boys. The Methodists had come to Tanunda too, in the form of a dozen or so Wesleyans with a seeder and combine. Their wheat purchased a plot and built a church on Irvine Street, away from the real business of a German god brandishing mettwurst and thunderbolts. The descendants of the twelve still made their way to Irvine Street every Sunday but they were the religious white trash of the valley.

Arthur Blessitt, out inspecting trial plots of strelitzia and Geraldton wax, heard the Langmeil bells, stood up, adjusted his tie and headed off towards town. Stopping in at Mr Wilmhurst's, Tanunda's gout-stricken blacksmith, he dropped off a pot of raw beef tea which he promised would have him up and about in no time. Passing the Savings Bank and Turner's dress shop, he turned into Langmeil's avenue of candle pines and crossed himself, over-come by a spirit stronger than an ocean of chamomile or reservoirs of barley water. '"Our help is in the name of the Lord,"' he whis-pered, making his way towards the steps, where Bruno Hermann shook his hand and handed him the order of service and hymnal, asking about the progress of his grandson's pillow box. 'One more week, Bruno, I promise. I was sold green wood. I refuse to work with green wood.'

Meanwhile, Joshua Heinz pulled the youngest of his six children off Menge's spotlights, a pair of Electricity Trust surplus spots rigged up in an enclosed bunker no one had bothered to fill in since the war. Anton Menge, trying to prove his, and his town's, loyalty during the Second World War, had painted the lights with crude Union Jacks held by an emu and kangaroo, in anticipation of stukas and dorniers on the horizon. Joshua stood behind his children and clapped his hands twice, saying, 'Walk on,' and smiling at Catherine, his wife. His children continued single file, along the road, up the avenue of pines and into the church.

Just as Ian Doms was about to give Edna Hermann the nod to start playing, he saw Seymour Hicks at the bottom of the avenue, unloading his family from a converted hearse he'd purchased at Syd Wenham's 1940 fire-sale. Seymour's wife, Mary, walked up the slight incline arm-in-arm with their daughter Ellen Tabrar, followed closely behind by her husband Joseph and their three children. Joseph was a Lutheran by marriage, a not-so-religious postal worker who still lived with his in-laws, although he had plans – to build, to move his family away from the Hicks', to bring his children up in a suburban paradise of couch and short-leaved fescue.

If Joshua was in William's left ear, Seymour was forever in his right, whispering how William was right to be worried about Revelations and its hidden dates. Seymour was the straight man, feeding lines, encouraging a friendship that stretched back thirty years. Seymour was six-foot-two and lanky, pot-bellied and unstable enough to sway in the wind at family barbecues. He talked softly but meant every word he said. Life was serious, the Bible said so.

'Seymour will be forever parking the hearse,' Mary Hicks said to Bruno, looking to Edna and giving the nod as her daughter seated the children at the back and asked Ian if Herb Medlin was still taking Sunday School.

Edna played her own version of *O Heilige Dreifaltigkeit*, a morning hymn, as the congregation hushed in anticipation. When she finished, Ian Doms stood up and asked the children to follow Herb Medlin and Mrs Fox into the vestry. Nathan watched on, newly graduated himself, wondering what he'd do when he replaced Herb, when the Goebbels of the vestry took two weeks off to visit his rellies in Brizzie.

Apart from Mr Wilmhurst, tucked up in bed with his raw beef tea, the congregation was complete. On one side the men, fortifying themselves with peppermints and Altona drops, on the other side the women, holding methane-heavy bowels closed against the cold of Langmeil.

On the men's side, at the front, a row of church Elders sat respectfully: Gunther Fritschle, an old-school Lutheran whom William had given up on, knowing Gunther himself had given up on Christ-made-real amongst them; Ron Rohwer, William's singing companion, the eternally flat baritone droning away in his left ear; Trevor Streim, the man who understood the elusiveness of the perfect pin, its form as unknowable as the face of Christ himself.

And the parishioners: Bruno Hermann, William's neighbour, and his wife Edna, straining to focus on sheet music she generally disregarded; Bruno and Edna's children and grandchildren, including Lilli Fechner, searching out Nathan across the aisle, Ian, Arthur, the Millers, the Heinzes and the Hicks', Julius Rechner and many more silent, featureless faces, in churches across the valley, summoned by imported Silesian bells, singing hymns in a dis-harmony as subtle and yet obvious as Menge's two spotlights.

Pastor Henry approached the altar and the congregation rose. '"In the name of the Father and of the Son and of the Holy Spirit,"' he intoned, straightening his robes and trying to conceal an un-movable beetroot stain. 'Amen,' the congregation echoed, as Edna adjusted her stool and started in on a hymn of Invocation.

The service continued via yawns and wandering thoughts, lofty messages sent and received in mixed and muddled ways. The Confession of Sins and the Introit, the Kyrie and the Gloria, mostly stolen and re-packaged from the Catholic church.

'"Glory to God in the highest,"' Henry sang, modulating through a variety of keys.

'"And on earth peace,"' the congregation replied, '"among men with whom He is pleased."'

The Salutation and the Collect, standing up and sitting down, fathers cuing sons and mothers cuing daughters, altar boys tempted by coin, the faithful careful to show they were adding pounds not pence and passing it on with a rattle and the knowledge that God had seen anyway.

After the business was complete, Henry climbed his pulpit and looked out across a nearly full church. His fingers ran across the smooth varnish covering some of Arthur Blessitt's best chisel work. The repairs dated back to when Arthur had been an apprentice to one of Ewald Graetz's sons. Although Henry could've chosen one of the Graetzes themselves, one night he found himself traipsing through Arthur's early experiments in floriculture, arriving at his door and knocking and saying, 'I have some work for you, Arthur.' Seeing as the Graetzes had plenty of work anyway, and Arthur was just starting off. Henry knew it was best to spread the work around, that was the Lutheran way, and strangely enough, the Australian way.

Henry smiled a smile which seemed to reach everyone. 'The Old Testament lesson is written in the eighth chapter of Deuteronomy, beginning at the first verse.' And with that he was off, explaining how the Bible, and God himself, had given men licence to live, increase in number and occupy promised land. Such as the Barossa, with its metaphor of vines as people made real, pruned by Jesus and harvested by God, the sinners thrown into the winepress to make cheap, undrinkable claret.

Meanwhile, in the vestry, Herb Medlin had his charges lined up, dressed like so many wise men in search of a star, swathed in flannelette sheets and Onkaparinga rugs gone seedy. The youngest Heinz had borrowed his father's pipe to try and look even wiser but Herb grabbed it from his mouth and said, 'You're in search of Jesus, not a pair of comfy slippers.'

Back in the church, Henry passed from the Epistle to the Hallelujah and eventually to the hymn of the day, *Ein Feste Burg*. William wasn't inspired with Henry's choice of material, dwelling in the church militant when he should've been more celebrational.

> *A mighty fortress is our God,*
> *A trusty shield and weapon . . .*

23

As Edna's organ drowned out Mrs Fox's piano in the vestry, the children walked in in a circle, holding up their hands in choreographed ecstasy. Herb ground his teeth but couldn't take it. He closed the piano lid without so much as warning Mrs Fox and said, 'Sit down children,' joining them with his hands in his lap, determined to wait out another three verses of Luther before he continued.

As they stood for the Gospel reading, Nathan's eyes moved from the peeling alabaster Christ-on-his-cross behind Henry to the rows of girls with their mothers and nannas: little girls in lace-up frocks and older ones picking chips from between their teeth, gathering dust like so many Russian dolls on a dresser. Bonnets, Bibles and Lilli's hands, describing the explosion of an A-bomb, mimicking William's obsession with the Apocalypse. Nathan looked at Lilli and her lips silently described the explosion. He smiled and looked back at his father but William's eyes were closed, his mind busy analysing Henry's words: '"And if so be that he find it, verily I say unto you, he rejoices more of *that* sheep than of the ninety-nine which went not astray."'

Lilli's expression turned sheepish, silently baaing, moving onto the lifted eyebrows and pouted lips of a dimly remembered Lollobrigida. She looked at the alabaster Christ on the wall and wondered if he'd ever been young, waking up beside the Dead Sea after a night of binge drinking. Looking into his face she couldn't imagine it. No trace of a man who could keep down three dozen oysters, turning water into wine as a party trick. Turning and looking at her family and friends she could recognise some of their own alabaster qualities. People whose lives were as solid and unchangeable as the Kaiserstuhl.

Nathan turned back to her but could see that her thoughts were elsewhere, her eyes caught up with the pattern of light as it passed through coloured windows. Her dress, worn loose, revealed nothing about her body but he was busy with her face in his hands anyway, kissing it all over, plunging his tongue into her mouth.

Seymour Hicks watched Nathan's head come around and saw

that Lilli had finished. Deciding to tell William after, he looked over at his son-in-law and back at Henry, who was saying, '"Here ends the Gospel,"' smiling as the congregation muttered, '"Praise be to Thee, O Christ."'

And to thee, Joseph Tabrar thought, staring at his father-in-law with contempt. He'd seen Lilli too, but had smiled, understanding Nathan's connection to her, more convinced every day that he had to move his family on soon.

After the service, as families re-grouped and gathered outside for morning tea, Harry Rasch distributed rehearsal notices for Liedertafel. William felt Seymour Hicks take him by the arm and listened as Seymour whispered in his ear. William found Nathan cutting honey cake and decided to have it out then and there.

Bluma, busy with Edna and the coffees, watched as Nathan put down his knife and walked off down the avenue of pines which had become an avenue of shame. William returned to Seymour and Joshua Heinz and the smile returned to his face. Watching, Bluma felt repulsed by her husband's grinning and laughing and arm slapping. Unable to explain this feeling she reconciled herself with the fact that her husband was a fair and balanced man.

Joseph Tabrar watched as Lilli slipped out through the graveyard, out and down the hill towards a nearly deserted Tanunda. He fancied he could hear her calling after Nathan in the distance but the spell was broken by the ringing of Bruno's bells.

After the women had gone some of the men gathered in the vestry to convene a committee: Farm Day 1951, prudently planned, costed and set out on paper, responsibilities shared out and new attractions considered. The Cambrai Leinerts had put forward a proposition for a light steam competition (the winner being the first to pump out a thirty-gallon tank) and one of Bluma's distant cousins had suggested a pet judging event.

'Too much competition,' Ian Doms observed, but William was bound to defend the idea on behalf of Bluma. As a string of disjointed conversations overtook the planning circle, William overheard Joshua Heinz saying to Pastor Hoffmann, 'And you believe this?'

'Of course not,' the pastor replied.

'Believe what?' William asked, and saw Joshua smile as he realised the whole group was listening now.

'Old Mother Falland,' Joshua said, and William joined the rest as they variously smiled, laughed or nodded their heads.

'Fritzsche's wife is beside herself,' Joshua continued, going on to explain how the Fritzsche woman was convinced the old witch Falland had laid hexes on her. Starting off with the fact that the wheel had fallen off her buggy last Wednesday as she drove past Falland's house, through to her cow's milk dropping off the very next day.

'Why would Mother Falland put a spell on Mrs Fritzsche?' asked Ian.

'She couldn't say,' replied Joshua. 'Maybe something about a land dispute between her father and Falland's.'

A local had suggested she slaughter a calf and hang its liver over her fireplace, but this had done no good. In desperation she'd summoned Pastor Hoffmann. 'Wear a red ribbon around your neck,' she'd warned him before his visit.

'My grandfather knew the Fallands,' Seymour Hicks interrupted, describing a falling-out and their own dry uddered cows. 'He put a little milk into the stump of a tree and everything was fine.'

William shook his head. 'Seymour . . .'

'Just stories, William.'

'Ma Falland is not in bed with the Devil,' Henry said categorically, tapping his finger on the list of Farm Day jobs. Unwilling to mention the fact that he *had* carried a red ribbon in his pocket when he visited the Fritzsches – how he'd prayed with her over a white bonnet she claimed had flown across her kitchen, how he'd explained the large shadows of birds over her house and the branches of gum trees which reached down to smack her over the back of the head.

Before they left, William checked the numbers for Bible study at his house the following night and Pastor Hoffmann confirmed who was down to do what for Farm Day. William and Bluma were to oversee the making of garlands for the Harvest Festival, with Bruno and Ian in charge of a charity car smash, a new event Joshua had suggested, having seen it done by the Methos at some other fete. Julius Rechner, asleep at the back, woke in time to promise a couple of sledge-hammers he'd seen in the school's grounds shed.

Lilli and Nathan walked the back way to Seppeltsfield, Lilli dissecting Gary Cooper's performance in *Distant Drums*. A bit of a belly behind the pistol belt, she explained, wobbly forts and quarter-caste Seminole Indians, but if that's what you like. Nathan explained how he didn't even like Gary Cooper, but how his father had an old clipping of John Wayne in *Dark Command* in his scrap-book of clues. They laughed about William and Nathan explained how, in a sense, he was the jazz trumpeter to his father's dreary hymns. 'We share a name and a roof,' he said, going to extremes to distance himself from William.

'Proud to call myself an atheist,' Lilli bragged, smiling, tempting Nathan to better her. 'There's gotta be a God,' he replied. 'But he doesn't eat honey cakes.'

'Weak.'

'Something's better than nothing.'

'Not if it's a fairytale.'

Nathan was stumped. He smiled. 'You're a disgrace to the Fechners.'

'Fuck the Fechners.'

The clouds parted and sun opened out across the floor of the valley. At length she said, 'It's all a crutch for the feeble,' kicking a bunch of dandelions, whose seeds floated into a whirlwind of warm, must-flavoured air. 'Oh look,' she laughed. 'Angels! Hosanna! Hosanna! Save me! Miller the rampant masturbator!' She looked him squarely in the eyes. 'Feeble.' And ran off towards the Seppelt mausoleum.

He ran after her, nearly but never quite catching up. 'So what if you're wrong?' he asked, but she just sped off ahead, calling at the top of her voice, 'Feeble,' racing up the steps towards the mausoleum at the top of the hill and tripping over. Nathan ran past her, up, opening his arms out towards the finishing line and screaming, 'Feeble!'

But then stopped, turning around and going back to her. Holding her ankle she moaned then looked him in the eyes, whispering, 'Feeble,' before sprinting up the remaining steps and hammering her hands on the giant wooden doors.

As they sat at the top she took off his shoes and socks and gave him the consolation prize of a foot rub, saying, 'God can't help you win, and he can't help you be happy.'

Nathan refused to answer, feeling she was both right and wrong. He could hear William ranting, explaining how man wasn't put on earth to be happy, just to prepare for Christ. As he looked over the valley, his eyes following the roads lined with date palms, he felt entirely content in the presence of both Lilli and his other God. And as though in recognition of this a breeze blew up, filling his nostrils with the smell of pot cake and his ears with the sounds of rustling sugar gums.

A bus pulled up at the bottom of the hill and a dozen tourists got out. Nathan stood to gather his shoes and socks, and they headed off.

When he got home that night, William sent him to his loft with a pen and paper and the Bible. Nathan copied and re-copied the usual, Hebrews chapter thirteen, until William told him he could put out his light and go to sleep. To contemplate the disrespect he'd brought to the Miller name. To clear away thoughts of the Fechner tomboy, with her predilection for everything brash, steamy and celluloid.

'She wants me to see a film with her,' he'd pleaded, but William knew what sort of film.

After William had gone out to his vines to check his Baume, Bluma smuggled Nathan a plate of sauerkraut and sausages. When

William returned he smelt the sausages and saw the empty plate and thought, He is a merciful God, reminding us in sin we're not beyond redemption.

Nathan's thoughts were torn between two Gods: one which made him feeble, and one which made him strong.

Chapter Three

Nathan's turn first. Sitting in a large copper tub Bluma would later use to wash their clothes in, he watched as the skin on each of his ten toes wrinkled and turned pale. 'Don't drown in there,' his mother screamed. 'Some of us have work to do.'

It was a busy time for William too. He'd decided to follow up some early rain by seeding two of his three stock paddocks. As he harnessed an old mare he'd kept from the knackery, he saw his son run half-naked from the wash-house, Bluma flicking him with a tea-towel and laughing. Sighing, William backed up the mare to Bruno's seeder, its seed bin nearly rusted through, and filled the American contraption with a mix of Machete wheat and vetch in a ratio Riedel the seed merchant had suggested. He'd been doing it this way for years, with mixed success. Robert had been the first Muller to go mechanical, giving up on Anthelm's method of hand-sowing improved pasture, hand reaping and stooking and stacking bales under a leaky green tarp.

One year, as William was stirring a mix of peas and barley in the seeder, he looked up to see a group of soldiers with rifles running towards him. Unsure what to do, he took flight, jumping the dry-stone wall to Arthur's place, only to find Arthur himself busy with a dozen or so soldiers.

Eventually the strangers introduced themselves. Nothing to fear if you've been a good Fritz, let's return to your house and see what's in the cellar. The military intelligence officers spent the afternoon looking at William's photos, considering his scrapbook and searching his house: the roof cavity, cellar and loft, right through the smoke-house and wash-house.

Eventually they returned to Adelaide and the Keswick barracks, confiscating some books from William's study and letting him know they'd be watching him. In the form of mail censorship and a not-so-subtle, on and off, personal surveillance by two men in an old Ford.

William traversed the rows, up and back, and even as the light began to fade he kept on with the whip. Eventually the animal just stopped and he left it there, refusing to unharness it, feed, water or even acknowledge it. After he'd washed up and eaten tea he returned to the horse and stood beside it. 'Tomorrow,' he whispered, making his way back across the muddy furrows.

As the cold of another early May night set in, Bluma watched as William stoked the oven in their black kitchen and returned to his Bible and scrapbook and other documents laid out on the table. Soon she retired to his study, the only other room in the house apart from their bedroom, with a *Weekly* full of ideas for the spring bride. As she marvelled at endless miles of lace and white organdie (she'd been all in black, according to the *Lutheran* tradition), Nathan sat at her feet with a copy of *Macbeth*.

'Surely this one's Bruno,' she said, looking at the husband of a confetti-covered bride running through Trafalgar Square.

'Bruno's never been to London,' Nathan smiled. 'I doubt Bruno's ever got past Gawler.'

'And here ...' Another groom in her magazine, the splitting image of Mussolini, with glasses, but nonetheless ... After which they immersed themselves in their own separate thoughts.

William welcomed Arthur, Joshua and Bruno and, a little later, Seymour Hicks with his hearse parked beside their smoke-house. Coffee was prepared and cake consumed and William opened with a devotion. '"And I saw an angel come down from Heaven, having the key of the bottomless pit."'

31

Bruno smiled at Joshua and said, 'Willy shouldn't be bothered with his seeding this year.'

'Or the harvest,' Joshua smiled.

William stopped and half-smiled himself. 'Bruno, you'd have us believe no one will need food.'

Bruno shrugged. 'Maybe we won't. Who's to say who'll make the grade?'

But this was something William refused to enter into. He went on to finish Revelations chapter twenty, explaining how Satan, escaped from his prison, was deceiving Seymour with his automobile and even Pastor Henry with his fundraiser film night. Which was the greater of two evils? Shoeless orphans or the devil invited into Langmeil itself? Arthur was warned off an electric lathe and, as for the Anglicans with their Guy Fawkes, *these* were the fires which would come down out of Heaven to devour them.

Luckily, Premier Playford had kept the sin of gambling at bay, but knowing the temperament of the average Australian, that too would have its day. Already had: lotto coupons in the papers, a new pool table in the Tanunda Hotel. In William's scheme of things even the new hot dog machine in the Black and White Cafe was a sign.

At which point he opened his scrapbook – to the accompaniment of moans and Bruno thumping the table. 'William, put it away.'

But William couldn't be stopped. The signs were there. The mare standing like a statue in the middle of his field, their children in defiance of them (although Nathan wasn't mentioned by name), fossils which the newspapers said were a million years old, chromosomes, genes, meaningless gabble set down by scientists who'd lost their way under the influence of the devil Darwin.

'William,' Bruno continued, 'this is Bible study, not your sermon.'

William waved his Bible about in the air then read: '"And I saw the beast, and the Kings of the earth, and their armies gathered together to make war against him that sat on the horse ..."' He looked at every man in the group. 'Who is the man on the horse?'

'The Saviour?' Seymour offered. Grabbing the lifeline, William looked to Joshua, who replied, 'I don't think the false prophet was worried about a hot dog machine.'

'Nonetheless,' William observed, unimpressed.

'I told you, William,' Joshua continued, 'people will laugh at you.'

But just then Bluma emerged from William's study, breaking the spell. Bluma cut the men a plate of pickled pig, set it adrift on a sea of pickled cabbage, then filled some of Arthur's wooden goblets (a present for their anniversary last year) with some of William's 1948 shiraz. As they ate she opened the back door and strolled into the moonlight. The night was cold and crisp, the stillness broken only by rustling leaves. Spying the mare in the distance, its shoulders sagging under the weight of the harnessed plough, she walked over and unharnessed the beast and led it to an empty paddock. As she ran her hand across the horse's neck and shoulders, a nervous twinge shot down its leg.

Inside, Joshua had taken a newspaper as the starting point for their discussion. By the end it was generally agreed, even by William, that the sale of Holden's five hundredth FX was not a sign of the End, that the flooding of Lake Eyre was just the flooding of Lake Eyre and that Bradman hadn't claimed any Christ-like properties. Then William started flicking through his old, worn copy of the *Augsburg Confession*, the central tenet of the Lutheran faith. He stopped at article seventeen: '"The Lord Christ will return on the last day for judgement and will raise up all the dead, to give eternal life and everlasting joy to believers . . ."'

The document went on to reject the ungodly men and devils and Baptists and Jews, not necessarily in that order. Then it explained how, after the End of Days (which William knew was just around the corner), Christ would rule over them on earth for a thousand years of bliss. Peace amongst men. A giant bonfire on which would be placed a million rolls of celluloid and a thousand hot dog machines. And in this Millennialist time men would flock to pay homage to William for the vision he'd shown – they would drink his shiraz and massage the calluses on his feet.

William himself would have Christ over for tea. Jesus would discuss the perfect seed mix and the tragedy of the *Titanic*.

Weeks passed and the rhythms of the valley flowed like the water which had mostly deserted Jacob's Creek. William helped a distant cousin clear the last three gum trees from his property and lost a night's sleep keeping watch over Arthur's Hereford cow as it struggled with a breach birth. On the Kaiserstuhl and its sister hills, sitting bald and velvet in a long line, dead grasses dropped their seed onto hard, lifeless soil.

It was before dawn and William was walking through a dark landscape which had no thoughts of admitting the sun. Birds here and there were starting in on their business and a few chimneys had started to smoke off towards Menge's Hill. A girl's voice somewhere taunted someone with gibberish but mostly William heard only a sleepy hush, broken by the rustling of callitris and breezes down from the ranges, skimming the plains. In a moment of transcendence, William felt it was only him in the landscape with God, in His various manifestations: orchids, a still pool in the trunk of a fallen tree. He felt as though nothing else in the world existed. Not scrapbooks, or dill pickles. Not Baume or Bluma's white-work. Even memories of his forebears were like skins shed in the grasses of a Tanunda morning.

And in this state, he stretched out his hand to walk beside God, in the same way he had walked as a child with his mother down the main street of Tanunda. Oblivious to direction and purpose. No one speaking. Just the shedding of more and more layers until there was nothing but spirit – neighbours witnessing a naked Miller dragging his feet through a dew wet carpet of sorrel.

He passed like this most of the way toward Angaston, toward Henschke's Hill of Grace vineyard. Gnadenberg was ready for the harvest – a mistake, William believed, seeing as there was still plenty of sun left to warm the sugars and finish the flavours of near-perfect grapes. But if that's what the Henschkes wanted, he would oblige. The extra money for a few days of picking would offset any shortfall in his own vintage. There was still talk of lino, or a new suit for Nathan, but the art of being prudential was something they'd all thank him for one day.

The Hill of Grace was a valley of grace, the fog still clearing as William, before any of the other pickers arrived, started filling a wicker basket and delivering the grapes to a German wagon. As the sun inched its way over the horizon the steeple of Gnadenberg church cast a long shadow down into the valley, across the rows of vines which had been growing there happily for nearly a hundred years. Bunches of grapes hung as heavy as ram's balls in expectation of another perfect harvest. The soil, according to Henschke, was as giving as the love of God himself – in fact, there was no way to make bad wine from Gnadenberg's miraculous vines.

As William looked out over the sea of vines he stopped to breathe, slowly, and think how, apart from Presbyterians and collar rot, his life had reached a stage of calmness and resolution, full of familiar smells and tastes and people with their bearable imperfections – like Bruno's Glen Miller records, broadcast the length of Langmeil Road every few weeks. And in this moment of clarity, the bells of Gnadenberg sounded in his ear. Bells unlike Langmeil's. Rung more consonantly than Bruno or Ian, with their complete lack of rhythm. Bells which echoed down through the valley, resonating through every grape and every sod of turf, dying out to nothing in the far distance beyond Graetztown Corner.

And at that moment God spoke to William. Not a white-bearded God of the sky, heralded by MGM-movie musical fanfares and Pears-print angels, but the God of a single white arum lily, growing between his legs. And as he bent down to touch it the lily spoke to him. Its words were in the form of ether, rising up out of the earth, venting through the copper-rich soil into the atmosphere of a clear Barossa morning. The ether entered his nostrils and filled his lungs and attached itself to every blood cell in his body, feeding every organ with the good news of Christ's return.

William sat on the earth and, through habit, looked up at the sky. 'What is it?' he asked. But the baritone of a younger Tauber or

Lanza didn't reply. Instead he had to search for the vibrations, like Brahms hammering away after a lost melody. Like extracting teeth through sheer will-power.

But then the voice returned, whispering his name, 'William Miller . . .'

Farm Day was State Fair minus Shirley Jones, show tunes replaced by folk songs, choreography by thigh-slapping, love interests by love interests and a decent-white-folks-in-the-middle-of-harvest feel by the Gemutlichkeit of a hundred squealing pigs.

The day started with Joan Lavner, daughter of the fortified wine Lavners, being crowned the Daughter of Bacchus pageant queen for the third year running. This caused some friction with Bruno's eldest grand-daughter, Christina (Lilli's sister) who, most agreed, had the higher cheekbones and broader forehead.

As William finished yarding the last of his stock display, the Tanunda Brass Band played the German and then the Australian national anthem, dying in the end around the *Long to reign over us* phrase, in a flurry of misfingered notes.

Bruno approached and handed William a piece of Stinkerkaese, a cheese made from curdled skim milk, and a beer in a coffee mug. As they looked around, William provided a narration that was of little interest to Bruno. 'The merino,' he began, 'is a wonderful animal . . . but not suited to the valley.' He rubbed his hands over the horns of Arthur's ram, explaining how the high rainfall would always rot their feet. 'Leave them for Ceduna,' he smiled, unsure of where Ceduna was.

They passed giant pigs, weighing as much as small trucks, wallowing in the mud of Tanunda oval mid football season, contemplating a future of slit throats and pickled pork. Cattle, again, selected to show off the breeding and husbandry skills of their owners: an Angus steer extruding shit like Bernard Zwar's sausage machine, a Hereford heifer with shoulders as broad as Himmler's archetypal superman and a couple of dried-up Friesians, destined for the abattoir if not purchased by four p.m.

There were goats and Tukidale sheep, chooks and chicks for the town kids to hold, an Alpaca, which was apparently the next big thing, and Shetland pony rides for a penny a piece.

'Have you noticed Nathan and Lilli?' William asked, as Bruno skirted around a minefield of pats which would never bother William himself.

'Lilli is alert up here,' Bruno replied, tapping his head and thinking of his grand-daughter. 'And so is Nathan.'

'Of course.'

'She reads everything: newspapers and timetables, the labels on jam jars.'

Going on to explain how this was the age-old dilemma of fathers and sons, and to a lesser extent, mothers and daughters: children outgrowing their nest in more than a physical way.

'Could they come to us to discuss their music?' Bruno continued.

'I can't think of what Nathan listens to.'

'He listens.'

William thought, I've done my best, but what good's that when someone else comes along and launches their waif of a child into the world to spoil everything for everybody else. 'Bruno,' he began, 'I understand Lilli is . . .'

Bruno scowled, reading his thoughts. 'William, we didn't create the times, but we have to live in them.'

William was silent, agreeing with him completely, imagining Lilli as a low-cut Sophia Loren, dragging Nathan into a mire which could only end in one thing – disrespect. The wood-oven-fired love of family replaced with grins and sarcasm, a culture as dried-up and worthless as the two doomed Friesians.

'Anyway,' William said, patting a Romney ewe, 'things will sort themselves out.'

'Kids,' Bruno replied, slapping him on the shoulder. William looked at him but in the end chose to keep the peace with his neighbour.

As the Tanunda Brass Band continued playing, Joshua came running down the hill towards William's stock display, taking him under the arm and saying to Bruno, 'Can you watch the animals?'

Before Bruno had a chance to reply, Joshua had William half-way up the hill, handing him his red, embroidered jacket and explaining how they'd been moved up on the programme. 'The horse-shoeing's off.'

'Why?'

'Don't ask me. There's a hundred people from Adelaide, waiting around for something authentic.'

'Joshua.'

'Would you rather lederhosen?'

'It's *our* Farm Day.'

'Nonetheless.' And with that he had William in the front row, buttoning his jacket and clearing his throat.

'All ready?' Ron Rohwer smiled, as Harry Rasch held his baton mid-air.

They sang for a full half hour, lusty at times, stretched beyond their range at others. As William looked at the crowd of mostly city suburbanites, he started to read their thoughts: *look at the German people, children, how terribly quaint* ... Caught up with this feeling his arms and legs froze, his neck muscles stiffened and his diaphragm weakened. But he kept singing – what, he couldn't say. His mouth moved and something came out, but he felt like a performing monkey inside a glass case, dancing on an electrified floor controlled by the deposited coins of these leering devils.

Their applause was a blur, a meaningless gesture. Their faces lit up as a lady from Swallow's Ice Cream, wearing nylon stockings and mauve lippy, led on a small choir of children with Mickey Mouse ears and coloured skivvies. The Liedertafel looked at each other but no one said anything. She explained how Swallow's were offering free iron-on transfers with every purchase, eventually turning to the choir and prompting them to start singing: *Who's the leader of the club who's there for you and me – M.I.C.K.E.Y. M.O.U.S.E. ...*

Before they could start the chorus, William stepped forward and attempted to pull the ears from a dozen or so heads. 'This is *our* Farm Day!' he said.

The crowd fell silent, convinced, again, of the German habit of ruining everything. After all, a few perfectly nice kiddies, and how was it *their* Farm Day anyway, this was Australia, not Berlin with its Reichstag and underground bunkers.

William used his hands to help explain his argument. 'This is a day we have to show off our agricultural produce, to each other.'

'What about us?' a voice asked.

'Of course, everyone is welcome . . . only . . . Mickey the Mouse?'

And with this he handed back the Mouseketeer ears, stopping short of apologising as the lady in nylon stockings ushered them off-stage, looking at William with a sideward stare.

Dill pickles and egg noodles, explained William, these were closer to his world. But at best, the crowd thought him pathetic, trapped in a past of wax cylinders instead of records, children instead of birth control. At worst they had their preconceptions confirmed. Driving home in cosy, American-inspired cars they took consolation in their Wynn's Estate at cellar door prices.

The afternoon continued in the same vein: feather-picking, sheath tossing and stooking, bienenstich, pickled cabbage and blutwurst. Sitting amongst his stock William took consolation in the honesty of his own display: real animals shitting real shit, making real noises, bringing pleasure to even the town kids. And as he sat he planned what he'd say to the organising committee: how all this 'dressing' would ruin them, leaving them selling wurst from roadside stalls like so many reservation Indians.

After a lunch of burnt waffles and white pudding, William joined forces with Joshua to beat the bejeezers out of an old Austin Seven as the Langmeil church choir serenaded them with an out-of-season *Alle Jahre wieder*. As William was starting in on the bonnet the head came flying off of one of Julius Rechner's sledge-hammers, narrowly missing the euphonium player from the Lobethal Band, which went onto a faultless rendition of *Watch on the Rhine*.

The Zilm Brothers, of anthropomorphic chair fame, variously

doubled on button accordion, tin whistle, flute, cornet and saxophone to produce a version of *Now thank we all our God* which had even William up standing, applauding.

Tomato and garlic chutneys were tasted and preserves consumed on toasted bread. Bluma's quilting circle had their wares on display beside the harvest-festival wreaths she'd made from Arthur's flowers on long, cold nights as William sat reading and writing beside the family Bible. Nearly every family had provided a garland for the festival, competing with each other to see who could find the whitest freesias and bluest helichrysum. This year Mary Hicks had done her garland entirely out of laucodendrum, a marvel acknowledged by all.

A Prussian ferris-wheel and steam engines, the pancake tent and stein-holding contest made William wonder whether he hadn't been too hasty. At the end of the day the St John's kindergarten children put on a production in the beer tent in which a tubby ten-year-old played Bert Hinkler arriving in Australia from London in his miraculous Avron Avian. The children bowed down as his cardboard plane landed and Bert alighted. One of the girls, a stand-in Lady Mayoress, stepped forward with a wreath and said, 'Bert Hinkler . . .'

And in this William heard the whisper of his own name at Gnadenberg. 'William Miller . . .' And wondered whether God mightn't arrive, after all, in a Trojan horse in the form of a giant Austin Seven.

Chapter Four

William and Joshua, their children at school, their wives in search of the perfect egg noodle, settled around William's table with a small bowl of shiraz and merlot grapes. In turn each grape was squeezed, split and sucked dry. William dissolved the juice between his tongue and the roof of his mouth and smiled. 'I think I'm ready,' he said.

Joshua had to agree. 'You could check with Bruno's refractometer.' But to William that made as much sense as checking the air they breathed, the water they drank. 'And what if it says I'm wrong?' he asked. 'Ninety years we've made wine, without Bruno's tool.'

'You could make better wine.'

And again he knew where Joshua was going: quality control and time and motion, chemists with bubbling beakers and temperature-controlled processing plants. 'As I found out yesterday,' he offered, 'maybe I'm a relic . . . still.'

Instead of getting straight to it, disinfecting crushers and fermenting barrels, repairing faulty bubblers and converting the house into a winery, he fetched a tawny port from their cold cellar (where soldiers had once searched for *Mein Kampf*) and joined Joshua around the fire of Bluma's kitchen, forever stoked, eternally warming the cottage.

After a while the talk turned to the past. William fetched his family photographs, tied up in a Blundstone boot box from his father's day. Sacred of the sacred was a photo showing his father, Robert, helping his grandfather, Anthelm, build the walls of the very cottage they were sitting in. 'Before then it was a wattle and daub cottage with a thatched roof,' William said, going on to explain how, as a boy, Robert would sleep beside contented cattle under the single roof which formed their home. In the background the Muller vines were already flourishing and the half-finished spire of St John's, at Ebenezer, was pointing towards a sky of hot north easterlies and unpredictable dust storms.

Another photograph showed Robert and Brigid, his wife, sheltering from a rainstorm inside a hollowed-out gum tree a family named Herbig had lived in for years. The back read *Newly joyned in God's eyes, 1898, Springton, B. Valley.*

William pulled out pictures of himself, excitedly explaining them to Joshua as he spilt his port and mopped it up with his sleeve, pouring himself another and topping up Joshua. Photos taken by cameras he wouldn't have in his own house: him as a part of the Lutheran Boy's Club, a group of serious kids in overalls restoring an early Thomas Carter stripper. Bluma and her sister working at Laucke's mill as girls, sewing up bags of flour. Nathan as a baby, being held by a nurse on the front steps of Scholz's Willow Hospital at Light Pass. A car wreck on God's Hill Road which had killed a young Latin teacher from town, six months out of college. Festival displays of wurst. Streetscapes. An old Turk who'd set up a trash and treasure outside the deserted Ampol on Murray Street. No one could remember anyone buying anything, until one day he was gone, taking his prayer mat and stubble with him. And finally, a serious portrait of Anthelm, clutching a Bible, now lost, in which Pastor Kavel, the valley's founding father, had supposedly written. Possibly explaining why he'd led his followers (Anthelm barely moving out of his shadow) from Silesia to England, across seas under hostile skies to Port Adelaide. There to settle amongst the gum trees and black fellas, experimenting with new forms of blutwurst beside the River Torrens.

And the only other shot of Anthelm, standing beside his wife

Margaret on a block of virgin land they would tame and make productive. Sustaining generations until Christ returned to reward them for keeping the faith. Establishing a thousand-year dynasty in which everything would remain much the same, cucumbers grown, preserved and eaten within the boundaries of their new Eden.

'Anthelm took me further away from the church, but closer to God,' William explained.

Because of Anthelm and Kavel, the Lutherans had been given the opportunity of bringing the *true* Christ to Australia. Spreading His word through Hermannsburg and Boundary Gate and a dozen other missions to black fellas, who, if the truth be known, were probably beyond salvation. But in the tradition of Luther and Kavel they had to try. When Christ returned he would ask them, 'What did you do to save others?' And they would have to be ready with a reply.

The last photo was Elizabeth Street, Tanunda, 1936, a whole convoy of tractors driving towards Nuriootpa. Joshua smiled and looked at William. 'You remember this?'

But William didn't reply, moving his glass into a puddle of spilt port and turning it by the stem. 'God spoke to me,' he said.

Joshua looked up. 'He speaks to all of us, William.'

'No, not in that sense . . . real words. He whispered my name.'

'When?'

'Hill of Grace. I was picking for Henschke. I had my basket half full. I noticed a lily and bent down and then I heard . . . *William.*'

Joshua put his hands in his lap and shrugged, unsure of a reply. 'Did he have a deep voice?'

'I don't know.'

'Was it everywhere, or just the . . . lily?'

'The lily didn't talk.'

'Did it say William, or Wilhelm?'

'Joshua.'

William threw back the rest of his port. 'I can't remember the words exactly, but I looked up . . .' He was looking for the words to explain but they were far beyond his grasp.

43

'So, what did he say?' Joshua urged, sitting forward, unsure if he should grin, or hail William as some sort of prophet. Surely if God was going to pick a messenger ... still, William was a reliable man, and messengers had to be reliable.

'I can't remember,' William continued, 'but it was something about spreading the message.'

'The message?'

'Christ's return.'

'It was that clear?'

'Yes.'

Joshua's eyes drifted off into the rafters. 'Like Ussher?'

'No, that was different. He was loopy.'

William was referring to the Calvinist Bishop who, Henry had explained to them one Sunday, had made a study of the Bible and come up with the very day and time God had created the earth: twelve o'clock, Sunday the twentieth of October, 4004 BC. His chronology had even extended to the day of Noah's flood, 1659 years later. This is what Lutheranism had saved them from, Henry explained. Dark Ages religion. The dates so misunderstood they'd even graced the margins of the King James' Bible. But what were dates, he'd concluded? Pure guesswork. This wasn't in the spirit of the Bible. The Bible was about two things: grace and love. And William was inclined to agree, referring to it at the following week's Bible study as Ussher's arrogance.

But this was a different thing altogether. He'd imagined Ussher, in his purple robes, sitting in his chambers dictating dates to feeble minded lackeys. *His* revelation was about the knowable, something written in every verse and rhyme of Revelations.

Joshua sat back in his chair and breathed deeply. 'And that was all?'

William tapped his finger on the table. 'He didn't give me instructions.'

'But what did you make of it?'

'That there's more I can do ...'

Joshua shook his head. He still didn't know what to make of it. 'Well ... there'd be no point him coming to me.'

William shrugged. 'So?'

'Henry says he speaks to all of us. Maybe to you his words just . . . clarified.'

'Maybe?'

'I'm sure they did.'

'I swear. These were real words, spoken by a real voice.' And with that he sat back and breathed deeply. 'I swear.'

'If that's what you tell me, William, I believe you. Maybe he wants everybody to have the opportunity –'

'Exactly!'

But William was still only a little more convinced himself. Joshua had rationalised the news with a less than ecstatic response. If William was going to convince others he'd have to convince Joshua first.

Joshua's revelation was nowhere near as profound as William's or as poetic as John's. The voice of God didn't speak to him and, as with most people, there was nothing new about the thoughts which passed through his head: his magnolia in full flower, the lemon scent of Bon Ami washing powder, the whispers of his children tucked up in bed; the almost musical snoring of Catherine, his wife, reclining in a sofa beside him, and the sound of tobacco burning up in his pipe as he inhaled.

Joshua, alone in his living-room, was thinking of William, alone in his cottage, staring down at his linoless floor, arms on his knees, muttering something incomprehensible. The words transformed into those of Roy Rene, scratchy through a vintage bakelite radio playing softly on Joshua's mantlepiece. *She calls me dear, she must be shook on me.* More lines, applause, play off, and the whole business of the apocalypse seeming so distant.

As the comedy faded to a chorus of Colgate promos, Joshua stretched back in his chair and closed his eyes. Reaching out for the tuning knob he by-passed 5AD's gardening hour and settled on a low, gravely voice with a Russian accent. He pricked up his ears. 'As we moved into punishment block we came across the whipping bench . . .'

Describing the marks of clawing fingers on the wood.

The Soviet film *Chronicle of the Liberation of Auschwitz, 1945*, was almost as powerful without the images. Joshua's mind created the portable scaffold which hardly ever worked, inmates being helped back up as if they were boarding a bus. And as the voice continued, he entered a sorting house known as *Kanada*: piles of teeth, hair and prosthetics, reaching to skylights which would offer no liberation. Spectacles and shoes, decoy tickets which spoke of places the victims would never see.

And through all of this a vision of God started to clarify in his mind. A pile of burnt bodies, still smoking, hastily re-burnt before liberation, like a clipping William had failed to find or stick in his scrapbook. An aborted foetus with placenta, dried up beside its murdered mother.

Where was God? He was there watching, shaking his head, despairing for human beings and their inability to see him through a haze of sweet-smelling smoke. Jesus too, looking at his watch, saying to his father, How long before I can return and sort this whole sodden mess out? But God was in no rush. 'Let them come to see me first, in lilies and Ajax, Roy Rene and the smashed shell of an old Austin Seven.' Otherwise, he explained, there would be no point in returning. People would just laugh when he said, 'Yep, it's me, Jesus of Nazareth. Nazis and Baptists to the back of the room, please.'

Which meant that if he were right, William was just as likely to be called as anyone else. Eventually the words ended and a Bach violin concerto began. In the play of instruments Joshua could hear voices struggling for dominance, forming a sonority and then receding; a chorus of all instruments speaking at once, and then a single voice, clearer and more pure than all the rest.

And in this state he stood and walked out his back door, leaving his pipe on a window sill, moving down through his garden in wet, muddy socks in the face of an approaching storm. Passing through rows of Seppelt's chardonnay the rain began to spit, and every drop was a bullet trying to stop him from reaching God:

bloomers at three and six, Victas and Tony Curtis in a zoot suit. The rain bucketed down. He pulled off his socks and, feeling the energy William had tried to describe, started to run between the rows. 'Lana Turner has written to me,' he screamed, and a few pickers, working late by gaslight, looked over the vines to see.

'Lana Turner, the movie star!' he called hoarsely, trying to overcome the noise of torrential rain. Tripping. Falling over and ending up in a puddle of mud. Looking up at the sky and screaming, 'Damn you!' Lying back down, yielding, his heart returning to normal as he licked water from his lips. Convinced that he did have some part to play in the grand scheme of things which, all in one instance, encompassed Auschwitz and Macackie Mansions.

The next day, as he helped William pick, they laughed over the story of his muddy socks. He urged William, again, to write something down, to describe and define the time he'd been told about.

'I have some ideas,' William replied, 'but numbers are unreliable.'

'Nonetheless . . .'

They worked on in silence, William watching Joshua and wondering if he'd risen above the rational.

William cleaned and rinsed his crusher and his first dozen barrels of blended red, with oak chips, were placed on the floor of the wash-house to start reacting with the yeast he had added in imprecise amounts. The barrels were wiped clean and covered with old cardboard boxes, salvaged from the Black and White Cafe, to keep out the light. Within days the bubbling would begin, carbon dioxide erupting in small hiccups of shiraz perfumed gas.

As he did at least once a week, Arthur Blessitt joined the Millers for dinner: lamb chops fried black in a frenzy of improvised hollandaise Bluma had read about in one of Mary Hicks' old *Weeklies*. He helped Bluma and Nathan clear away the dishes and wash up and they settled in for one of William's epic devotions.

Pulling up his sleeves and setting out pages in front of him, William began. 'God chooses us,' he said, as he looked at each of them. 'We become disciples through his grace. What am I talking about, Arthur?'

Generally a pious man, Arthur could think of better ways of letting his food settle. Still, there was no point trying to change William. When the Lord's name was invoked you bowed your head and savoured the smell of Bluma's rhubarb crumble, drifting over from a slowly cooling stove. There was nothing original about William's devotion – as with Pastor Hoffmann, you stood at the right time, made the sign of the cross and recited blank verse. Maybe it all meant something to God, but it probably didn't. There were better ways of expressing your love for the omnipotent. The full-size cross he'd started building in his workshop was an example of this. What he'd do with it or where he'd erect it when he was finished, he didn't know. Probably he'd just re-use it for scrap. The thought of being branded a heretic was too much for a simple man of flowers.

'Forgiveness,' Arthur replied, remembering a similar devotion from last year. Either way, the intoning of a few simple words was generally enough to keep William happy: sin, forgiveness, love, persecution, resurrection – once he'd even thrown in *sublimation*, and William had nodded his head in approval.

'Forgiveness was at the centre of the Saviour's life, this is what his disciples learned. Unconditional and absolute. Here in Matthew chapter nine, verse nine to thirteen ...'

William was off and running, rubbing the pages of Matthew between his fingers, reading slowly, as though the words might come to mean more. '"And it came to pass, as Jesus sat at meat in the house ..."'

But Arthur was off in his delphiniums, lovingly weeding between the drip irrigated rows. Nathan's thoughts were with Lilli, recreating moments on the Seppelt hill, as foot massages became other things in anticipation.

'Nathan?' He heard his father's clicking fingers in front of his face. 'Sorry.'

'Tell us about the disciples.'

Nathan furrowed his brow. 'The desertion. Peter's denial. Things put in the Bible to teach us about . . .'

'Grace.'

'We aren't naturally forgiving. We have to learn.'

'And this was the lesson of the disciples?'

'Yes.'

'And where do we hear about this?'

William pushed the Bible over. Nathan picked it up and flicked through Matthew, as though it was the *Weekly*, full of stories, tid-bits and cardigan templates, words that meant little beyond the obvious.

'Matthew eighteen, verses twenty-one . . .'

'Go on.' William sat back and folded his arms as Nathan read. '"Then came Peter to him and said, Lord, how oft shall my brother sin against me?"'

Arthur's stomach gurgled and he farted into a haze of warm rhubarb. Nathan stopped reading and looked up. '"Children of Israel, shall we forgive . . ."'

Just as Nathan knew he would, William sat forward, his hands on the edge of the table. 'Nathan.'

'What?'

Nathan continued reading, but he caught Bluma's smile as Arthur bowed his head in unspoken shame.

At last his father took back the Bible. As Anthelm's grandfather clock ticked away in the hallway and Arthur sniffed for the fading scent of Bluma's crumble gone cold, William canvassed the Bible's views on sin, passing on to how forgiving is not the same as forgetting but how, like the twelve disciples, we had to try do both. As the tired old metaphor of the vine and the branch was trotted out again, Nathan watched as Arthur slumped forward in his chair, waking with a start sometime around the, 'If man not abideth with me . . .' line.

'Pardon me,' Arthur said, excusing himself again, as Nathan grinned. William looked at his son.

'What, it wasn't me!'

Everyone except William laughed. 'We're reading the Gospels.'

'William,' Bluma scolded, 'your whiskers are sticking up.'

At which point the three of them lost it completely. 'You have the spontaneity of a mushroom,' Bluma continued, poking her husband's belly.

'Get off.'

Arthur had had enough. He stood up and took the crumble out of the oven, fetching a steak knife and stirring the coals for the kettle.

The following Friday, as Nathan waited with his father and mother on the Adelaide Railway Station concourse, Arthur deposited a bag of brown apple cores in the bin. Although he was way past it, Nathan read the poster for *Eagle* magazine as William considered a series of photos promoting the progress of the Snowy scheme. New Australians, with their single eyebrows and greasy hair, manned pneumatic drills on sheer rock faces, working for the privilege of being called *real* Australians.

Arthur returned via the cafe with Peter's Dandy ice-creams in their tubs. Wooden spoons were clutched as Nathan led them towards the River Torrens. Passing the city baths as the sun began to set he said to his father, 'This way, no turning back.'

For once Nathan was genuinely happy. All he needed now was Lilli, to witness what he was up to. Which was to follow up on his father's promise.

'I'm *not* stuck in the past,' William had said, as they sat eating cold crumble.

'Prove it,' Nathan challenged.

'I have nothing to prove. My focus is on God.'

'God won't mind.'

'So?'

And with that Nathan had closed his Bible and told him what happened every Friday night beside the Torrens. Brushing up against Anglicans and agnostics his father's capacity to celebrate life would be fully tested.

Passing through Elder Park – where Arthur had once come with a rug and thermos of coffee to watch La Stupenda sing *Rejoice Greatly, Oh Daughter of Zion* – Nathan led them onto the Pop-eye passenger boat and paid their fares.

Casting off, William could hear jazz drifting across the water, could see strings of fairy lights flashing blue, red and gold, reflected in the water of the Torrens lake. The Pop-eye approached the floating stage, docked and William's eyes lit up to a dozen or so musicians, all in tuxedos, playing a waltz he could almost remember. Joe Aronson and his Synco Symphonists, he read, on a painted backdrop, as Nathan helped him aboard the over-sized barge which bobbed lightly in the wake of the Pop-eye.

William stepped onto a dance floor which extended out in front of the orchestra. Tables and chairs were arranged in precarious clusters around the edge. Imitation flappers darted to and fro with watered spirits, West End in steins and frankfurts dished up with a dollop of sauce. An American flag refused to flap as a couple of teenagers from Mile End feigned Al Capone. Children invaded the dance floor, teaching each other something called the 'vertical stomp', leading Nathan's eyes and mind away from the oom-pah resonances of a valley childhood.

'Fine,' William said, sitting and smiling. But he wasn't impressed, convinced that Australians, in the absence of their own culture, were too quick to imitate others, generally choosing the worst of whatever was available. 'A swinging time,' he said, smiling, trying his hardest, although Bluma could tell his words were about as real as Joe Aronson's accent.

Drinks were ordered and Bluma was up first with Arthur. Nathan took over, twirling his mum about in improvised moves which had more of the Landler than the Charleston. After a time he whispered in her ear and she went over to fetch William. At first he refused to stand, but when the cheers of surrounding tables grew up around him, he had little choice.

As a dancer he stunk, his moves stiffer than the hired tuxedos. But in time he put his arm around Bluma (in a public display of affection which took some doing for a Barossa Lutheran) and they settled into a slow, gentle rhythm which seemed to respond to the waves of the Torrens itself.

'Matthew chapter . . .?' Nathan asked Arthur, his eyes set on his parents.

'William may yet learn,' Arthur replied.

'What?'

'Every man worships in his own way.'

Which to Arthur was a glass-house of summer chrysanthemum, or a freshly planed cross smelling strongly of Tasmanian oak.

When he sat down, everyone looked at William in anticipation. The voice of Gnadenberg and the feel of brittle pages between his fingers had faded, but the fake moustaches of the waiters reeked of an artifice he couldn't tolerate for too long. At best a novelty, this was a world of lost people, unsure of what to eat and drink, when to harvest or how to cure wurst. These were people with Mickey Mouse ears, out for a good time, with nowhere to go afterwards.

Still, he knew he had to try, at least this once.

As Aronson's baton came crashing down, the music faded away into the distant bamboo on the northern bank. Aronson stood up and, beaming a smile, asked the diners to check under their seats. There was a general flurry and at the Miller table, ecstatic cries as William produced an envelope. Bluma hugged him and accompanied him up to the podium.

'Open it,' Joe urged, in his fake Brooklyn accent.

William fumbled the envelope and read the writing on the voucher.

'Into the microphone,' Joe urged.

'"The holder is entitled to goods to the value of twenty pounds,"' he read. '"Courtesy J.N. Taylor's Homewares, Grenfell Street and suburbs."'

There was general applause and Joe asked, 'What will you use it for?'

Bluma jumped in. 'Lino.' And people mostly laughed.

William suddenly felt like he was a contestant on Pick-a-Box,

52

broadcast through crystal sets into the living rooms of a nation. The flickering of lights in the water became the illuminations of an all electric hell, the static through the microphone, the hiss of God's displeasure.

'I cannot accept this,' he said, but Bluma grabbed the voucher and headed back to their table. Again the laughs welled up. William slipped from the podium and everyone applauded.

All at once *he* had become the mouse. '"M.I.C.K.E.Y., Why, because we like you ..."'

Falling asleep on the train, grasping the envelope in a sweaty hand, Bluma felt the rhythms of the track through her feet, smelt burning coal in her nostrils and knew they'd soon be home. She watched as an Ovingham mother screamed at her children and returned to scrubbing the pedestal of a bird bath by the salvaged light of a hallway globe. Moths crowded street lights rusted to the sides of stobie poles and a gas man worked by torch light to uncover meters overgrown with honeysuckle. She looked at Nathan and said, 'Your father's right.'

Taking the voucher, she ripped it in half and slipped it out of the window. William watched it scatter and settle in front of a cemetery. Nathan looked at her but didn't speak. Bluma wanted to explain but didn't know how to say it in the same way William could. *Things* weighed you down. *Things* bred expectations of more things. *Things* were a barrier between man and God, and consequently, a man and his family.

As she fell asleep that night, Bluma wondered if tomorrow she'd regret throwing the voucher out of the window. She thought, why would God have this dampness forever in my lungs?

Later that night, William closed his study door and opened his Bible, reading, words falling from his lips in whispers. '"This know also, that in the last days perilous times shall come. For men shall be lovers of their own selves, covetous, boasters, proud, blasphemers ..."'

And stopped, closing his eyes, allowing comic book images to crowd his head. Miller as Aronson as the Devil, waving his baton wildly, screaming, in a giant speech balloon, '"Traitors, heady, high-minded, lovers of pleasures more than lovers of God ..."'

A bit of lino, Bluma thought, as she drifted off to sleep, how could he deny me that?

Chapter Five

The following weeks were a succession of sauerkraut and yeast, hands stained red and rain hanging perpetually above the valley. William and Joshua worked hard to finish the harvest before the mould took hold and swarms of galahs, descending between the rain clouds with shafts of sunlight behind them, settled on the heaviest bunches – eating a grape or two and letting the rest drop in the mud.

The morning mists floated weightlessly above William's cucumbers and the ants on his myrtle had disappeared into a hole somewhere. Returning to the wash-house with grapes, his pants would be soaked up past the knees, his socks wet through the eternally unrepaired holes in his boots.

As he put the grapes through the crusher they split and run, the must draining down a tube into a barrel. More yeast, a gentle stir and another batch sealed, fermenting on-skin until it was ready to be strained through stockings – the only time Bluma could be seen buying nylons, sheer and medium, which she stretched over the decanting tap of William's barrels, as the men removed sludge and skins in preparation for the secondary ferment.

After these few weeks Joshua and William's picking was finished, the barrels bubbling away happily in fulfilment of a promise God had made and William had done his best to honour. He figured he'd make just over six hundred bottles, up on last year's five fifty. Then there were the labels and the packing and the endless round of bottle shops in Seymour's hearse: Gawler, Kapunda and beyond, tardy publicans and shop managers saying, 'We *do* have an arrangement with Seppelts.'

But it wasn't just wine which had been filling his head. William had sent apologies to Bible study for the last three Monday nights.

'Unlike William,' Arthur Blessitt had said, when it came his turn to open up his home.

'He's deep in study,' Joshua commented.

'Study?'

'Dates. He's convinced. A clue here, a clue there. A word, a phrase someone missed. At least that's how I understand it.'

Eyebrows raised, coffee sipped, as if they'd just discovered William had a fetish for dressmaking.

But William's fetish went far beyond that. He'd started off by locking himself in his study at six every night, only emerging for custard cake and coffee. If nobody else was going to take the Bible seriously then he would have to.

The first book he studied was Daniel. In chapter nine there was a well-known prophecy of 'seventy weeks', a period of time extending from God's commandment to rebuild a broken Jerusalem through to a time when 'the anointed one shall be cut off'.

The following Monday, as Joshua, Arthur, Seymour and Ron Rohwer gathered in the Miller house for study, William set to explaining what he'd come up with. Study and facts alone, he stressed, had led him to this understanding. 'I say nothing that wasn't said in the Bible.'

The group looked at him, Joshua sucking on his pipe, already convinced. 'Remember,' he said to the group, 'William's picking up on research that's already been done. Aren't you, William?'

'Some.' Referring to some pseudo-religious 'facts' he'd seen in someone's old *Watchtower*. 'I've read the Bible three times in the last three weeks,' he said, as Ron thought, So what, lifting his eyebrows and whispering, 'A book in Chinese is just as meaningless after –'

'Different thing,' William interrupted.

'Not necessarily.'

They stopped, realising they sounded like a couple of school boys.

'So,' Seymour began, sitting back and folding his arms, 'let's hear what you've got to say.'

'Let's,' Ron joined, folding his arms.

'The starting point for the seventy weeks,' William explained, 'could only be the decree of Artaxerxes, which is in Ezra.' He took his Bible from underneath a pile of papers and flicked through. 'Ezra chapter seven, eleven through twenty-six. Does anyone know it? The decree was to allow Ezra to return to Jerusalem. Yes . . .? The rebuilt city?'

He stared at them in anticipation. 'People have tried to link Ezra and Daniel before, this is nothing new.'

'It's new to us,' Seymour said, sitting forward.

Seeing he had their attention, William pushed away the pile of papers and continued mostly with his hands. 'Next step, I took a day in the Bible to mean one of our years. Seymour, you're good at maths. If a day becomes a year, seventy weeks becomes . . .?'

'Four hundred and ninety years.'

'Correct. Now, according to the Bible, the decree of Artaxerxes was issued in 457 BC.' He looked back at Seymour, who smiled and bowed his head, saying, 'Four hundred and ninety on from 457 . . . that's 33 AD.'

William's eyebrows lifted, he extended his hands in jubilation and looked at each of them. 'The year of Christ's crucifixion.'

Ron nodded his head, unable to make sense of it. 'So, what does that prove?'

'457 . . .'

'457 . . .?'

'It might be a coincidence.'

'What might?'

'I went back to Daniel, and there it was, in front of me.'

It had been a sub-zero Thursday morning, one a.m., when he came running into Bluma, asleep in the middle of their king-size bed. Shaking her awake he said, 'Two thousand four hundred and nine . . .'

But she had just rolled over and gone back to sleep, and he'd returned to his maths. 'In Daniel chapter eight, verse fourteen,' he continued, sure that he hadn't lost any of his audience yet, 'there's a reference to two thousand four hundred and nine evenings and mornings which'd have to elapse before the sanctuary's cleansed.'

'The sanctuary?' Seymour asked.

'Where else? Here. Our sanctuary. And who's the one set down to do the cleansing?'

'Christ,' Arthur gathered.

'Yes. On his return.'

Which was William's way of referring to the atheists and agnostics with their Mickey ears and shiny fridges, the ching-chongs and pagans and witches, the makers of Horus heads and the chanters of Navajo spells. 'Again, if two thousand four hundred and nine days meant two thousand four hundred and nine years . . .'

By now they were hanging off his every word.

'And if we remember that the decree of Artaxerxes was issued in 457 BC . . .'

Seymour put his head down, fulfilling his role as the disciple of simple mathematics. 'Two thousand four hundred and nine minus four hundred and fifty seven . . .'

But even Ron could do this maths. '1952.'

William smiled.

'Next year?' Arthur asked.

'Next year,' William replied.

Ron Rohwer stood and pushed his chair in. Although he had no doubt that Christ would return one day, it was a bit much to believe it would be next year. 'You can work the figures any way you like, there's enough of them in the Bible,' he said. 'If it could have been done it would have.' Going on to explain how a monkey could accidentally type out *Hamlet*, given a billion years or so.

'I've looked at dozens of possibilities,' William defended, 'but this is the only one that makes sense.'

'It doesn't.'

And with that Ron pulled on his coat and walked out of William's back door.

Seymour Hicks believed faith and mathematics were two very different things. When he arrived home that night he was still attempting to reconcile them. Maybe, he thought, if the maths were beyond dispute the belief would follow. After all, it was as much faith as maths which had built the Sydney Harbour Bridge. Early visions of its two arms growing together had concerned many. But eventually they joined. This was the engineer's faith. That numbers would conspire to support thousands of tonnes.

Trying to create his own faith he scribbled on the back of the *Lutheran Times*:

$$2409 - 457 = 1952$$

Again and again, as if poor numeracy might lead to greater disaster. The next step was to go to Daniel and check the dates. Correct. The decree of Artaxerxes. Correct. For a moment he wondered if the dates had any relationship beyond the maths, but then dismissed this, guessing that William must have understood deeper reasons.

Seymour was contented to let the truth simmer. It would either burn or fill the house of God with wonderful smells. He ripped out the dates and placed them in his wallet, beside the article on Korea he'd kept to consider. Seymour's glueless scrap-book was for his own sake. There was no point convincing others if you weren't convinced yourself.

Nathan stood on the platform of Tanunda station, pulling potato sack undies out of his arse, adjusting the suit his father had lent him. The elbows and seat had nearly worn through, but William insisted there was a few good years in it yet. The pin-striped Nathan had all but resigned himself to looking like a hay-cutting Amish in a truck stop, but if that's what it took. A job interview with the Railways wasn't something to be taken lightly, William had explained. First impressions were crucial.

He heard his father's voice – 'Back from the line' – and shuffled away from the edge of the platform. Contemplating the shiny steel rails and oil-soaked gravel he tried to remember if chlorophyll constituted 6.6 per cent of shade- or sun-grown algae. And other questions, such as the possible vectors and intercepts of a line with the form $y = 3x - 1.7$ (ab). Protein synthesis in plant cells. Polynomials. The unfathomable differences between mitosis and meiosis. Pages of them. Staring up at him. Saying, in their own meaningless way, everyone else in this room understands, *they* spent their study day working.

Bluma adjusted his jacket and straightened his tie. 'Remember,' she said, 'if you're asked a question, no funny stuff.'

'Mum.'

'*Why would you like to work here?*' she asked, entwining her fingers.

'Mum!'

'Why?' William persisted, but Nathan could see his father's gaze had returned to the fog which hung heavy on the Kaiserstuhl, blurring any visions he'd had of his son the doctor or engineer.

'It's an ambition I've had, to learn a trade, to work with my hands,' he'd told his parents, but they both knew him better than that. He knew that William was thinking, Rubbish, it's because you let yourself down.

Geometry: finding three-dimensional points. Surds. Enzymes of the pancreas. Algebraic equations his father had explained a thousand times. Respiration. Fractions. Amino acids and the formula to solve trapeziums. The biology paper sitting in front of him, whispering, *Your father's going to kill you, running off with that randy slut. By the way, define autotrophic assimilation.*

Two papers. Graded in Mr Rechner's reddest ink. Maths: 17%. Biological Science: 23%. He'd just scraped through in English, German and Classics, but his marks would never be enough for uni.

And it had all been Lilli's doing. Not that he cared too much, as he saw the trace of smoke and steam in the distance, heard the big drive wheels and pistons of the loco heading down from Angaston. His fall from grace had been sudden but pleasurable, caught up as he'd been in the ecstasy of every imaginable sin under God's gloomy sky.

Formal lessons had ended on Tuesday. The seniors were told

to report back on Wednesday, for study day. Nathan had got up early, pulled on his clothes and headed off along a familiar path, his head already full of algebra and respiration by the time he turned into Elizabeth Street.

Where he came face to face with Lilli coming out of the Apex bakery.

'Honey cake?' she said, passing a sweet-smelling bag under his nose.

'Working?' he asked.

'No. Studying?'

'Always. Although today isn't a proper school day.'

She smiled and raised her eyebrows, his first temptation for the day. 'No no,' he grinned, 'I have two papers tomorrow.'

'And a father with chin whiskers.'

'Sorry?'

She passed the bag under his nose again, this time walking off along the Adelaide road.

Nathan stood his ground. 'I've completely forgotten my cosines.'

'Fuck your cosines.'

Tempted by the smell he was off, walking through paddocks and remnant vegetation, avoiding the road with its Lutheran spies and sales reps.

'Brother Miller,' she began, as they stopped to steal ripe strawberries, 'follow the whore to Hell. Partake of her honey cake and taste damnation, Apex style.'

Lilli had dropped out of school years before, choosing the smell of fresh pipe loaves over the stale sweat of St John's change rooms. She had told Nathan that her mother, Bruno and Edna's daughter, had gone on about it for weeks, urging her to hold off at least until she found someone to marry. 'Who will you find at the Apex?' she asked Lilli. 'And where will you be in fifteen years? Slicing bread.'

But Lilli didn't care. Things had a way of taking care of themselves. Anything but school. 'Who needs it?' she asked, as they kept walking.

'I do.'

'Why?'

He shrugged, unsure. 'The marks.'

'Gonna become a doctor?'

'Maybe.'

She smiled at him. 'Keep daddy happy.'

He didn't argue, wondering what he'd ever got out of school. To him it was a soccer game in which the sports teacher let the two biggest pricks pick the teams. Waiting and waiting, always picked last, which was some consolation he supposed. Then the whistle, and the three largest boys on each team holding on to the ball, the rest of the boys, like him, running around for no reason, calling, 'Here, here ... pass,' but never getting a turn. Running and calling, for four quarters of utter pointlessness. Fetching the ball when it went out of bounds but returning it to the biggest ape for the throw in. Finishing. Smelling bad. Showering in a room full of steam and wet singlets, dicks displayed proudly like so much pickled pig. Returning the next day for more, of nothing, no one thinking to explain or wonder why. Or dreaming up a better way of surviving until adulthood.

He tried to estimate the gradient of a hill which rose gradually above Jacob's Creek. An ironstone cottage, overgrown with weeds, lay mostly in ruins before them, a rusted camp oven in the fireplace telling stories of Silesian pioneers fed up with it all, taking their stuff and heading back to Adelaide. They reached the top of the hill and looked down over Tanunda. 'Hello, William,' Lilli waved, preparing for her next transgression. 'Me and Nathan up here, you know, ooh ...' Gyrating her hips orbitally.

They sat in the mouth of Johannes Menge's cave, a cathedral in quartz which had housed a monk-like Prussian mineralogist in the 1840s. For many years Menge had searched the valley with his hammer and pick for sapphires and rubies but had found none. Most agreed that he had been touched by the sun, taking his 'walking cures' and writing a tome in which he tried to link geology to Creation.

Lilli handed Nathan the honey cake and he raised it to his mouth. 'Yeast is sin,' she smiled, but he bit into it anyway, custard dribbling out the sides, down his hands and onto his blazer. 'That's it,' she said, 'you're going to Hell,' transforming herself into the snake he'd always imagined her to be, as his whole body glowed with anticipation of endless yeast, and sex. Lilli the guru, completely free of hang-ups, shedding her skin like a snake in a tub of spermicide. Although in the end it was just his imagination, quivering with the nervous energy which should have been preparing him for exams.

Trigonometric functions and chromosomes. Integers and the uterus, and oviducts and ovaries and cervix. He gave her the cake and grabbed his satchel. 'I'm dead,' he whispered.

'Not yet,' she smiled, stealing his old, leather satchel and opening it, producing Brodie's *Physiology of Algae* and throwing it as far as she could, out into the long, wet grass which led down to Gravel Pit Road.

'Christ!' he yelled, chasing after the book, picking it up and drying it off. As he did with *A History of the Black Death, Experimental Biology* and *Pure Mathematics 1.*

Standing up, Lilli took the last book, *A Bible Atlas*, tore out a page and screamed at the top of her voice, 'Strike me dead!'

Nathan had darted back and grabbed the atlas. 'Jesus. That's gonna cost me money.'

So here they were, a week later, waiting on the platform. William stood with his hands behind his back, his head bowed. 'How will you explain your exam results?' he asked his son.

Nathan shrugged. 'Not everyone's that way inclined.'

Back in Menge's cave, Nathan and Lilli had laid on the ground silently, Nathan unable to muster even a foot massage.

'You can be moody,' she said.

'Lilli,' he replied, 'I'm still at school.'

'Well go back.'

Silence. 'I got exams.'

'Go learn.'

And with that she started chanting, '"Hare Krishna, Hare Krishna, Hare Hare . . ."'

He stood up, repacked his satchel and headed back to town. As the chanting grew quieter behind him he thought how he'd fucked it up again – a bit of this, a bit of that, but not enough of anything. Perhaps if he'd stayed, the honey cake could have led to other things. As it was it was after lunch with nothing achieved. He turned to see Lilli, back on the hill and silent now, observing his slow progress.

Back at Tanunda station, the train pulled in and Nathan got his own compartment. Sitting down he read the reference that Arthur had hurriedly scribbled, attesting to Nathan's abilities with his hands, his proficiency with the lathe and chisel, in cutting and joining wood without splitting or fracturing it. Suggesting they couldn't do better than a boy with a brain like Nathan's, a manner the Lutherans were known for and a tenacity that would put Bradman's cricket team to shame.

As Bluma waved at the train becoming distant, William had already walked back into the empty car park, his head down, thoughts elsewhere, bubbling up like carbon dioxide through a cracked fermenter. God would return and Nathan would be saved too, regardless of chromosomes and integers. Refrigeration mechanics were as welcome as anyone in the garden of endless pickle.

Unless, of course, the Fechner girl got to him first.

'Where were you?' William had asked, when he found the absentee note in Nathan's school diary.

'Lilli was helping me revise.'

'Where?'

No reply, and William red-faced with a fire few of his neighbours ever saw. 'Where?'

'We went for a walk.'

Hitting Nathan around the head with the diary. But worse still when he presented them with his results: Maths 17%, Biological Science, 23%. And what else could William do but link these two

64

abominations? 'She helped you learn? Learn what? You've never had results like these before.'

'The work is too hard for me, Dad.'

'Nonsense.'

'It is.'

'Ask for help, from teachers. Not ... Fechner.'

Reminding himself to confront Bruno again.

'Dad,' Nathan had pleaded, 'I'm sick of study.' Although Nathan himself didn't know whether this was true or not. Whether it was the boredom of facts. Or Lilli. Chanting *Krishna* in her summer frock in the middle of winter, tearing up books he despised without compromise.

'From here on we work harder,' William had said, throwing Nathan's results into Bluma's stove.

'What about an apprenticeship?' Nathan asked. 'The government's sent around to schools.'

Adelaide apprenticeships. Boarding in town, coming home on weekends. The sort of disaster of a compromise which generally works between fathers and sons, William thought, allowing them both to save face, leaving the door open ... Avoiding talk of dreams, of writing poetry or making pottery – piano-playing ambitions left to shrivel in the shadows where they belonged.

As Nathan passed through Ovingham the city opened up in front of him: backyards full of soursobs and rusty bikes, Hills Hoists restrung with twine and teenagers cutting their toenails. Getting off at Islington works he found the appropriate building and had an interview with the works manager, who was turning an axle on a lathe the size of a Sherman tank. Nathan didn't get as far as producing his reference. Handshakes were exchanged and details taken.

That was it. He'd become a fridge mechanic.

Endless centrefolds above fitters' lathes promised ample consolation for the loss of an Eden of endless shiraz.

Tanunda was the epicentre of the vintage festival. On the Saturday after Nathan's interview, floats gathered in Goat Square for a procession of everything Prussian. Bluma, posed on a Dodge flat-top in a low tide of old lettuce leaves, was a Greek goddess in flannelette robes holding a vine-entwined staff. Children sat at her feet surrounded by semillon and chardonnay grapes as two third formers from St John's climbed a giant Grecian urn like natives in search of coconuts.

The same floats the locals had had for decades, courtesy of the Seppelt coopers and their apprentices. The Tanunda float (each of the Barossa towns was represented) was over-run with middle-aged Rhine maiden hausfraus courtesy of the Tanunda Hair Salon. Steps led up to an alfoil-covered throne where an unidentified Harvest Queen waved in the manner of the Princess Betty England. A giant papier-mache vine leaf in the shape of a sea shell extended its vascular network over the lot of them, protecting them from the rain which soaked their parade every year.

Except this one. A perfect day. Girls with shades of *Hitler-madchen* sprinkling rose petals before the parade as oom-pah bands struggled to keep their footing on the back of trucks. Traditional costumes and headware had been resurrected from bags of naphthalene and strapped on uncomfortably in counterpoint to gym shoes and thermolactyls showing beneath collarless jackets in the Bavarian style.

The major wineries had broken with tradition and organised a 'Chemistry of Wine' float, complete with scientists in lab coats testing wine in Pyrex beakers. This, a sign explained, was the future of their industry: the perfect pH and tannin, woodiness in predictable amounts, bags of tartaric acid hovering over the edge of giant stainless steel tanks which could each hold more than ten of William's vintages. William himself shook his head and muttered to a stranger, 'What's that got to do with wine?'

Nathan got in the spirit as a picker in traditional work clothes carrying a basket of shiraz grapes, distributing them to kiddies who lined the street in anticipation of something sweeter from the Apex float. Managing an almost sincere smile, he passed Joshua Heinz and his brood then Seymour Hicks and his daughter Ellen – Joseph, her husband, watching in the background from the steps of the Tanunda Hotel.

And Lilli. Standing with her grandparents, her mum and dad busy hamming it up on the Yalumba 'Four Crown Port' float ('The Port That Kept Mawson Warm in Antarctica').

'Haven't seen you round,' he said, placing his basket on the ground.

'Hear you're moving up in the world?'

Instead of replying he just smiled.

'You could've been a surgeon,' she continued.

'You could've been Prime Minister.'

'Conquering the ching-chongs with my custard cake.' She kissed Edna goodbye and started walking with him, the grapes forgotten in an ether of sexual chemistry bubbling from Penfold's Pyrex.

'I'll be coming home on weekends,' he said. 'I get free travel.'

'Goodness. How exciting for you.'

He looked at a fine wrinkle, permanently set across her forehead, and knew she was jealous. 'So we can catch up.'

'Perhaps.'

And the creases around her cheeks, forming small canyons of their own. 'Perhaps?'

'You'll have study, and church.'

He smiled. '*Feeble.*'

But she didn't respond.

'I should thank you,' he continued.

She frowned.

'For Menge's cave.'

'What's that got to do with anything? I screwed up your exams.'

'No.'

'Well why bring it up?'

'I could've just ... gone on. And then where would I be?'

She picked a bunch of grapes out of his basket. 'Chin whiskers.'

And although he smiled she just raised her eyebrows and, picking

67

grapes, sucking their juice and spitting them on to the footpath, returned to Bruno and Edna. Nathan wanted to say something but didn't, couldn't, dismissed again by someone close to him. It could've been lust, or love, or he might've just been an amusement, a pastime, a situation which he'd completely misread. Perhaps he'd become a challenge, a canvas on which she could paint over the algebra scrawls of his father. But, he figured, he was always analysing things too much, and his conclusions were generally always wrong.

Just because she was twenty-two and he was sixteen. He'd read about such relationships in Hollywood, men who mowed the lawns of bored, rich women. He didn't have a problem with this but, as it turned out, she wasn't as liberated as her manner or comments suggested, having him believe that she might dance naked in the mouth of Menge's cave as she waited for some Hindu god to swoop down and fuck her.

Nathan picked up his basket and walked on, smiling a barely credible smile as he got rid of his grapes as quickly as possible.

He'd spent the last few days repairing things with his father, working silently beside him in the wash-house. Blending different amounts of shiraz and merlot and trying them, spitting them into the concrete wash-basin and rinsing until they'd come up with something William was almost happy with.

Generally, at this point, William would seek out Bruno Hermann's opinion, sharing a glass of his first blend over the back fence. This year Bruno was forgotten, waiting, watching on his back porch as William returned to the wash-house without so much as looking at him.

Going inside, Bruno said to Edna, 'William is moody again.'
'Why?' she asked.

But Bruno didn't say anything, Lilli having already explained to both of them how Nathan had dragged her up to Menge's Hill when he should have been studying.

The following day was Pastor Henry's turn to have his say about Erntedanke, the harvest thanksgiving rich with the imagery of the vine and the winepress. The ladies had spent the previous evening decorating Langmeil church with their homemade garlands. The winning entry from Farm Day was given pride of place on the altar beside Henry. It was a controlled explosion of Arthur's gladiolus and lisianthus which Ian Doms' youngest had dreamt up as a tribute to the Blessed Mary. Who soon took centre-stage in a hymn of thanksgiving which finished in an exaltation to the great vigneron, imploring him to keep them safe from the Eyeties with their sparkling reds and the industrial chemists with their tartaric acid.

Thy word, O God, keep ever pure:
Protect Thy congregation;
Keep us untainted, and secure
From this vile generation . . .

Henry watched as Edna, bent over the organ, lost her spot in a coughing fit and Bruno sprung from his chair in anticipation of a very public Heimlich manoeuvre. Soon she recovered and continued, her rheumy fingers clicking like so many wishbones snapping cleanly in two. The front row grimaced as they listened, as they did every Sunday, suffering over the distorted blur of an improvised C sharp minor (she could only play on the black keys).

The Nicene Creed was invoked and a sermon, in Henry's most musical voice, led the congregation towards the lake of fire in which those missing from the book of life, at the End of Days, would be cast. What would the lake look like, he asked. The settling pond at the cement works, or the fountain in front of Yaldara homestead? Most probably like a slurry of hot, fermenting hops, indigestion bubbling up from the Sons of Darkness as they spent their eternities in perpetual copulation.

And then he began to improvise, smiling as he dared to descend from his pulpit to play the role of Christ, recently returned to earth in fulfilment of his promise. He had just appeared in Heuzenroeder's homeopathic shop as the elder Mrs Heuzenroeder was closing up. This got a big laugh, and the elder Mrs Heuzenroeder herself blushed in shades of red which Max Factor hadn't even dreamt of. Christ, unable to convince her of who he was, was sent packing down Murray Street, where he set up a soapbox in front of the Holden dealership.

'"It's me!"' Henry cried, re-mounting his pulpit as grandmothers farted beside their respective Stations of the Cross.

Jesus is crucified.

Henry took the voice of a heckler. '"If it's you, give us a sign!"'

Jesus is taken down.

As the Messiah, Henry explained, re-inflated a flat tyre on one of the dealership's FXs.

William, unsure if he should be alarmed at the levity, smiled a shallow smile he could explain away later if need be.

Henry waited until the laughing subsided and whispered, '"The peace of God, which passes all understanding, keep your hearts and your minds in Christ Jesus."'

And everybody heard him, replying in a hushed, communal whisper. 'Amen.'

As church was let out, Bruno stopped the Millers beneath the tallest of the candle pines at the top of the hill. Shaking Nathan's hand he said, 'We're all happy for you. And you too, William.'

Holding his neighbour's arm and rubbing it.

'Nathan's decided,' William said, curt. 'There's no good going on about it now.'

'About what?'

But William was already off down the avenue of pines, followed distantly by Bluma and Nathan.

70

Chapter Six

William popped his head into Arthur's workshop. 'Seymour's waiting.'

'I'll be right there.'

He waited outside with his hands in his pockets, watching a snail moving up the stem of a mostly dead larkspur. Inside, Arthur finished marking an arm of his cross with a hot poker: *What shall I render to the Lord, For all his bounty to me?* The smell of burning Tasmanian oak wafted out, through a plastic fly curtain, over to William as he picked up the snail and bowled it with his best Neil Harvey over-arm.

'Arthur!'

'Coming.'

Seymour Hicks, sitting behind the wheel of his hearse, tried to sound his horn but remembered it didn't work. Winding down the window he called, 'William,' as Mary rubbed away the condensation and said, 'It's like the good old days.'

'When was that?'

She kicked her husband's leg. 'The demister didn't work back then either.'

The hearse had been converted into a mini bus, of sorts, cushioned pews down both sides, feet resting on the metal receptacle which used to hold the coffins.

Joseph Tabrar, sitting beside his wife and three children, looked at his blurred reflection in a silver crucifix screwed into the roof. Then he turned to Ellen and asked, 'Have you looked?'

Referring to the brochure he'd given her on the satellite city of Elizabeth, a township about to be constructed in the outer northern orbits of Adelaide; promising 'all new homes and amenities, parks and gardens in a formal style ... modern hospitals and well-equipped schools'. All for the children of the migrants who Premier Playford would tempt over from the land of hope and hailstone, subsidising their fares in a hazy dream of Chips Rafferty with sheep. In reality a housing estate, doing horizontally what England had done vertically. Backyards big enough for cabbages and lettuces but little else.

'If we get in now ... pay a deposit.'

Ellen didn't look at him, staring ahead. 'David, did you bring your Brownie?'

Their middle child grimaced. 'It's Chas's too,' implicating his youngest brother. 'When do I get to use it?'

'All the time.'

Joseph looked into the clouded window. 'Quiet!'

'All those migrants,' his wife replied, trying to draw him out on her terms.

'So what?'

'I've always lived here.'

Close to Mary, her mother with her Barossa roots and a taste for white pudding. Close to Seymour, who'd always believed if it wasn't for him his daughter would have fallen into a great, dark chasm of Presbyterian shame and poverty. Ironing shirts in a tenement bed-sit for the dim-wit husband with his drinking problem (which would surely develop when they moved away) as their kids (with their filthy faces) crawled up the walls.

These were Seymour's thoughts, as he waited behind the wheel, looking back through the cracked rear-vision mirror, thinking, we all have a cross to bear. Because of the alternatives. Because of things we can't change. Nailing notices on church doors: *21. Life without Christ is stew without meat. 22. Dr Mosse and his Indian Root Pills cannot cure their way to Heaven. 23. Heaven is no seaside resort reached by steam train.*

Ellen turned to Joseph. 'I've read your brochure,' she said.

But now Joseph refused to answer.

'This can't go on forever,' he whispered.

Seymour thought he could make out Joseph's words. Unsure, he decided to say nothing, although he had before, late one night a year ago. 'If you're unhappy, leave, but if you think my daughter will go with you . . .'

Both Joseph and Seymour stared at Ellen.

'Don't be stupid, we're perfectly happy,' she replied, intent on damage control, taking Joseph by the arm and soothing his fiery temper.

Arthur opened the back of the hearse and climbed in. 'Sorry.' Followed by William and Bluma who, they claimed, had left Nathan inside with a book on the history of the Railways. The hearse set off, stopping next to pick up Julius Rechner, William telling the teacher how he shouldn't feel bad about Nathan, having only done his job.

'Nathan could repeat,' Julius consoled. 'He still has it in him.'

'He could, but he won't,' Bluma interrupted, shaking her head. 'I could talk to him.'

William shook his hand in the air. 'At that age, they can't be told.'

Detouring via Gruenberg they picked up Ron Rohwer and his young wife, then made for Lyndoch, only a few miles down the road, for the second outing of the Langmeil church's social club.

The first, they laughed and remembered as they drove, had been a trip to the South Australian Museum in Adelaide. Pastor Henry had shown them around the Micronesian and Aboriginal galleries, commenting how, although the Aborigines had been denied the good news of Christ, they'd nonetheless manufactured some very charming artefacts. Ian Doms, who couldn't come this year, had actually picked up a boomerang and said, 'They produced *this*, as Michaelangelo painted the Sistine Chapel.'

This missed the point altogether, Henry explained. Without the light of Jesus there could be no Sistine Chapel. Therefore, the boomerang affirmed the message of Christ even more.

But worse was to come. They were joined by a natural history guide who showed them around the stuffed animals, stopping in front of a wedge-tailed eagle and saying, 'In evolutionary terms, the birds of prey pre-dated most of our ... garden varieties.' Going on to relate this to Charles Darwin, the pigeon-fancier, who had compared the English carrier and short-faced tumbler, outlining differences and similarities in their beaks and skulls, explaining how their elongated eyelids and nostril orifices proved their brotherhood beyond a doubt.

Like the Negro and the Asian. Eskimo and European.

Moving on to Annie, Darwin's daughter, whose death the guide described in the most Dickensian terms. 'After she died, Darwin realised ...'

'What?' William asked.

'The purpose of all this.'

Turning on his heels and presenting them with a whole gallery of dead things, caught in the act of hunting and eating, preening and sleeping.

'The purpose being?' William asked.

'Nothing. Life was meaningless. God couldn't expect to take the credit for all Creation and at the same time strike down innocent children. It didn't add up.'

Silence. William shook his head. 'And all this came from Mars?'

The guide smiled. 'Perhaps.'

William stepped forward but before he could say anything else, Bluma was dragging him off towards the cafeteria.

No such dilemmas at Dinkum World, the social committee had decided. Here was a place, according to the brochures, where the best of Australia was celebrated. In the spirit of a Lawson story, read by a sheepless Rafferty around a roaring fire as cattle moaned in the distance – this would be the archetypal Aussie day. Visitors and migrants would go away understanding a little bit more about the wide, brown land.

A stobie pole painted with acacia-entwined slouch hats was

their first taste of Dinkum World. The hearse turned off and followed a paling fence covered with Aussie advertisements: homemakers with a Persil dazzle clutching their husbands' new Pelaco shirts.

Arriving at a carpark overgrown with asparagus fern, the group bundled out of the hearse and paid a sixteen-year-old the precise amount at group discount rate, pound notes tied up with a piece of Bluma's recycled string. Pastor Henry was there waiting for them, smiling.

First up, a man called Doctor Hamilton (this was never explained) showed the social committee how to attach corks to their hats. William improvised with one each side of his woollen cap. They were then led down a garden path, the joke having to be explained, and stopped before a replica outback dunny. When you opened the door and dropped a penny in a slot, the toilet seat lifted and a giant redback spider raised its head out of the pan. Bluma clung to Mary Hicks' arm and laughed. 'Who knows what's living down ours?'

'It may get a bit blue, ladies,' Doctor Hamilton said. They then continued along a path to the next exhibit: a nightie on a pole. Doctor Hamilton urged William to turn a handle and as he did the pole lifted and then dropped. They looked at the Doctor. 'Up and down like a bride's nightie.'

No response.

Jesus Christ, religious nuts, Hamilton thought, having had groups like this from the valley before. 'A real Aussie saying,' Hamilton explained, but no one was buying a word.

'Okay, this way to our wildlife exhibits,' the Doctor said at last, motioning towards the path.

As they continued Pastor Henry noticed a sandbox, the type used to stub out cigarettes. 'That's nothing,' Hamilton explained, but Henry was already standing beside it. Inside the sandbox was a small jam jar full of what looked like dog's hair; an old, winged nun's habit was arranged around it. Henry's expression turned from anticipation to confusion.

'What is it?' Bluma asked.

'This way,' Doctor Hamilton urged.

As they shuffled along, mostly in silence, Seymour pulled up beside William and said, 'I've checked all your dates.'

'And?'

Seymour smiled.

'Seymour, to me there's no doubt. I've had no theological training –'

'How's it possible then?' Ron Rohwer interrupted from behind.

'Faith,' William replied, turning his head back. 'Faith, the Bible, study, time . . . and a well worn *Cruden's Concordance.*'

'Setting dates is a folly,' Ron said. 'A sin. How does it go? "No man knoweth the hour or day, not the angels in Heaven . . . the Father only." Is that right, Pastor Henry?'

'Sorry?' Still caught up in the old Glen Ewin jam jar.

'"No man knoweth the hour . . ."' Ron repeated.

'Yes, Matthew . . . twenty-four.'

'William seems to think he knows.'

'Who's to say? The Bible's a very strange, a very imprecise book.'

'But it's the word of God.'

'And others.'

'"Take heed,"' Ron continued, '"watch and pray, you won't know when the time is . . ." or words to that effect.'

'"It is not for you to know the times or seasons,"' Henry said, '"which the Father have put in His power."' Going on to explain how they still knew when to pick grapes, when the leaves of the myrtle would turn, when the winter reached its equinox and the summer its most searing. 'I mean, we're not entirely stupid,' he concluded. 'Still, it's a big ask, William.'

Doctor Hamilton couldn't believe his ears. From *The Overlanders* to the Amish. More Fritz than the Chapman's factory, and a group discount too. Still, they'd paid. Goebbels was dead and part of being an Aussie was to take people as you found them.

'So,' Ron continued, 'you, William Miller, above all other men, know the exact year, month and day?'

'Kookaburras,' Doctor Hamilton whispered, as he pointed.

'According to the Jewish calendar,' William replied, 'it would be March twenty-one.'

'Nineteen fifty-two?'

'I believe.'

'What do you make of that, Pastor Henry?'

Henry stopped in his tracks, a confused Moses leading his tribe towards emus. The others stopped and looked at him. Even Doctor Hamilton stopped.

'As dry as a nun's nasty? Is that correct?'

Doctor Hamilton smiled, but everyone else was shocked.

Henry sighed. 'Well, at least that's *one* thing I know.' And smiled, walking on, taking the lead from Doctor Hamilton.

As they continued on through denuded scrub, overgrown with potato weed and horehound, Ron Rohwer took William aside and said, 'Just because someone exploded a bomb, doesn't mean the world's going to end. Every time's had its bomb.'

William was silent.

'There'll be a sign.'

'What sign?' William barked.

'Churches with Christ's face in the plaster.'

'Rubbish. Signs for idiots. Haven't come to nothing . . . anything.' Whereas William's path had been logical, mathematical, as well thought-out and balanced as an algebraic equation. He continued on without looking at Ron. 'We're all entitled to our own views, Ron.'

'Not to brainwash others, though.'

'Brainwash!'

Ron stopped but the others kept moving. '"No man knows,"' he whispered to himself, seeking higher consolation than Pastor Henry, who was caught up in a vision of someone harvesting their pubic hairs.

They were marched past an enclosure containing three lame wallabies that had been orphaned by a Holden. 'My daughter nurses them,' Hamilton said. 'When she's not busy in the ticket booth.' The Doctor explained how a Chinese panda, sitting motionless in a grassy enclosure, would be dead had Dinkum World not purchased it from the Chinese government when some zoo or other was about to close.

The pentothal narrowly avoided, thought William.

But suffering a sadder, slower form of euthanasia, as lorikeets and galahs from an adjacent aviary mimicked the sounds of his apocalypse.

The social committee settled in for their free sausage sizzle and the Doctor encouraged them to carve their names into a roughly hewn outdoor setting. 'Carved by our neighbour,' Hamilton said. 'A Yid, but by far the nicest Red Sea pedestrian I've ever met.'

Eventually it was time for a group photo. The Doctor stood beside William, smiled and said, 'Meine freundes, ha?'

William looked at his watch and sighed once again.

William lay in long grass in the late afternoon, watching drops of water trail down split tomatoes he'd told Bluma she never should have planted. Dusted regularly, but dying anyway. Turning a winter yellow of everything gone weedy, setting seed in a garden no one would bother about until spring.

He looked up, but then closed his eyes, his ears alert to distant trucks and sheep, a breeze through stray, wild oats. A Cessna over the High Eden Ridge transformed into the stukas of a nearly forgotten World War Two newsreel, screened for the town's benefit during the war in the Tanunda Institute. Then, days later, there were the trucks full of new street signs: overnight Bethanien became Bethany, and the Kaiserstuhl, Mount Kitchener. Pastor Henry had been ordered to pray in English and the Holy Cross and Gnadenberg churches were told to paint over their portraits of Luther, depictions of Prussian villages and narratives with decorative script, and to remove five statues of Jeremiah, Moses, St Peter, St Paul and Jesus, which were handed over to the Anglicans.

William was looking for a Wettebaum, a 'weather tree' that formed itself in the shape of a conifer in the high cloud formations which had made their way over from the west. The Wettebaum, it was said, would forecast the arrival of rain three days later. Another story said that if it rained on the twenty-seventh of June (three days time) then it would rain for the following seven weeks straight.

William had made out a Model T Ford, the face of Billy Hughes and even an olive tree. Close but not close enough. Mostly the clouds refused to solidify into shapes-as-signs, giving no indication of things to come, such as the council mowing of verges which always preceded their rates notice.

Bruno Hermann had always ridiculed William for his old-fashioned beliefs, but each time it had rained on the twenty-seventh it had just kept raining. Sometimes on and off, but without fail, for seven weeks, give or take a few days (*And no, it's not just the normal course of winter, Bruno*). On June twenty-four last year, as he was lying in this exact same spot, Bruno had come over to the fence and said, 'Look up there, William, it's a pencil pine ... or is it an Aleppo?'

Laughing. But William's eyes had stayed focused and he'd found one. Calling back to Bruno, busy on the throne, 'Look, perfectly formed,' not bending or warping as it made its way across the sky. 'I have to see this,' Bruno had said as he emerged, fighting with half a dozen buttons, to see William pointing at a giant pine tree stretched out across a blue canvas.

'Doesn't mean anything,' Bruno had muttered, but three days later William saw Bruno at his window, peering out at a sky full of dark clouds. William, vindicated, was doing the same, explaining to Bluma how Bruno had lost touch with his past.

But sometimes faith wasn't enough. The clouds had passed on without shedding a drop and that evening Bruno was at William's back door, explaining how the Siebenschlafer made about as much sense as life without electricity or gas. Still, he explained, we make worlds in our own heads and live in them, if that's what you want.

Bruno wasn't troubled with technology. Crushers the size of

B-17s, aerial spraying? No problem. 'Luther himself was a reformer,' he'd told William. Nailing notices to church doors. *21. My Kelvinator tractor is a rare and beautiful thing. 22. God would have us fill the bellies of starving kiddies, regardless of the means.*

And this is what William heard, laying in the grass in search of cumulus pine. Bruno on his Kelvinator tractor, emerging from his shed with Ian Doms' boom spray in tow.

He refused to sit up or open his eyes, or let Bruno spoil his day. He continued scanning the skies hopefully, picking up a viburnum-scented breeze from the Tanunda Road. And when Bruno engaged his P.T.O. and the air pump started charging the tanks, William lay back and thought of better ways of doing things: of neighbours (*real* neighbours) who used to help out with the hand-sowing, harvesting and stooking, and who would look after your children and share their extra lemons. Of preserving your own pears, avoiding tin cans leaching God-knows-what, and re-tiling your own roof.

Bruno opened the arms of the boom and re-mounted his tractor; opening the nozzles he engaged high range and started making passes through a paddock of Salvation Jane which he'd let go for too long. William had complained but it was too late now, the weed having set and dropped its seed. Up and forth, William trying to remain focused on the sky. Until a cloud of poison drifted over and settled on his face.

Spitting it out he sat up and wiped himself. He stood up and went over to the fence, waving at Bruno. Bruno left his tractor idling and came over to him. 'William, what were you doing in the grass?'

'What do you think?' Spitting. 'What are you using?'

'Glyphosate.'

From a brand new drum, purchased with his sheep dip and a bag of linseed meal for his broilers; bagged and delivered to the back of his ute by the new boy at Bennett and Fisher's. 'Say hi to Lilli for me, Mr Hermann.'

'How do you know Lilli?'

'We did maths together.'

'Oh.'

As Bruno's tractor chugged he leaned on a fence post and spoke quietly. 'How was I to know, William?'

'Look at the breeze, Bruno. People have washing out. That went straight onto our vegetables.'

'Can't hurt 'em.'

'The point is – '

'Alright, I'm sorry. Just the same, don't see snakes lying in long grass.' Bruno was tempted to tell William about Bluma, secretly dusting his cabbages and tomatoes when he was off at kegel or choir. Instead he took a deep breath and tried to keep the peace. 'Think you'll get your rain this year?'

'Have to wash these clothes.'

As if glyphosate was some mortal sin in liquid form.

'William – '

'People farmed a long time without – '

'You got shit on the liver.'

William stepped forward, indignant. 'I haven't got – '

'It's this business with Lilli, isn't it? She tells me it was your Nathan took her up there.'

'I'm talking about poison.'

'No you're not. This is because things haven't ended up like you wanted.'

'Pesticides stay in the body.'

'Lilli's got spirit, but she isn't what you think.'

'Which is?'

'A tramp.'

'It's Nathan's choice.'

Bruno's Kelvinator chugged uneasily and stopped. He looked around and back at William. 'I suppose that's a sign.'

'You're superstitious.'

Bruno smiled, folded his arms and thought about Bluma with her hand-crocheted covers that she pulled over mirrors during thunder storms to stop the collection and deflection of God's anger down hallways and through bedrooms, up into Nathan's sleeping loft and down into their cold cellar. 'Anyway, I gotta finish this,' he said, turning and walking off. 'All the best to Nathan for his new job.'

William stormed into the wash-house, slamming the door and sitting fully clothed. He knew where the problem was. It was Bruno's son-in-law, Peter Fechner, forever busy in Adelaide, who had neglected his duties as a father, allowing Lilli to drift through life without so much as a thought for the essentials: God, family, school. Allowing her to turn from a valuable member of their community into someone who didn't care. A child of her age, more than willing to infect others with the plague of apathy. Infecting Nathan whenever he was around her. Until he succumbed, Julius writing it up in his reddest ink: *Nathan lost his focus.* Just as much on God as Biology, or so William believed. And so he wanted to tell Bruno.

In the end it was best to show some discretion, lest things degenerate into a soap opera of carefully scripted replies, which ultimately led nowhere.

He pulled off his clothes and soaked them in the trough, taking washing powder from the cupboard and pouring it in by the handful. Then he filled a bucket with cold water and tipped it over his head, again and again, until he was shivering and his penis had shrunk to the width of a carpenter's pencil. Finally he set to his clothes, scrubbing, rinsing and draining. Again and again, until his hands were red and numb.

And then he opened the door and called out at the top of his voice, 'Bluma!'

'Yes?' Emerging with a scone cutter.

'Bring me some clothes.'

That night William left early for kegel, minus the Wettebaum which he'd probably missed as it dispersed across a pasture of blue sky thanks to Bruno's stubbornness.

Bluma helped Nathan pack his duffle bag: work boots and

T-shirts, hankies and freshly ironed underwear; a Bible, which he promised he'd return to from time to time; and a jar of pickled dill cucumbers for his host.

'Help with the washing up, leave the toilet lid down and don't talk politics.'

'Or religion?'

'Unless it's the Bible. They may be Methody.'

Bluma was trying to finish some white-work, improvising with a needle too big by half. This time, *Schlafen Sie Wohl*, for Nathan's hosts to hang above their bed. Nathan was reading what remained of William's newspaper when there was a knock at the door, followed by a head, and Lilli bearing a gift.

'Mrs Miller, how are you?' Kissing his mother on both cheeks like some impudent Frenchy.

'Fine. And your mum?'

But Lilli just smiled and handed Nathan the gift. 'For those long nights when you haven't got me around.'

Nathan looked at Bluma. Unable to explain what this girl was doing in their home, he shrugged and unwrapped the present. *The Golden Age of Steam*. 'Thank you. Just in case I haven't had enough during the day.'

'Just in case,' she smiled.

Nathan was confused, but he already knew that with Lilli what you saw wasn't necessarily what you got. Lilli was coming to resemble some barely believable creation from a radio soap. While Lilli sat and talked with Bluma, promising his mother free cake if she came in when it was quiet, Nathan tried to read her motives. Then he wondered if he wasn't becoming like his father, analysing agendas where there were none, sealing his observations away inside a glass brick wall where they could be seen but not changed.

Walking her home later that night he said, 'I can't win with you.'

'Do you know what that book cost me?'

'What?'

'Nothing ... it was my Dad's.'

They stopped inside the ruins of an old cottage and sat on rubble. 'Will you miss me?' he asked.

She smiled and almost laughed. '"Oh, Rex, my heart beats like the wings of a –"'

'Alright!' Throwing the handle of an old saucepan at her.

'It's not a gulag,' she said.

He looked at the moon on her face, settling on her high cheek bones. 'I'm sort of looking forward to it,' he said.

'That's what I've been saying. Do you know how backward this place is? Quaint.'

And all at once Nathan thought of his father again, William's anachronisms growing cheesier by the minute in contemplation, like so many remaindered postcards of places which no longer existed except in people's memory. Places in which the desperate clung for dear life, catching buses where they no longer ran and singing (mostly incorrect) lyrics from songs no one remembered or cared about. William's world had ossified. Nathan knew that he had to move on, because the alternative was death by hand harvesting. Memories had to be forged, made unique, otherwise they were just somebody else's.

'I'm not going to be here forever,' she said, as if trying to convince herself more than anyone. 'Oh, I forgot.' She pulled out a newspaper clipping and smiled. 'I found this … I thought if you had any spare time.' She used her best recitation voice, leaving behind the boy on the burning deck in favour of the Adelaide *Advertiser* classifieds. '"Greek goddess. Traditional recipes involved. Discount for the liberators of Crete."'

He shook his head. 'I don't understand.' She rolled her eyes and he slowly got it. 'Oh …'

'There's a number for you.'

'No, no, I have *The Golden Age of Steam*.'

'Those long, lonely nights.'

'I'm a school kid.'

'Not anymore.'

Where William had harvested news of the 38th Parallel, Lilli had cut out the Adult Services (William had found them too, deciding they should be in his scrapbook of signs, but deferring in the interests of decency). She kept reading, two columns of everything hot and spicy in bluestone Adelaide, cooking away under the nose of Playford and the moral majority, decent folks in frocks with cardies sipping bronchial cure and listening to *Blue Hills* as Mistress Josephine, severe and sensational, took endless calls on a PMG bakelite phone, alternating between home and a cottage in Wright Street which charged by the hour.

'This one's for you. "Male to male. Ryan. Tall, dark and gorgeous."' Nathan laughed and sat back, trying not to think about it. Eventually he crawled over the rubble and sat next to her. 'I'll take it anyway.'

'You wouldn't know what to do.'

'"Sheena. Well dressed ..."' he read, but stopped, watching as Lilli stretched back, like William in search of lost weather trees, emotionally neutral, curious.

Bloody hell, he thought, watching the rise and fall of her chest.

'Are you looking at me?' she asked, sounding detached.

'Of course. It's you or a pile of rocks.'

'Thanks.'

He moved on top of her. No words necessary. If religion was instruction then nature was instinct. *Michelle seeks pillion passenger. Hold tight, keep quiet.* He held her arms down and said, 'Who's feeble now?' feeling, for what seemed like the first time ever, completely in charge of what happened next. No morals to be drawn from the Scriptures. None of William's homilies.

He unbuttoned her blouse, quickly, confidently, and there they were, like a pair of Bluma's Berlei's hung out to dry, bulging like over ripe tomatoes about to split down the side. Verbal instructions followed, putting a momentary damper on things, but he quickly moved onto the fullness of her body as they rolled together over rubble and rusted tools, a broken mixing bowl and a baby's rattle.

As he sat on top of her, shirtless in the full moonlight, he wondered if it'd finish as quickly as it started, Lilli taking off into the night like Grable painted onto the side of a B-17.

And then suddenly, at a crucial moment, William appeared out of the darkness. 'Seven angels with seven vials full of plague,' he was saying to Arthur, who was skipping to keep up with him. 'Let's see: TB, polio, smallpox, syphilis, cholera . . .'

Nathan lay on top of Lilli as the men walked past the glassless window, so close he could hear his father breathing and Arthur coughing. He covered Lilli's mouth when she giggled, but then he started laughing too, rolling off her, ending up in the old fireplace, breaking up as William passed into the distance.

'I've had it,' he smiled.

She crawled over to him. 'Of course. Why did you come to Menge's cave?'

Unable to find the right words, he continued.

As far as trains were concerned, he guessed he'd either end up loving or hating them.

It all started on the trip down from Tanunda when the conductor, having found out where Nathan was going, started in on the history of the Brill railcar in which they were travelling. 'Built by the Railways in 1928, Islington workshops, by fellas just like you.' Taking Nathan up front to meet the driver, who explained the crunch gear-box and clutch, how the Brill would come to be seen as the pioneer of diesel railcars, moving on to a history of broad versus narrow gauge, which itself was a discussion of colonial politics, Federation and opportunities missed.

Nathan was saved by Islington station – a platform hemmed in by depots and workshops, parallel and criss-crossing lines filled with steam and diesel and rolling stock: eight-wheeled side loaders and four-wheeled sit-ups, the cafeteria car and the Governor's Vice Regal. Men in overalls sat in the sun against workshop walls eating stale sandwiches of corned beef and pickled onions beside white and red geraniums (to Islington what carob trees were to Tanunda).

Nathan was overcome by the smell of the place: coal dust drifting and settling like mist in the Flaxman Valley, into every pore in every man's skin, hair, car windscreens – floating through windows onto official SA Railways correspondence, over the fence and across Churchill Road, settling on the washing of the double-fronted red brick homes. As he crossed the tracks the smell of oil came up in vapours, emitted from gravel, quarried in Kavel's day, that had never seen weeds or grass or anything remotely green. A big, black loco moved off from taking water and blasted him; Nathan jumped and kept walking, feeling like a mite lost in the train-set his father would never build him.

Peering inside giant, cavernous workshops he saw men at work on axles and wheels and pistons and rods, welding, hammering, illuminated by arc lights and skylights and cathedral windows covering whole walls, the message of Christ replaced by the homilies of Commissioner William Webb: *The only basis of economy in railway operation is the reduction of train miles by the use of large capacity cars and the largest possible locomotives.*

Nathan, now kitted out in green overalls and workboots, was introduced to Bob Drummond, a lightly bearded man of about fifty with rampant nostril hair. 'Bob looks after the refrigeration apprentices,' a supervisor explained – teaching them, watching their work, keeping them in line and, in Nathan's case, having them board with him and his family during the week.

'I have a son a little older than you,' Bob said, 'he'll keep you busy.'

Nathan smiled. 'Busy?'

'Nothing your parents wouldn't approve of.'

And Nathan thought, I wouldn't be so sure.

He was led through the yards, through a door into the western end of a shed given over to refrigeration and hydraulics. 'S'pose it's a bit of a culture shock,' Bob half asked, stopping to look at him more closely. 'You from the Barossa?'

'Tanunda.'

'Nice spot.'

He means for day trips, Nathan thought, for a quick Sunday motor, wine-tasting and authentic yeasts.

'What's that little bakery?' Bob asked.

'Apex.'

'Yeah. Bloody beautiful. I could get you to bring some down on Mondays.'

'Sure.' Thinking how it'd be a good reason to visit Lilli, and how impressed she'd be with him in his overalls and workboots.

Bob took him into a side office and sat him on a sofa of ruptured springs. Seating himself behind a desk he went through the indenture papers Nathan would have to sign, and get co-signed by his parents. 'Miller ... you're not one of those humourless Lutherans then?'

Nathan paused and sighed. 'Actually, we were Muller before the war.'

Bob kept reading. 'I generalise. Still, you seem okay. You'll need a sense of humour to work in this place.'

'How's that?'

'These fellas are salt of the earth, no bullshit. Meat and three veg, football and milk on your back doorstep. Don't bring your ballet shoes, and leave your Bible at home. What you give is what you get and if you're a smart arse ... you don't seem like a smart arse ... you wanna learn?'

'Of course.'

'Make some money?'

'Wouldn't be bad.'

Bob paused and looked at him. 'Your lot have always stuck to themselves,' he said. 'I always thought that was strange.'

'They were persecuted in Germany.'

'Wouldn't a happened here.'

Nathan looked back at Bob, who was busy printing words in a slow, simple script. He looked at his mentor's sideburns and fat, pasty cheeks and imagined him sitting in his living-room, surrounded by Cornish seascapes and a portrait of the King. He imagined Bob carving corned beef (encased in fat) and dead-heading his agapanthus on a quiet Sunday afternoon. He wondered how comfortable he'd be losing his ironstone heritage.

'Tanunda is inbred,' he smiled. 'You find yourself fancying your cousins.'

Bob grinned. 'You're a bloody lunatic, Muller.'

'Sieg heil.'

'Just don't forget my bloody streusel.'

Nathan was set straight to work on an eight-wheeled Butcher van, a refrigerated Commonwealth Rail carriage which formed part of the Tea and Sugar train. This supply train, he was told, made weekly runs across the Nullarbor desert, stopping at sidings to sell groceries from one carriage and meat from another. The Butcher van featured a cool-room stocked with whole animals on hook, a pair of resident butchers cutting by request. Over time water had ruined the wooden panelling which lined the cool-room, holding in thick insulation which did its best against Nullarbor summers as compressors worked tirelessly to keep everything cold.

With gloves and mask he worked beside another apprentice, pulling nails and stripping back the wood. At one point the older red-head warned, 'Watch out, they'll be coming for you.'

'Who will?'

But the red-head just shrugged and wouldn't elaborate.

After they had stacked the wood and removed the insulation, Nathan was left to sweep out the carriage. Finishing up, he heard voices outside and then saw a group of six young men, all in green overalls, standing in the doorway.

It only took them a minute to strip Nathan, putting his boots back on and locking him in. The compressor clicked on and a cold vapour as thick as mist rose from the floorboards. For an hour he stood and sat, jogging on the spot, swinging from the stainless steel beams which held the carcases on hook, unsure whether he was pissed off or amused – either way, determined to laugh about it when they opened the door.

Which wasn't the ending he'd expected. Being carried across the workshop by the same six in overalls. Lowered into a 44-gallon drum full of cold, murky water and honoured with a crown of geraniums and a toilet-brush sceptre. Bob stood in the background smiling. Nathan could read his lips as he whispered, 'No bullshit.'

'Here stands the King of Kings,' the red-head mocked, and they all laughed uncontrollably.

Nathan shook his head. 'When do I get out of here?'

'When you've been judged,' the red-head laughed. And with that they led in half a dozen office girls, who took seats and settled in with smiles on their faces, obviously used to this game.

Nathan lowered himself into the drum until his shoulders were just above the water.

'We can wait all day,' one of the girls called, and with that the whistle blew for the fellas' smoko.

Nathan waited another ten minutes but by then his toes and fingers were numb. 'Is this for real?' he asked, and they all laughed, choking on sandwiches and fighting back tears.

Attack was the best form of defence. Nathan submerged his head and used his weight to tip the drum over. As the group leapt about to save their shoes he climbed from the drum and ran towards the office, making no attempt to hide himself, shouting Navajo war cries and leaping through the air like a gazelle.

(Just the same, one of William Webb's old secretaries made a sighting. She returned to her office with the others and typed up a memo which later appeared on every notice board around the works. Like one of Lilli's personals, it didn't pull punches, describing form, shape and general appearance. Bob Drummond asked for them to be taken down but Nathan said he didn't care.)

Walking home with Bob that first night, Nathan felt a thaw which extended beyond his fingers and toes. Bob said, 'If you give it, you gotta take it,' describing how Phil, his son, had mastered the art. 'This one time, he got me good. I couldn't afford to get power into the shed, so when I used to come home at night, I'd drive the car in until this tennis ball, hanging from the roof, touched the windscreen.' He smiled, remembering. 'So this one night, I'm slowly edging the car in and, crash, right into the back wall. Got out, scratched me head, couldn't work it out. Turns out Phil had moved the ball six inches forward.'

He kept walking, smiling. 'Never got it repaired. Use the shed for me wheelchairs now.'

Another story, Nathan guessed, as they walked on under crows balancing on power lines and someone somewhere starting up a Hoovermatic.

Chapter Seven

Pastor Henry's was a surplus government house from the twenties, red brick and crumbling, painted white here and there to cover up the salt damp. As William made his way up the driveway, he noticed horehound growing between cracks and through a hedge of camellia which grew below the kitchen window.

Pastor Henry had let things go. Piles of empty bottles, themselves overgrown, lay smashed beside a mountain of old newspapers smelling cat-pissy and soaked by the rain. Cracks from the driveway extended up the walls, revealing mortar and wiring Henry didn't give much thought to. Without the touch of a Bluma or Mary Hicks his life had become a domestic disaster, in counterpoint to the surplus home-maker magazines which Edna Hermann, his cleaner, had gathered from Dr Scholz's waiting room and left on his phone table.

William knocked on the door. Henry led him into the living room and it was all just as he'd suspected.

Earlier that morning, at church, the Elders had avoided him like the plague, walking away as he approached, cutting short conversations. And then Gunther Fritschle had come up to him and said, 'We'd like you to come to a meeting tonight, at Pastor Hoffmann's.'

'Why?'

'Seven perhaps?'

Walking away.

William knew what it was about of course. People who should have known better, choosing to bury their heads in the sand, following protocol in the established Prussian way. As he saw the Elders sitting in a row in the living-room, he imagined them with spiked army helmets, sent in service of the Kaiser. He sat down and Edna, finishing her cleaning, put a shot of something red and syrupy in front of him. 'How's Bruno?' he asked, in a scene from a Hollywood film which was going from bad to worse. 'That's something altogether different,' she replied – a bad sign no matter how you looked at it.

Edna was dismissed and Pastor Henry began. 'The Elders have made a decision, William.'

William looked along the row: Gunther, the old school Lutheran who saw him as some sort of heretic. Ron Rohwer, the droning, flat baritone who still saw Luther's translation of the Bible as an act of God. Trevor Streim, with his fetish for the perfect kegel pin, scratching his chin and watching a daddy-long-legs crawl across a spot on the front window Edna could never reach. And then there was Julius Rechner's brother, Franz, and a shop-keeper from Angaston he'd never said more than twenty words to. As well as Rohrlach, a *Vactric* vacuum salesman, as slippery as a bucket of squid, having worked his way up through the Langmeil hierarchy with favours on much-reduced terms.

'They ... we, would like you to stop talking about your dates,' said Henry.

Although he knew it was coming, William was still surprised. 'My dates are all correct,' he said.

Ron Rohwer shook his head.

'Let me finish,' Henry continued. 'I believe people are entitled to their own opinions ... frankly, I'd be quite happy if it was March twenty-one. Only, there's no one else saying this, William. I'm no academic – '

'*Cruden's Concordance* – '

'I know about *Cruden's*, and the Bible, still ... the Elders are the government of the church.'

'Christ is.'

'William ...'

There was silence as William looked at the row of Elders accusingly. Edna, listening from the kitchen, happy to see her Bruno vindicated, tried to remember the exact words to tell him later. 'I shan't stop talking about it,' William said, 'because it's the truth. The Bible isn't a static book.'

'Neither is it a book of spells, of hocus-pocus,' Ron replied.

Henry turned on him. 'Ron, please.'

'No, this is the real issue, Pastor Henry. William has put himself above the word of Christ.'

'I have not.'

'You have.'

'I bet this was all your idea.'

Henry stood up. 'Please . . . this is what we were trying to avoid. It's not a school yard. Everyone gets their turn.' Sitting down he looked at the ground and then back at William. 'Nonetheless, a vote was taken, William.'

'I shan't stop.'

'Joan of Arc,' Ron whispered.

'I haven't stolen your pulpit, Henry. I just tell those who ask, who listen.'

'William, it's out of my hands.' Henry moved a dead, potted aspidistra which had been sitting on his smoker's stand since before the war, and said, 'William, I've got a whole congregation to think about.'

'Exactly why you *should* be listening.'

'I'm not *not* listening. Cripes . . . who wants to say something? It's you fellas started it.'

Gunther opened a well-worn Bible to Matthew and read, '"Of that day and hour knoweth no man – "'

'Gunther,' Henry interrupted, 'we've covered that. Maybe if we could stick to personal impressions.'

Gunther closed his Bible and pondered. 'You're an honest man, William, a hard worker, but we've had these problems before.'

Referring to the schism last century between the moderate Pastor Fritzsche and the fire-and-brimstone founder of their church and town, Pastor Kavel. Kavel was obsessed with the End, Fritzsche

94

with growing the perfect cucumber, building the perfect fachwerk and being happy for the here and now. Valley Lutherans were bent one way or the other; this would dictate the church they'd worship in and even the people they'd acknowledge in the street. Families were split and communities divided over this very question. Some ended up moving interstate, one family even to America.

Gunther, whose father had been friends with Kavel, retold a story the moderates had used to ridicule them, completely untrue, told and re-told, becoming a gospel of its own. 'They said that my father had a vision of a giant, bloodied, fire-breathing Mephistopheles walking across the Kaiserstuhl on a wet and windy August night. He went and asked a blacksmith to make a tremendous chain which would hold the Devil for a thousand years. Later, Kavel and his followers took the chain and climbed the Kaiserstuhl in search of the Devil. But all that happened was it rained and they went home wet.'

Ron Rohwer opened his eyes, having heard the story at least forty times before. He wasn't so interested in the past as the future, he explained. There were better ways of teaching people about Christ and his eventual return. Take last year's musical production for example, going on to remind them of the twenty minute show which had been purchased from an American evangelical group. Apparently *they* knew how to get the punters in. He recalled the scene where all of the kiddies bowed down at the feet of a crucified Christ:

> *Walking in the shadows of your disciples,*
> *Sheltered from the hot, burning sun;*
> *I can go anywhere with you beside me,*
> *Now we've got the Romans on the run . . .*

Ron as director, drilling the kids every night, clapping and singing along in an attempt to resurrect Mrs Fox's forever slow tempos. 'Remember,' he asked, 'when the stone was rolled back from the mouth of the cave?' He continued singing, smiling:

We're all feelin' fine,
It's resurrection time;
Raise your voices higher,
And praise the new Messiah!

William slipped back in Henry's recliner and shook his head. 'If that's all the Bible means to you.' Box steps and cheesy grins, Mickey Mouse ears narrowly avoided.

'You're not Nostradamus,' said Gunther.

'He was mostly wrong,' the vacuum salesman offered.

Gunther sat forward. 'He foresaw Hitler.'

'Rot. He could have meant anyone.'

William stood, refusing his sherry. 'I shall say what I want to who I want.'

The other Elders were glad they'd avoided their turn. 'Just as well,' Henry said afterwards, 'it wouldn't have made any difference.'

William walked home angry, misunderstood, starting to see his church as a puritanical dictatorship of one view and one view only, like the society he'd seen described by the newsreel footage at the Institute during the war. Pastor Henry was a shambles, a man of God without God, a spineless jellyfish like the ones he'd pass through his fingers on their camping trips to Port Elliot – sitting on the end of the jetty with Bluma, Nathan and Arthur, contemplating God's creation in its infinite beauty and complexity, something only understood by *those who thought about such things.* Yes, Wilhelm Muller, still tackling the riddle of Revelations. He looked at the stars and saw a code there too but guessed it would take another William Miller to read it.

The next morning William was up a ladder, pruning a golden elm which each year exploded vine-like branches into the atmosphere. Why Anthelm had ever planted it was beyond him, but there it was, easier to prune than chop down, and it did give some decent shade in summer. Suddenly Pastor Henry was beneath him, steadying the ladder and asking, 'Why do you bother pruning it?'

William answered in the fewest possible words. 'Pruning is a habit. Like cutting toe nails.'

He heard Henry laugh – 'Last year when we had the washing of feet . . .' – and dropped a branch in the pastor's direction. 'I should get you to do my garden, cape honeysuckle everywhere, and next door's lantana.'

'Sarsaparilla vine will ruin everything.'

William felt Henry let go of the ladder and looked down to see the pastor bent over sniffing a scentless paperbark.

'My mother was hopeless. Rosemary everywhere. Although she did manage to grow a weeping fig.'

'Henry, you're not going to talk me around with plumbagos and bottlebrush. Just like Pastor Fielke used to do. Fire you up with every piece of rubbish under God's sun, then, watch out.'

Henry cowered from another branch but this time it was nowhere near him. 'They came to me, William. I told them there was no risk of a . . . fracture, but they insisted.'

William climbed down and moved his ladder. 'There was some business between Rohwer's father and mine.'

'It wasn't just Ron.'

William stopped and looked at him for the first time. 'He's in everybody's ear.'

'Well . . . like I said.'

'Henry, don't be so diplomatic. What do *you* think?'

Henry took the pruning shears and mounted the ladder. 'I can see their concerns. Thinking about that picnic we had on the Kaiserstuhl . . . thirty-six, thirty-seven?'

'No, it was during the war.'

'Remember the fall-out?'

'So what?'

'People would like to see us look – '

'Henry, focus . . . Jesus is listening. What's he think of what you're saying?'

Henry reached over for a branch and almost fell. William steadied the ladder, wondering if he was up to *any* job. Now Henry was peering down at him. 'William, I've got nothing to hide from Jesus.' Stopping short of saying what he'd given up for the Christian faith compared to William. 'Maybe it was thirty-nine ... anyway, it seems like we've only just put it behind us.'

'It wasn't an issue, Henry.'

Referring to the episode that began with a picnic service they'd had high on the Kaiserstuhl. Henry had led them up there like a budget Moses, surveying a spot with the best view of the valley. Picnics were laid out and enjoyed and children played. After lunch the men made a ring of stones for seating and Henry attempted to inspire his open-air congregation with a Bergpredigt, a sermon on a hill about the sermon on the mount. Jesus was invoked on the breeze which blew over them and a morning hymn was sung in praise of Creation.

And then Henry began. Holding up the periodical *Joseph's Best Paper*, he proceeded to slander the godless dogs who'd criticised (in language oozing sarcasm) the Barossa Lutherans for 'book burning'. In reality, this 'censorship' had just been a comment he'd made in a sermon a few weeks earlier, criticising Lawrence, Joyce and others. In defiance, *Joseph's Best Paper* was burnt and the smoke blown, by a hundred wheezing lungs, back towards the whore of Babylon which was Adelaide. Unfortunately for Henry, there'd been a spy among them. The cover of the next issue of the magazine featured a line drawing of their picnic, complete with Henry as Goebbels and a camp-looking D.H. Lawrence being boiled alive in a pot of sauerkraut as an unmistakable Picasso was beaten to death with sticks of mettwurst. The main article contained fictional episodes from the picnic, including book burnings of the periodical, Hitler sympathisers cursing the English in Barossa Deutsch and men in lederhosen whacking each other on the bottom with Lutheran Bibles.

The editors were warned by censors about the dangers of hysteria, the risk of defamation and general insensitivity towards German Australians. But by then the damage was done. Letters were written to newspapers, signatures gathered and German companies boycotted. Day by day Pastor Henry descended further into a Hades of his own creation – a hot, steamy place where even God himself couldn't venture and so-called 'intellectuals' played the role of horned devils.

Henry outlined his position in a letter to the papers but no one believed his pleas of innocence. A Fritz was a Fritz. In the end only time saved him. His job was never in question as the Elders of Langmeil supported him – a debt he could never repay. Church leaders voiced their support for the King, Union Jacks flew down Murray Street and when the trucks with their new street signs arrived no one said a thing.

Henry prayed publicly in English with his head bowed.

He looked down from the golden elm, covering his heart with his pruning shears. 'I learnt, sometimes it's better to keep things in here.'

William nodded. 'You were nailed up like Jesus. You didn't say anything wrong. God heard what you said. The bookworms will rot in Hell.'

'It wasn't what I said, but when I said it. Anyway, the Presbyterians banned the same books.'

'God walks with some of them too.'

'If I had my time over, William.'

William pointed towards the middle of the canopy. 'You would've said the same thing.'

'No.' Henry stepped on a branch to reach the centre. 'All I ask, William, is that you keep your dates in your study. I don't care if the world beats a path to your door. Even if you're right, which would be good. I could avoid the worst of old age.'

'The middle branch ... This is the good news, Henry. I can't lock it in my study. And if the bookworms and Rohwers of the world –'

Henry reached just beyond his balance. 'You don't hear a word –'

Slipping, coming to rest with blunt branches in his ribs, a bleeding scratch down the length of his neck. 'William ...'

'Henry, careful.'

Henry freed himself and climbed down, handing back the pruning shears and shaking his head. 'I hope you're right.'

William shrugged. 'I can finish off if you like.'

What Rose Drummond called 'chow mein' was cooked in her near-new Namco pressure cooker, whistling steam every minute or so in tribute to Saigons never seen and Shanghais never tasted. As Nathan buttered bread she explained how it was the latest thing: carrots, peas and top-grade mince, doused with Keen's curry and covered with as much cabbage as a Namco could hold, steamed down and served with bowls of rice beside slices of Kraft cheese on 'continental bread'.

'My dad would never eat this,' he commented, thinking how chow mein was the Joe Aronson of the mouth.

'And what do your people eat?' Rose asked, breaking off a piece of fig nougat and placing it beside him, immersing her hands in water the temperature of molten steel and scrubbing Bob's ashtrays lovingly as her favourite pittosporum rustled gently outside the window.

'Pickled pig is big. Ham, bacon, pork. Bruno, next door, does the killing for Dad.'

Describing the beast tied up by the back legs and strung up from the myrtle beside his old swing. Squealing and then calming, as its throat was cut and blood went everywhere, spraying out over Bluma's vegetables and into the Santa Anna William hardly ever mowed with his blunt and rusty hand-mower. 'Then Bruno cuts it up and takes some for his efforts, including the blood.'

Rose turned and frowned.

'Blutwurst, a sausage you wouldn't give your worst enemy. Then Mum's out with a knife and the Saxa – salted, pickled, and Dad carrying the jars into the cellar. Although it fries up okay, I suppose.' Going on to explain how anything tasted good besides his mum's pickled turnips.

'I could try some of these meals, if you like.'

'Don't worry, Mrs Drummond, it's not something I'll miss. Apart from the custard cake.'

100

'Ah –'

'Which is already taken care of.'

Rose then told him about her day at the Royal Adelaide Hospital, where she went most days as a volunteer visitor – 'talking the legs off any poor soul who's willing to listen to me' – beside a fellow volunteer called Terese, a newly arrived New Australian with a dozen words of English but no confidence to use them. Rose generally sent her to the cafeteria on errands. '"Give them this piece of paper and they'll know," I'll say as I scribble. "Turf Virginia, ten pack, ten shillings . . . now, you know how much change to bring back?"' Other times she'd try to draw Terese into the conversation. 'Now, Terese, tell us about your village – Vienna, wasn't it?'

Rose explained how both she and Bob were involved with the hospital auxiliary – Bob mending and restoring old wheelchairs in the shed of the shifted tennis ball, most nights after the *Colgate Hour*, and she as a Lavender Lady.

She stirred the cabbage, inhaling deeply and smiling at him. 'There are lots of jobs: the sweets trolley, delivering papers . . . but I just like to talk. Especially the ones that seem alone. You can tell 'em. Specially when everyone else's got family around.'

Rose of a morning, after Bob had left for work, setting off in their Vauxhaul for a specially reserved park; unloading another gleaming, mechanically faultless chair, wheeling it down to the basement as porters scattered imaginary rose petals in her path.

'I had a young lass this morning, lost her kiddy, mind you, this is all confidential. As it turned out it was just as well, seeing how her bloke was a . . .'

Nathan never learned about the father, his faults being passed over in a shower of curry. Eyetie or Arab, or maybe one of those wandering types, hanging around outside the Challa Gardens Hotel at closing, draped in black leather across a mechanically faultless motorbike he spent his days perfecting. Moving out at sunset to hunt the innocent, and the next morning, taking his clothes and 'splitting' before the sun rose and another disillusioned girl reached for her Balfours aprons.

'I tried everything to take her mind off it. Of course, the parents were off in . . . Czechoslovakia.' She stared down into her dishwater, unhappy with the temperature and suds, pulling the plug and refilling it, sparing Nathan the details of how the girl had let the little kiddy go hungry, for days, weeks, crying, and not a single neighbour, not a one mind you, knocked on the door to ask if they could do something. No, not the Australia I know . . .

'Cold hands, warm heart,' she whispered, as the water filled up. 'I've left my ring on.' Removing it. Thinking how cold dishwater could get nothing clean. 'Still, maybe it's all for the best.'

Seeing how lovelessness only led to more of the same.

'How's that?' Nathan asked.

She turned off the tap and looked out of the window. 'I talked about the movies, but even Rodney Taylor couldn't bring her around. The koalas at Cleland, which she remembered as a kiddy. The snake show near the children's hospital. As it turned out, she was one for the racing vehicle. Bob's taken us to Rowley Park speedway, but she said her people used to live there, so to speak, every Friday night.'

As she droned in his ear like an Anglicised Rohwer, Nathan looked up and saw a crucifix on the wall: Christ staring down at a stray pea, stranded in the middle of a melamine savanna. Explaining the most simple of spiritual conundrums: yes, he thought, William Miller doesn't own Jesus, or God – the Messiah lives on kitchen walls beside hand-painted enamel plates of Broken Hill. The Messiah is happy with Rose's chow mein. And no one has a monopoly on him. For all his dates and Bibles and books, my father has done less to spread the word of God than the Drummonds.

Eventually Rose stopped talking, something to do with the Myer silver-service restaurant she'd been to with Bob, however that related to anything.

'Are you Anglican?' Nathan asked.

She looked around, surprised that the topic had even come up. 'Bob's Baptist, but he keeps the Bible in the bedside drawer, if you know what I mean.'

'I know. My father's the opposite.'

She had no reply, searching for other words to skirt around it, like the topic of lost babies and why the Russians and Chinese were making bombs when all we wanted to do was get along. Not the Australia I know. Still, warm hearts rub off onto other warm hearts and for the kiddy there was still Heaven, praised twice yearly with a visit to St Polycarps (weddings and funerals aside). But mostly God was worshipped on her melamine altar, in the carrots chopped and scones kneaded lovingly to the confessions of *Blue Hills*.

Nathan was sent outside to fetch Bob, sitting in a shed of wood and fibro construction, built above a crumbling slab of concrete he'd mixed and laid himself before he knew anything about adding gravel. 'Tea's ready,' Nathan said, popping his head in uneasily.

If the kitchen was Rose's domain, then this was Bob's. It was a place for him to settle in an old arm-chair rescued from an eight-wheeled Bragshaw sit-up. Turf was smoked as broken spokes were re-soldered and split upholstery patched with a kit from the maintenance workshop. Wheels and handles and seats hung from every inch of the walls, forming a sea of parts around a work-bench full of ex-S.A.R. tools – as he stared out of the window, working, like Rose staring into her pittosporum.

'Come in.' Choosing to reveal himself rather than hide in a forest of brake cables hanging from the roof like rampant asparagus fern.

'You're well set up.'

Bob stood up. 'You could learn a lot about trains from wheel-chairs.'

'How's that?'

He just smiled. 'I can smell her chow mein.'

'Beats pickled pig.'

'She only has seven meals, in rotation, every two weeks: chow mein, stew, chops, corned beef, roast lamb, bangers and mash – then there's her off nights: bubble and squeak, fish and chips, baked beans and *I couldn't be bothered cooking* ... whatever you do,

103

don't suggest anything new. *I try my best* . . .' Nathan smiled as Bob locked the shed. 'Once I suggested she do a cookery course – '

'Bob!'

'Coming!'

As they went in, passing through a gap in a hedge of sword fern, Bob looked up at the stars and said, 'Know anything about constellations?'

'No.'

'Pity.' He limped as they went, coughing a few times and clearing his throat, explaining how it was an interest he'd like to develop.

Standing in the hallway, strong with the smell of Mr Sheen, Nathan looked out at what remained of the sky and thought, chow mein and continental, now I'm living. Which was his way of using the smallest things to describe the biggest.

Phil Drummond was legal and had grown sideburns to prove it. He sat forward in his chair, shovelling chow mein into his mouth and drinking milk he'd made cold with an ice-cube. 'See, Nathan, this isn't a society of poets and sculptors. I'd like to be an actor, but I'm told I'd need to go to London. So we dispense Bex, and sell Lux off the back of a train.'

Bob pulled a long string of cabbage from his mouth. 'What's wrong with that?'

'Nothing, only if young people – '

'You've got more choices now . . .'

Phil smiled. 'Thank you, o tribal ancient. You also didn't have chow mein in your day?'

Bob grinned. 'Exactly.'

'The thing is, Nathan, I'm happy in Kilburn, strangely enough, so I need a trade. Like my dad, and his dad, and his dad's dad's dad, and every Drummond that's ever drawn breath.'

'Or run out of it,' Bob said, with a full mouth.

'Therein lies a story.'

Rose came in with a pot of hot tea. 'Phillip, you're not being stupid?'

'Mother, please pour the tea while it's still drinkable.'

And because she insisted it needed longer to draw, he came around himself and poured his and Nathan's. 'You do drink tea, Herr Muller?'

Nathan choked on a lump of mince the size of a golf ball. 'Yes, please.' And clearing his throat, 'What's the story?'

Rose started eating with a knife and fork, piling a bite-sized portion over the prongs and eating, looking up to make sure Nathan wasn't shocked, putting down her knife and fork, wiping her mouth and placing her hands in her lap. A sequence she repeated with every mouthful, finishing a full half hour after the others.

'It has to do with Phillip's great grandfather,' she began.

Phil sat forward. 'He was riding his bike down a hill when a pheasant, escaped from someone's yard, charged his bike.'

'Why?'

'Territorial. Pheasants are funny like that. Straight into his front spokes, jamming the wheel, throwing him through the air. Crash, bang, head first onto the road. Three days in hospital but he never regained consciousness.'

Bob moved about uncomfortably. 'It wasn't a pheasant.'

'You told me it was.'

'Still, there's worse ways to die.'

'Anyway, *Ma'ma'*, I was just telling Nathan that I'm an actor on the side.' Phil went on to explain the acting role he'd just landed, as a bridegroom in *The Whitehorse Inn*, walking on stage with a Scot the age of his mother, staring adoringly into her eyes and repeatedly mumbling, 'I do,' followed by their big line together, 'We do.'

It was a small role, he was off in two minutes, but he had some business in the chorus as a waiter in lederhosen, and anyway, you had to start somewhere. The problem was, this was where most amateurs ended up too, mouthing the same lines forty years later, as eight rows of relatives on discount tickets nudged each other at the appropriate moment. 'If I don't have a lead role by twenty-five, I'll give up,' he explained. 'Either that, or would somebody please shoot me.'

Bob mopped up his chow mein with a thick piece of bread. 'Bob,' Rose warned, chewing each mouthful forty times.

'Nathan,' Bob said, looking up from under raised eyebrows, 'Rose would have you believe this is the South Australian Hotel, |but she knows,' turning his gaze to his wife, 'that if a man mops up his gravy he's not necessarily – '

'Children!' Phil waved his bread about in the air. They stopped and listened. 'Mother, your tea is ready.'

'Not yet.'

The meal continued with endless renditions of *The Goodbye Song* as Phil essayed the whole cast's inadequacies and how he'd been passed over through sheer jealousy, as tailors and butchers and stockbrokers sung mostly out of tune songs through their nose and unknowingly overacted with more ham than a Lutheran's cold cellar (having heard the story of the slaughtered pig). Sets that wobbled every time someone passed through a door and an orchestra which smelt of mothballs and had to be back at the Klemzig aged care by ten fifteen.

Apart from that he was having fun.

A lecture on new antibiotics was discussed besides Nathan's early progress as a fridge mechanic. Nathan explained his initiation and Rose scolded Bob for having taken part (in fact, having organised it) as she finally finished her meal and decided the tea was ready. Phil explained to Nathan how they hadn't come up with a new initiation in living memory and how there was really a lot of latent bum lust involved. Bob warned his son of the dangers of such things in the world of amateur theatre but Phil just replied, 'The closest I'll come to anyone's bum is a suppository.'

Nathan marvelled at the novelty of Bob and his son sparring, superimposing it on his own tea table and becoming depressed. William discussing bum lust and operetta, laughing, accepting and returning criticism, sarcasm wrapped in love – sharing his thoughts about the heavens, inviting him into his study and showing him around. Sons as friends, or sons as a source of disappointment.

After tea Nathan and Phil walked down the hill to Kilburn station, waiting beside a bed of neatly clipped geraniums as a Maori in white abattoir boots peeled a tangerine, ate it and sucked the juice from his fingers. An express went past and Nathan said, 'N-class.'

Phil looked at him, unsure, and grinned. 'You one of those, train types?'

'What's that?'

'You know, *the Bayer-Peacock special was fitted with new bogies in nineteen forty-one. Prior to this . . .*'

'No. I needed a job. Preferably not in Tanunda.'

'Thank God for that.'

On their way to the city, Phil stared out the window and said, 'My father and trains . . . generally he leaves it at work. Could you imagine the Romans obsessed by their carriages?' As they slowed through the Adelaide workings he cheered with the sight of city lights. 'Anyway, it'll be a solid trade for you, Nathan. Solid. Like me . . . happy and well the Laxette way . . . *when your child is crabby, naughty or nervy . . . tiny squares of nice-to-take milk chocolate . . .*'

Nathan showed his employee's pass as they walked onto the concourse. Phil said, 'Watch this,' and approached a man in a neat, blue uniform who was standing in front of a full-wall timetable in oak, with destinations and times clicking over frenetically beside a giant four-sided clock. 'Kilburn,' he began. 'Our movie at the Savoy Theatrette finishes at ten fifteen.'

The lines on the older man's brow furrowed. After a pause of a few seconds he said, 'Platform nine, ten twenty-nine.'

'We can't make it in fourteen minutes.'

'If you don't dawdle you will.'

'Thank you, sir.'

'It's my job.'

They briefly stopped at the men's and then set off, laughing at a sign that said GENTLEMEN – CHECK YOUR DRESS. Climbing the stairs at the city end of the station they crossed North Terrace, up Bank Street into Hindley. With time to spare they stopped at Sigalas' Milk Bar and Phil shouted Nathan a spearmint milkshake

('Available No-where else in the Southern Hemisphere'). Staring into the freshly polished vitrolite wall tiles, Nathan couldn't imagine ever returning to the valley again, couldn't believe that was where he was from, and had to return to. Couldn't even recall much about Lilli and their night together, although if anything could still draw him back . . .

Settling into the Savoy late enough to avoid the newsreels, Nathan chewed popcorn and drank Coke he'd bought on an advance from his wage. As the Three Stooges flickered, Phil farted and the lady in front of him complained. 'It's only natural,' Phil replied, explaining he had trouble with his bowels, as Nathan lay back and cackled in his hand. And when Mo started in on Larry and Curly he put his head back and looked up at all the phosphorescent stars glowing on the ceiling and thought, Where have I been?

At one point Phil leaned over and asked, 'Do you *really* believe in God?'

'Yes.'

Stopping to think, reaching over again and grabbing his arm. 'Have you ever done it with a woman?'

Nathan paused. 'Yes.' Unsure if Phil would actually believe him.

'Which is better?'

'What?'

'God or fucking?'

'Each has its own – '

'Liar.'

'What about you?'

'I'm a masturbating atheist. If I haven't screwed a woman by twenty-five I want you to shoot me. Does yours have a sister?'

'No.'

'You lot have a bent for that, eh? You could find me someone. Blonde and big-breasted. Sieg heil!'

Nathan kicked him and the lady in front looked around. 'Sorry.'

The boys reclined, watching the Stooges fuelling a rocket with olive oil. 'You could bring down more than streudel on Monday mornings,' Phil continued. 'Are you convinced I'm a degenerate yet?'

'No.'

'You will be.'

They made it to the station on time and the man in blue was still there. 'Platform nine,' he reminded them as they walked past.

Phil shook his head. 'A truly amazing man.'

Nathan stayed on at the Drummonds that weekend, helping Phil with his lines, learning to lay solder in straight lines, candying almonds on a Sunday morning of hymns and Hebrews avoided.

Back in Tanunda, William reclined in the back row of Langmeil with his arms crossed. He could see Pastor Henry's eyes searching for him at the front, moving back over the congregation until he found him. Happy that William had come, but obviously concerned that he'd changed his seat. William had never moved more than a few inches in fifty years.

William himself, refusing to acknowledge the Elders, imagined Nathan inside the pulpit beside Henry, forming a duo like Laurel and Hardy, reading one-liners from a script which moved the congregation away from a reality which daily faced them: the End of Days. The film monkeys Larry and Mo choking on their lines as they burnt.

Back at the Drummonds, Bob was concerned. From the way Nathan had talked about his father, he guessed it was more than fatigue which had kept the boy back. 'It'll have to be the rare exception,' he'd said, and Nathan had replied, of course, I'm going to miss out on seeing Lilli, so much for your yeast. Bob had had a situation like this before with a boarder from Tailem Bend who ended up staying every weekend, always ready with excuses. Eventually he asked the employment office to find him somewhere else. In that case an alcoholic father, but he couldn't let these things become his problem. He'd only reluctantly taken Nathan on, as company for Phil (he and Rose could barely keep up with their son anymore).

Phil spent the rest of the morning trying to convince Nathan to join the chorus of *The Whitehorse Inn,* but Nathan said he'd never be allowed.

'Why?' Phil asked. 'It sounds like some sort of cult. You sing a few songs and say a few corny lines and the audience laughs, how hard's that?'

Nathan shrugged. '*He* would say, it doesn't praise God.'

'Bloody hell, it doesn't criticise him either. It's an operetta. There's no discussion of the purpose of life.'

'Exactly.'

'So if that's the case –'

'I didn't invent the religion.'

'He'd never know.'

'No.'

Phil tempted him with a few bars of the title song but it wasn't enough. He cut his losses by showing Nathan a journal he'd started keeping of graffiti from around the uni toilets. Whenever he had a spare twenty minutes he'd lock himself in and scribble. Graffiti, he claimed, fell into either one of two categories: the extremely profound or the extremely perverted. He could prove this. He showed Nathan tracings of pornographic pictures he'd made on specially purchased tracing paper. And then he read a selection of work he'd copied from the Barr Smith library dunnies: *Where was God at Treblinka? Josie can suck your eyes from your sockets, cheep, 127 496.* All of the poetry Dryden had missed, he explained.

Nathan thought about them, Lilli and Phil, and what would happen if they ever got together. She'd have him worked out in no time – words, words and more words – or would it just be an explosive miasma of smut under the arc lights of the Barr Smith unisex?

At two a.m. the following Wednesday, Nathan was woken by Phil's alarm – his room-mate turning over, switching off the light he'd left on and kicking an analgesics text off his bed.

Nathan got dressed and had breakfast with Bob, who was busy sucking back a last minute Turf and coughing enough to wake the dead. They walked to Islington, as they did every morning, gathered their tools and boarded the employees' carriage for their trip to Peterborough.

They emerged from the loco depot behind 523 steam, a heavy engine with all the streamlining of a Glen Miller selection. Passing the tallow works and sheep paddocks of Salisbury, Nathan had to work hard to convince himself he wasn't headed home. Bob showed him a map of the state rail network, extending out from Adelaide in every direction like lantana, and Nathan knew (as surely as the crispness of the long, black lines) that his choices were becoming almost infinite.

Smithfield and Roseworthy, Wasleys and Hamley Bridge, lines shooting off here and there towards disused copper mines and the crabs of Port Wakefield, here the Nullarbor and via Hawker to the endlessness of the inland. Bob knew them all, having fixed every fridge and cold-store on the network. 'Once you hit Quorn, things change,' he said. 'Saltbush and gibber plains. But apparently there's things living out there. Country God didn't bother about.'

Burra to Terowie was an endless stretch of mallee, saltbush and corrugated plains stretching out orange against a sky of cloudless blue. Languorous melaleucas branched at ground level into explosions of purple and white pom-poms, their form reminding Nathan of black and white photos from school atlases, narratives of deluded explorers (megalomaniacal Germans with visions of inland seas) and stories of the big JC himself, talking with wallabies in the form of the Devil.

Peterborough was the last junction before the line headed east towards New South Wales. Beyond the border the world stopped, dropping vertically into a dark chasm of space they'd also described at school, full of half-human, half-dead vampires, lakes of fire and comets smashing into each other, sparks and showers of hot lava and an atmosphere of sulphur dioxide which could dissolve lungs in an instant.

Arriving in the Peterborough yards their carriage was detached and shunted and the loco reversed into an old round-house. Like the Islington loco depot, it was black with the smoke of over-worked trains, boilers lit and fed in the early morning ready to pull cattle-full rolling stock and dining cars with farmers off to town in suits that barely fitted. S.A. Railways men oozed from their carriage ready for work: relief crews, track work teams, a couple of diesel apprentices, smug in the railway hierarchy above refrigeration mechanics.

Bob and Nathan spent the afternoon stripping down and re-assembling a compressor full of bulldust. After cleaning up they were fed lamb in the William Webb Memorial Cafeteria and sipped long-necks of West End in the employees' van. Just after dark they went for a walk through town, looking in the sort of shop-fronts Nathan was mostly familiar with. A shoe shop with workboots and casuals, slippers and ladies' formals. Bob laughing, 'My mum used to have lace-ups like them,' as Nathan smiled, 'They're still catching up,' tasting the spearmint milkshake of Sigalas' as Joe Aronson and his Synco Symphonists echoed down main street, Peterborough, into the front bar of the Commercial Hotel, through into the men's with its noticeable lack of either profound or filthy graffiti.

Settling into a small park of perfectly manicured Kentucky bluegrass, Bob looked up at the sky and said, 'That one, I know, is the Big Dipper, and that one the Bear.'

'The saucepan constellation,' Nathan pointed, knowing exactly where to look for it.

And God, up there somewhere, perhaps. Bob refused to give voice to these thoughts, although he sensed Nathan shared the dilemma of the bedside drawer – unresolved feelings which Phil had rationalised out of existence. 'You could form anything out of the stars,' Nathan offered.

'How's that?'

'Dot to dot.'

Like imaginary weather trees, drifting across the sky, seen by some but not others, portents of rain or disaster, gods with mouths zipped up or not there at all.

To Phil it's just so much gas, Bob thought. 'Yes, that's an area of interest,' he said. Feeling small. Unable to mention God. (As William couldn't avoid it, at that moment drafting a speech he planned to read out in church, under the nose of those who'd deny the good news.)

Nathan and Bob walked back via a bakery smelling of pies and pipe loaves and a Christedelphian shopfront promising a public lecture, *Did Jesus Look Like This?*, a picture of a Neanderthal in Messiah's clothing. A mechanic laboured late into the night on someone's new Holden as his dog sniffed stobie poles.

They settled into bunks in the employees' van. If a star is a million miles away, Nathan thought as he drifted off to sleep, then what is God up to? Some time during the night they were coupled to the loco and taken home. Nathan woke with the world passing by in a dark blur, the certainty of static sleep passing away with everything else. He sat up and opened the window to let the wash of air pass over him.

Bless Dad ... I know, but bless him ... bless Mum, Lilli, Arthur ... bless Bob and Rose, and Phil, give him the ability to sing in tune. Walk beside me ...

Through the concourse with its departure times like so many stars in the firmament; and only the big fella in blue having the whole picture.

Chapter Eight

Nathan caught the late train to Tanunda after work on Friday night. He stared into small, weedy yards as his train picked up speed and he felt his mood drop. The smell of diesel and oil wasn't enough to save him from the thought of Tanunda. Getting off the train, William took him by the arm and said, 'You have remembered, the children's devotion?' And in an instant a cold fog descended on Tanunda Station, weighing him down in a gravity of things he'd tried to forget. Such as Bluma smelling his jacket and asking if the Drummond lady had been washing his clothes and, if so, with what, seeing as she probably had better – Bluma's leftover slices of Lux compressed together in the eternal drive for economy.

He spent Saturday helping out with the pruning, his mind drifting back to Adelaide, into Bob's shed and through a forest of cracked footplates and torn upholstery, mingling with stale smoke from the Ardath cigarettes Bob smoked. Going inside early he spent an hour on Ohm's law and electrical circuits. William arrived to watch over his shoulder, suggesting solutions. But again Nathan was dreaming Co-Co and Bo-Bo diesels, cabbage boiled senseless (avoiding any suggestion of sauerkraut), served up on best china in the Webb cafeteria. Bluma, returning from a quilting-bee in Angaston, brought home flake and vinegar-soggy chips as a sort of consolation prize, but the homecoming was soured by William refusing to eat anything cooked in a hundred per cent animal fat.

Waiting outside Langmeil on Sunday morning (William busy

inside with the bells, trying to teach Bluma some rhythm, 'Now, no ... now ...') Nathan grabbed Lilli before anyone noticed and dragged her into the church hall. 'It's my turn for Sunday School.'

They switched on lights in the vestry, lit heaters and sat down beneath a framed photograph of Pastor Hoffmann. Lilli smiled, crossing her hands in her lap, laying aside a dog-eared copy of *Lady Chatterly's Lover* and asking, 'So?'

Soon they'd come up with an idea. As she started scribbling messages on note-paper, Nathan wrapped them in endless layers around a presentation Bible. 'The Drummonds,' he began, 'are very different from the Mullers.'

Continuing with a description of Rose in her kitchen, Bob at work on his wheelchairs and Phil in the Barr Smith dunnies, copying thoughts at least as profound as Lilli's pass-the-parcel notes: *Jesus walks beside you ... he's the one with the sandals and food in his beard ...* Eventually she looked at him directly and asked, 'So why did you stay down? You oughta seen your dad last Sunday.'

Nathan shrugged. 'I don't care. Honestly. You could always come down, although I don't think they'd put you up.'

'I have some other friends, from school. One's at secretarial college, the other at uni.' She thought, yes, I'm still here, filling pasties with scoops of mixed vegetable, mixing topping for donuts and sprinkling hundreds-and-thousands on buns – slicing bread, endlessly, and ringing up sales from one end of the day to the next.

'Maybe I should stay,' she said. 'I love smiling at ugly babies and making small talk with drongos. Still, there's worse I suppose ...' As she thought of the options: sewing up bags at the flour mill, bottling wine, putting blue rinses through hair the colour of talc.

Nathan read her notes and smiled. 'If these kids blab, we'll get in trouble.'

'I don't care,' she mimicked, leaning forward and kissing him.

He pulled himself off. 'I have to think of Jerusalem.'

Taken by an idea, she smiled and started writing. *Mary Magdalene. My place or yours. Cheep. A wandering messiah and three children to support.*

115

William's head poked in the room. 'Nearly ready, Nathan?'

Lilli sat up. 'It's going to be quite a party, Mr Miller.'

William stared at her. 'Maybe Nathan would be better off running things.'

'I'm the hostess,' she replied, cocking her head, straightening her dress and returning her hands to her lap.

William closed the door and she grabbed the pen. *Alternatives to Christianity: Buddhism, Islam, Hindu, Pagan (fun, boiling mushrooms in cast-iron pots)*. She sat back and shared her week with Nathan. The Lawrence she'd found in the Tanunda Public Library, sitting abandoned in the Contemporary Fiction beside Patrick White's *The Aunt's Story*. She read him some extracts, underlined in hot, red biro, nowhere near as saucy as rumoured, falling well short of the *Advertiser* personals. 'See, Lawrence just skirts around it,' she explained. 'A bum to him is all marbled flesh, the schlong, *an instrument of love ... heaving breasts glow translucently in the moonlight...*'

She looked at him and laughed. He lowered his head and muttered, 'Jerusalem,' and she threw the book at him. Standing up, she selected *The Secret of St John Bosco* from a bookcase, and started drawing over the Archbishop of Buenos Aires and a priest named Don Cagliero, adding beards and moustaches, horns and elephantine cocks which passed from one page to the next. Nathan tried to grab it off her but she climbed to the ledge of a high window and sat in dust an inch thick. Scribbling. Smiling. Looking down at him and lifting her eyebrows as if to say, What y' gonna do about it?

William appeared at the door again. 'Pastor Henry's starting. Do you want to come and get the children?'

'Do we what!' Lilli replied, jumping down from her ledge.

Mrs Fox entered the vestry, cradling a pile of children's hymns in her arms. Lilli brushed past and said, 'We shan't need those,' walking out to make her announcement in the church proper.

The Langmeil bells fell quiet and pews creaked beneath the weight of a full house. Arthur Blessitt sat beside William, and beside Arthur, Joshua and Seymour. 'Join me today,' William had said, and since he was back in his spot in the front row, no one argued.

Arthur shifted his weight around to test some repairs he'd made: a full Tuesday afternoon, upturned pews and glue and nails and Pastor Henry fixing him coffee as he worked.

'William has finished his harvest?' Henry had asked.

'Yes.'

'This year he seems, preoccupied.'

'He has his dates. We've decided that it's inevitable.'

'He has.'

'We have.'

Henry rearranged a collection of Arthur's lisianthus on the altar. 'The thing is, if William's wrong, he stands to look silly.'

'Christ isn't coming unless we want it hard enough. That's what William says. Fixing pews is one thing, but there has to be an end to it.'

'You know what the Bible says about that.'

'Just the same.'

Henry had left him with his hand-drill and cold chicken sandwich, and retreated back into the vestry.

Henry looked out across the congregation. William's face was blank. Henry had no idea how many people William had got to. Joshua and Seymour probably, both prone to a bit of wand-waving and fireworks. Joshua had gone through an astrology phase, guided to horoscopes and star charts by a new stenographer in his office. For a while he carried around a satchel with maps, books and tables of dates, pulling them out at the slightest suggestion to check the best day for William to start harvesting or Arthur to pot up his carnations. It was a rhythm of nature which God had set in motion, he claimed, but no one was convinced. Henry visited to talk to him, to discuss the concerns of his friends. 'Who, which friends?' Joshua had asked.

Eventually he came to his senses, brought down to earth by Harry Powter, his boss, who didn't accept 'the stars' as a reason for missing three days work. 'Something terrible could've happened,' Joshua said, as Harry explained how it already had for the stenographer, newly replaced by his sixteen-year-old niece.

Henry looked about for the support of Gunther, Ron and Trevor and the others but guessed he was all alone, preaching a Jesus firmly stuck in his sphere.

Back in the hall, Mrs Fox started playing and singing, '"Jesus, friend of little children, be a friend to me . . ."'

Lilli, sitting in the middle of a ring of children, stood up and began talking over the music. 'Mrs Fox, Nathan and I were given the responsibility of organising today's devotion.'

Mrs Fox stopped but didn't move her eyes from the sheet music. 'It's standard practice to have a children's hymn.'

'Stand up children, musical chairs. Mrs Fox, do you know a tango, a foxtrot?'

Meanwhile, Henry worked his way through a standard mass, watching how William refused to drop any coins in the offering. The congregation stood as the offering was presented to the altar, all except William, who sat with his arms crossed, smiling. Bluma looked over and knew what was coming. During the offertory, Arthur bowed his head, burning Henry's words into the wood of his cross: *What shall I render to the Lord, For all his bounty to me?* William was unfazed, watching how Henry kept looking down at him.

In the hall, Mrs Fox was doing her best to improvise a dance tune from *Gott ein Vater*, stopping on Lilli's cue. One of Lilli's cousins lost her chair and started crying. 'Don't be a sook,' Lilli said, dismissing her with a twist of the ear. Mrs Fox turned around. 'Lilli . . . is there a point to this?'

Lilli smiled. 'Survival of the fittest.' Raising her eyebrows.

'I mean, how is this a devotion?'

'For goodness sake. Alright children, as you've been taught: "Our Father, who art in Heaven . . ."'

Mrs Fox bowed her head and joined in but as Lilli's speed became supersonic she looked up again. 'Are we finished here?'

'No, the fun is just beginning.'

Lilli produced a box of donkey's tails cut out of butcher's paper, and removed a half-sized portrait of St Sebastian from the wall. 'Pin the tail on the martyr. Who's first?'

The children eagerly lined up, even though there was no prize on offer, leaving tails on shins and elbows and ear lobes. Halfway through, Mrs Fox gathered her music, closed the piano and left. Climbing awkwardly past legs and over bags she reached Bluma, sat down and whispered, 'That Fechner girl is causing trouble.'

Bluma looked over at William but there was no point worrying about it now.

Back in the hall, Lilli got the children in a circle and said, 'When the Schoenberg stops, take off a layer and read out the message.' She began banging away on Mrs Fox's piano, picking random notes and clusters and narrating ad lib sprechstimme. 'Round and round and round it goes, where it stops, nobody knows.'

The first child unwrapped the present and read out his message: '"Hare Krishna, Hare Krishna, Krishna, Krishna ..."' Lilli encouraged the group to join in, '"Hare Krishna, Hare Krishna ..."' She returned to the piano with gusto, using her forearm percussively to explore new sounds.

Back in the church Henry looked up, smiling, 'Sounds like a different sort of devotion.'

But William didn't smile, choosing his moment, clutching his speech in his sweaty hand and finally standing up. He cleared his throat. 'I have something to read to you.'

Henry looked down at him. 'William.'

'It'll only take a moment.'

'Wait for the benediction.' The pastor looked around for the support of the Elders but they were willing to sit back and let things take their course. After William had dug a big enough hole, they'd just have to fill it in. Henry sighed. 'Go ahead, William.'

'I, and a few friends of like mind' – he indicated the length of his pew, unclear of where his following stopped.

One of the Linkes, sitting towards the end, said, 'Who?'

'Mr Blessitt, Mr Heinz and Mr Hicks.'

Mo, Larry and Curly, not disputing William, but hardly vocal in their support. 'We have come to an understanding of things as they stand. Of how the present business of the world is about to be wound up.'

Silence. 'This is best left for some other time,' demanded a voice from the back of the church. 'Who agrees?'

Mixed responses, but then another voice. 'Let him finish.'

William flattened his speech against his chest, held it up and started reading. The slight trembling of the paper was almost audible above the silence, which was disturbed only by the clatter of improvised Schoenberg through a thick, plaster wall.

'I, William Miller, again to be known as Wilhelm Muller, have read and studied the Scriptures for some years now. The figuring of dates is not as important as some suggest. Nevertheless, if you take the trouble to ask, I'll explain . . .'

On and on, explaining how he'd decided to leave the congregation – to hushed sighs of relief – and continue his worship from home. How anybody who'd like to join him was welcome. How, on the twenty-first of March next year, Jesus would return to earth via the Muller home, and various other places, gathering disciples to sit beside him in his thousand-year reign on earth. How he, Wilhelm Muller, wasn't here to judge anyone, except that the signs were there, and Jesus would ask about such matters as faith, unlikely to let things ride with the equivalent of a library fine. How the 'abominations of desolation' could be known by all those who wanted to understand and be ready for His coming. 'I am fully convinced that on March twenty-one next, according to the Jewish mode of computation of time, Christ will come and bring all his saints with him, and then that He shall reward every man as his work shall be.'

Silence. Henry looked at him. 'You finished, William?'

'Wilhelm.'

Lilli's cousin emerged from the hall, screaming and crying, pointing back and saying, 'Jesus' wife made babies for money.'

She found her mother and collapsed into her lap as everyone looked back at William. He left his speech on Henry's pulpit, walking out of the church, down the avenue of pencil pines, never to return. Bluma followed close behind, tripping over legs and apologising as a hundred or so voices passed sentence. The children drifted back into the church and Henry finished his benediction. Lilli and Nathan exited via the rear of the hall, damage done, Lilli with the copy of Don Bosco she was going to finish illustrating for him.

Later that morning, Henry stacked the chairs in the hall as St Sebastian, pock-marked with red and yellow plasticine, smiled down on him. The scribbled notes scattered on the floor spoke of a day when even the sun was unsure of its trajectory, burning through high cloud and laying itself across the cold ground of the Eden Valley. Seymour Hicks appeared behind him and said, 'Pastor Henry . . .'

Henry used his foot to crush a bin full of butcher's paper. 'Seymour . . .' Pausing. 'You looked very uncomfortable.'

'We didn't know what he was up to.' Seeing how they were really just props for a highly polished performance.

'Don't worry, Seymour, no one's judging you,' Henry whispered.

'We didn't think he'd . . .' Wondering if Henry thought he was hedging bets. 'I'm on the door next Sunday.'

'Very good.'

'Henry . . .'

'What's done is done. To me, Seymour, faith's not a matter of dates.'

'He's explained it . . .'

'I know . . .' Thinking of St Rita, the patroness of Impossible Causes, who longed to suffer like Jesus, pleading until she was struck by a thorn from a crucifix, the wound turning septic and killing her. Like William, wishing too hard for the wrong thing.

Nathan and Lilli took the scenic route past Traut Heim, a villa-turned-guest house that boasted the valley's first 'Scandinavian-style spa bath'. They crossed a rope bridge over the North Para River and passed the Byhursts' property with its two dozen rusted car bodies awaiting their own apocalyptic salvation. They followed the path along the creek, through Arthur's bottom paddock and into the Miller vines. Eventually arriving at the wash-house, they grabbed two bottles of shiraz from a crate ready for Seymour to deliver, and retraced their steps.

'I know a good spot,' Lilli said, fumbling in her pocket for Pastor Henry's corkscrew. Passing down Elizabeth Street and Langmeil Road, she hid the bottles up her blouse whenever they passed someone on streets which couldn't handle cars going both ways, crumbling cottage and workshop walls forcing pedestrians to go single file on footpaths collapsing into cobble-stone gutters. The fault of people who drove cars instead of carts, blocking laneways and filling cottage gardens with exhaust.

They crossed into the recreation park and sat in the shade of already ancient Moreton Bay figs showering over-ripe fruit. The stench of decay was heavy in the air as sulphur-crested cockatoos went crazy on the soft flesh of a sleepy Tanunda Sunday. Families set out picnics on Onkaparinga rugs as one of Nathan's old teachers whacked the hell out of golf balls he had no intention of retrieving.

Nathan sat on a swing and worked his way up to a semi-circular arc. As he did he saw nothing of William's vision of roof tops and tree branches flying through space in the company of redeeming angels. He couldn't recognise children's voices as screams, or air past his ears as a vortex of sulphuric acid, pulling him down a plughole into a hell as hot as the Simpson Desert. To Nathan, the air smelt only of rotting fruit, dried-up water holes and chimneys smoking down laneways of cracked bitumen.

They sat high in the grandstand, overlooking football games avoided and distant tennis games of a lifetime ago. 'Although it just seems like a few weeks,' he said, drinking and wiping his mouth on his sleeve. 'Not bad ... a little young.'

'As if you'd know.'

He imagined a football game on the oval below. Phil Drummond in one of Bob's wheelchairs, sunk into the soggy turf as St Sebastian on a butcher's-paper donkey chased him across the oval, throwing lumps of yellow plasticine and singing the *Veni creator*. Phil replied with choruses from *The Whitehorse Inn* and his only line, 'I do.' Spliced with quotes from Schopenhauer's *Indestructibility of Being* and definitions of Class A and B drugs.

St John Bosco, with his twelve-foot elephantine cock, looked back at Nathan from the front row of the grandstand and said, 'God spoke to your father on the Hill of Grace . . .' St John becoming Lilli, gurgling wine and gulping it down. 'No shit, I heard it from Sarah.'

'Sarah who?'

'Sarah Heinz.'

Nathan looked confused. 'So?'

'I'm not making it up. God appears to your dad and says, "Jesus is coming back, but I'm only telling you. Now, go to the Bible and work out when."'

Nathan lay back and let the world start to spin. 'It's made up, they wanna make him look stupid.'

'No, Sarah's not smart enough for that. The thing I find funny . . . if I was God, which I'm not –'

'No.'

'Why would you go to all the trouble of blowing your cover, and then leave out the details?' She climbed into the time-keeper's box. '*Nathan Miller, I have chosen you, to spread the message, from Yunta to Kyancutta . . .*' Standing on the time-keeper's desk. '*Praise me!*'

Nathan placed his feet flat on the ground but it was still unstable. Nodding his head he said, 'He might've *thought* he heard God . . .' And after some more deliberation, 'No, you're right, he's not all there.'

She returned and sat next to him. 'Just what I heard.'

'It'd explain his obsession.'

'But indicates a sort of . . .'

'Lilli . . . believing is like, it's a state of . . . it's like being pissed. What seems strange to one person . . .' He shrugged. 'Sometimes, when everyone's singing, it all seems to make sense.'

'Feeble, Miller.'

'Perhaps . . . but nice, in its own way.'

'Like *The Magic Faraway Tree*.'

'What's wrong with that?'

'It's a story.'

Looking at her. 'Good sense only gets you so far.'

'Reckon?' She shrugged. 'Small reward for big lie. The voice of God?'

'I know, feeble.'

The bottles sat empty before them and Nathan put his head between his legs. He felt Lilli slap him on the back and saw her walking up and down the rows on the backs of seats. St John Bosco, flooded by a spectrum of diffused and pure colours, looked around at him and said, 'Your dad's gonna kill you.'

Far below, Phil Drummond was wrestling in the mud with the martyr of yellow plasticine. Lilli slipped, grazing herself, revealing her hairy legs to him again. A caretaker appeared at the bottom of the stairs and said, 'Come on you two, we're locking the gates.'

Lilli took him home past the bakery, writing an IOU for PK spearmints which would fail to hide the smell of wine from William.

Sitting in his loft that night, copying and re-copying Hebrews 13, Nathan couldn't reconcile the person he'd so recently been, with what he'd become. Failing exams had been a disaster and a God-send, the same with Lilli and Phil and Bob and Rose and even the corned beef sandwiches in the Webb cafeteria. Still, there was no turning back. The heavens would have to explode and scatter before they ran out of momentum. Even then gravity would shrink them back into a pin-prick the size of a sub-atomic particle. And then what? A heaven of hymn singers? Nathan fixing fridges in the broad-gauge city of Babylon?

PART
Two

Chapter Nine

Nathan walked to Tanunda Station in the dark. As the grey of morning broke in a grainy light, thoughts of Sunday in the grandstand, under Moreton Bay figs, slowly evaporated like tepid puddles in a Murray Street gutter. (In the grandstand a cat sniffed the empty bottles and passed on, leaving them for a third-grader from the Lutheran school who'd find them, packing them in his satchel beside *The Magic Pudding* and the weekend's aborted long division.)

Passing the Evans' Wursthaus, Nathan stopped to stare in the window and wonder if he'd ever return. He had visions of William, walking the streets of Kilburn, looking for number seventeen Church Avenue, calling, 'Nathan, I demand you return home at once,' to endless Hebrews copied mindlessly in his loft, his resentment growing by the minute. As it had last night – peering down at William gluing his articles, Bluma snipping and smoothing a review of *Quo Vadis*. He'd been tempted to call down to his father, 'You really believe you heard the voice of God?' But chose to let his resentments simmer, cooking through slowly like a stew.

William again, with a photo of Lake Eyre in flood, still wondering if it wasn't God's doing – stands of eucalypts marooned, slowly drowning in a giant, brown puddle which showed no signs of receding. And a cocky in a boat, floating among it all, apparently looking for something. William wondered aloud if it mightn't be the puffed up corpse of the Fechner girl, or Rohwer. Bluma scolded him, saying who gave him the moral high ground, just because of the Langmeil business. Jesus didn't judge, she said, he offered salvation. That's where the church had gone wrong, teaching kids about the fear of Hell and an unwashed face.

Nathan passed along Ferdinand Street, leaving peppercorn and carob trees behind, watching for the steam and smoke in the distance which would indicate a change of scene, of sight and smell, and of a rigid Lutheran mindset which guided his every thought and decision.

The train moved slowly toward town. Over creeks so small they didn't warrant names, past Rowland Flat with its patchwork pasture and vines, Lyndoch, Sandy Creek and beyond. Passing through paddocks scarred by Highways Department graders which would become the new suburb of Elizabeth. The signs already up: The Satellite City of the Future. Rockets penetrating the rings of Saturn as astronauts contemplated Victa mowers. The slab of a hospital and civic centre poured, stobie poles raised in anticipation of bridal creeper and geraniums. Nissen huts salvaged from Woodside army barracks, for the first of the ten-pound Pommies, due any time. Newly seeded parks watered, but dying anyway, littered with monkey bars freshly welded and set in concrete. Excavations for a swimming pool which would chlorinate the eyes and infect the ears of a thousand sunburnt children.

Passing into the outer suburbs he retrieved his *Secrets of St John Bosco* and perused the amended illustrations, meaning to show them to Phil. He suddenly thought, Shit, Bob's cake. He was racked with guilt for the rest of the journey, trying to think how he'd explain his thoughtlessness to the man who'd let him stay on, who'd shared his shed and jarmies and candied almonds.

Arriving at Islington he made for the Webb cafeteria but the best he could find was a finger bun. Presenting it to Bob before clocking on, he said, 'To be a honest ... I've been a bit of a dick-head.' Going on to explain his disaster of a Sunday, inebriation (a slip-up, he promised, restricted to home), Lilli, Hebrews and a father straight out of the SS. But Bob had already absolved him, throwing him the overalls he'd left behind (which Rose had washed) and saying, 'I'll expect twice as much next week.'

Regardless, Nathan felt bad for the whole day, wondering what Bob was really thinking (although in truth it didn't cross his mind again).

William started the day picking mushrooms from the grass flats sloping onto the Blickinstal hillside. Waders wrapped around his shins kept him dry as he popped mushrooms into a cotton bag embroidered with Bluma's white-work: *Gemutlichkeit* – although there wasn't much of that this morning. Just the feeling of another day closer to the End, Nathan off on his own orbit, people everywhere letting him down.

The North Para River meandered slowly along water courses carved from soil and limestone; granite ridges, protruding like moss-encrusted flying saucers from the hillside, reminded him that a lot of time had passed without an apocalypse. Billions of years, he'd read somewhere, an article suggesting that all of human history would fit into the last ten seconds of the universe compressed into a calendar year. Which just went to show how much scientists really understood, creating theories with more holes than Bluma's potato strainer. He was confident he was right. The End was as real as the oats and Salvation Jane stretching up the hillside, the smell of must, the blinding dazzle of sun off the river. He hadn't even bothered saving the article, refusing to believe that anyone could take it seriously. He walked on, picking and deep-breathing as he approached the Basedow Road weighbridge.

He returned home for a breakfast of fried sausages and a prayer. Soon Seymour arrived and they started loading crates into the back of his hearse. William explained how 'all that business yesterday' hadn't come out of the blue. After his meeting with the Elders at Henry's house he had got up the next morning and walked down to Tabor church. He'd waited a full hour before he was told Pastor Ewell had needed to pop out.

'When should I return?'

'This afternoon, after lunch.'

He'd waited another hour then before they let him in. Sitting down, he had said, 'I wish to change churches.'

Pastor Ewell ran his hand through his hair. 'William, have you thought this through?'

'Of course.'

'You are still welcome at Langmeil.'

'I am not.'

'William, churches are families . . .'

William picked up another crate and looked at Seymour. '"Families," and he said, "No one is ever asked to leave a family." Ha!'

Seymour picked one of William's cucumbers and bit into it. 'But they're made to feel unwelcome, eh?'

'Exactly.'

'And you told him that?'

'I did. He said, "If you're unhappy there you'll be unhappy here."' William sat next to Seymour on the back of the hearse. 'I didn't want to hear any more, so I left. Without so much as a thank you. It was obvious others had already been in his ear.'

Seymour kept crunching. 'You're right to have done what you did. He should be reported to the church bosses.'

'They're all the same.' Going on to paraphrase the letter he'd returned home and written.

Pastor Ewell,

I was spoken to by God. Whether you believe me or not doesn't matter. I KNOW. He said He would send His son to me and tell me about it. I believe the government of God will return to earth. Maybe not just here. Maybe in Brazil some miner or shop-keeper knows, or an eskimo, having heard the voice like me. By treating me so and listening to wrong voices I dont know how He will like you. Wearing the cloth is not enough. Many will be cast down. Shot like dogs. Wilhelm Muller.

He told Seymour how at St John's and St Paul's the next day he got as far as explaining his calculations, but how they'd said the same thing, return to *your* church, *your* family – and how at the end of the day they'd left him with no choice but to sit down and write his speech, his resignation, from the Langmeil family. He felt like Nathan, sent to the loft to copy Hebrews chapter thirteen, over and over, so that he could stay in *their* family on *their* terms. 'Which I wasn't willing to do,' he said to Seymour. 'They'll all be cast down, Rohwer, Fritschle . . .'

Although Gunther's hell would have a climate control. William looked at Seymour. 'I appreciate your support.'

'William, it was the same in His time. And look what's happened. I think, though, the misguided will be forgiven. Otherwise it'd just be you and me . . .'

Convinced of the maths, at last.

William smiled. 'Perhaps . . .'

Standing in his workshop later that night, Arthur showed William how he'd salvaged a wheel from an old wheel-barrow and attached it to the base of his cross. Making it a portable cross, more suitable for carrying across the shoulder, especially with the aid of an old cushion. Harnessing up, he went once around his bottom paddock for William's benefit, walking, breaking into a trot, a budget Jesus on his way to a Kaiserstuhl crucifixion. William wasn't sure what Jesus would make of it, but after Arthur explained it was to know His suffering, William himself was persuaded to drape a hundred pounds of Tasmanian oak across his own shoulder and walk. Eventually becoming so caught up – 'And all this with the pain of thorns and open wounds' – he convinced Arthur to let him start off towards kegel.

By the time they passed Langmeil he gave the cross back, refreshed, walking tall in the Messiah's footsteps. 'This is a fine idea, Arthur, it will help us teach people about Christ.'

'For teaching? That wasn't quite what I intended.'

But William wasn't listening.

Arriving at the Kegelbahn, William herded all of the members outside, reclaiming the cross to demonstrate, handing it around like a Hoover demonstrator. Trevor Streim misbalanced and had it down on top of him as he lay laughing in the shit and mud of the stockyards. 'Arthur,' he said, 'you need some training wheels for us beginners.'

Ron Rohwer stood in the background, arms crossed, smiling but refusing to participate. 'C'mon,' Julius Rechner joked, dragging him by the arm. But Ron just leaned against the corrugated iron, nodding his head and eventually becoming serious. Seymour arrived just in time for his own circuit, suggesting they all build one and organise races, but Arthur said that missed the point entirely.

As the group stood around admiring the dovetail joins and bevelling, Arthur's hand-burnt quotes and the faultless varnishing, William watched Ron duck back inside, unobserved, setting up pins in the absence of any ladies. He wondered if he should just be gracious, if he should go in and offer his hand, talk through their differences, agree to disagree: grace – such as he'd been shown in Henschke's vineyard, made clear by the voice of God.

But it was more than that. It all went back to an argument his father had had with Ron's, sometime in the twenties, when the elder Rohwer had taken Robert's spot in the Goat Square markets. This was a spot Robert had inherited from Anthelm, who had originally helped other pioneers level and lay out the area last century. But there was Rohwer one Friday morning, set out right in the middle between Linke's cakes and a long-lost pottery maker, both of whom had pointed out the problem. When Robert and Brigid arrived with their hand-cart full of cucumbers and tomatoes, cabbages and lettuces, everybody watched to see their reaction.

It was on for young and old. Robert confronted the elder Rohwer and demanded he move; Rohwer replied that there were no reser-vations and in the absence of any organising committee, he could do as he liked. Robert had never been spoken to like this, especially by a Johnny-come-lately whose family had only been in the valley for twenty years. Again he demanded Rohwer move. No. By now the whole market was silent, hushed in anticipation. Realising that Rohwer couldn't be reasoned with, Robert up-ended his table, scattering vegetables, preserves and crockery everywhere – and what was worse, little Golgotha landscapes in a snowdome, glitter in water raining down on the three crucified figures, and a label: *The Place of Skulls, 1'6,* the whole lot smashing open everywhere. Robert walked off in disgust, the young Wilhelm following, while everyone looked at the elder Rohwer, as if to say, We told you so.

And that was just the start. Every Friday for months, the elder Rohwer and Robert arrived progressively earlier, the winner setting out his stall in an otherwise empty market-place, laying out his produce and lighting a fire to cook breakfast. The runner-up set up as close as possible, but never quite on Anthelm's spot.

Eventually the town council was asked to step in, settling things by instituting a permit system for stalls, placed randomly around the square according to a lottery draw which, strangely, never saw Robert or Rohwer getting his old spot.

William stepped towards the door of the Kegelbahn but stopped himself. Like his father, he had nothing to apologise for. Sometimes you just have to sit on the egg you lay, regardless of its chances of hatching.

Arthur leaned his cross against the wall and they headed inside. It was William and his followers (although no one would call them this) against the rest. Trevor sent for his son to stand the pins and as they waited they sampled some of his latest grenache. Julius, Ron and Trevor started off with perfect scores, and the Millerites had nothing to offer in response, Arthur guttering the ball three times.

Julius was the one to bring up the topic they'd all been avoiding. 'Where to now, William? Is it William?'

'Wilhelm.'

'Tabor or St John's?'

'Neither.'

'Why?'

'They're all the same.' Trevor and Ron were still unwilling to buy into it. Julius bowled another strike. 'Gnadenberg?'

'Too far.'

'So?'

'My dining table is my church now. And as I said, anyone who's willing to join me ...'

133

Ron tabulated the scores on the blackboard. 'Your turn, Seymour.'

Three pins down, and Arthur only a few more. It was up to William, again. Taking aim at pins the shape of Rohwer's head, he launched the wooden ball with every ounce of his energy, scoring a strike and looking up at Ron.

'Don't worry, I won't cheat,' Ron said, pushing on the chalk so hard it snapped.

'Your people have always been at Langmeil?' Julius asked.

William felt like telling him to shut up. 'Yes.'

'Your father was an Elder?'

'No. We've always been more concerned with Christ than politics.' Avoiding, he thought, Ron and Trevor's eyes as he said this.

But Ron, like William, was every bit his father's son. 'Robert, William's father,' he said to Julius, 'was heavily involved with Langmeil, Elder or not. As an example, I remember he led a group of parishioners to the Vectis Mission rally in Lyndoch in nineteen . . . when was it, William?'

'How should I know.'

'Nineteen twenty-two, I think.'

Ron launched a slow ball which missed the pins completely, but he showed no sign of concern. 'I was there, a lot younger, much more hair. The pastor was on the back of a truck in an empty paddock, surrounded by a ring of cars and Christians of every denomination. He said, Who amongst you will give testament to his belief? Remember, William, Wilhelm? Anyway, Robert got up.'

William had been standing in the paddock, listening, more embarrassed than anything else, watching his father, in his overalls and gum boots, about to make a fool of himself.

For the first time that evening Ron laughed. 'I remember Robert said, "I have heard the voice of God, and he has told me about the return of his son . . ."'

The young William had looked up, shocked. The elder William now felt the eyes of Arthur and Seymour on him, waiting for him to refute the story, to expose Ron for the liar he was, like the stall-thief his father was, money-lenders bringing shame to the temple of God with their Golgotha snowdomes.

William took another ball. 'He was caught up in the moment, people were fainting and talking in tongues ...' It was more, he explained, than the laying on of hands and simple prayer. The Vectis people were tricksters, getting people to say things they'd later regret. Good theatre from the back of a Dodge truck.

'Robert later denied it?' Ron asked.

'No, but he never spoke of it again.'

And William had always wondered, afraid to ask in case Robert had just been a little drunk, or a little touched by the sun. But deep down he guessed Robert must have heard a voice, or at least thought he had. It was the fault of the Rohwers and Streims of the world that his father had never shared his thoughts again. And it had always puzzled him – what were the clues Robert had been given, were maths and dates involved? And if so, when was *that* apocalypse? He guessed maybe, all these years later, that Robert had been given a long-term forecast of the event *he* had divined.

Ron wasn't about to give up, scoring another strike and settling back in his chair. '*He has told me about the return of his son ...*' Laughing.

William frowned at him. 'Alright, you've made your point.'

'Mightn't a been an Elder, William, but he was a visionary, like you.'

'My father didn't have the learning to work out what it meant. But he was sincere, in his own way.'

'And so are you.'

Julius looked at Ron. 'That's patronising, Ron.'

'It is not.'

William ruled off and started to add the scores. He had looked up at his father on the flat-tray and thought, My God, he's an idiot, even as Robert had continued to say, 'I don't know when, but we'll know it in our lifetime.'

I'm the best and worst of my father, William thought, blowing chalk-dust from his fingers. If he was wrong then I'm wrong, if he was right then we'll both sit beside Jesus.

Ron started stacking chairs, feeling he didn't need to comment on the winning score. 'Maybe if Robert could've lived a bit longer,' he smiled to William. 'What would he be, a hundred or so?'

'Eighty.'

And almost singing: 'So it's not inconceivable.'

The Millerites waited until the others had left, locking up and standing around in the dim yellow light of the showgrounds. A large plywood board with the letters CENTEN sat behind the shed, faded, broken up for other uses, left over from the 1936 Show. It had been part of a diorama of Tanunda, painted by a local artist to celebrate the state's one hundredth birthday, and had formed the backdrop to a inclined map of the state made from agricultural produce: grapes for the Barossa, oranges for the Riverland, golden wheat for the two peninsulas and papier mache rump steaks for the far north. William had offered some of his cucumbers, but the committee went with a slab of Bruno's blutwurst, claiming the valley was only so big.

William looked at the others and said, 'We should have nothing more to do with Rohwer.'

Seymour looked surprised. 'Why?'

'He doesn't follow the Bible, only committees and their rules. He's a small man.'

They walked down familiar roads, cutting across vacant blocks, over trampled grass. William was still fuming. 'If God tells me to walk to the top of Eden Hill, I will. Rohwer would form a committee to discuss this. Just like his father. Both caught up in their own importance. If God says walk to the top of High Eden Hill . . .' He stopped. 'Would you, Seymour?'

'Of course.'

'Arthur?'

Arthur adjusted the cushion between his shoulder and the cross. 'If God said to.'

And that was enough for William, changing course and leading them towards the gentle slopes of the Eden Hill. Encouraging them to sing as they went.

The hosts of God encamp around
The dwellings of the just:
Deliverance he affords to all
Who on his succour trust

Like so many boy scouts on a mission for a bemused, indifferent God. Arthur having trouble getting his cross over granite outcrops, pleading to Seymour for help as William marched on ahead. Halfway up Seymour said, 'He didn't actually want us to do this?'

William stopped and turned back. 'No, but what if he had?'

'Yes, but that's another thing.'

In which case William was happy to compromise, helping them rest Arthur's cross against a vertical cliff face, where its endless layers of varnish could reflect the moon (in its clear, cold winter sky) over the length and width of the Barossa.

They knelt down on one knee each and William prayed, quoting from Hebrews thirteen, remembered from a thousand nights in the loft, copying and re-copying for a stony-faced Robert below, sons as sons, disappointments handed down. Copying across the page in one direction and then over the top of it in the other. *Obey them that have the rule over you, and submit yourselves . . .*

Seymour felt assured in the confidence of William's delivery, but for Arthur it was not so much immolation as imitation, hearing Robert on the back of the Dodge truck.

Bible study was at William's house the following night. As they got under way, William paced Bluma's lino-less floor as he read from a heavily underscored Bible. '"And I saw a great white throne, and him that sat on it, from whose face the earth and the heaven fled away: and there was found no place for them." Joshua, what do you make of this?'

But before Joshua had a chance to reply, William was explaining. As he did every week, becoming two and three times a week, until at last they *thought* they were beginning to understand. Until he thought he was getting through to them, until the code of the

Four Horsemen was as clear as the tuning on Seymour's radio. Until the seven angels, with their vials of plague, actually appeared before their eyes covered in small pox, cholera and typhus. Until a Jerusalem of precious stones was before them to reach out and touch.

At the very same time, in one of the numerous spare bedrooms in Seymour Hicks' home, Joseph Tabrar stretched out in his singlet and shorts beside his wife Ellen, describing the garden of their Elizabeth home. He imagined a jacaranda which had grown to full size since they'd moved in, escaping, he thought to himself, Seymour and his crackpot mates. A canopy of purple flowers had broken open and emptied themselves across a carpet of Santa Anna, making a rectangle of mixed hues where Vicky and David used to play.

She stirred. 'Did you check them?'

'I did.' Running his hand across her belly before she sighed and turned over, refusing, it seemed to him lately, to discuss anything except overtime and the kids, the Lutheran school and why he always moped at Langmeil. Followed by the inevitable conversation about compromises, his, which she quickly turned into a discussion of hers.

A row of wine palms, he said, in cut down barrels, to remind her of Tanunda. Colourless and odourless, thriving in full sun, full of untouchable spikes with their religious connotations. 'What do you think so far?'

No reply. But Ellen was awake, staring out of the window at Gruenenberg's distant spike, listening to Mary in the lounge with Bob Hope barely tuned into Seymour's radio. '"Thanks for the memories . . ."' And thinking, Corny, except that life had moments like that. Mary spilt something and cursed – 'Shit' – and Ellen smiled, stopping as Joseph, explaining how these warm, winter days triggered something, crawled around in search of her lips.

David opened the door and stuck his head in. 'Mum . . .'

Joseph rolled back. 'Back to bed.'

But Ellen brought their son in and laid him between them, as a buffer, as Joseph turned to face a blank, mortar wall. Continuing nonetheless. 'Along the path, fuchsias and gardenia . . .'

'Joe, we need to get some sleep.'

Joseph closed his eyes and saw addresses, other people's – he knew every street and house and every peeling letterbox. He could imagine gardens – weedy, not thought-out like his – and children, distracted from street cricket, approaching fat, jolly posties (like W.C. Fields in shorts) and taking their mail. Running up pathways between heavily scented fuchsias, past wine palms, slamming fly-screen doors and throwing the letters down on the phone table.

The paradise of *his* Elizabeth, in twenty years time. Oak- and elm-lined streets, shading imported European vehicles, kids playing with neighbours' kids, the neighbours themselves sharing nectarines grown in the inexhaustible soil of their social experiment come good. Marx and Sartre discussed along paved footpaths which were swept daily by over-sized industrial vacuums. But even if it ended up a slum, it'd still be *their* slum. Seymour and Mary would come to visit and say their told-you-so's – Vicky pregnant at fourteen, David done up in a zoot suit, doing his best to look like Tony Curtis.

Joseph smiled at the thought of it. He stood up and put on a dressing gown, walking out to the front porch and sitting in a love-seat. Seymour stood in the shadows beside his broken letter-box, sorting his mail: PMG, church business and a land agent for Joseph. He raised the agent's letter to the moon but then saw Joseph himself, huddled against the cold. He walked towards him. 'Joseph.'

'Seymour.'

Inside, Mary sung along to Weill's *September Song*, more static than music. Seymour sat beside Joseph in the love-seat. 'For you.' Handing him the letter. 'Ellen mentioned Elizabeth.'

This time Joseph was short with a reply.

'You're welcome here,' Seymour continued, '. . . as long as you want.'

'Or at least until next March,' Joseph smiled, looking up at him.

Seymour looked down at the ground and played with his mail. 'Yes, but he'll live amongst us, like a neighbour.'

'Still, sorta defeats the purpose of real estate.'

'Well . . .'

'Unless he's wrong.'

'I don't think so.'

'Lotta others said the same thing, Seymour. Ended up looking very silly. I was always taught the End would be like a big plane crash.' In which everyone's kids got killed. Fire and retribution. Disasters which proved that Seymour's God was a loveless one.

'No,' Seymour continued, 'business as usual.'

'Convenient.'

'What about land around Tanunda, or Nuri?'

Joseph was as silent as the sexless Ellen in their bed. At last he looked over. 'This is your home, Seymour, you have your own ways.' Thinking how the radio was always tuned to Seymour's station, the salt and pepper in shakers as Mary liked them, pictures of Kavel and Luther hanging above the children's beds. 'I'd like some Beethoven occasionally.'

'Just say. If you don't tell me . . .'

But in Joseph's home, he wouldn't have to ask, bowing his head as he sought favours from others. 'Elizabeth sounds as good as anywhere.'

'You're crazy, look what you've got here.'

'Just the same.'

Silence. In time Seymour went in, opening and cursing his phone bill. Singing along with Mary, '"My heart belongs to daddy . . ."'

Joseph sat staring into the night sky, trying to work out how so many small compromises could have added up to this. 'Why rent, you can live here for next to nothing. Think of the money you'll save.'

Ellen dreaming endless afternoons of baking with the mother she'd never have to leave, the father she'd never have to disappoint, the children she'd hardly have to discipline or inspire with the Bible.

140

And how you just got stuck in a place and a time, sorting other people's letters.

The stage door to Union Hall, on the grounds of Adelaide University, was crowded with stage-struck plumbers, hausfraus and solicitors sucking back Capstan and Turf in a nervous frenzy of half-remembered lines and dance steps. One, a Scottish grandmother from Brighton, practised a waltz she'd later fluff in front of her friends from the Glenelg East Bingo (having worn out a perfectly good Axminster getting it right).

Phil led Nathan up the steps and into an ante-chamber of lederhosen and mock Bavarian dresses, recently finished with lace salvaged from the *Kismet* shrouds. He found a program, still smelling of ink, and showed Nathan his name, inserted alphabetically beside thirty-seven others who (according to the directions of Frank Fargo, the director) would walk on stage on cue and deliver their box-steps and four-part harmonies in a 'homely, natural style'.

Nathan stood back and smiled as Phil, mingling with the rest of the chorus, got laughs by imitating the director. '"Here, you, what's your name, never mind, if I see you up-stage from the principals again I'll have you removed."' Continuing, as Nathan examined the props table: fake plastic cakes and yeasts which wouldn't look out of place in the Apex bakery, artificial flowers and garlands to decorate the inn (again, good enough for the harvest festival), old suitcases for the guests and a dozen beer steins.

'"Your acting is *woody*,"' Phil continued, noticing Nathan and dragging him over. 'Nathan, though, is the real thing, a Barossa Lutheran.'

Nathan smiled, unsure if he had anything to be proud of. One of the chorus asked, 'How do we look, authentic?'

'We're an agricultural community: overalls and workboots. Still, I think, if we returned to Silesia wearing this . . .'

'Prosit! Ich habe *gemutlich*,' one of them smiled, acting with a stein, comfortable with the thought of a plywood inn and corny accents, refusing to consider realities which were still mostly rubble.

Nathan shrugged – '*I have cosy*, I don't think so' – but Phil had him by the arm, leading him on-stage through sets smelling of Hi Gloss, overlooking the Tyrolean lake of St Wolfgang which, within a few days, would be a sea of fake furs and blue rinses, suits that gents had worn to meet the Governor and christen the children. The rehearsal pianist struggled through *Salzkammergut* on a clunkety piano in the pit as the palm trees from the Foreign Legion scene were raised and lowered repeatedly in the inn's lobby. His Imperial Highness, Franz Josef, pencilled on his sideburns as the SM cut cheese under an eerie red light.

Nathan followed Phil downstairs, lingering outside the female dressing room and descending even further into a chamber of the bizarre: pot-bellied men wearing foundation and blusher, powdering their hair, warming up on scales of less than an octave and adjusting their scrotums in full view. A waiter, fully made up on the top half, naked on the bottom, scratched his pubic hair as his neighbour practised lines in the style of a Gestapo interrogator: '"Ve have your room ready, valk this vay ..."'

Phil fetched his costume as Nathan sat down in the corner, feeling more lost than ever, a kid from the country, naive beyond his years. If he tried to fit in it would just be pretending, his theatricality as real as prop yeast. Phil, though, was at home here, able to unleash the bit of him which was always acting. Raising his voice above the din of the dressing room: 'Quiet ... please ... thank you ... for those of us who care about the craft of acting ... I need some input ... where should the emphasis be, "*I* do", or "I *do*".' Going on to ask how they thought Olivier would handle it, if he ever bothered to get back to the roots of his craft.

Nathan wandered upstairs and settled into the back row of the theatre with his program. *The Davy Clarke Singers present, The Whitehorse Inn, starring Rex Pattison* ... the principal, a fifty-eight-year-old land surveyor with the Water Board, raised on *Die Fledermaus* and weaned on *Showboat*. Closeted in a private dressing room (he'd demanded) of leaking water pipes and steam valves. Busy emoting his character as others were having a good time; chasing the truth of Leopold, the love-sick head waiter, as others were busy chasing laughs.

Directed by Frank Fargo . . .

Formerly Frank Bleschke, an immigrant butcher's son raised on vaudeville, launching himself on-stage in a frenzy of black face and other people's lines, but dying a death by whispered mutters from the gods, retiring to the Grace Brother's suit department and a twilight of amateur theatre. Screaming from the stalls, 'Act, make us believe you,' as Nathan slipped back into his chair and smiled, and Rex and his love interest exchanged secrets over a garden wall. '"The moon sharpens my desires,"' Rex said, clutching the script he'd only partially learnt.

'This is a dress rehearsal,' Frank screamed. 'When will you have it down?'

'That's the easy part,' Rex replied.

'Not in my theatre. You won't be prompted.'

'Fine.'

Frank sat down, fuming, as his assistant continued massaging his shoulders. 'Every year there's less to work with.'

Phil, meanwhile, fully done up as a bridegroom, had locked himself in the basement lavatory with his pen and notebook: *High baritone seeks relationship with like-minded* . . . None of the profundity or poetry of the library toilets, affirming his belief that the theatrically bent were all trivial by nature, substituting the real for the imagined, one-liners for anything remotely spiritual.

The SM came onto the intercom. 'Bride and bridegroom, one minute.' Phil fumbled with an unfamiliar fly as he tripped up steps, knocking over a pile of fake rifles and searching for his bride in a small sea of hotel guests. 'Here.' He found her deriding him in front of her friends, arms crossed, frumpy. He dragged her on-stage like a reluctant heifer as he tried to stare longingly into her eyes.

Frank ran up onto the stage. 'Late.'

Deidre, the intended, was quick to point the finger. 'I was there waiting. He was off God knows where.'

Phil dropped his hands. 'I made it.'

Frank. 'Late.'

They all looked at the hotel staff, lined up in anticipation, as the terrified pianist vamped. 'Quiet!' Frank screamed, and she stopped. 'You've been late every time,' he continued, staring Phil down. 'We'll just have to replace you.'

'Me?' Phil imitated Frank, pointing out Rex and his overweight love interest. '*Woody, I've seen better waiters . . .*'

Frank called down to his assistant. 'What's this fellow's name?'

Phil stepped forward. 'Drummond, of the Kilburn Drummonds. Heard of us?'

Frank returned to him. 'If you're late one more time you're out.'

Phil breathed deeply. 'We are volunteers you know.'

'Continue!'

Method acting in the extreme. Phil returned to Deidre, and the deep (empty) wells which were her eyes. They walked towards Rex, the head waiter, who asked a series of questions: double bed? facing west? breakfast? – to which they muttered their famous line. After a few moments of low comedy, Phil decided to improvise, throwing off his jacket and saying, 'I don't know about you, darlin', but I got the hankerin'.' Clutching her around the waist as she tried to push him away.

'Please,' she said, the spell of stage-love forever broken. Frank was up on the stage in a moment, handing Phil his jacket and telling him to get changed. 'Come back when you want to take it seriously.' Taking a stray spot and calling down to his assistant for a suitable replacement.

The chorus was marched on en masse, each pretending to be interested in market stalls of plastic mettwurst and azaleas. They suddenly came together on cue, sucked centre stage like water down a drain, to waltz, banging up against each other and singing as hotel guests waved from windows and a costume donkey got laughs for all the wrong reasons.

Nathan, still patiently sitting in the back row, couldn't help but smile as Frank approached him and asked, 'Who are you?'

'The bridegroom's friend.'

Thrown out of the first theatre he'd ever been into.

He waited for Phil at the stage door of a thousand borrowed lines. They walked to the station along the path behind Government House, the sound of The Chordettes' *Mr Sandman* drifting down from the vice-regal digs. Phil ditched his script over the fence and said, 'Just like Rex: dead-beats in costume.'

They crossed King William Road, the syncopations of Joe Aronson still wafting across the Torrens and over the lawns of Elder Park. Phil said, 'Is there any Australian theatre?' but the sounds of Ellington's *Giddybug Gallop* seemed to suggest otherwise. He laughed, continuing extemporaneously, 'Is there any *Australian* theatre, or, is there any Australian *theatre*?'

Platform eight, ten fifteen, the man in blue resting on a stool, Phil with his head out of the Brill's window as they passed Dudley Park Cemetery with its cracking memorial wall. 'I do!'

The driver stopped at Islington to come back and quieten them down. The rail-yards were oblivious to the night, steam and diesel refusing to sleep, skylights bleeding arc light back into the universe as engineers ground axles to within a thousandth of an inch of their lives.

Kilburn. Red-brick dreams heavy with lantana, and Rose pulling back the boys' beds, discovering *The Secrets of St John Bosco* and sitting down for a giggle, taking it out to the shed to share with Bob who put it down to Phil.

The boys in the driveway, and then in the lounge of exploding tea and laughter, narrating the farce of theatre Fargo style, Phil describing the bride as a Wagnerian whore (while Rose crunched candied almonds in ignorance) and the director as a cross between Oscar Wilde and Goebbels.

That Friday, over bangers and mash in the cafeteria, Nathan asked Bob if he could stay down again. Bob channelled gravy through a canyon of finely mashed potato before saying, 'We don't mind you staying, only, it's what your mum and dad want.'

'They wouldn't care.' Going on to explain how much work he'd been given at trade school, his cold turned green, heavy, dark clouds, cold mornings and exhaustion.

'How they feel about you skippin' church?'

'Dad does, if he's got something on.'

'Yeah?'

Seeing how Bob understood that skipping church wasn't a mortal sin, having done it himself for thirty-odd years; seeing how it was just a case of being practical, God understanding that kiddies needed their wheelchairs, citrus its white oil, lawns their weekly trimming. Anyway, there were Rose's hymns on the radio – passing out through fly-wire which had to be cleaned, windows polished – serenading his near-ripe nectarines with the voices of angels from the Methodist Ladies' College.

And this is how it was that Sunday morning: Phil in his bathers, on a towel on the lawn working on a winter tan, Nathan beside him coughing, phrasing and re-phrasing definitions for torque and motive power, converting between pounds and stone, perch and acre, Bob staring through a lattice of gardenia into the sky, secateurs idle, silently mouthing the words to a distant *My Redeemer Liveth*. Thinking how, if the sky was a jigsaw, no one would ever solve the riddle of the blue bits, cloudless, featureless, stretching out forever – so many disjunct shapes refusing to come together, the poetry of what Handel had achieved in music eluding him.

William sat at his table, waiting for Bluma to stop coughing, receiving the usual complaints about dampness but explaining how this was neither the time nor the place – their table becoming their altar, demanding the same concentration and focus they gave at Langmeil.

'"And He showed me a pure river of water of life,"' he read, but Bluma couldn't take it seriously. Church wasn't church without Edna's rusty fingers, without the Stations of the Cross to study or your bum going numb on Arthur's resurrected pews; without hymns to sing along with or the smells of ladies doused in talc,

146

children slurping Turkey lollies in paper twists or the back of Mary Hicks' head full of dandruff and God knows whatever else. 'Coffee?' she asked, but William just looked up at her with a deadly stare, smoothing his page and continuing.

Bob finished pruning his six rose bushes, snipping the branches into twigs the size of cigarette butts and raking them into a compost pile of his own design: a border of railway sleepers containing everything from lawn clippings to broken egg shells. Drummond compost, he claimed, was the secret of plants which lived longer than a Bulgarian grandmother. Poking Phil's stomach with his rake he asked, 'Haven't you got exams to learn for?'

'All in good time.'

'When's the first?'

'Tomorrow. Listen, it's under control. You squeeze too much in it's likely to build up and rupture.' Showing how his head might explode all over Bob's buffalo grass.

After lunch they all walked down Carpenter Street towards the station. God had been satisfied (receding back into the box hedge for another week) and creamed corn toasties consumed to the gentle, persistent rhythm of the ABC's stock report. They walked past a sprawling Federation villa on a hill, Bob raising his hand to greet an old lady sitting on the porch. A goat grazed the un-mowed front lawn, tethered via a chain to a stake.

'Story has it,' Phil said, as they passed on, 'she was taken to the Queen Victoria Hospital, heavily pregnant, ready to pop. "Here comes the head," the surgeon says, but when it emerges . . .'

Rose shook her head. 'People might have stories about us.'

Phil imitated a goat. 'No joke. She arrives home with a goat, but no baby.'

Rose nodded. 'She lost the baby. The goat was a distraction.'

Phil laughed. 'Who gives a goat as a . . . grieving gift? A dog perhaps.' He remembered riding around on his 'bitza' bike with friends, hiding in the acacias across the road from her, imagining Satan reclining inside with his Best Bets and a lager – calling for her to come in and join him. They'd call out to her, 'Darling, I'm ready,' and she'd pack up her knitting and go inside, proving it beyond a doubt. Crawling under her window to listen they'd only hear the hum of an old Singer, but this was just put on to fool the innocents.

Arriving in Botanic Park they strolled among the crowd, gathered in close around speakers on the backs of trucks or standing high on piles of fruit crates. The speakers were generally done up in tie and jacket, preaching Communism and Temperance on ninety-day permits. Agitating to crowds comfortably numb in a paradise of Kelvinators and melamine kitchens free of garlic and spring rolls. The only ones taking it seriously were a pair of detectives, standing out like rams' balls as they scribbled in their notebooks: *Clyde Cameron, speaking at the Comm. (Soviet) ring. Discussed situation at Port Adelaide. Mentioned how men were organising and being drilled by returned soldiers.*

Beside the Communists were the single-taxers, for whom Bob cheered in support, confiding that most people were unaware of what they paid in indirect taxation. Then there were the Douglas creditors, the Socialist Labour Party and a religious group called the Rationalist Society. But for value for money, most people were drawn to the ladies of the Temperance Union, standing before a large banner of what seemed to be an inebriated pony thrown down at the feet of Christ. The first speaker identified herself only as Mary, Mother of Temperance, and declared that spirits worked by dissolving the very cells of the liver and kidney.

Phil couldn't believe it, calling from the back, 'Where's the research?'

'Oh, there's research alright. Visit our headquarters and we'll supply you with copies of papers from Europe, written by professors of biology and medicine.'

Bob tripped over a small sign, planted into the grass, announcing Peter Laundy, a pastor who described how the black man was being saved, taught the values of thrift and hard work in a network of missions throughout South Australia and the Northern Territory.

Removed from alcoholic mothers (gins sleeping around with multiple partners) so that they might amount to something; given clothes and a bed and a roof over their head, and if they so desired, education to 'the very highest level'. Briefly reminding the crowd of what their fate might have been otherwise: '"For *without* are dogs, and sorcerers, and whore-mongers, and murderers, and idolaters . . ."'

Phil nudged Nathan and whispered, 'Is this why you stay down?'

Nathan smiled. 'This one's a nut.' But wasn't so sure, conjuring up William on a soapbox, spewing forth the very same lines.

Bob looked at Nathan and wondered if it wasn't time he made contact with William himself. He watched as Phil, nudging Nathan again, said, 'Six months with me and you'll be throwing tomatoes at this fella.'

Nathan laughed, explaining how this place would bring out the idiots in any group. 'We're just like the Baptists,' he said. 'Nice sing-along and a prayer.'

But Bob wasn't so sure, remembering how his old man had taught him to recognise a Lutheran – walk into a pub and tell a joke, he'll be the only one not laughing.

Sitting in the 'switch-back', watching teenagers jumping mounds on stripped-back bikes, Bob could still hear Pastor Laundy above the other speakers, more convinced than anyone else of what he was saying. He felt glad, irrespective of the dramas, that they could give Nathan a buffer from the endless devotions and prayers and thanksgiving of the existence he'd described on their walks to work through Kilburn.

Eventually they bought ice-creams and tuppence of lollies from an old Afghan at the zoo gates and headed back into the city. Phil was left at the university library to study and Nathan stayed with him, content to catch up with the papers.

In the late afternoon – as the sun started setting west of the Torrens, streaming in the Barr Smith windows through an opaque, yellow film – Nathan left the newspapers behind and wandered aimlessly through rows of shelves pregnant with books. Rows which stretched as far as Arthur's bottom paddock, the full length

149

of Murray Street, holding more information and facts than he thought the world contained. Row after row, reaching up to a ceiling of spray-on concrete. Six or seven shelves per row, each with a few dozen books – African mystical cults, Micropaleontology, Common Algae of the Great Lakes. And when you were finished on one floor there was another. Silent. Heaters humming. The buzz of fluoros heard above water dripping somewhere. Almost devoid of people. Like the promised End had come and gone. Leaving behind books.

Each of the thousands of books was a world unto itself. Sitting silently, refusing to reveal any of its secrets unless someone picked it up, read it, and thought about things. Like his father's Bible. But that was only one book – one in an endless sea of words in which he stood, drowning in the smell of old paper, overwhelmed and overcome as he was sucked under. Each book seemed to contain its own truth and reality, quoting research and references, so that the Bible itself seemed to be lost among them, unable to support its own wild claims.

If this place represents all knowledge, he thought, then there's no way the Bible is right. What would be the chances of that? People as smart as Phil, working for thousands of years, having and sharing ideas, doing it all honestly and without bias and sentiment, testing them, rejecting them, trying again. Or on the other hand, water into wine and feeding the masses with some old bread.

He stopped randomly, opening a text on Climatic and Biotic Evolution, and although he didn't understand a word, realised that after so many books even your faith in God couldn't be a certainty.

Which led him to Phil, cramming in the medical library, suddenly aware of how much he had to learn before tomorrow. But Phil still wasn't worried, it always worked out in the end. 'Exams are a game of chance,' he'd told Nathan. 'There's only so much they can put in and after a while you work out what it will be.'

Nathan held a text and tested him. 'Stock solutions – G is equal to . . .?'

'Shit . . . yes . . . MWv over a thousand.'

'Where M equals?'

'Molarity.'

On and on like this, surprising Nathan at every turn. 'Enzyme kinetics?'

'No, they won't put that in.'

'Relative potency?'

'No ... maybe ... the dose of an unknown drug, U, divided by the dose of a standard drug, S.'

'Nearly.'

'The log of the relationship?'

'What's a log?'

'A bit of dead tree.'

They ignored the five-minute bell but were eventually evicted by a cleaner. On the way home, Phil's thoughts drifted out of the railcar's window, leaving molarity and enzymes behind in search of other things. Nathan watched him and, not in a competitive way, felt jealous. To think he had the contents of at least a few dozen of those books in his head, and yet, wasn't interested in using his knowledge as a tool to influence or control others. Phil was at peace with himself and what he did and didn't know. Dismissing it all as 'so much rot you'll eventually forget anyway'. As if he sensed that the important things were mostly unsaid and unwritten.

'"For *without* are dogs, and sorcerers ..."' he intoned, quoting the soapbox pastor and turning back to Nathan.

'Yes, there are some like him.'

'Some?'

'Lots.'

'What about your old man?'

Nathan turned his head towards the window, smiling, suddenly struck with his own apocalyptic visions on the back of toilet doors (Phil had given him the grand tour, the originals far exceeding the tracings: a nun exposing her breasts, ten times the size of her head, filled with sharks swimming as though in a gold fish bowl). 'What can I say? My old man believes in the end of the world.'

'Really? When?'

'Next year.'

Phil followed the progress of a conductor. 'You're kidding ... how's he worked that out?'

Nathan put on his father's voice. '"The dates are all in the Bible."'

'And he's found them?'

'Yes.'

Phil smiled. 'You know what this means?'

'What?'

'I can't date a Catholic.' Presenting his ticket and settling back in his seat. 'It's alright for you, you've had a root.'

Chapter Ten

Late on a Tuesday night, after the staff had gone home, the Millerites stood around in the *Tanunda Oracle*'s hand-press studio. Its editor, a valley newcomer named Juan Pascoe (his beard and hair as wild as Ned Kelly's, forever in untucked shirts and Levis) had given them a crash course on the iron hand-press, locking them in at ten p.m. and asking for things to be left as they were for the morning shift. He had no idea what William Miller was printing, but his money, a collection taken from the whole group, was as good as anyone's. 'A brochure?' he'd asked, showing them how to ink a form, but William had just replied, 'Along those lines.'

William had spent the afternoon in the back of the *Oracle*'s offices setting out his form, varying letter size and style, inking and checking each paragraph as he went. Eventually he printed a proof, read it and made corrections, cleaning down the galley with mineral spirits before setting it in the press and heading home for tea.

Sitting in front of Bluma's potato pie, he had said, 'In a few days we can start delivering,' explaining how he would draw up maps and assign streets to the others, spreading the word of God in line with the modern age. When she asked why a press was more acceptable than a vacuum he just mumbled something about the Hoover not being in God's plan.

God's improvised plan, Bluma had thought, the gospel according to St Muller.

Seymour, Arthur, Joshua and William stood in front of the

Washington Imperial No. 1 press, a relic dating from 1839 which was imported from Pennsylvania by one of Kavel's sons. William said, 'Alright, who's doing what?' and they all looked blank. 'Seymour, haven't you done some printing?'

'Yes, but that was a star press.'

William stepped towards the beast with its rib rungs and cheek stops, coupling rods and bar braces, and thought, Now you're working for me. Running his hand over the paper bench he said, 'Okay, this is how we'll do it.'

And before long they had the rhythm: Seymour as press-man, inking the form for each of the individual leaflets, Arthur as paper-handler, pre-pricking sheets of blank paper to fit the points on the tympan. Seymour pulling on the bar to lower the press. Re-charging the roller as Arthur removed the printed sheets and handed them to Joshua for checking. William double-checking every word for broken letters and defects before putting them in the humidor to dry.

They worked past midnight and into the early hours, barely a word spoken between them as they laboured for the first time as a team. Others would have been doing it for the money, to sell curtains or cars, freak-shows or a cricket match at which Bradman would be present. But they were publishing a warning. That the End was nigh and there were dark forces (even here in Tanunda, people you'd never guess) whose sole mission was to distract them from 'this present business'.

The Figuring of the End
Wilhelm Muller

I, Wilhelm Muller, have heard the voice of God at Gnadenberg on 24 May in the Year of the Lord 1951. He has told me that the time of his Son is near. Immanuel, Saviour, Lord of Heavens, will appear amongst us (at an unknown time and place) on March 21 next. Truly Good News. Dates derived from the book of Daniel and Revelation ...

Going on to explain his figuring.

> *Rejoice! Christ will make a Heaven on Earth! He will walk amongst you and talk as simply as this. The Scriptures suggest he will live in the Holy Land ...*

The leaflet unwilling, or unable, to explain how Jesus would get around to visit the Saved. Perhaps in his own version of the royal yacht *Britannia*, greeted by red carpet and oom-pah bands as he came ashore at Port Adelaide. Or maybe levitating, like a GI Joe doll with a NASA rocket backpack, appearing just as Bruno Hermann started sanding down his corns, 'Ah, at last, we've made pot cakes especially, just let me put on my socks.'

> *Those who wish are welcome to worship with me, at my house off Langmeil Road. There is no day or time, just knock on my door. I no longer sit among Congregation as I was told to bury these views. They were not buried. They are in your letterbox. All men have been told and He will know your mind and actions. We will all be judged in the End. Among my present supporters are Hicks, Blessitt and Heinz but I know there will be more.*

It had even crossed William's mind to put in how he would make up a final list of followers on March twenty next, presenting them to Jesus the next day as a definitive statement of those worthy. But Joshua and Seymour had talked him out of it, explaining how some might see it as arrogance, turning against him when they might otherwise have supported him.

At two-thirty a.m. Bluma walked down Murray Street, Tanunda, with the valley asleep around her. Carrying a flask of coffee in one arm and a basket of bread and cheeses in the other, she stumbled, picking herself up and swapping the basket to the other hand. Walking on she called, 'Coo-ee!' but it failed to echo off shop fronts, out of gutters or down Murray Street as she'd hoped.

Arriving at the *Oracle*'s office she knocked on the door and Seymour let her in.

William warned they shouldn't stop as they had less than three hundred done and only four hours before the staff arrived. Bluma relieved them in turn as they sat down beside a broken Albion press and sipped sweet coffee. 'I can imagine the surprise on a lot of faces,' Seymour said, as he stretched out and let the blood return to his feet, attempting, unsuccessfully, to sponge ink from a shirt not twelve months old.

Like the surprise on Pastor Henry's face, after he hobbled up his broken driveway in flannelette pyjamas, opening the letterbox, unfolding the pamphlet and reading. Thinking, I warned them about William. Turning to his neighbour and asking if she'd got one. 'Oh yes, put there by Vicky, the Hicks' girl, late last night. I thought it was a prowler.' Asking her what she thought. Promising she'd consult with her Bible and get back to him. 'Doesn't seem right, though. There was that lot in America. What came of them? And what do you think, Pastor Henry, all this business about the decree of Artaxerxes?'

'That's true enough. Still, I could predict this fence'd fall down tomorrow, and even if it did, doesn't mean I knew it was going to.'

'Let's hope it don't.'

'Seems to me that's how people are going to start thinking about William. Pity, his people were original. 'S like catchin' the cancer. Random. God acts like that. Bingo. He's up there callin' people's number.'

'Reckon William's come up.'

'Yes. Might be a touch of shell shock.'

Like an exploding bottle of William's red, corked too early.

Seymour stood up and reclaimed his roller, charging it with ink and returning to William's cast-iron negative. After they'd all been spelled, Bluma sat down, yawning, waiting for William to excuse her. 'You can start folding the dry ones,' he said, taking a pile out of the humidor and placing them beside her. And what could she say? It was God's work, even if it was after three in the morning.

William continued checking the bite in random sheets, reminding them to keep a constant pressure on the bar. He was imagining Ron Rohwer at his letterbox, reading the pamphlet and smiling, folding and slipping it into his pocket for the alternative Langmeil Bible study he'd organised. Bringing it out and reading it the following night at Fritschle's house. 'And then he says, can you believe this, "He will know your mind and actions . . ." William believes none of us have got it right. Don't we bow low enough, or sing high enough? And to think Henry wanted them to stay on.'

Or maybe it'd just be Ron with a box of matches, burning a pile of leaflets he'd gathered, as everyone emerged from Sunday service to see the ash blow down between the avenue of pencil pines. Smoke in their nostrils. Bruno starting in on the Langmeil bells. William and Bluma at home praying, deserted by Nathan, forming pacts to hasten the unrealised End of Days.

Just after six the sun started colouring the street. William cracked the whip but they were evicted half an hour later, walking home with nearly six hundred leaflets in Bluma's basket. The following night they returned and increased the total to a little over eleven hundred.

Towards five a.m. on the second night, Arthur, arms sore from pulling the bar, said, 'I think I've done enough.' William looked at him and said, 'Enough is when everyone in the valley has a copy.'

'That'd take weeks, and my arms are finished.'

William returned to his work, half ignoring him. 'Are you planning on going home?'

Arthur picked up his jacket and put it on. Seymour and Joshua kept working silently. Arthur stood staring into the back of William's head. 'I'm tired!'

And this time William ignored him completely, cleaning built up ink off the tympan with a rag. Arthur sighed, took off his jacket and returned to a half dry roller. After they'd continued working in silence for another fifteen minutes, William said, as he emptied the humidor, 'We're all tired . . . but it's His work . . .'

And there was no reply from anyone, the press clunking away into the night.

The following afternoon all of William's friends and their families gathered at his house. Groups were formed, maps distributed, streets assigned and leaflets packed into shopping bags. Mary took her daughter and Bluma and started on the northern end of town, passing beneath the sugar gums of Auricht Street with their flowers dropping pollen and anthers into their hair. Seymour took his grandchildren in his hearse, allowing Joseph to drive as he flitted between letter boxes in a long-lost athletic frenzy, competing with the children to see who could deliver most. Arthur set off on foot towards Bethany and William joined with Joshua to cover the area west of the hospital and south of the park.

Two nights later it was done and they settled in to wait for the response. If there were rumblings of discontent, William didn't hear them. Bruno smiled as he told him he'd stuck the sheet on his fridge; a retired butcher from Koblenz Avenue stopped him in the street to tell him he had it all wrong. But apart from that, nothing. William wondered if the various congregations had been warned off, told that making a stir would just encourage him. But he knew it must have got some people thinking and he was willing to wait for them to knock on his door.

The great silence that followed in the next few weeks was disconcerting. No one. Weren't these the descendants of Kavel and his followers? He'd stop people in the street and ask if they'd received his leaflet and they'd say, Yes, very interesting, but it's not something I'd like to discuss. In the end, he guessed, it might be a case of presenting his argument more convincingly.

The following week he blitzed Nuriootpa with the spares and asked his friends if they'd help him print more for Angaston, Moculta, Lyndoch and beyond. But the consensus was that leaflets were too easy to throw away and forget.

Something more solid was needed.

Ellen, marooned on the Hicks' front lawn, turned towards the Langmeil Road and crossed her arms. 'Have you finished?' Joseph walked around to face her. 'The only time you're not miserable is when your mother's around. Otherwise it's . . .' mimicking the sour expression she always seemed to have lately. 'You don't even notice it. Last night I asked you a question and you just kept staring at your mum.'

Looking high over the ranges which encircled the valley, she remembered the scene. Joseph coming over to her, placing his finger on her chin and turning her head towards him. As if to make up for it she turned her head towards him now. 'I was thinking.'

'You were waiting for her to answer for you.'

'Rubbish.'

But he went on to quote more examples – the time they were discussing Chas' piano lessons: Edna couldn't be trusted, short-tempered, didn't have the theory, yes, there had to be better. Until Mary entered. 'Edna, no, she studied at the conservatorium.'

'Well, in that case.'

Ellen couldn't remember; she turned away from him again. 'I didn't say that.'

Joseph moved around, hot in pursuit. 'You did. You find it simpler to let her decide.'

Mary, busy with her crochet, turned down her Golden Voice to hear. Chas came charging out the front door with a wooden B-17 Arthur had given him last birthday. He started playing at their feet. Joseph shook his head and returned to nailing up loose pickets on the Hicks' fence. Ellen came over to him and almost whispered, Mary straining to hear. 'They have experience in things. It's no harm –'

'It is. I'm a bloody accessory. *I* have experience!'

Ellen turned and walked back towards the house. Mary switched off the radio and sat forward. Joseph followed his wife. 'I'm their bloody father and I'll decide things.'

'Keep your voice down.'

At the top of his voice. 'I'll decide –'

Tripping on Chas' toy, falling and grasping his big toe. 'Jesus, Chas, I told you about leaving things –' Trailing off. Chas running up to Ellen and burying his head in her dress.

Ellen turned to him. 'What have you done?'

'Broken it.'

'You have not.'

'If it was your bloody mother... have an ambulance here by now.'

Inside, Mary turned up the radio and sat back with her handi-work. Seymour emerged from their bedroom in his best suit and tie. 'How do I look?'

'Fine,' Mary replied, looking towards the door. 'If you're going out ...'

But Ellen came in first, slamming the screen door behind her and taking Chas into her room. 'Everything alright?' Mary called, but there was no reply.

Seymour smiled. 'Lovers' tiff,' making his way down the hall and out the front door. Joseph was still on the grass, a shoe and sock off. Seymour stood on the porch. 'What y' done?'

'It's coming good.'

'Leave that fence.'

'It's nearly done.'

Seymour walked down the path, under an arch of rampant bougainvillea and up the road towards William's place.

Joseph slipped on his sock and shoe, picked up his hammer and returned to the fence. Chas appeared to apologise and ended up helping him pull the old nails, asking, 'Dad, what's a Flying Fortress?' as Joseph put his face in his son's hair, breathed deeply and kissed him.

Ellen, standing hidden from her husband by the window frame, let the curtain fall and walked out to sit with Mary. 'That the jumper for Arthur?' she asked.

'Yes, seeing how he's always making toys for the kids.'

Seymour stopped to gather lemons from a tree in a vacant block off Kalleske Street. He took off his jacket and filled it, tying it up by the arms, making his way to William's and emptying the lemons onto Bluma's table. 'Who planted it I don't know,' he smiled, 'but it's the best fruiter in Tanunda.'

Walking out back he found William in Arthur's stock paddock, the pair of them chasing a ewe with a stuck lamb. Seymour walked up to them as Arthur held the ewe and William rolled up the sleeves on his best white shirt, handing Seymour his jacket and undoing his tie. 'Here, I'll only be a minute.'

The lamb was already dead. They left it for the foxes in the tall grass as the mother licked the placenta and eventually drifted away. William walked with Seymour to his wash-house, cleaning up and saying, 'It's a miracle Arthur still has a farm,' by which he really meant the weedy oats, vinegar wine, undrenched and unvaccinated stock, and flowers. 'I've never heard of anyone making a living from flowers,' he continued. 'Flowers you can grow in your own garden. Who needs to buy Arthur's?'

Sleeves were adjusted, ties tied and jackets straightened as they set off towards town. Seymour carried a pile of spare leaflets and William his Bible. Seymour said, 'Fella on the radio reckons all this is atoms.'

William laughed. 'He would. Apart from the Methos, radio's full of funny men and frog dissectors. Pity they see it that way, there's a whole world of lost people.'

Which was the purpose of today's mission – to walk up garden paths and knock on front doors, and explain this fella Jesus to people. How he was portrayed in the Bible and what he did, his smell, the tone of his voice, the way he laid his hands on lepers and allowed himself to be crucified. To save the home-owner in question, whether he or she knew or admitted it. And how He was about to return, as the Bible had promised.

'This fella reckons,' Seymour continued, 'that the whole universe was as big as a pin-head and one day it just went bang.' Describing the expanding universe with his hands. 'And it's still moving away from the centre.'

William knew that the radio pushed God to the edge of the

universe. 'You should get rid of that thing, Seymour,' he said. 'It's like an open sewer running through your living room.'

'I would, only Mary loves the music.'

They passed the Tanunda Hotel and Juergie's Restaurant, full of lost townies feeding their gullets with whiting. This, to William, was proof of *his* scenario – stillborn accountants and plumbers left for the foxes in Christ's east paddock, warned, but choosing to believe in a universe of atoms. Eventually they stood in front of the gate of number one Edward Street. 'Feel like the Watkins and Rawleigh man,' Seymour smiled.

A young man in a singlet opened the door and said, 'What you fellas sellin'?'

But even William wasn't corny enough to say, Have we got a bargain for you, eternal salvation, absolutely free. Seymour showed him the leaflet and asked, 'Did you get one of these?'

The man smiled. 'You the fellas sayin' the world's gonna end?'

William cleared his throat. 'That's a common misunderstanding. Jesus will come and live amongst us. You can still grow your tomatoes and peas.'

'Thanks. Bit strange if you ask me. I always thought God was on about lovin' your neighbours.'

'He was, is. He predicted epochs, times when everything would be brought to a close. Times when people would be judged.'

'Like a spring cleaning?'

'Sort of.'

'And what about me, am I out in the rubbish?'

Seymour realised that the worst thing they could do was to preach, to appear to be passing judgement. 'It's not our job to say,' he began. 'People have their own ways. We just want people to know His message.'

The young man smiled again. 'So we can't say we weren't warned.'

Seymour shrugged. 'You're looking at it in the wrong way.'

'No, no, you said: People will be judged.'

'Yes –'

'And if they're not hollerin' hymns they're going to . . .?'

William couldn't see the problem. 'Hell.'

'So you fellas have got the nerve to come onto my land and tell me if I don't agree with your ways, then I'm gonna be boiled in oil for eternity?'

The missionaries were silent. Again William shrugged. 'We don't know, but it may be something like that.'

'You people think the valley's yours, but this is Australia, mate.'

William pointed out that Kavel had settled the valley first, starting with the township of Langmeil. The young man replied, 'We found the bloody place, built the roads. We been quite happy. Don't see us startin' no world fuckin' wars.'

Seymour took William's hand and led him back down the path, saying, 'Thanks for your time,' as the door was slammed and a female voice inside broke up with laughter. William had to gather his thoughts and calm himself before the next house.

'Is this the best way after all?' Seymour asked.

'It'll be fine. The thing is, I suppose, people have already made up their minds.'

'So there's no point getting your blood pressure up.'

Seymour shouted William lunch at the Zinfandel tea rooms, introducing him to Cornish pasties with chick peas and 'vegetables that were still growing this morning'. Talking with his mouth full, as usual, he said, 'This fella reckons we just broke off the sun, and spun around till we made a ball.'

'They've got answers for everything. But where did the elephants and wombats and whales come from?'

'Ah, then they get onto that Darwin fella.'

'I know.'

Seymour was more of a thinker than William, often wishing the Bible could have explained things in greater detail. 'How did he do it? Was it like magic? In the end they worked out Houdini's tricks. So it must've been more like a big chemistry experiment, God mixing everything together and then, bang! Maybe that's what the fellas on the radio meant . . . no . . .'

Stopping, remembering that whenever he followed this logic

he ended up confused. Did God have any help; what were the mechanisms, electrical, chemical, mechanical? Were there great storms in the universe that He charged with electricity, producing elements that produced matter? And who was God, and how did he get there? If cause and effect was true, if everything had to start from something, then who made the big fella? An even bigger fella? Who? Where did *he* come from, and where was he now? William, it seemed, had none of the answers; at least the fella on the radio was trying. And, it seemed to Seymour, if you couldn't reconcile science with what's come before then you're certain to end up with trouble.

The afternoon passed with general civility, 'Yes, I did receive your brochure, thank you, haven't quite had a chance to read it,' people uncomfortable with religion on their doorstep instead of locked away behind ironstone arches. 'I'm not willing to have it out here,' one woman said, closing the door on them, as William replied, 'Jesus walks Calleske Court.'

'Leave your literature under the mat.'

Why next year, many people asked, and William replied it had to be some time. Like elections, the mood had to be right. They were the democrats of Paradise, sent forth to persuade the swinging voters.

There was coffee at the Rechner's and more English tea at the Doms'. Obvious homes were passed over: Rohwer and Fritschle, Streim and Pastor Hoffmann. Gardening advice was given in Aughey Street and a chook held down for Ma Traeger and her blunt tomahawk, William having to finish the job properly.

Next door a middle-aged man, whose people neither Seymour or William knew, greeted them in nothing but underwear.

'Would you like a minute to get dressed?' William asked.

'Do I offend you?'

Passing on to a discussion of prophecy. 'The Bible foretold of Israel. But it also predicts that Russia will invade and take over,' said Seymour.

'Because the Reds are atheists?'

'Perhaps.'

'You lot are paranoid. Russia spent the war shooting Yids. It hardly wants their country.' The man scratched his pubic region; Seymour tried to ignore it as he continued.

'There are other signs.'

The man folded his arms, emphasising a pot-belly. 'Go on.'

'Take, for instance, the seven plagues of Revelation.'

'Such as?'

William, sensing Seymour's hesitance, took over. 'Typhus, cholera, smallpox, tuberculosis, polio . . .'

'That's five.'

'The cancer.'

'None of which existed more than . . . twenty years ago?'

William felt his heart racing again. In desperation he opened his Bible and turned to Revelations.

'I don't want to hear that,' the man said, hitching his under-pants. 'That says the world's six thousand years old. At that rate the Grand Canyon would still be a creek. And what about the dinosaurs? You'd have to be a bit simple.'

'It's a matter of faith.'

'Faith? What about the limestone under the Simpson Desert? How'd all of them shells get there? Six thousand years? That musta been underwater about the same time my old man bought his first Vauxhall. You'd *have* to be simple.'

William shook his head. 'What's so hard to believe?'

'I feel sorry for you. You're lost.'

William turned, storming off and setting course for home. Catching up, Seymour asked, 'Is that it?'

'I'm afraid so. We can't help these people.'

'We can help some.'

'Not enough.' Thinking how when Jesus preached he didn't have radio telescopes and astrophysics to contend with, or the devils Darwin and Marx. There'd been a Judas-Rohwer and a Pilate-Hoffmann but that was to be expected.

Arriving home Bluma fixed them black coffee and strudel

and they retired to a seat on the back porch. Seymour asked if they should pray for the souls they couldn't touch but William just said, 'Maybe later.'

Saturday was recycled as the new Sabbath. Between them, the Millerites agreed to meet at William's each week for a service and late lunch, a ceremony they would institutionalise as their own special time. This was William's idea, an attempt to develop a small ritual, the smell of pig-on-a-spit and Bluma's fresh bread spreading out over Tanunda, its radios droning football and the Gardening Hour. He was also being diplomatic. William didn't want to insist the others stop attending church; if it came down to that, Mary would just get in Seymour's ear and that would be the end of it. Joshua, too, he suspected of having a bet each way. But among the whole town Arthur, Seymour and Joshua were the only ones who had stood up to be counted. If they had their weaknesses he would have to forgive them; this was the lesson of Christ and the twelve, arguing amongst themselves, full of conceit, daily disappointing him.

And this is how it would continue up to the End, when they'd be interrupted from their pumpkin soup by sparks in the sky, a valley full of bells going crazy and an unbearably intense light. Dropping to their knees a great wind would blow up and overturn Arthur's newly made outdoor table-chair combo: a pair of old pews, mounted face-to-face on a frame, a table of his best Tassie oak in between – a movable ark for both praying and eating.

William sat opposite Joshua, who smiled at him. 'You'll never send it in, William.'

And as if to spite him, William started writing. *Previous name*: 'Miller, William'. *New name*: 'Muller, Wilhelm'. He signed the bottom, folded it and slipped it into an envelope. 'Do we have any stamps, Bluma?'

She looked at Joshua. 'Of course he'll never send it. William, it's been twelve years. Who's going to go back to calling you Wilhelm? It sounds like the Kaiser.'

Joshua laughed. 'You're an Austrayleeurn now, William. You have to try fit in.'

'I've been Australian for a hundred years. Doesn't mean I've ever stopped being German. Bluma, stamps?'

'No.'

He placed the letter in his jacket pocket. 'I'll fix it up on Monday.'

Bluma laughed, basting the side of pork the men had hung over an open fire. 'You'll need a sign around your neck: "Wilhelm, *not William*".'

'Finished,' Mary Hicks said, tying off the last row and holding up a crocheted jumper. An angular, blue Australia floated in a sea of variously coloured leftover wools and on the back, an even more angular kangaroo sat in a field of green two-ply. 'Arthur.'

Arthur dropped his paint-brush and walked over. She sized it against him and he tried it on, smiling, shaking it onto his body like the skin it'd soon become. 'Many thanks,' he said, but Mary replied it was little compared to what he did for them, for all of them, running her hands across the finely sanded oak of the table.

She ordered him not to wear it for painting, although he didn't see the problem. His bedroom was full of piles of paint and grease splattered clothes sitting unwashed on the floor.

Removing the jumper, Arthur returned to the banner (one of Bluma's donated sheets) on which he and Nathan were helping the other kids paint PLAY FOR THE APOCALYPSE: the title of the play William was writing, coming to life in thick, black letters. Between pencil lines Nathan had scored with his new drafting set, the six Heinz children, led by the eldest, Sarah, helped Victoria, David and Chas do their best to stay within the lines. Nathan re-filled paint jars as Arthur attached bamboo poles to either end of the sheet. When it was finished it would form the backdrop to a stage-on-wheels which Arthur planned to build – like his cross, a movable show which could be taken any place, any time, in search of an audience.

William laid the first draft of the script on the table. It was conceived as a children's play, with Nathan the returning Christ and the other children the saved and un-saved. Special effects and music would be involved, but it was still in the planning. At one o'clock, Mary and Catherine Heinz helped Bluma lay out the salads they'd all contributed. Arthur's ark was covered with the traditional and the *nouveau* (Mary's Mexican carrot salad), sharing their smells under a big, blue winter sky. William sat at the head of the table – content, sure that God was looking down and blessing them as everyone else in the valley sat indoors beside radios, re-smoking rollies and wandering outside to contemplate sickly agapanthus.

Like Bruno, standing at the fence watching them. 'Where was my invite, William?'

William refused to look over, buttering bread and shaking his head. 'It's your choice.'

Bruno read the words on the banner and thought, maybe not. 'Edna's frying me up some sausage.'

William whispered loud enough for the others. 'Enjoy it, Bruno. Goodbye.'

The Millerites giggled. They watched Bruno turn to go inside, and heard him mumble, 'I hope you choke on it.'

Bluma appeared from the kitchen with the last of the salads. 'Wash your hands,' she called, and the children flocked to the wash-house where Nathan was waiting to make sure they used soap.

Settling in around the table they all joined hands and William began, 'In the name of the Father . . .'

They passed onto a twenty-minute devotion which seemed longer in the presence of food, Bluma swatting flies and chasing a stray from their yard as William returned to Revelations. Explaining how the great wall with its twelve gates, each with an angel, was their way into the Kingdom: a city of pure gold and precious stones, the gates themselves pearly and a great temple in the middle.

As William prayed, Nathan looked around at the bowed heads and wondered. He caught Sarah Heinz's eye and mimicked death-by-endless-prayer, but she just bowed her head and closed her eyes. He wondered where Lilli was, and wished he was with her;

he knew that of the several lives he led, some were better than others. As Nathan had expected, William dominated proceedings. Seymour was his straight man, the Stiffy of Tanunda feeding lines to a reluctant Mo. 'Eh, William, what about Fred Murray?'

Bluma placed the meat on the table and William started carving. 'We asked Fred if he got our brochure,' William said. '"Yes, sir", he says. "But it's like this ... I wrote three hundred odd songs for the stage, and any of them what mentioned Jesus flopped."'

Seymour started taking plates and laying out pork. 'Next thing you know, we're in his music room. Fred sits down at his piano and says, I wrote this one for Alec Hurley:

I've found a lovely little tart,
And every night and morning I go to court 'er;
When waltzing around the town, I fairly take 'em down,
With Mary-Anne the 'addick smoker's daughter ...'

Without looking up, Nathan said, 'They used to bring him to school to perform for us.' Unaware of why their concerts stopped, the piano lid lowered during a rendition of *They Went to the Usual Place* in front of Mrs Powell's combined 4-5s.

Nathan macerated a pile of egg noodles with his fork and wondered what Phil was up to. Probably road-testing a Melchior double-wheel chair for Bob, he thought. Racing up and down the Drummond's crumbling driveway at dangerous speeds, occasionally losing his balance and ending up in Rose's petunias, fluffing up the flat ones before she noticed.

'How are your new living arrangements, Nathan?' Catherine asked, spooning herself some of Mary's coleslaw.

'The Drummonds are groovy.'

William looked at him through a forest of food. Groovy. Not the Nathan he knew. He put it down to the son, described by Nathan variously as a young Errol Flynn and a down-market Einstein, stopping Speaker's Corner with comments the dimwit Lefties and Rationalists couldn't counter. At other times Nathan had described him as a Mahatma in corduroy, awakening thoughts he'd never had, like how Japan was offered up as a sacrificial lamb, reduced to rubble as a warning to Stalin, and how Hitler could've been stopped, but how he was more valuable as a buffer to the East.

'Where does he get this from?' William had asked Nathan the previous night. 'At sixteen he understands politics better than anyone?'

Spooning herself some carrot salad, Mary said, 'He's a lively one. Bluma says he keeps a diary of toilet scribblings.'

Nathan looked at her and rolled his eyes. 'Graffiti.'

William stopped eating soup and wiped his mouth. 'Graffiti?'

'You know, "Playford couldn't run a raffle", "The end of the World is . . ."'

Silence. William shook his head. 'What would be the point of that?'

Bluma slapped him on the arm. 'You have your cuttings.'

'But they're facts. Things actually happening.'

Nathan shrugged and started eating his egg noodles. 'These are people's opinions. I suppose he thinks people are more honest in the privacy of a cubicle.'

For the first time, Joseph Tabrar showed some interest in proceedings. 'There are limits to what people can say, and think.'

His wife Ellen looked strangely at him. 'Like what?'

'C'mon, look around, this country bans more books than any other.'

Nathan offered Lilli's *Lady Chatterly's Lover* as an example. Ellen looked at Joseph, convinced he was only skirting around bigger issues. 'What else?'

Joseph smiled and shook his head disbelievingly. 'Your friend Phil,' he said to Nathan, 'is a rare sort, stick with him.'

Ellen still wasn't happy, but guessed it was best left until later. William, comfortable in his spot at the head of the table, wasn't so coy. 'Joseph, you mean things happening here?'

'Where?'

'Here, around this table?'

'William, if everyone at this table could say exactly what they thought . . .'

William pursued him like a dog. 'What are your concerns then?'

'I'm concerned that you're full of . . . you're telling lies.'

'What lies?'

'God throwing people into burning pits? What about the children? What about the millions who've never heard of God?'

William stood up, leaning over the table. 'That's why we call for missionaries.'

'I'm concerned that you're brainwashing my children.' Looking at Seymour but stopping short.

William opened his arms graciously. 'Take your children then, I won't force anyone to do anything.'

Ellen looked at her husband and shook her head. 'Have you finished?'

Joseph lowered his head. William sat down. Silence. He pointed his finger at Joseph. 'Don't be afraid to say it . . . if you don't agree with me.'

Joseph stood up and walked off. Ellen stood to follow him but Mary cleared her throat. She sat down and William whispered, 'I won't have people say I'm a bully. I'd rather one person who believes me . . .' Looking after Joseph.

In the silence that followed everyone was waiting for someone else to leave. Nathan kept his eyes down, feeling like he was already copying out Hebrews. Bluma was a lemon tree, sending out roots at the base of a giant, stone wall, seeking shelter from the wind but unable to grow in the absence of sun. Joshua said, 'We're with you, William . . .' starting a chain of joined hands. Seymour didn't know what to say. 'Joseph's a good Christian.' Later pleading with William to forget today's business, if only for Ellen. Like most, he explained, Joseph was uncomfortable trusting in the prophecies of the Bible.

William led them in prayer and then said, 'My play is finished, if anyone is interested.' Outlining the story and asking the children to stay with him to workshop ideas.

Arthur led the others through a tour of his garden. Standard and spray carnations formed a sea of colour around an experimental hydroponic set-up. Arthur showed them how he dissolved nutrients in a tank of water which fed into pipes watering individual pots. Mary was surprised to find the plants growing in sawdust and crushed quartz, although Arthur insisted Tanunda topsoil was as good as anything. 'Growing chrysanthemums this way, we could supply the valley for Mother's Day,' he smiled. 'And beyond that . . .'

The adults arrived back in William's yard to find the banner raised, Joshua's two youngest fighting the breeze to keep it aloft. Arthur's ark was moved and quickly filled by an audience hushed in anticipation.

William stepped forward and read from his script. '"Play for the Apocalypse, a children's drama in progress. Blessed is he who hears these words and keeps those things which are spoken, for the time is at hand . . ."'

Sarah Heinz and Vicky Hicks took the stage, a dead square of grass between William's myrtle and Bluma's vegetables. 'The scene is a department store,' he continued. 'Sarah and Victoria are at the sales.'

'These shoes are a steal,' Sarah began. 'I'll look six inches taller.'

David Hicks approached and helped her try on the imaginary shoes. 'I can give you these cheaper than sale price, if that's what you want.'

Arthur's ark sparked with fits of laughter. 'C'mon, Sarah,' Catherine called, 'you can always give them to your mother.'

'There was more to this salesman than meets the eye,' William said. David looked at the audience and smiled like a pantomime villain, greeted with boos and hisses and a pickled onion thrown by his younger brother.

'These will do just fine,' Sarah continued. 'Can I have an account?'

William continued with a not-so-subtle description of the accounts we all keep, and how they'd have to be settled with the big finance manager in the sky. 'In the end it is easier for a camel to pass through the eye of a needle . . .'

The girls passed through a succession of departments: white-goods and cosmetics, jewellery and women's fashions, receiving discounts from other salesmen (played by Joshua's sons), stumbling around with arms full of imaginary parcels, stopping for coffee, complaining about their husbands and laughing at those less fortunate, relegated to the Woolies basement. Finally they sat down for a rest, taking off their shoes and rubbing their feet. Nathan walked towards them, picking up imaginary cans from the ground and smoking someone's leftover butts. 'Spare a penny?' he asked, grinning and doing his best Quasimodo.

'The beggar who appeared before them was also not what he seemed,' William read. 'His smell repulsed them. His manner sickened them.'

'A penny?' Nathan repeated.

'Go away, you repulsive creature,' Sarah began, turning up her nose and looking away. Vicky felt in her pocket and found a penny, giving it to him. 'There.'

Sarah frowned. 'I can't believe you gave him that.'

'It'll do him more good than me,' Victoria replied.

William's narration went on to explain how the beggar then gave them some advice. How all the wars of their time were signs, how Luke had predicted nation would rise against nation, kingdom against kingdom. How earthquakes and famines and floods had also been predicted. How the only way to escape the terror of their times was to give up worldly things and surrender to Christ. 'Which of you will throw away your parcels?' Nathan asked.

Sarah looked at Vicky. 'He's simple.' She stood to gather her parcels. 'Coming?'

But Vicky looked to Nathan. 'I'll walk beside you . . .' And leaving her parcels behind, exited stage left with him.

Sarah shook her head and strutted off in the opposite direction.

'And so Christ saved another soul,' William read, beaming. 'At the End of Days no one shall stand before the pearly gates with his account unsettled. Christ is the greatest book-keeper of them all.' And that was the end of Part One, William explained, stepping up to take a bow with the children. Bruno Hermann, watching from his kitchen window, shook his head and said, 'Next he'll be building a church.'

Nathan excused himself early. William, feeling more than ever in charge, threw a few mulga logs on the fire and asked where he was going.

'Walking.'

'We haven't finished here.'

William was aware that small stirrings could cause an avalanche; he was interested to see if he could keep the momentum going. 'I was going to ask if anyone wanted to stay on ... we've more than enough.'

Seymour bit his finger nails and looked over to Mary. She smiled at William. 'We should get the children home,' passing the ball to Catherine Heinz. 'Yes, it's too cold to have them out late.'

And William, looking back at Nathan. 'Go on then.'

Curt. Nathan feeling the need to explain himself. 'Mr Drummond said he'd like some ... yeast.'

No reply.

Standing, disappearing up the side of the house. Passing Joseph and Ellen sitting on the front porch, under galvanised iron rusted through, patchwork sun settling on their hair and face. 'See y' Joe, Ellen,' Nathan mumbled, jumping his great-grandfather's picket-less side fence and heading up Langmeil Road.

Nathan could smell chimneys smoking – burning eucalyptus and melaleuca, ti-tree and old shingles salvaged from deserted cottages. He floated in a snowdome past rusted mangles and crank-shafts displayed on the porches of ironstone cottages with sage and rosemary in pots. Quaint, he thought. But if that's what people wanted. Like the Davy Clarke Singers, always choosing the pretend over the real.

Back on William's porch, Joseph sat with his hands in his lap. Ellen was turned into him, holding his hands and looking into his eyes, lost on the High Eden Ridge – on hills of green velvet pulled tight, clumps of gum trees where their parents' parents hadn't reached with sharpened axes. Ellen looked at the whiskers growing out of her husband's nose and said, 'Joseph, what do you want?'

He turned to her and replied, 'I want you to listen.'

'I do.'

'Me first, mother second.'

'Joseph, if we accept their help – '

'Charity.'

'No. If we accept their help we can't say, Oh good, you'll babysit, but you'll have to let them stay up, no baths, no smacking Chas if he pees in the hallway.'

She smiled. Joseph leaned forward. 'How much longer?'

She shrugged. 'When we've saved enough.'

'How much do we need?'

He knew she thought it was his fault. Low-skilled worker. They'd warned her; and when she'd shared this with him he'd said, 'And yet, if I was a chicken boner, a *Lutheran* chicken boner . . .'

She released his hands and leaned back, watching a shunt in the distance pulling grape bins towards Seppelt's. 'It's really about William, isn't it?'

He used his hands to express his disgust. 'It's about how your dad allows William . . . have either of them asked me, you, but when it comes down to his . . . play, "Oh, I'm sorry, I wouldn't force them to do it."'

'Fine, I'll tell them: church okay, Mr Apocalypse . . .'

He shrugged. 'He's a nut case.'

'Eccentric.'

'Nut case.'

'When they grow up they'll look back and laugh.'

'Maybe.'

When they got home that night Mary started saying the same thing. 'Joseph, don't be so precious, it's an outing for them.'

Ellen took her mother's hand. 'It's not a case of being precious, Joe feels no one's bothered asking him.'

Mary shrugged. 'If the world ends it ends, if not, we've helped Willy empty his cellar. The kids love the play . . .'

Joseph frowned. 'It's what the play's about.'

'Why should you care? It could've been *Snow White* – doesn't mean they'll turn into dwarfs.'

He wasn't sure whether Mary was unconcerned or if it was one of her ways of getting around him. 'I'll put on a play,' he continued. 'I'll get William to play Satan, the children can be fallen angels.' Imagining the backdrop of an inverted cross, goat heads tied on with twine and a pentagram of his very own blood.

'Now you're just trying to make a point,' Mary said.

'Of course.'

'It wouldn't bother me, Joseph.'

Ellen shrugged and returned to a pot of boiling noodles. 'You decide, Joseph.'

He stood behind her. 'And if I keep them home, will you stay with us or go to William's?'

No reply.

Nathan sat on a fallen log beside the North Para River. A bridge ran nearly directly overhead, its stone piers rumbling as cars and trucks passed by. He looked out over the low, soggy paddocks, full of sedge and weed, periodically flooded by storm-water – according to William, only good for the ching-chongs and their rice. Something his father said every time they went collecting mushrooms. A childhood of vitamins in a brown paper bag, William listing them alphabetically as their pants and socks got wetter and wetter. At which point William would pass on the family story of how Anthelm had encountered Aborigines out here, two or three dozen, in loincloth and war-paints, their women with mutilated breasts and their children hungry.

(In reality, before Anthelm had embellished the story for Robert, a single elder walking with his son, wearing an old suit from the government camp at Willunga, on the coast.)

Anthelm, in his usual way, had tried to shoo them away but

176

when this failed, approached them, saying how it was his land now and how there were places provided for the native. Places where they'd be introduced to God and agriculture, learning to grow food and raise livestock in ways they'd failed to work out for themselves. 'Out,' he called, shooing them again.

The son in the suit, wearing a bowler hat with cigarette stubs he'd collected in the band, laughed and said, 'Has the Kaiser come with you?' Or words to that effect.

The elder led them towards the creek and, through his son's broken English, explained how his father was buried here, and where is your father buried?

'Posen,' Anthelm replied, thinking how he'd been chased out of his own native land, and of how that's just the way life was. 'The police will remove you if they find you,' he said, but the old man just started gathering wood for a fire. 'I will fetch him, I will fetch the policeman,' Anthelm continued, as the son sat down and removed a pair of leather boots he'd found on a doorstep somewhere.

Unable to convince them, Anthelm sat down with them, eating his own mushrooms, eventually sharing them and trying to explain this Jesus fella the son had heard so much about. 'Soon he will return, and if you have listened to us you will be saved.'

'Saved? How saved?'

'From Hell. From eternal punishment.'

The son's eyes had lit up. 'Ah, we have a story like that.'

'It's not a story.'

Apex would be closing. Nathan jogged towards town, along a dirt road of crushed sleepy lizards, of endless corrugations bordered with a white-work of winter irises, finished with masses of pink flowering sorrel and harlequin.

The photos on the wall of the bakery showed a nineteenth-century cottage with multiple chimneys smoking from wood-fired ovens. They showed the same scene, taken every few years, all featuring the owner, Peter Fechner's grandfather, standing in the same spot with the same pose, his handle-bar moustache unchanged through the years. Photos showing stability, cooks and store-girls inheriting their parents' jobs like real estate. Stability. Endless slabs of coffee cake and bienenstich walking out the door in warm paper bags.

Until Ute. Years ago Ute Hrirbar did to the Apex what Picasso did to portraits. Ute was the first and last of a new breed of decorators in the valley. A painter by trade, he'd deserted off-cream, mauve and pale blue for orange and every green from Brunswick to Aqua-tint.

And it was all the Fechners' fault. They hadn't bothered checking his work before they hired him. When he'd said, 'Something fresh, with a touch of the modern,' they thought he meant melamine and wood veneer. Instead, he'd started off with the exterior in Hi-Gloss white, 'Apex' in stencilled plastic letters (raised above pink lights) in the style of Himmler's 'Arbeit Macht Frei'. Inside it was lino all around, a thousand mis-matched lady bugs glued down onto polished cedar floorboards. The walls were striped red, white and blue with an imitation chrome finish around the door and window frames. Within months it was known as Fechner's Automat. When he was asked to explain, Ute said, 'It's twentieth century.' The Fechners refused to settle and a lawyer was brought in to strike a compromise. The Fechners still planned to redecorate their shop. The daily question from tourists – Isn't this a German bakery? – suggested sooner better than later.

Lilli wrapped the yeasts and put them in a bag. Placing them in front of Nathan she said (in a mock German accent), 'Also in ze valley, ve have bratwurst and leberwurst.'

Nathan smelt the bag. 'You're paranoid.'

They locked up and walked with Thea, Lilli's off-sider, down Murray Street towards the Tanunda Club. The girls walked ahead, Nathan relegated to little brother status, and when a couple of cocky's sons looked at their bums and whistled he started to feel like excess baggage. The girls joined arms and talked between themselves; Nathan couldn't believe she was meant to be his girlfriend.

They stood at the back door to the club. Thea's bar-man

boyfriend was quick with a few bottles of beer, seeing her off with a bite on the ear and some mock heavy breathing. Nathan followed behind again, settling for an occasional swig from Lilli's bottle. At one point she turned back and said, 'Nathan's dad's waiting for the Messiah.'

Thea looked back at him and said, 'He's one of those idiots with the pamphlets?'

And Lilli: 'He *wrote* the pamphlet.'

They sat on a pile of bricks behind the railway station as Thea described her boyfriend in terms of a Cary Grant persona and Johnny Weissmuller physique. Nathan wasn't really expecting Lilli to respond with a glowing account of his own body, knowing that this was something the girls probably did in private. Still, some sort of acknowledgment of his existence would have been good.

'I'll have to go in a minute,' he said, but Lilli just replied, 'Why?'

Things should've been different. They should have been defacing library books or ripping at each other's clothes on the banks of Jacob's Creek. They could have been back in the Langbein grandstand, back into William's plonk he *thought* he'd gladly steal for her any day.

The girls were whispering. He couldn't hear what they were saying. Suddenly Thea looked at him. 'Heard you fucked up your exams?'

He shrugged, glanced at Lilli and back at Thea. 'That's okay. Something better came out of it. In Adelaide.'

Thinking, not that you'd care, being caught up in the centre of the universe.

The Apex universe. A budget Sigalas' without spearmint milkshakes. A universe of pot cakes floating about in snowdomes.

'That's a pity,' Thea continued, looking back at Lilli.

'How?' Nathan asked.

'So close.'

'So?'

'Don't get defensive.'

'Well say what you mean ...' He looked at Lilli; she was

trying to smile, but it was a smile for Thea. He thought, Fuck you, and all at once felt like Lilli's hobby again. What he needed was Phil, speaking his mind. He'd demolish Thea in a minute flat.

'I don't mean anything. You're paranoid.'

But he knew what Lilli had said to her. She'd described how this little sixteen-year-old had followed her into the hills the day before his exams. Like a puppy. After twelve years of school, like he didn't realise what he was doing.

But he did. And that's why he felt so let down, again. Alone, like his only family was his Adelaide family.

He stood and walked off towards Murray Street. Lilli didn't follow him. He heard them laugh as he went and felt so angry he could have thrown the yeast against the platform.

But he didn't, the warmth and smell, signs of better things to come. He heard Thea calling, 'See you, Nathan,' but didn't stop. When he was on the other side of the station he lowered his back down against a wall, putting his head on his knees, unsure of his thoughts.

After a few minutes he saw Lilli walking alone, coming in his direction. All of a sudden he knew how she saw him: pot-bellied and stiff-dicked, pallid, sweaty hair glued across his forehead, red cheeks and the lips of an angel, and teeth so white he had to be using All-Glo.

She walked past without seeing him, on towards town. He didn't say a word. He could do better. Whether it was in the dressing room of the Union Theatre or the shade of a Moreton Bay fig in Botanic Park. She was as surplus as the broad gauge axles the Railways had left around to rust.

William rested on Nathan's swing, watching individual drops of rain falling out of the sky, as if in slow motion, following a trajectory whipped up by the southerlies. Drops growing bigger on the leaves of Bluma's agapanthus, until they had enough weight to roll, exploding into shit-rich earth, reacting with nitrogen and phosphorus and potassium and moving osmotically into the roots of yellowing tomato plants, ready to be green-mulched when he found some time.

The bells of Langmeil rang softly, but there were no clues. They didn't have the urgency of a Doms or the randomness of a Hermann. Maybe it was Henry himself, with a few of his young nephews: one two three, and pause, one two, and pause . . .

Nathan, sitting at the kitchen table, looked up as his father came in and sat opposite him. 'Would you like to help me pick lemons?' William asked.

'I suppose so.' Sighing. Caught up in Lilli's pants, two sizes too big, hitched up every minute or so, unconcerned that the elastic from her knickers showed or her cuffs had frayed beyond repair. A fine silver necklace and a ring she'd never explained. Clips holding back black hair she claimed was entirely natural, although he'd never seen a black-haired Hermann or Fechner.

'You don't have to,' William continued.

'I will.'

Nathan had spent half of the night awake in his loft, staring up at rafters planed by Anthelm and bolted by Robert, thinking how he just needed to get her alone, how he'd seen her as a follower for the first time but how everyone had their moments of indecision. Still, he wasn't about to go chasing after her, and if she appeared under his lemon tree . . .

'"In the name of the Father, the Son and the Holy Spirit . . ."'

Bluma sat down and they bowed their heads. Nathan was busy running his finger behind Lilli's elastic, applying words such as grace and forgiveness and sin to his own situation, making Lilli the whore on the hill of fish and loaves, gathering up what she could carry to sell later. Held down by the faithful and stoned, but absolved by the wandering Messiah.

Grace. The promise of constant forgiveness. This is what still sustained Nathan. No one else promised and no one else delivered. *In the beginning was the Word, and the Word was with God, and the Word was God.* If you stepped back beyond that there was only darkness. You might be okay without the Bible for a day, a week, a month – but what about the times when you were tested? When you needed your faith? How would Bluma have sustained herself, lying in bed at Willow Hospital sixteen years before, blessed on one hand by the baby in her arms but cursed by the scar on her abdomen, where one of Mr Scholz's best had cut to find her uterus, bleeding from a haemorrhage three days after Nathan's arrival. Carried away in a stainless steel dish covered by a tea-towel as William watched them, up to their elbows in blood, threading and sewing and asking for surgical sponges. Whispering consolations from Hebrews chapter thirteen, '"Make you perfect in every good work to do his will, working in you that which is well-pleasing in his sight . . ."'

Nathan was a blessing, it was as simple as that. Bluma would forever curse the gingham tea-towel, but that was God's word and the word was with, and was, God.

And his son. William's devotion passed onto a celebration of Jesus, describing moments of healing and miracles such as water into wine. Jugs and jugs of the stuff. No one sure if it was cabernet or grenache, but wine nonetheless.

Nathan looked across at his father and frowned. William shrugged. 'What?'

'I'm not so sure.'

'What?'

'If it was meant so literally.'

William looked confused. 'If what was?'

'Like *Jack and the Beanstalk*, no one actually believes – '

'Nathan,' Bluma smiled, trying to stop him before it was too late.

William sat forward. 'But that's a fairytale. This is the Bible.'

'True. But they were still stories. Stories with a message. It was a better way of getting it over.'

William looked at him. 'These are not even your thoughts.'

'So what?'

Bluma shook her head. 'Nathan.'

But Nathan wasn't finished. 'Apparently, in Jesus' time, only the rich could afford wine. So what the Bible was *suggesting*, was that Jesus wanted them all to share.'

William shook his head. 'The Bible says that water was turned into wine.'

'Perhaps, but the Bible's full of this stuff. The burning bush. There's this shrub in the Middle East that produces a flammable vapour. Like petrol fumes. And every so often, on a hot day –'

'Nathan, none of this is true.'

'It is. Doesn't mean it's . . . all, wrong.'

William sat back, defeated more by Nathan's insolence than his facts. 'It's this Drummond boy, isn't it? He has books –'

'So?'

'Written by whom, eh?'

'People. Scientists.'

And as he always did, William resorted to the Bible, licking his fingers and flicking pages. 'What good is science if it sets out to destroy our faith?'

'It doesn't.'

'Why doesn't science cure disease?'

'It has, it will, what were your seven plagues?'

'I wouldn't mind if you'd worked these things out for yourself.'

'What about . . .' His father pointing at his Bible, slamming it shut, sliding it in front of him. 'Pencil, paper, the wash-house.'

Nathan pushed it back. 'I'm not going to keep coming home to this.'

'Who pays for your board?'

'I earn my own money now.'

William stood and pointed at the door. 'The wash-house!'

Nathan took the Bible and pen and paper and walked out. Bluma took William's hand but he stormed into his study.

The next morning Nathan rose early, slipping on his boots and overalls and taking breakfast with his mother. 'Think of your father,' she said, packing his clean washing. 'All you have to do is keep the peace, I've been doing it for years.'

On the train on the way down he found a pure-maths text

someone had left behind. In the jumble of scribbles and formulas he guessed there was even more his dad would reject. The conservation of angular momentum was apparently going on at that very moment: vectors and parabolas – all ways of describing Creation.

Arriving at Islington he dodged a Bo-Bo diesel and made his way to Bob's office. He put the cake on the desk and Bob looked up smiling. 'What have we here?'

'As promised. To make up for last week.'

At smoko both slabs were demolished in minutes flat, passing from greasy fingers into mouths of smoke-yellow teeth. Washed down by tea in tin mugs. Returning to copper pipes and solder and flux. Small things real and knowable.

Chapter Eleven

Bluma said very little as her hair was set. A girl, an apprentice with the surname Steinbusch, rolled the curlers too tight and sprayed on a fixative which smelt like William's sterilising agents. Then a hair-net full of other people's hair and a dryer which hummed quietly to the accompaniment of Edna Hermann getting her weekly trim, her hairdresser, a girl named Keane, struggling to find anything out of place. Edna was all for a short and practical cut, although she wouldn't trust Bruno with a pair of scissors, fringe lines like line graphs of GDP in some African nations.

'Leonie Munzberg,' she said, looking at a copy of the *Oracle*. 'Don't you remember, Bluma, she used to do the accounts for Chateau Tanunda?'

'No, though there was Mrs Fielke.'

'She's still there. Leonie Munzberg left years ago. I'd barely heard her name till now.' She straightened the paper and read: '"Mrs Munzberg was apprehended by police at West Terrace cemetery after the caretaker noticed her regularly placing flowers on the grave of the Somerton mystery man. His body was found on Somerton beach on 1 December, 1948 and, despite extensive investigations, never identified."'

Edna looked up and smiled. 'See, our own bit of intrigue. How exciting.' Continuing as Miss Keane tried to steady her head. '"Mrs Munzberg claimed she believed the body to be her father-in-law's, washed ashore after a boating accident." Likely story.'

The apprentice adjusted Bluma's dryer and said, 'Wasn't there something about *The Rubaiyat?*'

Edna lifted her eyebrows. 'Yes. His clothes were found in a locker at the railway station. They found a torn page in the pocket.' She found the place in the article. '"The fragment carried the words *Taman Shud*, meaning 'the end' or 'the finish'."'

Bluma reached out for her cold coffee and finished it in two gulps. The end of what? William would be interested ... no, he'd read all manner of things into it: Bulgarian sailors throwing themselves off freighters, suicidal angels as characters from Revelations, a spy, a Russian dancer, a frustrated local ending it all with untraceable barbiturates.

'So spooky,' Edna concluded, turning the page. Eventually Miss Keane finished and brushed her off, summoning a cloud of baby talc to engulf and sanitise the mystery man of Somerton beach. Edna set off for the Apex to check on Lilli. After she'd gone, the Steinbusch girl swept an almost hairless floor as Miss Keane removed Bluma's dryer, unrolling curlers and teasing her hair with a brush. 'You'll feel all fresh, like Doris Day,' she laughed, but Bluma felt as stale as an old Arrowroot biscuit.

Standing at the door, the rain came down in buckets. Miss Keane handed her an umbrella and, putting up the CLOSED FOR LUNCH, helped her down the steps, locking the door behind her. Bluma walked quickly down Murray Street, pausing to shelter under a carob as she fought to open the umbrella. She ran on again, stopping under the *Oracle*'s verandah. She resorted to brute force and the umbrella opened out in front of her, immediately blowing out of her hands and down Murray Street towards the hotel.

Pulling her coat up over her head she ran, cursing William as she went. Where other ladies had their menfolk to pick them up in Oldsmobiles and Austins, hers just sat at home in a haze of Hebrews and things as they'd always been. No thought of how it affected others. Like the lino she was sure would save her lungs from an old age of wheezing and spluttering. But no, lino was not necessary, inasmuch as anything was not necessary if March 21 was right. The End. *Taman Shud.* Although what Omar Khayyam meant as poetry, William took as revelation. The end to what? Meanwhile she had to feel guilty if she had her hair set or bought a block of Cadburys chocolate.

William, I sacrifice a lot, she'd say.

But he'd reply that the Last Days were a test, sin and vice everywhere, temptations laid out to lead the unwary into the bargain basement.

She rushed in the back door and stood dripping, hanging up her coat and kicking off her shoes. William sat at the table in candle light.

'Where have you been?'

She shrugged. 'To have my hair set.'

'Set? What's that mean?'

'A permanent wave.'

He looked at her wet hair, clinging to her head, her perm ruined. 'What did they do?'

She took a mirror from her handbag and looked at herself. 'You wouldn't read about it.' She rushed to the linen press, took a towel and wrapped it around her head. 'They had to close right then.'

'When?'

And with that the rain eased. 'Curse them.'

She removed the towel and teased her hair with a comb, staring into the mirror. There it was, a full head of hair sitting flat against her scalp. 'Ruined!'

William was walking around her, staring at the top of her head. 'A permanent wave? How much money was this?'

'What's it matter?'

He shook his head. 'You'll want your money back.'

'I can't ask for my money back.'

'You can. You will. What made you even think of a ... permanent wave?'

'I wanted something ... fresh.'

The only word she could think of. Fresh like Doris Day. More

187

like the photo of the corpse on Somerton beach, Edna holding it up and saying, 'There was a fella at the Strathmore. They found a bag of hypodermics in his room. But he'd checked out the day before.' Everyone hushed. The face of the corpse lingering in Bluma's head. As lifeless as the hair that clung to her scalp, even after it'd dried. 'Their chemicals weren't strong enough,' she said, teasing it vainly.

William sat down, scanning his papers by candle light. 'A permanent wave, eh?' Thinking how he'd stick it in his scrapbook if he could. She fixed him firmly in her gaze. 'I don't get much, William.'

'If that's what you want to spend money on.'

'It is. I'll go back, they'll fix it cheap.'

'They'll fix it free.'

'William!' she pleaded.

'You pay money, to look like a . . . monkey?'

She sighed, dropping her head.

'Check the bank book,' he continued, 'there's not a lot spare for . . . perms . . . like we were movie stars.' He started cutting the paper.

Bluma put on her shoes and stood up. Pulling on her coat she opened the back door and stepped outside, her husband not even looking up. She walked up the front path and out the gate, and as she started along Langmeil Road, the rain began again. Soft at first and then showers, spreading out into a squall. Soon she was soaked to the skin. She kept walking into the wind, head bowed, purse dangling, not in the slightest bit rushed. If anything she went slower, wondering where to go.

Meanwhile, Mary Hicks moved around her lounge room, dusting, listening for her daughter. Whispers. And then Joseph laughing. She paused by their closed door, calling, 'Anything I can get you?'

'No, Mum, we've nearly finished . . . cleaning up.'

Two o'clock on a Monday afternoon, locked in their room, what was a mother supposed to think? How do you clean up an already clean room?

Joseph moved his plastic glasses (with Groucho Marx nose and mo) down to the tip of his nose, 'Let me see,' he whispered, 'what have we got here?' Slipping Ellen's blouse up over her head. 'Just as I suspected, they'll have to go.' She giggled and he hushed her.

'What do you care?' she asked.

'She'll find some reason,' he replied, imagining his mother-in-law standing in the open doorway as his pants dropped to his ankles.

'These are always in the way,' he continued, unlatching her bra with an expertise he hadn't learnt at the PMG.

Just as Joseph was getting serious, the front flyscreen rattled and someone turned the bell. 'Ellen, could you get that?' Mary asked, right outside their bedroom, earlobe touching their door.

'I'm just getting changed.' Joseph rolled his head on Ellen's chest, dragging his mouth over her breasts, his tongue leaving a snail trail of curried egg and lettuce.

Mary opened the front door. 'Bluma.'

Bluma stepped in and stood dripping on her rug. 'Thought I'd pop in. You're not busy?'

'No.' She marched Bluma into the bathroom and covered her in towels. 'Don't you have an umbrella?'

'The wind took it.'

Mary fetched dry clothes and left Bluma to get changed. Passing the door she listened again and said, 'I'm putting the kettle on for Bluma. Who wants coffee?'

Joseph put his lips to Ellen's ear and whispered, 'Yes, thanks.'

Ellen laughed and drew close to his ear. 'She won't barge in now.'

Joseph, smiling. 'No?'

'Could you imagine, *Oh, Bluma, they're working on their next.*'

'Coffee?' Mary harped.

'No thanks, Mum.'

Joseph bit her ear. 'So?'

Bluma appeared from the bathroom wearing one of Mary's old work dresses. They sat down at the kitchen table and Mary made chamomile tea. 'Best for your immunity. Getting around in wet clothes could trigger a cold.'

Bluma stretched her hand out over the table and Mary took it. 'This is my new perm.' Teasing her hair.

'Oh, love, you should go to that new place in Nuri. Everything tested, scientifically. God knows what they use here. Looking at that, could be vinegar.'

Bluma smiled. 'I come home like this and what do you think William says?'

'I could imagine.'

'Said I looked like a monkey.'

And with that Bluma lost it, dropping her head onto the table and spilling her chamomile everywhere; sitting up and trying to fix the mess. 'Sorry.'

'No, leave it.'

Bluma looked her in the eyes. 'All he says is, get your money back.'

Mary pulled her chair over and put her arm around Bluma. 'That sounds like William.'

'Fair enough, her chemicals were weak, but it was the *way* he said it.'

'I know.'

Bluma started to hiccup and Mary rubbed her arm. 'Come on, forget it, they're all the same. Don't think before they say something. Seymour's the same. Doesn't like something you're listening to on the radio, *What yer listening to that for?* Like you're stupid or something. It's not worth letting 'em get to you.' She threw a tea-towel over the spilt tea and rocked gently. 'The stories I could tell you about Seymour.'

And then she heard noises, like furniture being dragged around the room. 'You two alright?'

No reply. She improvised stories about Seymour the uncaring husband, lest Bluma work out what was going on and broadcast it across the neighbourhood. 'Every time I cook something new,' she continued, urgently. 'I had a paella? You had a paella? Rice with peas and so forth. I bought some spices. Saw it in the *Weekly*, give you a copy. Anyway, Seymour just sits there, *what's this . . .?*'

Joseph fell back on the bed. 'D' you think she'll believe I was fixing the floorboards?' Ellen took his hand and led him down onto the rug; she moved on top of him, feeling his belly full of hot tea and sandwiches.

Bluma breathed deeply, unable to shake the hiccups. 'I walk out the door. Not a word. Doesn't so much as look up.'

Mary didn't know what to say. There were no more noises but they wouldn't come out.

Bluma looked at her. 'What are they doing?'

Mary bowed her head to think. 'Looking over some plans.'

Bluma smiled. 'Oh ...'

'A new house.'

'Where?'

Mary stopped to think. 'Haven't decided.'

'You won't know yourselves.'

'If ... they do it.' Trying to cover her tracks, although she realised it was too late. 'If ...'

Bluma sat forward, reviving. 'Joseph said something about Elizabeth. That'll be the place to go.'

Ellen lay on top of Joseph, motionless, listening to the women talking. 'Do you know anything about house plans?'

'Just some brochures. Perhaps she wants to get rid of us.'

Bluma and Mary moved out into the garden as sun broke through the cloud. Rows of yellowing, unpruned roses stretched out along fence lines, dropping their last few red and white petals into a knee high sea of sour-sobs. 'Black spot, aphids,' Mary complained, as they walked, 'but no one's got the inclination during winter.'

'You should see the new varieties,' Bluma said, smelling what was left of the roses. 'Apricot, two-in-ones – white, like Chantilly lace, with a deep red heart.'

'Still smell the same.'

'Apparently not ...' Bluma searching for words which would describe scent, clumsy words like peppery and woody, bitter and acrid.

Mary looked through Ellen's window and saw a bare shoulder; the curtain closed and a crucifix swung from the rod. 'This is the worst time of year,' she said.

'It'll soon be spring,' Bluma replied.

'And another year, and another, and then Seymour will be changing my nappy.'

Bluma smiled. 'Imagine William feeding me.'

Ellen appeared from the back, smiling, hands dove-tailed across her lap. 'Hello, Bluma, how are you today?'

'Thank you, dear.' Without actually saying.

'Could you turn the taters on,' Mary asked her daughter, taking Bluma by the arm and leading her towards the camellias.

'Sure,' she replied, following them.

Bluma looked back at her. 'Big place is it?'

Ellen frowned. 'Sorry?'

'Your new house?'

Ellen looked at her mother. 'Yes, big, three bedrooms and a formal dine.'

'Cost you a packet.'

'Joe's got it under control.'

William, sitting on his front porch, pulled on his workboots and football beanie. A roll of masking tape and a pile of leftover leaflets sat beside him, each with a line of extra scribble along the bottom: *Come and hear. Paddock opposite my place. This Wed. after-noon. 4.00 p.m. Wilhelm M.* Bluma had helped him finish them, having worked late into the previous night, buoyed by thoughts of a perm to sustain her through the dormancy of another valley winter. William had checked each leaflet. 'Write bigger. No one will see.'

He headed off for the barrel-house at Seppeltsfield, starting by handing out leaflets to bemused workers. He worked his way past the presses and through the new labs the festival float had depicted. He continued through Administration before he was asked to leave by an office manager in a cheap tweed suit. He repeated the whole exercise at Chateau Tanunda, nearly skittled over by a shunt as he argued with an agnostic picker.

Then he moved on to Murray Street, working his way along, shop by shop. Wohler's Furniture, Art and Gifts. 'If I could place it in the window, here, visible when people come in.'

'No thanks, William, this is a business. Some will disagree.'

'So?'

'Their money's as good as anyone's.'

Refusing to argue, slamming the door and continuing on. House Proud Decor Centre. 'Here, I'll stick it up for you.'

'No.'

Looking at the other notices the shop-keeper *had* allowed. *Quilts for Sale, see Rob for my number.* That was Harry Rasch's wife. But worse still, a pair of urban ring-ins from Edinburgh Avenue: *Eurhythmics, tues thurs school term, phone* . . . Pottery classes and yoga, exercise bikes and a pair of week old wire-haired terriers . . . William looked at the man. 'Give away pups? Have you read my leaflet?'

'Everyone's read your leaflet.'

'So?'

'I offer my window as a community service.'

'You should paint this message across the front of your store.'

The shop-keeper laughed. 'The End is nigh! Maybe I should give it all away.'

William could argue but it wouldn't do any good. He was already lost. From a street of several dozen shops he managed to convince five, and three of those, he noticed, were taken down after he'd gone. So what, the money-lenders and their Murray Street temples are lost too. Standing back in front of the Tanunda Club he thought, There must be a better way. On with the gloves. Graffiti was man's way of saying, How come no one's discussing this? Profound or perverted, there must be some way of getting your message across.

WCs were plastered at the club and the Tanunda Hotel, the railway station and the public lavs on Elizabeth Street. The Langmeil toilets, St John's, Tabor, Gnadenberg and Holy Cross.

St Aidan's and the other denominations were visited – hall doors, columns, archways and even church doors used to display William's message. Smoothing down masking tape and scampering like a truant, passing through the Tanunda school un-noticed, leaving his apocalyptic song-line on park benches, the windows of the council chambers and civic centre and even a statue of a crucified Christ in the recreation park. Going home for tea but returning after dark to tape his message across the windows of the money-lenders. Walking home smiling, every shop in Murray Street carrying his message at last.

Continuing the next morning with the remaining dozen or so leaflets. The door to the kegelbahn. Trevor Streim, busy practising his spin, coming out to see what all the fuss was about. Reading the leaflet and laughing, 'Four p.m., and who do you think will be there, *Wilhelm?*' ·

'Probably not you. But then at the End, when Jesus asks me . . .' He pointed his finger directly between Trevor's eyes.

Trevor only smiled. 'We've all tried to help you, William. After this,' pointing out his proclamation, 'people will desert you; and when you walk down the street they'll whisper and laugh. *How could he have believed such a thing? Is he simple?*'

William refused to argue. 'How did you become an Elder?'

But Trevor wasn't finished. 'At least think of Bluma, and Nathan. If you approached the Elders and explained. The church is your family. You can always come back.'

William shrugged, showing him the remaining pamphlets. 'I've got to get finished.'

'None of this makes it right, William . . . here, give it to me.'

Trevor took the leaflets and the tape and started sticking them to the door, one by one, until they covered the iron completely, hanging loose here and there, overlapping. He finished the roll, making sure they were well and truly stuck down, working without saying a word as William watched. 'There,' he said, finishing, handing back the empty roll. 'All of this isn't going to make it happen . . . William, I'm trying to help you.'

To save you from yourself.

'Afterwards, we'd still have you back, but things would be different.'

William threw the empty roll on the ground, turned and walked off as Trevor returned to his shed, walked the length of the alley and set up the pins.

As William slept deeply that night it started raining. The next day, dozens of blank, pink sheets were found taped up around town. A council worker named Alberts was sent to remove them, saving the paper for the floor of his guinea-pig hutch.

Wednesday afternoon. The threat of rain wasn't enough to deter William. In the great spelling test of life, he would sound out God's name regardless: S A L V A S H U N. Wet or dry, hot or cold, hoarse or full-voiced, his belly full of fire, captivating the crowd with the unassailable logic of the Bible, summoning sweet venom like Pastor what's-his-name at the Vectis Mission Rally. 'At the consummation of the world, Christ will appear.'

And all at once, several thousand voices. 'Amen!'

William was wondering whether he'd be up to it. His perform-ance at Langmeil had been scripted and woody; he knew now he should have just said what was in his heart. And the business of the name change, what had that got to do with anything? No, today there'd be nothing written down. He'd let God speak through him, through the Bible he'd brandish like a sword in his left hand.

Arthur helped him wheel his movable ark up the garden path, across the road and into the empty paddock. It was council land but they'd never looked after it, slashing it twice a year in antici-pation of the housing development no one had ever built. There'd been some talk of a fertiliser works but Bruno had gathered signatures from everyone on Langmeil Road and threatened to move all of the Hermanns out of Tanunda. The council gave in, turning to Laucke's to set up a new feed mill, but they'd found cheaper land out along the highway.

So now it was just weeds, stretching out towards Anthelm's mushroom flood-plains and the North Para River. The council's agents put up a FOR SALE sign which William and Bruno were forever knocking over, so that in the end it was just left in the mud.

William positioned the ark and climbed on the table, jumping up and down to test it. Reciting Hamlet's soliloquy, he sent Arthur back towards Langmeil Road to do a sound check. Eventually Arthur stopped, listened and applauded, but William thought, So many bodies are sure to absorb the sound.

At three-thirty Bruno and Edna brought kitchen chairs out onto their porch and settled in with a thermos, determined not to miss a thing. A reporter from the *Oracle* walked up Langmeil Road and called to them from the fence, 'Can I come in?' Settling in at their feet he asked them questions about William. 'No no, *Wilhelm*,' Bruno smiled, and the reporter started scribbling madly on his pad.

At four p.m. exactly the show began. Bluma and Arthur stood on either side of the ark, facing the listeners. They banged saucepan lids together and Bluma blew on Nathan's scout whistle. William climbed onto the ark and Bruno remarked that it could have been Golgotha, minus the crosses. The reporter scribbled again, mumbling something about a crucifixion by-line, standing, thanking them and wandering over towards the paddock.

Seymour and Joshua stood together, applauding, turning around to encourage Mary and Catherine and the children to do the same. Sarah Heinz sat drawing pictures in the mud with a stick, sitting up and smiling as the reporter approached her. 'Hi.'

'Hi. Do you know Mr Muller?'

'Muller? No one calls him that. Miller.'

The pencil trailing short-hand across the page. Sarah patted the ground for him to sit down. 'I'm Seymour Hicks' daughter. I have a big part in William's play.'

'His play?'

'Yes, *Play For The Apocalypse*.'

She continued whispering to him as William got into full stride. The thirty or so listeners sat, knelt or stood about in small groups.

William gave them the once over. There was no one from Langmeil or St John's. No Pastor Henry, or even the Elders, at least willing to hear him out. Although it could have been worse, William thought, it wasn't a turnout of Vectis proportions. They were the good old days, before the radio and the *Weekly* got to people. Pastor what's-his-name was blessed with an audience that cared; instead of a half-empty paddock of Salvation Jane and sedge, wild oats and a car body dumped during the Depression years.

William quoted the Augsburg Confession, about how the Anabaptists would suffer eternal pain and torment and how the Jews were lying (as they always had) when they said Jesus would choose godly men to annihilate the sinners. Strange how the Jews themselves had practically been annihilated. But that's what you get for messing around with the Bible.

From then on it was the usual stuff: the seven plagues, angels and seals, all of which he'd studied and could explain, although not here and now. Then there were the dates, the decree of Artaxerxes and a few simple sums scribbled on an old blackboard Rechner had supplied, held up by his two lieutenants as he repeatedly broke pieces of chalk.

It was like Einstein explaining Relativity to the Nuriootpa CWA. No one argued because no one knew if he was right or wrong. Either way, it sounded logical, and there was no denying that he'd carried his tens to the proper column. Maybe if they prayed and bowed their heads they might scrape in next March by the skin of their teeth. And if they were wrong, almost no one need know. As long as they were careful to keep their name out of the *Oracle*.

William opened his Bible and read: '"And he showed me a pure river of water of life . . ."' Looking up. 'Amen.'

Silence. The reporter stood up from transcribing the plot of William's play. William looked at him. 'Are you with us?'

'No, the *Tanunda Oracle*.'

Seymour turned around and smiled at his wife, whispering, 'We should help out.' Leading to a small chorus from the Heinzes and Hicks'. 'Amen.'

197

William looked at them as if to say, Take your cue from me. Turning back to the reporter. 'Are you going to write about the Truth?'

'I'm going to write about your rally.'

'But are you going to write about the Truth?'

'That'll get a mention.'

William shook his head. 'Just because we're few in numbers.'

'Is this your whole following?'

'We're a young movement.'

The reporter shrugged. 'Taken, but people would tend to either agree or disagree. You've been at it for some time now.'

William seemed unconcerned. 'Most come around slowly.'

'Surely not.'

'We need to explain ourselves.'

'And this is where your . . .' he looked at his notepad, '*Play For The Apocalypse* comes in?'

'Yes.'

Seymour turned around and looked at Sarah. She shrugged, mouthing, What'd I say?

'I'm looking forward to your play,' the reporter continued. 'Perhaps you could do a preview?'

William realised he was losing his momentum. 'It's not an entertainment.' He opened his Bible and continued.

Bruno and Edna wandered across Langmeil Road with their chairs. They set up just within ear-shot at the back of the paddock and topped up their mugs. 'There,' Edna said, settling in, 'he won't be able to see us from here.'

William wiped spits of rain from the page as he read. '"To him that overcometh will I grant to sit with me . . ."' But as he read, he thought of other things. Like how it wasn't his fault, how no one could inspire a bunch of duds like this, how Pastor what's-his-name didn't have Satan with his short-hand in the audience, how Vectis was a product of its time and how this was a product of his. But how this was another sign, how the low, contented hum of a world caught up in other things was a test set up for him. Which meant that when a car pulled up and two council inspectors alighted, he was ready for a fight.

'Mr Miller, do you have a permit?' one of them asked.

'A permit? Why? For standing in a paddock?'

'Regardless. I'll have to ask you to stop. I have an application form you can fill out.'

He produced a yellow form and waved it in the air.

TANUNDA ORACLE, 2 AUGUST 1951
A SOGGY START FOR THE MILLERITES

... at which point Mr Miller-Muller produced a document entitled Augsburg Confession. He quoted a section (apparently based on Acts chapter five) which said Christians were obliged to obey civil authority only insofar as it agreed with the Bible. But when 'civil authority cannot be obeyed without sin, God rather than men must be followed'.

At this point the inspectors, Mr Snow and Hobbs, explained to Mr Miller-Muller that if he continued they would be forced to fetch the police. 'Dramatics,' Mr Miller-Muller replied, explaining how the council was stacked with many of his detractors, several of whom were also Elders at Langmeil church ...

The reporter chose not to bring their names into it, going on to explain how council had already turned a blind eye to Mr Miller-Muller's posters and leaflets.

As the inspectors drove off, rain started to fall in a light shower. William was undeterred. 'Jesus wants to know how much you love him: wet or dry, one or two arms, crippled with polio or riddled with the cancer. Jesus is Lord! Amen!'

And again, principally the Millerites. 'Amen!'

The reporter covered his head with his jacket and kept writing. Bruno and Edna took their chairs and scurried back across Langmeil Road. A few of the onlookers competed for space under three umbrellas Bluma had handy, but when they ran off she gave them to Mary and Catherine and the children. Arthur, Seymour and Joshua shared the rain with William, standing with their arms crossed as they soaked through.

Bluma held the blackboard above her head but it did her no good. C'mon, William, she was thinking, we've heard it all before. But he wouldn't be moved. 'This is a baptism of the faithful ... rain down, rain down!' Looking up to the sky and opening his mouth. 'Amen!'

The chorus had given up, defeated by cold rain which stuck shirts to backs.

Mary and Catherine had had enough. They took the children and ran back to Bluma's house. Bruno and Edna watched from their porch and couldn't believe what they saw. 'It's like a cult,' Bruno whispered.

A police car pulled up on Langmeil Road but no one got out. Mary and Catherine and the children ran past them, slipping on the wet grass, splashing mud and laughing. The reporter saw the police, ran over and climbed in the back. 'G'day, Dave.'

'What's goin' on?'

'Jesus this, Jesus that ... I wouldn't get yourselves wet.'

At last William stepped down and stood beside his wife and three friends. 'Unconventional,' Seymour said, smiling. As they walked back towards the house the rain stopped nearly as suddenly as it had started. An *Oracle* photographer arrived in time to snap William and the others talking to the police.

The next morning's paper showed this picture. The headline read 'Millerites Defy Police'. Shaking his head as he showed it to Pastor Hoffmann the following night, Ron Rohwer said, 'See, we were right to have done what we did.' Pastor Henry agreed, reaffirming how they'd tried everything to save him from himself.

... Mr Miller-Muller continues to spread discontent within the Lutheran community. Some would say the debate he has generated is healthy. Not so, says Pastor Braunack, head of the Lutheran church in South Australia. He was one of the few who braved

the weather to hear William Miller-Muller speak. He said, 'Mr Miller's reasoning is all wrong. He has distorted the chronology of the Bible to suit his needs. The Bible is full of dates which can be read in a variety of ways. Unfortunately we have no control over Mr Miller, he is a free agent. I only hope that those who listen to him develop a healthy sense of scepticism . . .'

William bought every copy of the *Oracle* he could find. He kept one copy of the article to stick in his scrapbook and burnt the rest in a pile in his backyard.

The next morning Bruno walked to the offices of the *Oracle* and, finding the reporter, told him what he'd seen.

TANUNDA ORACLE, *3 AUGUST 1951*
EARLY GUY FAWKES FOR MILLERITES

. . . an anonymous source reports that William Miller-Muller pur-chased more than three dozen copies of this newspaper yesterday. The story as reported was entirely based on fact. Perhaps this is what Mr Miller-Muller fears . . .

A few days later William wrote a letter to the editor threatening legal action. The reporter argued he hadn't even come close to defamation but was warned off anyway. Soon after, William saw Bruno in Murray Street. Stopping to shake his hand he whispered in his ear, 'You'll be the first, Hermann,' and passed on.

Bruno returned home shaken. So convinced was he that William was wrong, he spent the rest of the week planting a row of oleanders down the fence-line. In a few years he'd be free of him.

Over the next few days, William's thoughts turned to Pastor Kavel, and how he'd been killed by the doubters of his own day. The story had it that Kavel suffered a stroke and was rushed to Dr Scholz's hospital. An Adelaide newspaper, the *Register*, believing him dead, published an obituary which concluded with the words: 'Pastor Kavel's one folly was to predict and preach a second coming of Christ . . . to many of his followers, and the public at large, this made him a figure of ridicule'. The next day, Kavel, sitting up in his hospital bed, read his own obituary and started to fume, throwing his breakfast dishes across the room and dragging himself out of bed. He got to his feet, stood momentarily and dropped down stone dead, the blocked vessel around his brain breaking wide open like a split grape.

Chapter Twelve

William's vines started early. Buds opened and offered fresh, green shoots to the air; finding it warm enough, they mimeographed themselves into small leaves, tendrils and what would become new canes, growing out from rods and spurs which had been happily sleeping since May. It was enough to warm his heart, walking up and down between rows, re-tying loose canes and encouraging new leaves with the tip of his finger.

The sun came in the kitchen window, lying itself across Bluma's hands and up her arms as she washed dishes. The black kitchen's flagstones were forever cold, bringing up dampness from earth the sun never reached. It left the house with a musty smell she'd carry to her grave, like the miner's dug-outs she'd seen along the Burra creek on some dimly remembered holiday. Fire, or the smell of cooking food couldn't shake it.

Nathan had a week off, on full pay, something Lilli and the Apex mob couldn't boast. Bored by the end of the first day, he made for the Tanunda library, bypassing Marx and Mies van der Rohe for a volume of Bruegel paintings he guessed had never been opened, the spine cracking like dry chicken bones.

Apparently Bruegel had been to Tanunda. Edna was there as the *Head of a Peasant Woman* and the *Parable of the Blind* was a picture of the Millerites, stumbling down Langmeil Road on a Saturday afternoon, feeling about with sticks and falling over each other, staring up into the sky with skin-fused eyes in search of a God who'd abandoned them. The *Allegory of Lust* was Goat Square, market day, togs off, every man for himself. Nathan smiled as Seymour-as-a-lizard tweaked Lilli's nipples and his father, half pig, half fish, mounted a squealing Thea from behind as he ripped at her Apex uniform.

On Wednesday, the second day of spring, he accompanied his parents to the market in Goat Square. As they moved from stall to stall, tasting preserves and over-priced gourmet cheeses, Nathan said to his father, 'Mr Drummond says my papers need to be done.'

William felt a cucumber and replied, 'He does, does he?'

'Have you read them?'

'I've read them.' Talking to a young boy who'd been left in charge: 'These are soft, you shouldn't be selling them.'

The boy shrugged. 'They look okay to me.'

Passing on, William ignored his son, whispering to Bluma, 'Was a time people would be ashamed to put that out.'

'Dad.'

William toyed with him some more. 'Your indentures? These oblige you for six years. Six years . . . not so long ago you couldn't commit – '

Bluma took his arm. 'William.'

'No, I'm not convinced – '

'Dad, you just have to sign them.'

'I have to do no such thing. I have to exercise my judgement. If I don't believe . . .' He trailed off, stopping to haggle and eventually purchase glass-house tomatoes. Nathan watched him count his coins and wanted to push him into a pile of fruit boxes. Hate was a strong word and, considering his up-bringing, he thought he was a pretty reasonable person; but hate was the only word he could think of. Or was it disgust? William's fat, unshaven cheeks flapping like the waste of air he'd become.

As they walked along Nathan said, 'I need my papers signed to continue.'

'I know.'

'Does this mean you won't sign them?'

'For now.'

Nathan stopped. 'They won't wait.'

But William kept walking.

In the middle of the square, where Maria and John Streets met, a group of Aboriginal women followed Pastor Henry towards a patch of crumbling concrete and stood waiting. They wore loose, billowing dresses which were dyed vibrant greens and yellows and reds; the parts of their bodies that showed were painted with Dreamtime water-holes and elongated wombats.

Earlier, they had emerged from the Langmeil rectory bare-breasted and Henry had had to explain to Pastor Flint (who'd been up north too long) that it just wouldn't do. Improvising with costumes from the Christmas Passion they soon had them covered, walking towards Goat Square bearing myrrh, incense and rhythm sticks. A pair of which Henry appropriated, clanging them together in a way the Rainbow Serpent could never imagine. 'Thank you ladies and gentlemen.'

For a while the commerce stopped. Hats were adjusted, displays rearranged and tills counted as Henry continued. 'Today we're lucky to have, as our entertainment, some ladies from Hermannsburg, in the middle of Australia. These ladies are from the Aranga –'

Pastor Flint stepped forward. 'Aranda.'

'Aranda tribe. Pastor Flint has brought them down in his bus.' Henry stepped back and put his arms around Pastor Flint and everyone applauded. 'David, would you like to say a few words?'

The Aboriginal women stood staring into the sky, oblivious, the twelfth time in just under a week they'd been shown off. The Lutheran Synod had insisted it would be inspirational for those in the south. It would give them the opportunity to see the Lutheran church at work: moving dynamically among those less fortunate, spreading the promise of salvation. Later, Flint would explain to Henry that he considered them a lost cause: lazy and ungrateful and, truth be known, doomed to extinction. Still, you did what you could. There was hope for the kiddies, some of them, if they could be removed and have the black bred out of them. The rest, those who weren't full of clap, could be fed and taught some useful habits.

'Each of the ladies before you,' Flint began, 'has accepted Christ into her life. Either myself or Pastor Kempe has baptised each one personally. To them, the Hermannsburg Mission has meant clothing, shelter, food and of course, God. It promises a brighter future for their kiddies.'

The Pastor prompted one of the girls to step forward. 'Big fella in the sky,' she said. 'He tells the Pastor what to do for us. We very thankful for our togs, and the Pastor's white sauce.'

Applause. Nathan looked at his father smiling, despite the fact that Henry had organised the event. At the end of the day, Nathan thought, Lutherans were all the same. Stripping down engines in a different order, killing pigs and pickling them according to different recipes, blitzkrieg or sitzkrieg, either way, harnessing their will to a cartful of cucumbers and pulling them towards the ends of the earth.

Pastor Flint quietened the crowd to say his last few words. 'We don't seek to rob the Aranda of their culture. They can use their own ways to praise God. I have left some paintings with Pastor Henry, traditional pieces ...'

So many red and yellow and black dots coming together to form a vision of God. Ochre crosses receding into a background of blurred meaning, snakes and earth serpents diluted, as if by metho, into a wash of colour and formlessness.

The ladies were left to do their thing: '"Mine eyes have seen the glory of the coming of the Lord ..."' Stamping their feet on the concrete and following each other in a circle like so many elephants trunk to tail. Clanging their rhythm sticks and droning in the best Langmeil tradition, moving onto the spokesman in her own solo, '"Amazing Grace, how sweet the sound, that saved a wretch like me ..."'

But that was it. There was pickled pig and fresh lamb to be sold. The ladies were led back towards Langmeil in a line, not talking, tripping on kerbs and gutters. Arriving back at the rectory they changed into cotton dresses of their own making and squeezed into Pastor Flint's bus for the trip to McLaren Vale.

Nathan pursued his father. 'This is because of Lilli.'

'Partly.' Going on to explain how it was a little like killing a pig. You had to know where to cut, how to turn the knife and later, how to skin it and remove the blood and organs so nothing was wasted. And the meat itself. Preparing and salting the right cuts in the right order. 'Maybe, Nathan, another twelve months.'

'Twelve months?' He looked at his mother and she looked at William.

'William, are you saying Nathan should leave his job?'

William had started tasting cheeses. 'It's up to them, but if they're asking me . . .' He shrugged.

Nathan stood staring at him as he kept walking. Bluma took his hand. 'It's just your father's dramatics. He'll sign.'

Nathan turned and ran off towards Murray Street. They didn't see him again until nine o'clock that night, when he walked in the back door, opened the door of his father's study and stepped inside. 'What have you heard about Lilli?'

William refused to look up from his book. 'Not as much as I think you think.'

'I've scored top marks for all my tests. Tomorrow you can come with me and we'll call Bob, Mr Drummond. He'll tell you how I've been working.'

'Nathan, I'm not stopping you.'

That's exactly what you're doing, Nathan thought. He stared at the bald patch on the top of his father's head. The old bastard was playing with words again, saying one thing but meaning another, trying to make everyone do what he wanted, when he wanted, how he wanted.

'I've done everything at home,' he continued.

'I know you have.'

'The weekends I missed I was busy.'

No reply. Bluma appeared behind Nathan. 'William, just sign the papers.'

No reply. Nathan stepped forward. 'If you stop me in this, there are other things.'

William slammed his book shut and stood up. 'I won't be threatened.'

It was enough for Nathan. As his mother clawed at his arm he packed his clothes in his duffle bag. 'I'll spend the rest of my holiday with the Drummonds.'

'And next weekend?'

After a few hours in the Langbein grandstand, watching a pair of foxes sniffing out a dead tabby in the Tanunda Titans change room, Nathan wandered along Murray Street, down an alleyway beside Wohler's furniture shop and through an unlocked window. Making a coffee in the tea-room he set up a gramophone beside a locally made divan and slipped in between factory fresh flannelette sheets: Bach's *Brandenburg Concerto Number 3* was enough to send him off. The record finished and the stylus clicked over as the turn-table turned and Nathan dreamt Axminster dreams of steam and copper piping and the squeal of stuck pigs.

The next morning he woke with a hand on his shoulder and one of the Wohler sons standing beside a policeman. 'You Miller's son?' the senior constable asked, and Nathan shook his head. The policeman and Wohler's son retreated into an office. Nathan sat up, pulling on his shoes and sneering at a couple of girls from his old school who were staring in the front window with their noses squashed flat.

'We'd only be making his problems worse,' the constable said, staring out at Nathan, reminding Wohler of the pamphlets and all of the business in the *Oracle*. 'He's not a bad kid. I say we don't drag the religious nut into it.'

Which is how Nathan ended up spending his morning loading deliveries. Just before lunch he was dismissed with a combination lecture-commiseration. At one o'clock he waited on the platform of Tanunda Station, watching Mr Fritschle pick weeds from between cracked tarmac. Looking up, the older man said, 'You fix a fridge yet?'

He smiled. 'Most things.'

'Handy to have a fridge man around town. When you finish up you could set up here.' Gunther grinned, as if to say, Six years, don't you think the Railways would've known about Revelations?

After all, the Railways knew about everything: the man in blue, giving platform numbers and departure times which extended well beyond next March.

Nathan smiled back at him but didn't voice the thought they shared. Broadcasting it to Fritschle, and beyond, would be a final burning of bridges with his father. To disagree was one thing, argue another, but to go behind his back . . .

Just to be sure he sat at the opposite end of the carriage, avoiding eye contact and studying a Gravox ad. Coal smoke blew in the window and he felt assured, moving through a landscape of endings into one of beginnings. Fraction equivalents. Three eighths equals 0.375, a row of red ticks on a trade-school paper – even the smallest details were a consolation: a crack in the glass of the emergency stop, hastily repaired with electrical tape, a list of rules and their equivalent fines, foul language coming in above fare evasion.

Arriving at Islington he searched out Bob and explained his predicament. To Bob it was history repeating, more melodrama than *Blue Hills*, taking on problems of other people's making. Busy wrestling with a pipe bender he said, 'You'll just have to sort it out with him . . .'

Nathan stood staring. 'He won't change his mind.'

'Well . . .'

'Is there some way around it?'

Bob dropped the pipe. 'I don't know, go see personnel.' But Nathan knew he meant, I don't care, it's not my problem, I have enough of my own. When Bob locked the pipe in the vice and started bending it again, Nathan turned and started to walk off.

But Bob just couldn't do it; next he'd be leaving nuts off of wheelchairs, returning them with broken spokes and treadless tyres. 'Eh, strudel boy.'

Nathan stopped and looked back.

'Give it a week or two.'

Nathan nodded his head. 'He won't change his mind.'

'Okay . . . you want me to talk to him?'

'Arthur, next door, has a telephone.' He returned and put his hand on the pipe. 'If you tell him the papers can't wait . . .' And shrugged.

'Okay, now piss off, you're meant to be on holidays.'

Nathan walked home past cottage gardens in the first throes of spring. Tulips, freesias and lisianthus; coloured beds of dying sour-sobs and potato weed. Barely warm soil promised a regeneration of life for the folks of Kilburn, grown fat and pale and wheezy over a winter it seemed would never end. Unpicked lemons dropped from tree tops, hitting the earth with a thud, waking up leaf mites and ants drowsy with morning frost. The smell of jasmine blew over from a trellis around someone's water tank and shrivelled passionfruit hung heavy over broken, paling fences.

Rose, busy cutting recipes out of the *Weekly* and sticking them into a scrapbook, was so surprised to see him she knocked over a vase of white geraniums. Phil, giving up on a drug text, wondered aloud how anyone could've had enough of Tanunda. As Rose put on the kettle, Nathan started explaining himself, using Bruegel as a descriptor of lesser hells in which his father became the ogre of Goat Square. Ending up with an edited version of his argument with William and a description of the night at Wohler's.

'So Dad says, Nathan, don't you think I've heard about this whore – sorry, Rose – this girl you've been going out with? And I say, What have you heard? And he says, She's the local . . .'

Rose looked at him and smiled. '"Bitch."'

Phil covered his ears. 'Mother.'

'She's the local bitch,' Nathan continued, modulating his voice into tones of fire and brimstone.

'Maybe you should introduce them,' Phil said, continuing an assignment.

'I know,' Rose smiled, cutting outside the lines, 'rumours multiply like bugs in a small town.'

'Like bacteria, mother.'

'Bugs.'

Phil ran his finger over the page of the text, smiling at Nathan. 'Lithium. Just perfect for your dad.'

Rose turned the recipe over and started gluing. 'Phillip, it's none of your concern.'

But he read anyway, grinning, '"Taken to treat and prevent mood swings, either up or down, mania or depression ..."' Continuing until he found something to support his argument, reading it slowly and loudly, '"People with manias are liable to destroy relationships and jobs in bouts which may last for weeks, followed by even longer periods of depression. They may be talkative, sleepless, irritable, egocentric and *prone to flights of fantasy* ..."' He looked up at both of them, 'I could arrange for some.' Checking. '"Dosage: slow release tablets ..."'

Rose didn't look up from a diagram of a whiting skeleton. 'Phillip, would you talk about your own father that way?'

'If he started a cult.'

'Phillip, people disagree on things, doesn't mean they want to do each other in.'

Phil couldn't see the problem. 'It's an option.'

'Nathan might be angry, but I'm sure he doesn't hate his father, do you, Nathan?'

Nathan looked back at Phil and smiled, '... no.'

In her head Rose was filleting, a skill she'd never properly developed. Taking a knife she opened the flesh down the spine and started removing bones. No matter how hard you tried you'd still miss some and Bob would just about choke, coughing and spluttering and gurgling cold tea as he recovered from another brush with death.

'If my dad doesn't sign,' Nathan continued, 'I *will* hate him. He can see it's something I want to do. If you do that to a person they'll never forget.'

'Oh, you'd be surprised,' Rose said, searching the fillet for stray bones. 'After the first war they said it'd never happen again.

211

Lessons had been learnt. Then came the League of Nations. Then came Hitler. So . . .'

Phil looked up. 'What's Hitler got to do with an apprenticeship with the Railways?'

Rose sighed, obsessed with a single bone, somewhere, that she'd missed. Realising that humans never quite got it right, fussing over things which probably didn't matter anyway.

'I think hate could be the word,' Nathan concluded, 'if it came down to it.'

Rose started to feel the weight of other people's problems – this time, not things she could leave behind in the Coronary and Surgical wards. It could have been worse. Nathan was a good kid, but when they took him on they took on his father. There were some things the extra money couldn't cover, like the stress from so many *Weekly* sagas made real.

The sun tumbled in the window, settling across a lace tablecloth full of bread crumbs and gravy stains. Rose found the recipe for an Asian soup and started clipping. Chances were that Bob, with his pockets eternally full of antacid tablets, wouldn't let it past his lips, but at least now it was three onto one. And anyway, she guessed, if he played up, there were still cans of chicken noodle dating back to before the war.

Phil's eyes lit up again and he looked at Nathan. 'I think this is what you're after.' Reading. '"Pentobarbitone. Barbiturate sedative used to relieve anxiety and promote sleep . . ."'

He looked at Nathan again and lifted his eyebrows. 'This is the good bit. "Accidental overdoses are common and characterised by a loss of consciousness, shallow breathing, weak pulse and low blood pressure. Shock and kidney failure follow . . ."'

'Phillip.' Rose looked up, brandishing a stick of glue.

After tea Rose washed the dishes and settled in at the phone table with her best friend Lorna. Lorna had introduced her to the League of Health and Beauty, Prospect branch, a group formed by and for the betterment of Christian women in their 'post-motherhood phase'. Rose was telling Lorna how much she'd enjoyed their eurhythmics on the floor of the Presbyterian church hall. Stripped down to their black satin briefs and undershirts they'd moved their bodies about like 'wild flamingos in a dying frenzy' (Rose's words), combining ballet and gym in previously untried combinations.

'Is it every Wednesday?' Rose asked, as Nathan listened impatiently from the lounge. It was nearly nine before he brought it up again, looking at Bob and saying, 'Do you want me to speak to my father first?'

Bob stood up and took the phone from his wife. 'She'll call you back, Lorna, I've got a business call.'

Arthur stood on the porch of the Miller house shaking off rain, which was coming down torrentially, and scraping mud from the soles of his slippers. He knocked and Bluma told him William was riding Shanks' pony.

'Who is Shanks?'

'The toilet, Arthur.' Smiling.

Arthur tightened the cord on his dressing-gown and sprinted down the side of the house. Knocking on the toilet door he called over the rain, 'William, a phone call, from Adelaide.'

'Who?'

'Nathan.'

'Tell him to ring again ... no, wait ...'

Arthur hung his dressing-gown over the back of a chair and placed it in front of his stove. William came in, wiping clusters of wet hair from his face. 'Sorry to disturb you, Arthur.'

Nathan heard the voices from the kitchen and breathed deeply. When his father came on he said, 'Mr Drummond said he would explain, how the indentures work.'

'Nathan, I don't –'

But Nathan had gone.

Bob took the phone from him. 'Mr Miller?'

'Mr Drummond?'

William's voice was colder than Bob had imagined. 'Nathan has asked me to explain the legal aspects of his uh, apprenticeship.'

Nathan sat down on the arm of the lounge and listened eagerly.

Arthur sat down on his own chair, leaning into the stove, reading a volume of Steinbeck he shared with a nest of curious mice.

'I understand,' William replied, 'but sixteen's too young for a person to decide their future.'

Bob paused, not wanting to agree, not wanting to disagree. 'Everyone's different, Mr Miller. The thing is Nathan – '

'The papers are asking me, do I think he's ready? No. That's why I haven't signed.'

There was no other way to say it. 'Mr Miller, I've worked with Nathan – '

'And I'm his father.'

'Other supervisors I've spoken to – '

'The papers ask me, I say no. If you think he is, all well and good.'

'But Mr Miller, he can't continue without your consent.'

'Mr Drummond, I didn't draw up your contracts.'

Bob looked at Nathan and shrugged. Phil, laying back on the lounge with his eyes closed, whispered, 'Barbiturates,' but this time Nathan couldn't laugh.

'Mr Miller, I keep copies of Nathan's work from trade school.'

'I have no doubts they're good. Nathan was drilled in maths and science. It's not a question of marks.'

Or dates. So many numbers, meaningless in some cases, profound in others. Cleaned from the collective memory like graffiti from a cubicle. From thirty-foot dicks to the Apocalypse.

'Mr Miller, if you don't mind me saying, there seems to be a separate issue – '

'Nathan has told you this?'

'No. I've gathered.'

'You're wrong. You'd have to know everything about us. And anyway, to say I can't keep things separate … if it's the girl he's mentioned, he's wrong. I look at everything. That's something you can't do from Adelaide.'

Bob knew there was no point arguing. After a few, empty moments he said, 'Maybe I'll send you the results anyway, and get his supervisors to write something down.'

No reply.

'Mr Miller?'

'It's up to you. Apart from this, I'd like to thank you for looking after Nathan.'

The strangeness of this comment struck him; William was just as Nathan had described. After he hung up he said to Nathan, 'There's always a way.'

'How?'

But he just looked at him as if to say, Innocent child.

After the commiserations of a shared, communal cuppa, Bob went out to his shed, coughing from a cold he said he couldn't shake, and Rose returned to Lorna and the League of Health and Beauty. The boys stretched out on the lounge-room floor with Phil's doctored version of Monopoly, the Strand becoming Syphilis Street, Westminster Herpes, Bond Gonorrhoea . . .

William left Arthur buried in Steinbeck. He went home, peeled off his wet clothes and stood completely naked in Bluma's black kitchen. 'Telephones,' he whispered. 'Who'd have 'em, bringing bad news into your house.'

On Friday, Nathan had the Drummond house to himself. He rose early and cooked everyone breakfast, burning bacon in a frypan Rose had picked up for a steal in the Harris Scarfe basement. After he'd waved them off at the door, he attacked the dishes, scrubbing with a rusted, limp Steelo; he cleaned the WC and hand-washed Bob's overalls, the familiar smell of kero, turps and everything diesel in his nose.

Just before lunch he sat down with a clean, white sheet of paper and tried to summon words. *Dear Dad . . .* no, too familiar for his purpose . . . *Father . . .* melodramatic . . . *William . . .* he'd never called him William, that denoted an equality they didn't have. Eventually he left it out all together, starting simply: *Regarding our conversation, and the phone call Mr Drummond made on my behalf . . .*

He finished the letter and found an envelope in Rose's drawer of everything that doesn't go anywhere else. After feasting on a lunch of stale bread and jam, he locked the door and headed south towards Churchill Road. Stobie poles stood rusting silently in the half-sun, their foundations overgrown with capeweed or tarted up with geraniums and asparagus fern, either way, a compendium of dog piss as unknowable as the Enigma code. Turning into Churchill Road, he stopped to look in the window of an old funeral parlour turned white-goods showroom. It would never happen in Tanunda, he thought, imagining the guts of Langmeil church full of grocery-lined shelves or agricultural chemicals, the spirits of the dead retreating from the rafters in horror.

He bought a stamp at Wagner's deli and licked it, positioning it geometrically in the corner of the envelope, as if this might impress his father. Eventually he took out the letter, sat at a bus stop and re-read it. *I can see that you're determined to have me home. Why, I don't know, as there's nothing for me there. I could never go back to school now and our farm, as it is, could never support us both. And anyway, it doesn't interest me . . .*

Going on to explain that a compressor was no less profound than a bottle of shiraz, one set of skills no more important than another, but how it was *the way* you spent your days. And what he meant was, the people around you, their way of talking, of kidding you, of seeing you not as a son, eternally driving through life on a set of learner's plates, but as a complete and fully formed person, reliant, derived or reminiscent of no one else. *If it's a case of having me around to help fulfil your prophecies, forget it. Christ is coming, maybe, but God's quite content to let us go on running railways . . .*

And Hoovering rugs, growing orchids, entering lotteries we'll never win (Rose was religious with her Tatts), repairing wheelchairs, making conversation with patients too deaf or nutty, or both, to know what we're saying, but continuing anyway, sure that something will get through. A God content to let us go on eating chow mein, share memories of relatives no one had seen for thirty years, take the wrong job or marry the wrong person; to let us go on living until an artery blocked or a bus swerved somewhere.

. . . the thing being, Dad, I won't come home until you come to your senses. I know you're probably cursing me, but there it is. I could come home, but I'd be full of resentment. I don't want to be. I don't feel that way here. And anyway, why should I give up what I've worked for? You wouldn't . . .

A bus pulled up and the doors flew open. The driver looked at him strangely. 'It's an hour service.'

'No thanks.'

The driver shook his head and, revving the engine, pulled out in front of traffic. Nathan opened out a near-perfect electronics test and checked the answers, knowing it wouldn't matter anyway. There was a hand-written note from his lecturer and a brochure on the benefits of working for the S.A. Railways. Nathan knew that superannuation, sick pay and a job for life would mean nothing to William compared to the promise of March 21.

Anyway, Mr Drummond says there are ways. Failing that I can wait. There are shops to be cleaned. I will find money. I will continue. Please make it easy and sign my papers. Sincerely, Nathan.

So be it. He sealed the envelope and dropped it in a post box. Walking back into Wagner's deli, he bought a pack of Craven A and started off down Churchill Road towards the city. At five o'clock he met Phil and they managed to sneak into the Imperial Hotel. By six they were nearly pissed, chatting up a pair of twenty-something office girls in search of a reliable man. 'I'm nearly a chemist,' Phil said. 'Chemists hold people's lives in their hands.'

He cupped his hands, anticipating something more than Bex, and they laughed at him. 'Where do you ladies stand on the 38th Parallel?'

The manager rang a bell. 'Time, gentlemen.'

As the girls climbed the stairs to King William Street, Phil called after them, 'Let me shout you some whiting.'

But they both knew communism and youth were no match for a solid income, even when Angelakis' Fish Cafe was involved.

'How would you have afforded whiting?' Nathan asked, as Phil lead him towards Rundle Street.

'I would've improvised,' Phil replied, going on to explain how they were probably private school girls, beyond pre-marital corruption. 'What we need are a couple of girls like us.'

'Like what?'

'Unbound by . . . moral considerations.'

'Speak for yourself.'

Phil smiled at him as they paused at the Beehive corner. 'Nathan, dear boy, five minutes horizontal beside the Torrens and you'd forget your Proverbs.' As Phil imagined giggling voices and wet, hungry tongues, as Joe Aronson drifted across the water. 'The Beehive is where they meet.'

'Who?'

'Girls. Before the flicks.'

Phil was a collector of human refundables, thrown into the bin of his good fortune. But tonight was a quiet night. After twenty minutes Nathan said, 'This is useless.'

Phil persuaded him to do one circuit of Hindley Street. Eventually they returned to the train station and the consolation of new-season bikinis in Rose's latest *Weekly*.

The next day, as the Millerites sat on Arthur's ark in a lukewarm pool of gemutlichkeit, involved with Mary's pretzels and Catherine's lighter-than-cumulus potato salad, Bluma asked Mary what had happened to their son-in-law Joseph.

Mary shrugged. 'He has work.'

'On a Saturday?' William asked.

'This is what he says,' Mary responded. 'What about Nathan?' she asked, as if in retribution.

'Study,' Bluma replied.

Instead of Revelations, Bluma felt like their time was becoming a salad of half-truths and bluffs, things people didn't want to discuss. And at the centre of it was William, the Anubis of Tanunda, weighing up souls and finding them wanting. It could be anyone next. The best you could do was bring a salad and keep your mouth shut.

After lunch they gathered in the shade of William's myrtle, kneeling before a cross Arthur had built them and erected in place of Nathan's old swing.

'See,' Bruno said to Edna, staring out of the window at them. 'This is how those cults start in Africa. Should've closed them down.'

'Who should've?'

'The government.'

'What can they do?'

Bruno was thinking how they should've put William in Loveday, and thrown away the keys. 'Not a proper religion. Shouldn't be allowed.'

'Y' sound like the Russian fella, with the mo.'

'Stalin? So?'

'Down to Korea, be here next.'

Bruno parted the venetians, raising his voice. 'Eh, William, keep it down.'

Edna pulled him away from the window. 'Bruno.'

The Lord's Prayer stopped and they all looked up. William saw Bruno moving around inside but said nothing, bowing his head, '"... Thy Kingdom come ..."'

The following Tuesday, William stood beside Arthur's cross, a can of varnish in one hand, a brush in the other. Bluma approached him, holding Nathan's letter. William, knowing what it was, continued painting as she read the letter aloud.

'So?' she asked, when she'd finished.

William half-smiled. 'I'm not going to let it affect my blood pressure.'

'Damn your blood pressure, what about me?'

'Bluma, it'll work itself out.'

'It won't. He's determined. Sign the papers and let's have peace. Otherwise it'll go on forever.' She paused, staring at him. 'My brother didn't talk to my sister for seventeen years.'

'No wonder.'

'We don't all measure up, William Miller.' She used his full name on purpose, explaining how you didn't throw away underweight tomatoes, how they were the ones that had the flavour.

But William was unswayed. 'It'll work itself out.'

She stamped her foot on the ground. 'William, I want to see my son.'

He pointed his paint brush at the letter. 'He's the one with the dramatics. The door will never be locked.'

'Tell me why he should come home, to this.'

William just kept painting. Bluma stormed off, half dreading she'd never see her son again, half believing that William was right and it would work itself out.

That night William locked himself in his study and wrote a letter to the 'Director of Adelaide Railway'. Although Bob Drummond had been doing a good job with his son's accommodation, he explained, he was failing to reinforce family values. Some days later William received a letter back saying that Mr Drummond had been consulted, and that host families had the right to run things their own way. Mr Drummond had done his best to consider Mr Miller's wishes but in respect to 'grey areas', Mr Miller was advised to resolve differences with his son directly.

As there was no definition of 'grey areas', William didn't know what had been said, or by whom. He wrote back (THIS SHALL BE MY FINAL CORRESPONDENCE) saying that the Drummonds of the world could be teaching their children anything.

'I'm not responding, then we'd be at his level,' Bob said to Rose, showing her the copy of the letter, lighting it and throwing it in the laundry trough and making her promise never to mention it to Nathan.

It was true, they'd ended up in the middle of another soap opera, but Nathan's best hope was the Railways, and a fresh start. He couldn't imagine asking Nathan to leave.

William had created a mental folder. Into it he'd placed Rohwer and Fritschle, Streim and Bruno Hermann, allowing his various poisons to drift into his realm. Doms and Rasch and Pastor Henry were in there too, although not so deeply. The Drummonds and the insipid little mail sorter, and now his own son. It was getting full. His chances of retrieving people from it were getting fewer. He'd tried nearly everything, but in the end there was little he could do. In a way the whole world was in there, except for those of like mind, who lived across the oceans somewhere, who he'd eventually get to meet.

In another folder were his followers, and there were degrees of those too.

Chapter Thirteen

Saturday a.m., Joshua Heinz preparing himself for worship, increasingly unhappy that he should lose nearly an entire weekend praising God variously through Miller-Muller and Hoffmann. It was okay for William, he was self-employed, weeding his turnips and pruning his vines in his own good time, but for those who kept more regular hours ... But Joshua was only left with the vacuum that was a Sunday afternoon, managing to fix a few tiles or spray a few roses before dark, devotion, in the name of the Father, Catherine's curried sausages, bakelite Mozart, the *Oracle* in its third re-reading, sleep and then insurance.

Joshua worked out of Strehlow's offices in Sobels Street, daily packing his satchel and setting off on a door-knock of a different kind. 'Yes, I am a friend of Mr Miller, but that's not why I'm here. You have a husband?'

'Yes.'

'He works?'

'He does.'

'Have you ever wondered what would happen if he had an accident ... or something more permanent.'

'Death?'

'Yes. You have, how many mouths to feed?'

Canvassing the options of house fire, automobile accident or flood damage, all very real and regular. 'Although no one thinks so until it happens to them. I could prepare a package of options which would allow you to sleep soundly at night.' Something they couldn't do after the images he'd invoked: mothers clawing the sides of trees as they listened to their babies scream from inside homes engulfed with flames; wives visiting husbands in hospital wards, trying not to look at the place where their arm used to be; half-sized coffins; burnt out Austins sitting in police compounds; roofs blown into cow paddocks by the one-in-a-hundred wind they hadn't seen since the days of Kavel.

Joshua employed scare tactics to make a good living, selling more policies than the rest of Strehlow's office cobbled together. And yet, doing a real public service, giving people protection they hadn't realised they needed ('We grow complacent in our valley, Adelaide people wouldn't *dream* of being without cover. And what's it cost, a few lousy pieces of copper ... c'mon, you'd spend that on a bar of Cadburys').

Apart from eating into his weekend, William's work hadn't made Joshua's job any easier. Now, when people realised who he was, they'd say, 'You, selling insurance?' And he'd have to explain how Christ was returning to establish a thousand-year ministry. Legs will still be broken, cars crashed, windows smashed. But for most it seemed a bit rich. At least once a day someone would say to him, 'Wouldn't it be one or the other?' and although he did his best to explain the need for post-apocalyptic protection, he was starting to see a real down-turn in numbers.

Not that he'd tell William. He knew this was just one of the prices he'd pay for a comfy seat in eternity, for a spot for his whole family. Nonetheless, that week he'd started introducing himself as Joshua Heinemann.

'But aren't you Aaron Heinz's boy?'

Laying his policies across various kitchen tables, stopping to explain his dilemma and apologise for a little white lie and say, 'I realise most people don't agree with us–so, why should I put myself out of business? I still have a family to feed, and a house to keep going.'

As the morning warmed up, Bruno Hermann closed his front door and crossed the road to the vacant land. He jumped a small picket fence he'd helped William and Arthur erect, paint white and, for most of the years up to now, maintain. It was hard to think of them doing it now, working together in the summer sun with their shirts off. They had built it to keep their cattle in, leaving them there to graze native grasses as their own pastures grew. Come October, they'd lead them back across the road, leaving a trail of hot, sloppy shit the colour and consistency of Catherine Heinz's curried sausages.

Bruno drained a cattle trough and used his hands to muck out grass and mud. Checking his three Hereford steers and Angus heifer he stood contented, lighting up a recycled rollie and farting. The weeds were all there, flourishing – it would never be used as a proper paddock again: spurge, echium and capeweed, three-corner jack and paddy-melon. A few sugar gums survived here and there but they were mostly pale, lignin skeletons, branching low, vainly sending coat-hanger limbs into the atmosphere. Every day salt seeped up through a landscape of outdated agriculture, still prac- tised by Bruno and others with the aid of tractors and twelve-tine ploughs.

Arthur Blessitt was deep in his flowers, cutting gypsophila and tying it in bunches to take to the florist. In the distance he saw William, waving and pointing to his watch. 'Have to finish,' Arthur called, but William couldn't hear him, continuing to pace and look back every now and again as Arthur whispered, 'The world doesn't stop for you.'

In the Hicks' lounge room, Ellen Tabrar switched off the radio and said to her husband, 'Are you serious?'

Joseph smiled. 'Yes, I am bloody serious.'

Mary Hicks tried to leave the room but Ellen grabbed her arm. 'Mum, talk to him.'

'Ellen, they're his children too.'

Joseph crossed his arms. 'Too bloody right.'

Victoria, David and Chas sat in ascending order of age on the lounge, dressed in their best Sunday (Saturday) clothes, hair combed, shoes polished – legs dangling, sometimes swinging like pendulums marking time. The routine of warring parents was becoming so familiar that they didn't say a word, frown, sigh or even listen.

'What is it?' Mary asked Joseph.

'I've decided to take them to Adelaide, to the pictures. Tarzan, eh, Chas?'

And with that the youngest beat his chest and imitated Tarzan's call.

'There's Mario Lanza,' Vicky sighed, looking longingly at her dad, but David elbowed her in the ribs and nodded his head in disgust.

Ellen looked at her mother. 'He could go any time, but he picks today.'

'Any time, they've got school!' Joseph replied.

'And holidays coming up.'

'Every Saturday they have to sit there listening to *him*. Tarzan makes as much bloody sense. What would they rather?'

The three adults looked at the children. Ellen folded her arms and sneered back at Joseph. 'It's not a case of what they'd rather.'

'It is.' Thinking, you heartless bloody bitch. Waiting for her to turn to her mother, which she did.

'Maybe this once,' Mary replied, to keep the peace. And with that Ellen stormed into their bedroom and slammed the door.

Waiting at the train station, Chas asked his father, 'Is the world really going to end?'

But before Joseph could reply, Vicky said, 'Of course not. Don't you listen to people? Miller's the village idiot.'

'Vicky.'

'He is.'

At which point Joseph became the diplomat and explained to his youngest how some people just go off the tracks, but how they had to try and get along with them anyway.

'Why?' Vicky asked.

'Because he's your grandpa's friend.'

'So?'

'Your grandpa married your grandma, she had your mother, I married her and we made you. Blood's thicker than water,' whispering, '... apparently.'

Vicky smiled, 'I heard that.'

'Just don't repeat it.'

Sitting in the dark at the Regent, Vicky decided she did like the world of African jungles more than Saturday at the Millers. Still, the old crackpot's play was a lot of fun and she was sad to be missing their final rehearsal. In the end, popcorn and Coke were more than enough consolation, Johnny Weissmuller's abs a dream more vivid than any apocalypse.

William, sitting at the head of Arthur's ark, passing the potato salad to Seymour, could feel his folder getting thinner. Seymour, who hadn't known about the excursion until they were gone, insisted it wouldn't hurt as it was something the kids seldom did.

(But when Seymour saw Joseph that night, he repeated Ellen's words. 'You had to take them then?'

'Yes.'

'But they love their afternoons with the Heinzes.'

'They loved their afternoon at the Regent.'

Seymour started shaking his head. 'Ellen was quite distressed. She barely said a word. Think of what it looked like for her.'

'To whom?'

'William.'

'Seymour, please ...')

Around Arthur's ark the remaining followers joined hands to pray but somehow the spell was broken. William thinking, How can I sustain this when there's so much against me? Whispering to his ever-diminishing ring of supporters, 'Lord, let us be true believers. Let us pray for those who've turned away.'

Rising early the following Wednesday, market day, William and Arthur pulled Arthur's movable stage down Elizabeth and then Maria Street, setting up on the crumbled concrete of the Tanunda corroboree. Bluma raised the children's banner as Arthur chocked rocks under wheels salvaged from a shopping trolley dumped in the North Para River.

At ten a.m. the market was buzzing, the price of lettuce and tomatoes mingling with whispers. 'He's determined to make a complete fool of himself', 'Fancy humiliating the children in such a way.'

At the Hicks' house, Ellen saw Joseph off to work without a word. When she was sure he was gone, she helped the children iron their costumes. Mary helped her herd the kids into the back of the hearse and Seymour drove the family to Goat Square.

Locking the door of Strehlow's, Joshua Heinz took his lunch break early. He stopped by the Apex for a dozen Cornish pasties and hurried to meet Catherine, Sarah and the rest of their children beside the stage, where they shared their lunch. Some of the children were already pulling on costumes and one struggled with a bottle of Rosella tomato sauce which would double as blood.

Just before lunch, when the market was at its busiest, William mounted the stage and started clanging a wooden spoon on one of Bluma's best saucepans. 'Welcome,' he called, 'to our *Play for the Apocalypse*. Our story is not a prophecy. It is fact. If you haven't heard of us, then *this* will explain our vision. Afterwards, you have two choices: return to your sausages and flowers, or come and talk to us. We're a friendly group that meets of a Saturday at my house. We'll continue to do this until the great day of Christ's return. At that time, we'd like you to be there with us.'

'He's comin' to my place first,' a voice rang out, and the crowd laughed.

William smiled and raised a finger knowingly. 'Do you know what Hell is, sir?'

'Listenin' to you.'

A variety of comments were called out, most of which William couldn't decipher. The young cast stood in the open-air wings, taking it as a bad sign. Lilli Fechner, on her own lunch break, called, 'You dirty old man, you should be ashamed.' Ron Rohwer stood beside Gunther Fritschle, both with their arms crossed, refusing to join in the derision – William could dig his own grave without their help. Pastor Hoffmann stood at the front, beside a grinning Bruno and Edna, silently observing William's impending humiliation.

Part one went off smoothly, with William himself taking Nathan's part. The only incident was a tomato thrown close to the kids, William stopping the show to explain how people could lose eyes. Part two started with David and Chas reclining in a 'cinema', as Vicky swooned the part of Maureen O'Sullivan in leopard skins. On the other side of the stage, the Heinz children variously worked their fields, read the Bible, prayed and, in Sarah's case, ventured north as a missionary. Addressing an imaginary native as she clutched a Bible, she recited, 'Have you heard of Jesus Christ, Lord of Heavens? No? Well, sit with me as I read you this book.'

'Not all that bad,' Bruno said to Edna. She had to agree: the kiddies were well turned out and none of them muffed a line. They were having fun and it showed. When Vicky and Sarah knelt in fear before the appearance of the archangel Gabriel, the crowd erupted in laughter at a scene reminiscent of Laurel and Hardy. Lilli dropped her defences to applaud and the Rohwer-Fritschle combination called out, 'Good on you kids,' as if the presence of Miller and his agenda could be temporarily overlooked.

After Gabriel came the big fella himself, Seymour as Christ bearing script. 'Who among you have heeded my words?' he asked, and all of the children stood around him with their arms raised. 'I have a test,' he continued. 'Like eggs in water, the rotten ones always sink.'

Lilli couldn't resist it. 'Is that the best you could come up with?'

William thought he recognised the voice, but couldn't be sure.

'Your metaphors stink,' she continued, and the crowd laughed again.

Seymour, desperately searching for his place, looked up and said, 'A bit of respect, please,' and their audience laughed even louder.

And then, exactly on cue, the children started running about on stage, screaming, squeezing pork sausages open to simulate human viscera, smearing sauce across their faces and tearing at their clothes. As an apocalyptic vision it was more Hoovermatic spin than Bruegel – an attempted miasma of smell, screams, crushed bodies, trees and houses and livestock flying through space, human devils being cleansed from the earth for ever, faeces in motion with blood and vomit and Coca Cola, all drawn from William's experience of swinging on Nathan's swing.

Ellen, Catherine and Mary stood around the stage popping party streamers and throwing confetti, banging saucepan lids and adding their own screams of pain. Catherine, taken by the spirit, started casting alfoil-covered thunderbolts at the children, careful to avoid her own.

William stood up in front of all this, and spreading his arms, said, 'It's not so far off. Are you prepared? Like water being sucked down a drain, *there is no way to avoid it.*'

And after the judging, who would be left, he asked. As if in reply, David, Chas and Vicky screamed and cast themselves down dead on the stage. The noise and motion stopped and everybody looked at their bodies. Lilli nodded her head, 'Oh please, spare me,' but most of the market crowd seemed determined to see the story out.

'There's no secret to salvation,' William said, 'it's just hard work. Nothing comes from nothing. The Bible has all the answers.'

And with that the saved souls joined hands and danced around the bodies, joyous but not gloating. William explained how this was his mission, to save people from themselves. This time next year they'd be thanking him. Buying and selling vegetables in a market place of many empty stalls. He had studied the Word and seen these things.

Joseph Tabrar, on his lunch break, walked down John Street into Goat Square and couldn't believe what he saw. Fighting his way through the crowd he made his way to the stage and told his children to stand up. 'Home,' he said, pointing, and they ran off without a word. He looked at Ellen and then at Seymour and then at William and said, 'That's it.' Catching up with his children he grabbed their hands and pulled them down Murray Street towards what they called home. Throwing open the door, he told Vicky to run a bath for the three of them and take off their ridiculous costumes.

'But it was fun,' she pleaded.

He made no reply, settling in on the lounge to await what it was he called his family. 'Clean up,' he demanded, 'then I'm taking you back to school.'

Back in Goat Square, Lilli Fechner watched the remaining Millerites pile their costumes and banner on the stage and start wheeling it back towards Arthur's place. Pathetic bastards, she thought, checking her watch and seeing she was ten minutes late. Walking back towards Apex, she realised that Nathan *had* proved himself, drifting away in a lifeboat from William's comedy of high farce. *She* was the one left behind, drifting, slowly sinking.

Seymour and Ellen, walking in the front door, were met by Joseph's stare. The splashing and laughing from the bathroom attracted Ellen but Joseph stood up. 'No more Miller,' he said.

Seymour laughed. 'Is that for you to say?'

Joseph walked towards him. 'It is.'

'What about Ellen, and what about the kids? You weren't there, you didn't see how much they enjoyed it.'

'They're meant to be at school.'

'One morning, come on.' Seymour didn't flinch.

'They're my children.'

'And it's my house.'

Joseph moved even closer to him. 'So?'

'You can't have it both ways. You need to compromise.'

'*They are my children.*'

'Don't raise your voice to me.'

Ellen stepped between them. 'Stop.'

Joseph paused for a moment then walked off to the bathroom. 'No more Miller.'

'We'll see,' Seymour replied.

Joseph closed the bathroom door behind him just as Mary

came in the front door carrying a pile of dirty costumes. 'Guess who gets to wash these?' she laughed.

Ellen knocked on the bathroom door. 'You better get back to work. I'll take the children to school.'

The door opened and Joseph appeared, refusing to speak to any of them. With little of the dramatic flair they'd displayed, he walked down the hallway and out the front door. Ellen looked at her mother. 'Don't ask.'

That night, William, Bluma and Arthur formed a production line. At one end, William, the editor of the *Last Days*, a boy's own adventure in which he explained how the British had already picked a site for the detonation and fenced it off, herding up the black fellas but leaving the possums and kangaroos. How a crew had been picked and a bomber flown out for trials. How it was probably academic as the Russians or Yanks would use their bomb first, and how he had a suspicion when – the Cold War warming to a new year's climax some time after the Christmas sales but before Easter.

Bluma was the cutter, Arthur the paster, smoothing down the newsprint, cleaning off the excess glue and writing annotations according to William's strict format: *The Tanunda Oracle, September 15, 1951. Page 3, halfway up.* They were all clues to the future, hidden away in the bottom corner of page twelve so no one would notice. Except William. Looking at a page three spread of atrocities from the Korean War: stunted, grinning, mud-covered Reds holding up severed heads, bodies slumped in shallow trenches, two American kid-soldiers about to be executed, unsure whether to look at the camera or the rifles.

William moved the paper over so Bluma and Arthur could see as he tried to think of a link between communism and atheism and dead bodies frozen in contortions in the best Pompeii tradition. He tried to convince them that people could be brainwashed, lost, over-running the earth in a frenzy of evil justified by the need for shared capital.

He prayed, improvising, but after, worked on in silence, trying to work out what would happen to the innocents. So many of them, screaming into a void as empty as the Flinders Ranges, their voices echoing and fading without reply. God as a mighty river red gum, unmoved, forming growth rings as the years passed, each with its own unwritten history of birth, death, love, smog and betrayal. Man had been given free will and it was up to him how he used it. William knew that God couldn't be blamed for everything – we couldn't have it both ways, one minute starting revolutions and then looking for someone to blame when it all went wrong. 'We're such a disappointment,' he mumbled, at last, imagining the faces of the Commies in their quilted uniforms as those of Rohwer and Fritschle.

Bluma could guess what he was thinking. 'The kiddies'll be back,' she said.

William continued turning pages. 'I hope so.' Thinking of Joseph holding three, small, severed heads, grinning.

Arthur sat forward. 'It must be hard for him though ... as a parent ... if I had children ...'

William looked at him. 'He'll tear that family apart.' And not for the first time, Arthur stared at him, becoming alarmed at the evolving drama, wondering if it wasn't William's fate to scorch, or slowly poison, anyone who ventured too close to him. It shouldn't be like this, Arthur wanted to say, but couldn't. It should be about simple things: wood sorrel growing in irrigation ditches, sitting on the porch with the sun on your cheek, the smell of freshly turned wood. Praising God daily by being alive, participating, accepting ...

Arthur had begun to suspect that he'd been misled. Two and a half thousand people, in Tanunda alone, couldn't be wrong. And out of the few believers William had scraped together, his group was shrinking at an exponential rate. Here was a man who could turn his back on people who'd shown him nothing but trust and friendship: Pastor Henry with his policy of God for everyone, Bruno, sharing endless sticks of wurst and homebrew, Trevor, happy to spend the night setting up everyone else's pins. All of them Christians. But not Christian enough. Failing one of the many tests William had set up for them somewhere along the way. So that the few remaining, Arthur felt, were no better than the brainwashed Reds, mouthing someone else's thoughts, chronically unable to think for themselves.

Arthur knew William wouldn't stop at destroying a family. With Joseph gone, Seymour would bring the rest of them in line.

'Those kiddies had the time of their life yesterday,' William said. 'Problem is, you can't make people like Joseph see sense . . . Tabrar, isn't that a Yiddish name?' Going on to recall that Joseph was a valley ring-in who'd never made an effort to adapt. 'Did the post office transfer him, or did he want to come?'

Bluma shrugged. 'He got that job after.'

'Nonsense. I'm sure he wanted to come. Which makes you wonder why. He's never stopped complaining.'

Arthur put the lid on the glue and spoke softly. 'He was transferred here.'

'Same difference. Work for the PMG you'd expect it. Local people should expect *them* to make an effort.'

'He did,' Arthur defended. 'Married local, settled down and had kids.'

'Settled down? Ha.'

Arthur wiped his hands on his pants. 'We haven't been here all that long, William.'

'Long enough.'

'William, if you want to get people behind you . . .'

William looked at him, surprised. 'What do you mean?'

'You shouldn't be so . . . selective. You make it hard for people.' Arthur had a vision of William at the door of his very own church, checking identity papers, birth certificates, racial profiles and character references of potential worshippers. Going inside and preaching to a church empty except for the reliable few.

The next day Arthur found himself back beside William, harvesting cabbages and pulling weeds from the Miller vegetables. It

233

was no good saying he'd try to see less of William. Living so close there was no way around it. Waking up with a tap on the window, there he was, pushing open a louvre that had never been locked. 'Couldn't spare an hour or two?' And what could you say? That's how things were done in the valley – pull some weeds in return for a couple of cabbages, carnations for Bluma's table, leftover shiraz for digging a ditch.

It was a hot day. When it came to vegetables, William knew no shame. With his shirt off, his stomach hung heavy over a belt which had missed nearly every loop, working its way up to his pubic region, half-exposed through an open fly which wouldn't have bothered him even if he knew. Arthur was more conservative, pulling his sleeves down to protect his arms and making a hanky-hat in the accepted English style.

'Hey, Arthur,' William called, cutting cabbages at ground level with a razor-sharp knife. 'Ever thought of changing *your* name back?'

'No.' Barely looking up from bent-grass which was beyond the help of any fork.

'Maybe it's been long enough.'

'I'm happy with my name,' Arthur whispered, wiping his forehead.

'Only, it's not your name.'

'It is.'

They worked on silently. Artur Weidemann, who'd changed his name on William's advice, had never missed the clunkety, Germanic handle he'd inherited from countless generations of cabinet-makers. Blessitt had been chosen for its poetry, its grace, its ability to move him away from the squareness and solidness of a silky oak Weidemann past. Then there had been the case of a European Weidemann, a mass murderer or child killer or some such, and people remembered, tracing genes back as far as it took to make a connection. Blessitt was a new beginning, an Australian beginning, a beginning of fresh lisianthus and carnations, the type of thing his dying father had warned him against but suspected he'd do anyway. 'What's become of Wilhelm Muller?' Arthur asked, without lifting his head.

234

'I've filled out the form. Persuading people's another thing.'

'Why don't you stick with William? It's not so bad.'

'But I'm not William, I'm Wilhelm. This is all Hitler's fault. I won't have him ruining everything.' William smiled and stood up, straightening his back. 'Eh, imagine it at the pearly gate. St Paul says, "There's no Wilhelm Muller here," and I reply, "But I swear, I changed my name back, didn't they send you the paperwork?"' He laughed, but Arthur still didn't look up, wondering whether this was from William's sermon of the empty church.

Bluma emerged from the house and approached them, holding out an open letter to William and waiting. 'What is it?' he asked, slashing the knife to within an inch of his fingers.

'Nathan.'

He worked on silently.

'Are you going to read it?'

No reply. She paused, returned it to her apron pocket, turned and went inside. The two men worked on without a word, sweating, stretching, wiping salty water from their eyes. In time Arthur asked, 'How's the apprenticeship going?' and when William ignored him, he decided he'd had enough of Mr Muller.

He finished his work, throwing his weeds onto William's compost pile and walking home with an armful of cabbages. Sitting at his kitchen table, wiping his face with a cold flannel, he knew what he had to do. He took a sheet of paper and a pen and wrote. When he finished he cooked tea, ate, cleaned up and sat on his back porch with a jug of home-made lemonade. At ten o'clock, when he knew he wouldn't be seen, he walked over to William's back door and slid the note under.

William found it the next morning, whispering to Bluma over his oats, 'Arthur is no longer with us.'

'What do you mean?'

He handed her the note and she read it. In it Arthur explained how his God was a living, breathing, gentle being, full of love and forgiveness. But how, since his time with the group, he'd been unable to accept an image of God as Gestapo man, promising a hell of fire and pain to everyone who didn't subscribe to certain views. He closed by asking if they could still be friends, as their families had been for generations, but thought it unlikely, considering the way William had treated his own son, for instance.

Next morning, when Arthur was out getting water from his tank, he looked over to see William back at work in his vegetable patch, pulling weeds, oblivious to any part of the world beyond his fence.

Chapter Fourteen

Nathan realised how easily life could become one of Rose's romance novels, read and re-read until its very cheesiness became real through familiarity. Standing in his room, staring out of the window at Bob's severely pruned iceberg roses, he listened to Rose singing along with Nat King Cole. '"Unforgettable, that's what you are . . ."' And although to her it meant the laughter of kiddies at the hospital, chow mein, almonds candying on a late winter morning, Phillip's eternal harping in her ear – to Nathan it was just Lilli.

As the high violins floated below the cracked ceiling and the clarinets passed into wardrobes and sock drawers, he imagined Lilli serving coffee to a couple of kidless townies seated on a table outside the Apex. He could see the faulty neon of the Fechner automat blinking pink and bright blue, and Lilli slamming the door in disgust as she went back in.

He opened his bag, put it on his bed and started packing: spare socks and pants, T-shirts and a jumper of his mother's creation. Phil walked in and said, 'Christ, how long we going for?'

'You've never been camping before?'

Phil grabbed Nathan's Bible from his bedside drawer and started flicking through the pages. 'Never been. What's it involve? Lying on a rug and falling asleep. Pissing on a tree and crapping in a hole. Douglas Mawson had nothing on you.'

'You should pack some dry clothes.'

'Ha, if it looks like rain we can just chant some of this stuff. Maybe we should hold a rally?' Phil closed his eyes and smiled.

'*Brothers and sisters* . . .' Looking at Nathan and saying, 'The Salvos play in the middle of Rundle Street, every Sunday night, I gotta take you . . .' Choosing not to finish with, It'll be a big laugh. 'This thing got any prayers for rain?' he continued, sitting down on his bed and looking through Ephesians and the Gospels.

'It doesn't work like that.'

'It should. A religion should be practical. American Indians could pray for anything: harvest, death of unwanted relatives . . .'

'But did it work?'

'Did it matter? Or the Egyptians, had hundreds of gods, kept people's interest. This lot it's just, hymn number twelve and pass the butter. Where's the bit about the end of the world?'

Nathan took the Bible and turned to Revelations. 'Chapter twenty.' He handed it back and watched as Phil read through, half-grinning, half-annoyed.

'How do they get from that to the end of the world?'

'It doesn't end. Christ returns and the sinners are cast off.'

'Cast off?'

'Into Hell.'

'Which is?'

'Fire, showers of molten lava.'

'But does it actually say that?'

'Not in so many words.'

Phil smiled and placed the Bible on his bed. 'Of course not. I could write something like this.'

'No you couldn't,' Nathan replied, shaking his head.

'I could.'

'Even if you did, how would you persuade half the planet?'

Phil stopped. It was a good point, bit it didn't make a wrong thing right.

'I don't believe it'll happen like this,' Nathan added.

'I'm relieved.'

'But lots do.'

And Phil thought, How could so many human beings be so stupid? The atom was split, antibiotics perfected and space mapped, but half the planet still believed in the seven seals. 'Humans worry me,' he concluded.

Nat King Cole persisted in gravy-soaked air, wafting in as some sort of consolation, explaining away the universe in Rose's peculiar way. The idea of religion depressed Phil, there was nothing good about plagues and angels, it just proved that humans failed to meet their potential. There was no way a lifetime of dispensing drugs could change that. It was his destiny to help keep them alive, so they could go on being stupid. 'I could write that,' he repeated.

Nathan smiled. 'I look forward to reading it.'

The sound of a car mis-firing in the driveway distracted them from God. Emerging from the front door, they found Bob inspecting the engine of a near new Whippet, borrowed from the works manager who'd bought it on the proceeds of a recent inheritance. 'One of them spark plugs is kaput,' Bob began, looking worried. 'He didn't mention any problems. Now it'll be up to me to fix it. Typical.'

A small mutt jumped about at Nathan's feet. 'He comes with the car,' Bob explained. 'Rides on the running board, y' oughta see it.'

After tea, Bob climbed up into the roof cavity and retrieved three old sleeping bags, hanging them on the rotary and getting the boys to bash the life out of them. Then he packed his .22 rifle, babbling on about the rabbit stew he used to survive on as a kid, while Phil explained the world of myxomatosis. They spent the rest of the evening around the radio. The mutt was let in and when Bob was in the kitchen toasting jubilee cake, it settled into his recliner. Returning with a tray of Bushells and bun he prodded the dog in the ribs but it refused to wake up. Eventually he left it and settled at Rose's feet, caught up in the consolation of orange peel, raisins and the ABC's *Evening of Light Classics*.

In the middle of a Mozart clarinet concerto, Bob turned to Nathan and said, 'Hey, I forgot to tell you, I talked to the works manager . . . the top dog, the fella who loaned me the car.'

Rose looked up from a crossword and grinned. 'Always asks your advice, eh, Bob?'

'Sometimes. You'd be surprised who's in my ear.'

Phil put a bookmark in a volume of Robbie Burns. 'You mean you're in *his* ear.'

'Same difference. The thing is, I told him about our little problem and he said, Let me think about it. Well, today he comes back and says, How long till the boy's seventeen? I said, A few months. He says, At seventeen he can sign himself on. I said, I was aware, but can it wait that long? Well, he smiles at me and says, I was wondering, what if we put him down as a work experience student up till then?' Bob was grinning, ready to bust with his own cleverness. 'It's perfect, you can continue with your study and your work but because you're not technically an employee . . .'

Nathan sat on the floor to get at Bob's level. 'But if I'm not an employee I won't get paid.'

'Who's gonna tell the pay office? By the time anyone's caught on you've signed your own papers.'

Nathan started toying with the crusts on his plate. 'What can I say? Thanks . . .'

Phil sat forward, smiling. 'Herr Wilhelm won't say anything if he doesn't know. Tell him they're waiting for his signature, draw it out, make it sound like you're depending on him. Then pow, sign on the bottom line and stuff you Mr –'

'Phillip!' Rose stood up, collected the cups and plates on the tray and said, 'See, Nathan, for all his many, numerous faults, my husband does get things done.'

Nathan breathed deeply and sighed. 'And they'll do this for me?'

'Of course. We're a very practical lot at the Railways, you should've learnt that by now. Always find a way.'

'Thanks, Bob.' And went on to explain, as Phil cracked up, how it wasn't his way to hug another man.

The next morning Bob and the boys started early. Pryor, the mutt, lived up to his reputation and rode the running board all the way up Unley Road as they headed for the hills. When they stopped at the lights the dog jumped off, ran around the other cars barking, and hopped back on just before the lights turned green.

Phil and Nathan fed him Arnott's biscuits as they drove. Sniffing the breeze, balancing and licking crumbs from his whiskers, Pryor was a miraculous sight, full of an endless energy drawn from spring sunshine, yapping enough to drown out car radios.

As they moved into the foot-hills, Bob changed down into third and whispered, 'C'mon, Betsy,' as the engine struggled on three cylinders. Just before Mitcham the temperature gauge moved into the red and he pulled over. Popping the bonnet, he noticed that the radiator had started to steam. 'Who'd pay three hundred pounds for this?' he asked, and the boys had to agree, there were better ways to waste your money. In the end he decided they couldn't risk taking it up into the hills. Luckily Torrens Park railway station was only a few blocks away, and after some discussion, they decided it'd be a waste to turn back now.

As they headed up to the hills in an eight-wheel sit-up, Bob grew concerned about the dog. 'Anyone could stop and steal him.' He moved his rifle uncomfortably across his knee.

'Who steals a dog?' Phil asked, as they passed through tunnels and up inclines.

Nathan surveyed sheer cliff faces which rose above them, dropping occasional chunks of granite and limestone into wire barriers. Caves had formed, each as impenetrable as the memory of Menge's, leading him into a haze of all-things-Tanunda – Lilli, wood sorrel and an over-full septic cart moving down Murray Street.

Early in the afternoon, just as Nathan was imagining the Millerites gathering around Arthur's ark to pray for lost souls, Phil, Bob and Nathan left their gear beside a creek of rocks and soup cans in National Park, setting off on a hike which Bob had promised to use to showcase his knowledge of native flora.

'This one here, a river red gum.'

'Dad, we know.'

'And this one, the golden wattle.'

'Dad.'

'But where have you seen it before?'

'The national coat of arms.'

'Very good.'

Bob managed to find and name the same six plants he'd shown Phil on the same hike eight years earlier. 'And here, xanthorrhoea, or black boy. Look at that seed pod, amazing.' Especially to a man who spent his days covered with grease and smelling of turps, insulating cold rooms in the cathedral of darkness that was Islington. 'Casuarina, known by what other name, Phil?'

'Sheoak.'

'And over there, look, callitris?'

'Native pine?'

'Exactly.'

At three they returned to their campsite and started unpacking. Bob took his rifle and set off in search of rabbit, insisting he could cook the myxomatosis out of anything.

When Phil was sure his father had gone, he unzipped Nathan's bag and retrieved a copy of the *Field Guide to the Agarics* he'd hidden earlier.

'Agarics?' Nathan asked.

'Fungi,' Phil smiled, taking his arm and leading him beside the creek.

Mostly they just found common field mushrooms, their speckled white caps and brown gills bringing flavour to a thousand kitchens of boiled and burnt meats. Although the guide didn't say as much, Phil had been told *Cortinarius australiensis* was the collectors' favourite, laced with a compound resembling lysergic acid and unmistakable thanks to its bulbous base and rust-brown spores. 'We touched on Mycology in first year,' Phil said, as Nathan smiled. In the end they found a specimen which looked close to the one in the book, and since they'd ruled out the poisonous ones . . .

Eventually they found a dozen, took them back to camp and started a fire. Phil crushed them up in a foldaway saucepan and boiled them in water as Nathan kept watch. Hearing rifle shots in the distance, they guessed it was safe.

Phil went first, sniffing and then gulping the brew down in a single swallow. Nathan wasn't so sure, sipping some and spitting it out in disgust. Throwing away the evidence, they settled in around the fire to see what happened.

They closed their eyes and crossed their legs and Phil started reciting the Vajra Guru mantra from a card he kept in his wallet. Before long Nathan broke up laughing, rolling on the ground and intoning Hebrews 13 as a sort of counterpoint: '"Be not carried about with diverse and strange doctrines . . ."' Phil picked up a log and threw it at him, 'Pipe down, God boy, I want to see what happens.' Apart from getting a cramp, the closest Phil came to an hallucination was the memory of Davy Clarke's *In Salzkammergut*.

Bob returned an hour later, minus a rabbit, but with a summons from a ranger for hunting in a National Park. They cooked toast and ate it plain. An hour after dark, as Bob was pointing out the major constellations, Phil complained of a stomach ache and started vomiting. A few minutes later it started to rain. Minus any shelter, they ran back to the station to find they'd missed the last train. 'What we need now,' Phil said, his arms on his knees and his head between his legs, 'is a good dose of Revelations.'

They all laughed, spending the night talking, analysing the Gospels and eventually falling asleep on the benches of Belair station as the rain eased.

The next morning when they got back to the Whippet they found Pryor lying dead on the front seat, his tongue sticking out of his mouth. Bob was convinced he'd left the window down and when he returned the car, later that morning, he told the works manager some bastard must've come and put it up.

Arthur had started off cautiously. On the first day he walked the length of Langmeil Road, turning back before the intersection with Seltzer Road, where the bitumen widened out into a carpark in front of a sprawling reserve of sugar gums the pioneers had forgotten to clear. On the second day he made it down Murray Street as far as Angas Street and on the third, to Burings Road, which was almost halfway to Nuriootpa. On the fourth day, nursing a sore shoulder and blistered feet, he made it as far as Nuriootpa

High School, deciding the only thing limiting his progress was having to return home every night.

So that night he packed a can of baked beans and a bottle of water in his swag and strapped it to the base of his cross. The idea was to start off with an over-nighter, then two, three, four nights, a week, months, maybe years, traversing Chile or Greenland or the United States with his cross over his shoulder.

It was a Thursday afternoon. He'd stopped just an hour before to grease the wheel on the base of his cross, but it squeaked, like the pedal on Edna's old Singer. He adjusted the pillow on his shoulder and reholstered the cross, walking, tripping on fig roots and hidden drains.

Jimmy Hoffmann, a sixty-two-year-old cousin of Pastor Henry who rode his bike between valley towns collecting bottles in a gunny sack, stopped on the opposite verge and called out to Arthur over the traffic: 'Hey, what's that for?'

Arthur turned to him and smiled. 'I carry it for the love of Jesus.'

Hoffmann looked at him, trying to decide if he was genuine. 'Where you going?'

Arthur shrugged. Hoffmann shook his head, re-mounted his bike and rode off towards the Coke bottle paradise of Tanunda. Arthur walked on, whispering to himself, 'For the love of Jesus.'

It had come to him after the split with William. The message was simple: God could be found in olive groves and marketplaces, on the Graetztown Corner, walking beside the stone walls of Henschke's Hill of Grace. These were the places he'd find God, and these were the places he'd go, seeking out people and telling them the News. And in searching these people out, he'd experience his own revelations: baked beans more divine than Bluma's rhubarb crumble, nights as still and peaceful as childhood sleep-outs on the Pewsey Vale Peak. Along the way he could speak to people about *his* God, the god of grace and forgiveness who rode along beside Jimmy Hoffmann, protecting him from moving vans and strays.

It wouldn't be a mission as such. He'd be happy to leave it at a smile or a wave, sharing cheese sambies on the steps of the Seppelt mausoleum. No preaching or using the Scriptures to argue a point. That was the old way. He'd carry his Bible, but that was to pray for the ones who wanted it. 'Give me a dose of the Gospels, Arthur,' they'd ask, holding his hand, seeking consolation from things last heard at the Metho Sunday School. In this way God would travel the valley and beyond, doing what the disciples had done as they wore out endless pairs of sandals. Doing what William had failed to do.

An old Ford pulled up on the verge, chugging uneasily in the afternoon sun. A hand motioned for Arthur to approach and he went around to the driver's side. A small man in a suit and tie looked out and asked, 'You're Arthur Blessitt?'

'Yes.'

'I'm Scholz, Doctor Scholz. My grand-dad had the hospital at Light Pass. Homeopathic. You use Altona drops?'

'Sometimes. Used to be rheumy in the knees, but one day it just cleared up, all of a sudden.'

'Thing is, I got the cancer, in me bowels. They put me in a nappy. I ain't scared to tell you that, Arthur. I ain't scared cos I got Jesus.'

'Amen.'

Jesus, sitting on the torn upholstery beside him, studying road maps and suggesting short cuts, watching his speed and ushering him towards the grave.

'Pray for me, Arthur, pray for me.'

Something Seymour or Joshua or Arthur himself had never asked William to do, although he did it anyway. Arthur put his hand on Scholz's arm and prayed, and when he finished, Scholz put a five-pound note in Arthur's top pocket and drove off without speaking.

Arthur knew he wasn't the first. Years ago he'd read about a fella who'd gone through seventeen pairs of shoes walking through Africa, spreading his message to the lost tribes. He'd been attacked by baboons in Kenya and a green mamba snake in Ghana, chased by elephants in Tanzania and gorged by a crocodile in Zimbabwe. He'd eaten squid in ink in Djibouti as soldiers with machine guns watched him suspiciously. He'd had his cross thrown under a truck and stolen in Capetown. The next morning he'd found the blackened wheel in a cold campfire. But he'd found a carpenter and had another one made, going on to feast on monkey legs in Chad and rat soup in Mozambique. He'd set up in the middle of shanty towns and spewed St Paul in technicolour verse over bemused black fellas with three words of English. Still, this evangelist had believed, watching the sun rise over Mount Kilimanjaro, he was doing the right thing, and would be rewarded.

Misguided, Arthur thought, transmuting the example of Christ into arrogance, telling empty stomachs what they'd done to deserve hunger.

That night he lit a fire in a clearing adjacent to a road-side rest stop. After he'd finished his beans he went for a walk and found a deserted graveyard, the headstones broken and overgrown by weeds. He tried to read the fragments of names and dates, indecipherable apart from *Hier ruhen in Gott* and *Schlafen Sie Wohl*. An impression of a vine-encrusted anchor was still intact, still attached to an ironstone cross as impermanent as his own. Returning to the camp, he cleaned his cross with a rag, so that the inscription he'd burnt into it – *What shall I render to the Lord?* – could be read from a slow-moving car.

He settled into his swag until, just after dark, a moped-riding reporter from the *Oracle* pulled into the rest stop. He got off and came over to Arthur.

'You're the fella wrote that article?' Arthur asked.

'Mr Miller's mission?'

'Yes.'

'I just wrote what I saw. Mind if I join you?'

'No, go ahead, I only have beans.'

'I've eaten.' The reporter sat down, scanning the camp site for copy – narcotics, religious pamphlets, anything. 'I came looking for you,' he said. 'Pastor Henry said you've fallen out with Miller?'

'If that's why you're here – '

'No, honest, I've said enough about him.'

Just then Seymour Hicks' hearse slowed down and pulled over

on the opposite side of the road. Arthur stood up and waved as Chas and David wound down the back window. 'Hello, Arthur.'

'Pull up the window,' he heard Seymour scream, tooting his horn in the absence of a better insult, and speeding off. Arthur sat down, somewhat taken back, staring into the fire. The reporter sat forward. 'Yer not breakin' bread with him either, eh?'

'That's personal,' Arthur replied.

'Sorry. When's their big day?'

'March.'

'You changed your mind?'

'I said I don't want to –'

'Okay. Well, let's talk about this,' said the reporter, pointing to the cross and extracting a notepad. 'What are you trying to say?'

'Nothing. Jesus said, "Take your cross and screw on a wheel." So I did.'

'Jesus actually said this to you?'

Arthur spoke slowly, trying to remain calm. 'No, listen, I know what you're after. Why don't you just say it as it is?'

'Which is?'

Arthur moved about uncomfortably on the ground. 'Yesterday this big fella stops his car and comes over to me. He takes the cross and lays it down and lifts me up in the air by the scruff. I say, "Hey, you look like a big, strong fella, can you help me carry my cross?" And five minutes later he's carrying it towards Springton. We stop at a deli for a coffee and someone has to drive him back to his car. That's what I'm doing. I'm putting up a big billboard, Come Try Jesus! Some people stop and say I must have a lot of guts, but it's not me, it's Jesus.'

'But that's what Mr Miller said.'

'Listen, you don't have to stop if you don't want to.'

They moved onto a discussion of where he'd go next and Arthur explained he was getting tired and might head home for a spell.

'And after that?' the reporter asked.

'Getting my steam up. Maybe head off towards Adelaide.'

'What would they think of you there?'

'Jesus goes everywhere.'

On his way home the next day, Arthur stopped in at the *Oracle*'s offices and had his picture taken in front of the press on which the Millerites had printed their leaflets.

(An irony which escaped him. When William read the article the next day he cut it out and stuck it in his scrapbook, finishing it off with a border of red exclamation marks and the comment, 'Take up your cross?')

Two days later Arthur set off for Adelaide. By the time he returned, six weeks later, he was a minor celebrity, having featured in both daily papers several times, each time with a bigger photo and cornier caption: 'I walk for the love of Jesus', 'Jesus walks beside me on Main North Road'. There was none of the angle they'd tried for in Tanunda, none of the village idiot or religious freak. One mother, having brought her child to be kissed, claimed he was a modern miracle. But when an article appeared claiming he was gaining cult status, he'd decided it was time to head home.

During all this time, William Miller bought the Adelaide papers daily, searching them for any reference to Arthur and reading the articles aloud to Bluma. '"One guy shot at me from a pickup truck. Apparently he missed." "Apparently" – what does that mean, is he trying to be funny?' Snipping and gluing away, trying to make sense of how such an idiot could be so loved.

Nathan Miller read the stories to Bob and Rose, explaining how Arthur used to push him on his swing. One day Nathan set off with Phil to find his old babysitter on Churchill Road. The *Advertiser* had started publishing a 'Where's Arthur today?' timeline, hour by hour, but Arthur had caught on and decided to change his route. The boys waited with a dozen others for about an hour but Arthur was nowhere to be seen.

When Arthur arrived home at last, the Langmeil Elders – along with the mayor, the local, state and federal members, the CWA president and Rotary representatives – started visiting him with presents of yeast and woodworking tools, asking him where he was off to next and if they could walk with him for a way

248

(along with a photographer or two). Pastor Henry claimed it would be good for the church, imagining photos of Arthur and the Elders between the Langmeil pines, proclaiming their faith and way of life and the fact that God walked with *them*. A writer from a women's magazine contacted Arthur asking about perseverance and inner strength but again he just said, 'No, not me. Jesus did this.' (She had no idea what he meant, dropping the story in favour of an 'at home' with Rock Hudson.)

In time it would all die down and he could be off again. This time he decided he'd go somewhere quieter, inland, or the south-east. Somewhere where he could find people who hadn't heard about him, joining him to pray in front of post offices and public toilets.

After Arthur had been home a week he went to sit in the sun on his back porch. His flowers were overgrown and needed harvesting, but all in good time. He looked around and saw William Miller staring at him from across the fence. William bowed his head and walked inside. Arthur could see where the Millerites had worn out the grass worshipping in front of his other cross.

PART

Three

Chapter Fifteen

Summer turned the wild oats golden from St Kitts to the Potter's Field. Down Murray Street the carob trees sagged and fig trees wept, dropping fruit into the back of double-parked utes. Old couples walked slowly, stopping to rest in the shade, to remember the smell of beer-wet carpet from the couplings of the Tanunda Hotel. Dust blew up from between the graves in front of Langmeil, settling across the road and on the grass of the Lutheran school, its sprinklers laying out patterns to nourish weeds along cracked footpaths. In the hospital, wedged between the swimming pool and endless vines, porters wandered basement corridors, hiding in storerooms to escape the heat and smell of boiled cabbage. Bruno and Edna Hermann bought a Kelvinator cooler and hung it out of their kitchen window, shutting their blinds and locking themselves away for days at a time. William Miller, trying to fall asleep with his window open, couldn't ignore the noise, storming onto his front porch and calling, 'Some of us have no choice!'

But the Hermanns were snoring, hermetically sealed in a sarcophagus of recycled air which Bluma could only envy as she lay awake sweating, listening to William pacing the verandah.

Church Avenue, Kilburn, had transformed too. After the first few stinkers, people emerged from their red-brick ovens of an evening, dragging Onkaparinga rugs and carrying teddy-bears and eskies full of Bickford's cordial. Settling in on the freshly cut lawn on the reserve, they shared stories from a long, cold winter – who'd died of what, who'd married who and if it was true that Premier Playford had the cancer. Late at night a few would resort to war songs, remembering the time, not so long ago, when they dug an air-raid shelter where the council had since planted hydrangeas. Eventually everything would fall quiet, the still night filled with the music of crickets and someone's dad jogging home for a trot-stop.

Milk warm in leaky fridges, ice-boxes forever dripping on lino. Houses left open as voices distantly mingled to the tune of a radio someone had set up on the end of seven extension cords. Mo amongst the hibiscus, a sparkling new N-class loco whistling off down the hill towards Islington. And someone saying to Rose, 'That boarder of yours, he don't never go home.'

'I know. His people are zealots.'

Receiving a look of, *I'm sure you know what's best.*

In mid-December, as most of the valley folk were harvesting pines and pickling pig for Christmas, William continued his program of door knocking. On a bright, clear, blue-skyed Tuesday, as the sun warmed the footpaths of Munzberg Court, he walked along in polished black shoes, real leather soles taking the heat up into his feet. Every step was a step closer. Aching corns and doors slammed in his face were a sure sign of salvation. He wore his father's grey suit and a tie Bluma had bought him for their anniversary. Which one, he thought, wood, tin, opal? It was before the war, but after the worst of the Depression. Time was like that, blurring in giant swathes, a million little memories transforming into one, small victories inflating like a prize pumpkin at the Tanunda show.

He opened a gate and navigated a weedy yard, tapping on a fly-screen door which was mostly all holes. 'Hello,' he called, softly, down the hallway.

'That you, Sue?'

'No, my name is William Miller, I was wondering if we could talk.'

He heard furniture shifting and a kettle whistling, the clang of metal and then silence. A budgie, hanging on the front porch, flitted around its cage trying to escape the sun. William took it down and placed it in the shade. 'Hello?'

'I'm comin' . . . is it important?'

'Yes.'

'You're after money?'

'No.'

William sat down on a petrol drum and waited. Time was on his side.

Further up the street, Joshua Heinz stopped, looking at a piece of paper and saying to his youngest son, 'Two more streets, if not we go home.'

'Dad.'

'Two.'

They kept walking, Joshua tapping his pipe on the sole of his shoe, walking, tapping, almost tripping over.

William stood up. 'Joshua.'

'William.'

As the Heinzes joined him on the porch, William set to straightening the young boy's tie. 'Joshua, you told me one o'clock.'

'I would've been. I was stood up. They figure I need their business. You watch, tomorrow there'll be a phone call.' He sighed. 'What you waitin' for?'

William called down the hall. 'Hello?'

'Hold on.' And then came the sound of hammering.

Joshua looked at his son. 'Don't be so glum. What are we here for?'

'Jesus.'

'And what's he gonna do?'

'Save us.'

Joshua spat on a hanky and wiped the boy's face. 'You tell people – '

The door nudged open. A man of about sixty, wearing a singlet and stooping so much he strained his neck to look up at them, shuffled out to the porch and squinted. 'Haven't done a fuckin' thing with this yard. Apologise for the mess.' When his eyes adjusted he looked at Joshua and said, 'Didn't you sell me a car once?'

'No. Maybe it was some insurance.'

'Maybe.'

'You up to date?'

The man laughed and smoothed his singlet down over his belly. 'You gotta be kidding. Does it look like I got insurance?' Taking a moment to look them over, he continued: 'That what you here for?'

William stepped forward. 'No, we've come to talk about Jesus.'

'Fuck. Dunno what's worse. What's the kiddie for? You lot always bring your kiddies. Think we might feel sorry for yer?'

The man walked down his front steps and into his garden. Bending over to pull a thistle he nearly fell over. Joshua took him by the arm and he became defensive. 'Get off. Done alright without you lot up to now. Always round when yer not wanted. Never when yer needed.'

Joshua smiled. 'Mr Grosser.'

But Albert Grosser was bending over to the little boy. 'You talk, or you just for show?'

Joshua's son stepped back and caught himself on the roses. As he untangled himself he said, 'Next March, on the twenty-first, the Bible says these days will come to an end.'

'What days?'

Joshua stepped forward. 'Mr Grosser. I remember I insured your house for fire.'

'And it didn't burn down.'

'It might've.'

'Do I get my money back?'

William pursued him through a hedge of rosemary. 'Mr Grosser, Jesus Christ is *your* insurance.'

'Spare me.'

'Do you deny the truth of Revelations, of the Bible itself?'

'All I know's you lot are never round when you're needed. Just when a man's tryin' to take a piss.' He looked up at William. 'I got your bita paper in me box.'

'Yes?'

'You're a fuckin' idiot.'

Joshua looked at him, picking dead heads off carnations which were nearly dead themselves. 'Albert.'

'It's my fuckin' house.'

William asked him why he was so angry and that's all it took. Albert was off, telling them about the orphanage at Goodwood and the Marist Brothers with their God is Love and their bamboo canes. He showed them an article he kept in his wallet, stolen from the State Library reading-room, yellowing and broken where it was folded, dated September 1893 and entitled 'Baby Deserted'. It told the story of how an unidentified mother had abandoned her baby on the floor of the ladies lavatory at the Royal Adelaide Hospital: a small, hairless male done up in a dress and wrapped in a shawl; and beside him, neatly folded, a pile of new clothes for a baby girl. Albert claimed he could still remember the smell of polished floors and disinfectant, could still see light reflected off polished brass and mirrors, could smell the shit and hear the flush of nearby heads.

'Whoever she was,' he said, 'the one who left me there, chances are she'd be dead by now. Good riddance to bad rubbish. And if some fella put her up to it, maybe God pushed him in front of a truck. God would've punished them, eh?' he asked William.

Who couldn't say yes.

'Exactly. So just leave me with my fuckin' roses. Take the kid next door. That Davies woman'll be eatin' outa yer hand in no time.'

William had his standard argument for this type of situation, but it was no use. Albert had made his choices. A lot more started off a lot worse and still found God. Still, if there were latitudes of Hell, Albert would end up in a temperate zone, fanning himself with the raffia fan of lost opportunities.

Mrs Davies gave Joshua's son a piece of Cadbury chocolate. By some strange arrangement, it turned out she was living with Trevor Streim's uncle. 'William,' the uncle said, standing over him, 'you got bigger worries my friend.'

'How's that?'

'You're out there on Langmeil Road?'

William followed his eyes back across Tanunda. Off to the west a giant plume of smoke rose into the air, mushrooming like a budget Nagasaki, dispersing and blowing back across the town. The bells of the Tanunda fire service rang out from Murray Street and people appeared from their homes to watch. Joshua put his hands on his son's shoulder and said, 'Walk straight home. Tell mum I'm helping Mr Miller.'

The boy headed east, looking back over his shoulder, wondering if this wasn't Mr Miller's apocalypse come early. The two men started off with a fast walk, then a jog, breaking into a sprint as they pulled off their ties and cursed their choice of footwear.

The volunteer brigade, as it was, soon pumped the tanks of their '39 Ahrens-Fox dry. Their leader, a bare-chested Henschke in suit pants and hard hat, ordered Harry Rasch to run a hose back to the closest hydrant in Elizabeth Street. In the meantime, Bluma, Bruno, Edna and Arthur, whose homes were most at risk, helped unload hessian sacks from the fire truck, run them to garden taps and thoroughly soak them.

Arthur Blessitt and Bruno Hermann were soon out with the first line of volunteers, trying to keep smoke from their eyes as they attacked the flames with the bags. Others filled backpacks from the Millers' garden hose, spraying flames twelve feet high which were feeding off the weeds and uncut grass of the Langmeil Road paddocks. A wet winter and a dry start to summer had created the disaster William had predicted. The site of his washed-out rally had become a fireball, filling his home and vineyards with smoke as thick as winter fog on the Kaiserstuhl.

The police, and neighbours from several streets away, did what they could, joining garden hoses like extension cords, filling watering cans and buckets and praying in the traditional Langmeil way. A photographer arrived from the *Oracle* but soon put down his camera in favour of an old bed sheet Edna had soaked in her laundry trough.

William and Joshua jumped across the picket fence and into

the paddock. William took off his jacket and soaked it with a garden hose, starting to beat at the flames which were still burning towards Langmeil Road. Stepping back to get his breath, he looked over and saw Arthur, staring at him, pulling off his shirt and starting in again. William moved up behind him and put his hand on his shoulder, speaking directly into his ear, 'Where are the other units?'

'I called. They're on their way.'

'What happened?'

Arthur shrugged. 'Kids . . .' Throwing caution to the wind and smiling. 'Maybe it's a sign.'

In the smoke and noise William was off guard too, smiling and returning to the flames with his father's jacket. After a few more minutes, Harry Rasch returned, waving his arms, and the appliance's pumps roared to life. Bruno helped a volunteer bring the hose forward and William helped his neighbour pull it across the paddock, freeing it from snags as the flames fell black and smoky in a line not more than fifty feet from their front doors.

By the time the Nuriootpa appliance arrived it was all over, men shaking hands and putting on their shirts.

In the throng of white, sweaty bodies, Arthur stepped forward to talk to William. Whether he didn't see him, or ignored him, Arthur couldn't be sure. But within minutes, as the last of the hoses were reeled in, William walked back to his house with Joshua and Bluma, fire out, all bets off.

Christmas approached. Although William wouldn't say as much, he was lost without the Langmeil community. He felt set adrift without Henry and his knack for organising a committee for this and that, the ladies making Advent wreaths, setting them out around the church with four small candles in the middle, the children weaving garlands from tree branches and flowers which Arthur had supplied: calendulas and lisianthus, gerberas in four colours and bundles of gypsophila. As usual, William knew, a group had been organised for a cooking night at Apex, producing six dozen honey cakes the night before the night before Christmas. All of these parts would come together under Pastor Henry's baton at a Christmas Eve service which was the highlight of the worshipping year. A decent dose of God and the Gospels, a few hymns and then the carols. And then everyone standing and shaking hands and drifting into the hall for supper.

Bluma would be there. Refilling the urn, shooing children from under foldaway tables. Topping up the sugar and milk, cutting coffee cake into generous slices and complaining how Joshua's pipe was triggering her asthma.

But not this year. This year they would have a quiet night.

William would have been climbing a ladder to open church hall windows, rusted shut since the twenties, calling for Seymour to get his crowbar from the car. Working until he had them all open, letting in the breeze, carrying the congregation's voices out across the burnt paddocks of West Tanunda.

But not this year. This year they'd have coffee with the Hicks', wandering home down Elizabeth and William Streets, kitchen flues already smoking in anticipation of whole pigs and lamb, fowl and a side of beef ordered from Linke's last Easter. The smell would pass down hallways and out front doors, mixing with jasmine and tempting them as they walked home. As Bluma thought, Surely we can't sink any lower. Although she could. March 21, 1952. The only consolation was that if *Wilhelm* was wrong, then people might take pity on her, inviting her back to their quilting-bees and coffee clutches.

So they sat around in the Hicks' living-room, dutifully, singing in uninspired, monotone voices: "'O Christmas Tree, O Christmas Tree, Your boughs can teach a lesson ...'"

Mary played piano and Seymour turned the pages. Ellen, William, Bluma and the children sat around them in an arc, Joseph slouching against the kitchen door. Ellen turned and motioned for him to sit down but he shook his head. "'That constant faith and hope sublime, Lend strength and comfort all the time ...'" Eventually Joseph joined in, conducting mock-Toscanini as Chas looked at him and smiled. "'O Christmas Tree, O Christmas Tree, Your boughs can teach a lesson ...'"

William knew this wasn't the time for lessons. As Joseph disappeared into the kitchen they joined hands and William prayed one of his shortest prayers ever, evoking Jesus as a chubby, giggling baby, filling nappies 'just like any mortal man'. He held open a bag and Bluma produced gifts wrapped in plain, brown paper. For the children there were wooden toys: trains for the boys and a stove set for Vicky. 'They won't fall apart,' he promised. 'Not like the stuff you buy these days.'

Joseph opened the kitchen door and walked out into the garden, leaving the dishes half finished. He set off towards the Tanunda Hotel, guessing it was probably closed. Back inside, William presented Seymour and Mary with a leather-bound Bible, inscribed to 'My True Friends', the plural 's' added as an afterthought in entirely different ink.

William walked the Hicks family to Langmeil, up the avenue of pines, past Kavel in his plot, awaiting imminent resurrection from a grave of sandy loam. William wondered if the earth would shake and open up, two hands reaching up as Kavel emerged. William helping him up, dusting down his frock-coat and offering him a comb for his chin whiskers; telling him about Henry and Streim and the others and how things had gone downhill since his time, but how the big fella was waiting for them back at his place on Langmeil Road. Kavel would squint, watch the cars buzz by and wonder why they'd built a zincalume garden shed almost on top of his grave.

Vicky read the inscription on Kavel's gravestone to her brothers, '"He shall stand in his allotted place at the end of the days."' She looked at them as if to say, You don't think Mr Miller's right? After all, if it was written in stone then it must be true, Miss Jacka, their teacher, had told them as much. Why would someone go to all the trouble of publishing something, chiselling it or setting it to music if it wasn't true, she'd asked them. It wouldn't make sense. Therefore the Bible was right. Then the Gurkis boy had asked, 'What about the book that Hitler wrote?' and she'd had to stop and think. 'Readers away. Algebra texts out.'

As the roar of Edna's harmonies filled the church, William shook Seymour's hand and wished him a merry Christmas. The chorus sung an evening hymn and in the stew of voices, William fancied he could pick out, one by one, Trevor and Bruno, Arthur and Ian, Gunther and Pastor Henry himself.

Bluma hugged Mary and almost cried. Mary whispered in her ear and she smiled, sighing, clutching her empty bag and peering inside the church. As usual, there was the Christmas tree, a native cypress which reached up into the rafters. Arthur had built a base and a large wooden frame to support it. His movable cross had been cleaned down and put on the altar next to a list of all the places he'd visited. In the foyer there were photos. But he'd left it at that; if anyone was interested they could talk to him and he'd tell them why he'd done it. One reply and one reply only: For the love of Jesus.

Seymour, Mary, Ellen and her children went into the church. The Millers lingered for a moment then walked off down the hill, through the old graves which William would sometimes stop to read. When they got to the road they held hands and walked home, down streets deserted in favour of worship: Tabor and Langmeil, St John's, Gnadenberg and Holy Cross, each as full as a Catholic school, people celebrating their oneness through hymns, *Silent Night* and *Hark! The Herald Angels Sing*, leaving hot houses full of hidden presents unlocked.

In the reserve off Church Avenue, Kilburn, people sat around on parched, dying grass singing hymns with all the lustiness of the Tanunda Lutherans. They were gathered in what had been shade, although the sun had gone, leaving its heat behind. They were singing *O Holy Night*, Bob Drummond leading them as a sort of spastic conductor. Nathan was matching Rose's lusty alto in the way he used to complement his mother's soprano. Things out of kilter. Finding their own equilibrium beside a hedge of hydrangea bushes which desperately needed dead-heading.

Back in the Millers' cottage, still ten degrees cooler than the outside world, Bluma descended into her cold cellar to fetch meat for tomorrow. Just enough for two.

No cut small enough. Standing beside the pork, holding a knife, she felt unable to go back up to *Wilhelm*.

Meanwhile, Arthur sat on the front pew of Langmeil church holding a long, hollow pipe. Small candles on the Christmas tree would occasionally catch and he'd raise his pipe and blow out the flame. The candles' heat rose towards the ceiling, turning orna-mental wheels of angels circling central stars, a project the kiddies had done after the disaster of Nathan's Sunday School.

Night was invoked with an evening hymn, made lusty by the smell of honey cakes and sausage from the hall. Arthur closed the service, fittingly for many in light of what had happened in the last few months. He told the story of how a tyre company had offered to sponsor him, painting their name on his cross, photographing him holding it as it had a wheel alignment. Pastor Henry knew how to leave his crowd on a high, sacrificing a final benediction in favour of an encore from Arthur.

Bluma came up from the cellar, placed the meat in a pan and covered it. William looked at her and whispered, 'I know it's hard to understand, but these are little things.'

She wiped her hands and said, 'They're not ...' Returning to a vacuum of memories which had overtaken her, trying to find the words, and strength, to explain how she felt. How if they lost Nathan, they'd lost everything. How she didn't care about the End anymore. How even six months ago she could never have imagined it would be like this – Nathan a part of another family, a happier one. She sat down, but none of these words came out. She looked at William and sighed. After a long pause she said to him, 'I need to talk to our son.'

William didn't argue. She stood up and walked out of the house, crossing into Arthur's yard and remembering he was still in church.

William sat silently, still. There was no noise. There were no smells apart from the lingering odour of smoke in their curtains and bed clothes.

Bluma re-appeared in the doorway. She stood staring at him and finally sat down, saying, 'I'll try in the morning ... will you talk to him?'

'On Arthur's phone?'

'We'll find another.'

She saw a piece of paper in the middle of the table. She picked it up and slowly read. It was a receipt for underlay and lino. William said, 'That's your present. I was going to show you in the morning.'

It had been a secret visit to Wohler's, William served by the younger Wohler, the one who'd found Nathan.

William handed him the measurements and he did a quote. 'That's fine,' William said, producing his grandfather's purse, counting the notes and coins.

'You want to pay now?'

'Why not? It's my wife's asthma.'

Wohler wrote a receipt.

'Does that include installation?' William asked.

'Of course ... how's that boy of yours going?'

'He's in Adelaide.'

'Doing what?'

William didn't answer, standing up, folding the receipt and walking from the store. And with that, Wohler knew he'd done the right thing by helping Nathan out.

Back in her cottage, Bluma re-read the receipt but didn't feel as happy as she knew she should have, as she might have a few months ago. She went around to her husband and kissed him on the top of his head. 'Thank you.'

'You need to go select a pattern. Then they'll make a time.'

'Of course. This is a lot of money.'

'You only have one pair of lungs.'

She returned to her seat and made every effort to smile. 'I'll put the kettle on.' William was silent. She fetched the kettle and went out back to the water tank. Standing, waiting, as it slowly trickled, she wondered how long she could be happy about linoleum.

The next morning she went into Arthur's and talked to Nathan for an hour and a half as Arthur topped up her coffee, trying, in his own way, to show her that things hadn't changed so much, that all of William's confusion would sort itself out in the same way that his had. And then Nathan would come home, and they could return to church.

In the way Nathan talked, and what he talked about, she sensed she hadn't lost him. William was barely mentioned and when he was it was in the same vein as an Abbott and Costello film they could both have a laugh about. Rose came on to wish Bluma season's greetings and assure her, not in so many words, that she and Bob knew about the ups and downs of family life and that whatever and however long it took, they were willing to help. 'And anyway,' she concluded, 'it keeps Phil out of our hair. We've never had it so good.'

At the end there were promises of more calls. Nathan said that after March, 'Dad should come good.' Either way, he was happy, healthy, working and earning a decent wage. The rest would work itself out.

Within a week she'd had two more calls and her lino laid. Some consolation for her worst Christmas ever.

Arthur had pinned a map to his kitchen wall. His various journeys were marked in red texta, most noticeably a line which followed the road through Rowland Flat and Lyndoch, Gawler and Elizabeth, down the entire length of Main North Road towards the city. An arrow pointed towards another map, of the city itself, his route pockmarked with little numbers in circles which showed where he'd slept. Corresponding to the numbers were photos he'd taken with his box brownie: road-side rest stops, parklands, the banks of the Torrens on one of Joe Aronson's quiet nights. Each showing Arthur with his cross and sleeping bag, warming beans on a fire or posing with a local, such as the policeman he'd talked out of evicting him from the David Jones carpark. There was always someone willing to take the photo, to stop and talk and share hot, strong coffee.

But Adelaide was ancient history and he knew he couldn't rest on his laurels for long. It was time for another journey. He traced the road north with his finger: Greenock, Kapunda, Riverton, Auburn and Clare. Or whichever detours took his fancy; the destination wasn't so important.

On a Tuesday night, just before the new year, he decided it was time. Packing his few things in a swag, he rolled it tightly and strapped it on his cross. Singing leftover Christmas carols he oiled his wheel, attached a reflector for night walking and gaffer-taped a cushion to the cross's left arm. The following morning he pulled on his long, white walking socks, gym boots, skin-tight footy shorts and polo shirt. Pulling on a terry-towelling hat and coating every inch of exposed skin with zinc cream, he shouldered his cross and set off down Langmeil Road.

Passing the Apex bakery he found Bruno cracking peanuts on a bench, throwing them into the air and catching them in his mouth. Resting his cross and settling down, Arthur asked, 'Edna inside?'

'She is. Where you off to now?'

'Clare.'

'They say it'll be hot before the end of the week.'

Arthur shrugged. 'Packed me Zam-Buk.' Bruno offered him a peanut. Soon it was the best of five, then ten, Arthur dropping nuts but picking them up and eating them anyway. Bruno managed a perfect score until Arthur said, 'Hey, what if your life depended on catching the next nut?'

Bruno looked at him scornfully then tried again. For the first time in three years he missed, his tongue attempting a late save. 'Bloody hell, Arthur.'

Arthur was doubled over with laughter when one of the Angaston Teppers came out of the bakery and said, 'Mr Blessitt, we read about you.'

Arthur smiled and Bruno continued throwing nuts in the air.

266

Mrs Tepper pulled her string bag closed and continued. 'They say you were offered a radio show.'

Arthur smiled. 'I wouldn't know what to say.'

For the second time in so many years, Bruno nearly choked on a nut. Mrs Tepper leaned forward and kissed Arthur on the cheek and said, 'This'll be good for the valley,' and then began to stroke the cross herself. 'It looks bigger in the photos. Is it heavy?'

'Tasmanian oak, but the wheel takes most of the weight. Unless, of course, it's a bad road.'

But Mrs Tepper was lost in the inscription, afraid to ask for an explanation lest he give one. 'Yes, very nice, we have a dresser like this.' Arthur signed her Apex bag and she passed on towards the Black and White.

Bruno said, 'They have no idea. Most of them think you're a bit loopy.'

Arthur shrugged. 'Perhaps I am.'

'One minute they see you with William ... then ...' He threw a peanut at the cross and it hit Arthur's swag. 'Still, I think you got out just in time.'

Unsure, Arthur looked at him. 'How do you mean?'

'Well, how's it gonna look for the kiddies, Joshua's lot, and Ellen's and ... what's his name?'

'Joseph.'

'How's it gonna look after ... the big fizz?'

There was silence for a minute or so, broken by a muffler blowing smoke on Murray Street. Bruno offered him another peanut but this time Arthur refused. 'What if he's right?'

Bruno laughed, putting down his peanuts. 'Those that stay around Goebbels too long will regret it. Them kiddies will be the ones that suffer. I'm not telling you anything new, am I, Arthur?'

Arthur sighed and crushed peanut husks under foot. 'I suppose not.'

'He'll turn out to be one of the worst things that's happened to Tanunda.'

'More than Tanunda.'

'Perhaps.'

At length Arthur said, 'What's happened with Nathan, that's what's got me.'

'There you go. I used to watch you lot, over there on a Saturday, and I'd think, how can they allow themselves to be led? Intelligent people, like Seymour. He's got a diploma in something.'

'What?'

'Electronics . . . or was it floristry?'

Which meant that Arthur knew what Bruno had been thinking about him, and maybe still did. 'I was never comfortable,' he continued, 'but it's always been my weakness, following. That's why I'm gonna keep to myself now.'

Bruno nodded. 'I used to watch you over there, hammering away, building this and that. And then when William spoke, everyone was hushed, and I'd think, Spare me.'

In his defence Arthur said, 'It was a hard business for me to break with him. Our families have been close for years. His dad and mine.' Still, time has a way of fixing these things up, he thought. Looking at Bruno he wasn't so sure others would understand; he might have got out just in time, but apparently he was still tarnished. No amount of lugging around a lump of Tas oak could change that. According to Bruno it might even make it worse.

'People do understand,' Arthur said, wiping dust from his cross. 'They tell me, this is what the preachers should be doing.'

Bruno turned his head and smiled slyly. 'What people say and what they think . . .'

Arthur stood up. He wasn't going to be defeated again, Bruno's lack of faith substituting for William's excess. 'You still on to water my lisianthus?' he asked.

Bruno started tossing nuts again. 'I'll water your lissies.'

'Say g'day to Edna for us.'

'Where'd you say you were going?'

'Clare.'

Bruno smiled and nodded his head. 'They'll find you dead beside the road.'

268

Arthur walked off towards Murray Street, smiling, singing, '"We wish you a Merry Christmas, We wish you a Merry Christmas ..."' Gunther Fritschle, driving his near-new Vanguard ute, crunched gears, sounded his horn and waved. Ron Rohwer, sitting beside Gunther, looked up from tuning the radio and said, 'That man's a marvel.'

Their cabin was filled with the static of the Talmadge Sisters attempting Lerner and Loewe. 'He'll end up with the bucket back,' Gunther replied, watching Arthur stumble in the rear-vision mirror. The sisters started an upbeat number as the Langmeil Elders turned down Hobbs Street towards Joshua Heinz's house. Pulling up in front of number seventeen, Gunther waited for K,K,K, Katie, Beautiful Katie to finish before he switched off the ignition.

Joshua's second youngest ran out and opened the gate for them. 'Are you here to see Dad?' he asked.

'Yes, is he in?'

'He's practising.'

Joshua was halfway through Franck's *Panis Angelicus* when Ron, mounting the front steps, matched him with a harmony of a third. Joshua was oblivious, climbing to the crescendo, '"Hear us, hear us, hear us when we cry to thee!"' Sarah, his eldest daughter and accompanist, struggled to find his variable tempos, tapping out, as she always did, the beat with her foot, calling, 'One two three *and* ...' but eventually giving up. Like Ron, unable to match Joshua's top C with his creaky baritone.

When Gunther eventually knocked he heard Joshua say, 'Bloody hell,' stamping down the hallway and peering out into the light. 'Gunther, Ron, come in.'

Joshua showed them into his study, smelling of port and Butter Menthols, clearing insurance quotations from a sofa and assuring them the chocolate stains were old. A newspaper was spread across his desk, an article on Freddie Bartholomew's lost millions sitting half read under the children's crayon renderings of the Adelaide Baths. 'I can't get Franck out of my head,' he said to Ron. 'I need Harry here, and the other voices, otherwise I get lost. Do you find that?'

Ron smiled. 'To be honest, I don't practise.'

'Neither should I.'

Sarah and a few of the children returned with lemonade. 'The little ones made this,' she said, 'but I can vouch for it.'

The boy who had met them at the gate toppled a glass but Joshua only laughed, passing Sarah the newspaper to blot it. He lit his pipe. It went out straight away and he put it back on his desk.

'You're friends with Bruno Hermann's grand-daughter?' Gunther asked Sarah, although he knew quite well.

'Yes.'

But no mention of Gnadenberg, or Henschke's with its endless stone walls, or how she'd got hold of William's secret and given it to Lilli, Nathan and beyond. 'Mr Miller's neighbour, isn't he?' Gunther asked, probing.

Sarah frowned. 'Who?'

'Bruno Hermann.'

'Yes.'

Joshua was curious. 'Why do you ask?'

Gunther drank some lemonade and said, 'No reason.' But then looked back at the young girl. 'William Miller has some very . . . peculiar ideas.'

She shrugged. 'Are you asking or telling?'

For Gunther it was too much like disrespect, just what he'd expect from a Heinz. Sensing this, Ron Rohwer took over. 'How do you feel about all this business, Joshua? Are you looking forward to – '

Joshua tapped his pipe in a bakelite ashtray. 'Thank you, children.'

After they'd gone, Gunther explained how they'd just been to see Seymour Hicks. How the conversation had started off amicably until they'd mentioned what they'd come for. How Seymour had refused to talk about William or their prayer group. How he was unwilling or unable to discuss what they believed. How they'd said that if an idea couldn't be talked about, then it couldn't be taken seriously. And finally, when they asked him how he'd feel after March, how he'd stood up and shown them the door. 'It was very hard to understand,' Ron explained. 'We just went as peace-makers. Next thing he's slamming the door behind us without so much as . . .'

Joshua looked at them. 'He knew you wouldn't see our side.'

'We were willing to talk.'

'Pastor Henry asked you to do this?'

Gunther shook his head. 'No, just the opposite, he wants to let it all blow over. Only, we don't think it'll be that easy for you and Seymour . . . and your families.'

'Look at Arthur Blessitt,' Ron continued. 'People have already forgotten that he was . . . involved.'

Joshua straightened up a pile of paperwork. 'You've come to talk, or give me an ultimatum?'

'Joshua,' Gunther protested, 'we all know Tanunda, and the valley, and how people think. William will never live this down. He's wrong, and deep down he knows it. He needs others to . . . flatter him.'

'Gunther, please,' Joshua replied, shaking his head.

'I didn't mean you.'

'I'm with William because I believe what the Bible says.'

'But it doesn't say that.'

'Have you ever listened to his explanation?'

'Of course, it's nothing new, people have been playing around with dates for centuries. A hundred and twenty years ago there was this fella in America, said the same as William, managed to persuade hundreds. Most of them sold their farms and came to live with him. No one doubted what he said because he was convincing.'

Joshua sat stony-faced, refusing to do what they'd accused Seymour of doing. Ron Rohwer took out his Bible and turned to Matthew 24, repeating and repeating how the hour and day no man knoweth. 'Look, here, read it. It's what the Bible *really* says.'

'But it says other things.'

'Indirectly. But here it's clear.' Turning to Acts he read: '"It is not for you to know the times or the seasons . . ."'

Through all of this Joshua sat motionless, focusing on a toy stethoscope his youngest had left in his bookcase.

Outside, the Heinz children tuned Ron's car radio, keeping watch for Moses and Aaron and sneaking a few chocolates from Gunther's Old Gold assortment.

'It's a matter of faith,' Joshua said at last.

'That's not the point,' Ron replied.

'It is.'

'We have faith. We believe the Word. But it doesn't mention March twenty-first.'

Joshua started to feel like he was following a script. 'What about the signs?'

'Joshua.'

'The A-bomb?' He knew he was on shaky ground, he only hoped they didn't know about William's scrapbook. 'And what about the Reds, taking over Asia, blowing up temples?'

Gunther sat forward. 'And Mussolini, and Hitler and his gas chambers. Didn't mean the end of the world.'

Joshua stopped, his head full of the images that had got him started. Piles of glasses and shoes, gold fillings and bodies they hadn't managed to burn in time. And in the realisation that life goes on, he wondered whether he had been right. 'What do people say about me?'

Ron sat forward, sensing they were making some progress. 'They say you were misled.'

Joshua took a long, deep breath and then exhaled through his nose. He could smell sausage cooking in the kitchen and hear the voice of his wife Catherine laughing with Sarah. He could see the colour and movement of kingfishers outside of his window.

The children struck gold: Gunther's half-eaten Violet Crumble in the glove box and Rudy Valle on the radio.

Joshua was running through the vines again, slipping in the mud, lying in filth, looking up into the sky through rain and cursing God. For not making things clear. For promising and then taking away.

Chapter Sixteen

Another hot day. Mary Hicks sat in the darkness of her bedroom, her feet in a bucket of water, a vinegar rag across her forehead and cucumber peel on the back of her neck. As she cooled herself with a bamboo fan she longed for distantly remembered gully winds, southerlies come to save them from over the Kaiserstuhl. Shadows and blurred shapes filled her bedroom, light cut into slices, laying itself across near new Berber courtesy of blinds as sharp as the Apex's bread slicer.

In the kitchen a puddle of water sat in front of the Hicks' new all-electric fridge, its condenser broken, wet towels draped across its shiny, new enamel in an attempt to keep their food cold. If only Nathan was still around. That's what the valley needed, she thought, people with skills, skills for the modern age, more electricians and fridge mechanics and less barrel makers and bakers.

Joseph walked in the front door, sweat spreading osmotically from the armpits of his PMG shirt over pockets and through collars. 'Hello.'

Mary sat up, pulling her frock over her shoulders, wondering if she should close her bedroom door. 'That you, Joe?'

'Where is everyone?'

'They've gone out.'

Joseph stepped in the puddle on the kitchen floor and placed his lunch box on the table. 'I was going to take the kids to the movies.'

Mary stopped to think. 'Maybe they forgot.'

'Where did Ellen take them?'

Mary knew how he'd react, she'd seen him growing moodier with the passage of every hot day, saying things he'd formerly left unsaid, like, 'There's no future in this town, if you had any sense you'd get out too, Mary,' although what his plans were she wasn't sure.

'She went with Seymour.'

'Where?'

A dozen places rushed through her head: the Black and White, the supermarket, Linke's, a walk ... but on a hundred degree day? No point. Everyone knew everything in Tanunda, handbills or no handbills. She only risked getting him even more off-side. 'I think they just went to see William.'

No reply. She heard his bedroom door slam and a few minutes later the front door. Waiting until the house was clear and looking in his room, she found his work clothes thrown into a pile in the corner, a bottle of California poppy left open and the smell of Rexona lingering. And in a piece of predictably bad timing, the voices of the children and Ellen and Seymour coming up the street.

Joseph walked down Murray Street towards the Institute. Sitting on a bench beside Wohler's he listened to the rantings of the God-man, Tanunda's occasional speaker on matters theological. Like William, he was a member of no church, but unlike William, he didn't claim to have any bigger or better ideas. He stood before a placard which read, *About 1930 I had a gathering of children at the Nuri high school. Children made decisions for the Lord Jesus Christ. I am wondering whether anyone remembers this occasion?* But if they did, they weren't saying.

God-man was a rarity, appearing two or three times a year, in pouring rain or fierce dust storms, year after year, wondering why no one knew about the children after so many years of asking. 'I just spoke to them and said that if they agreed to believe in the Lord Jesus, to hold up their hands, and many of them did.' Joseph listened to the tone in his voice: like Arthur's, full of longing

274

to know more about Christ. 'I pray for the children who held up their hands, and that they'll keep believing.'

At seven o'clock he passed into the Institute in a better frame of mind. After drinking from the water cooler and wetting down his face and hair, he bought a ticket and went into the hall. Fabric had been taped over the windows and tarpaulins rolled out over the skylights. Despite this it was nearly as bright as outside. Flies buzzed in a low orbit through an ether of rising damp, naphthalene and poppy oil. Families lingered in aisles to catch up as children ran up into a balcony of stored filing cabinets. Joseph sat down in the back on a pew salvaged from Tabor, after they'd gone the way of chrome and vinyl. In his hands he held five paper bags he'd prepared that morning, each with a banana and sherbets, a couple of coconut ice and a Brockhoff biscuit. As the newsreel started to flicker and people scurried to their seats, he opened the first bag and started peeling what would become his tea.

Francis the talking mule, with its stupid voice-over and tormented sidekick, had got them started. But Joe could remember laughing anyway, sitting in the very same possie with the very same brown bags. Chas laughing on Vicky's shoulder, the half fake laugh he remembered all of his kids having. All of them eating their food within the first five minutes and asking for Coke.

This time it was *Francis Goes to the Races*, an even cornier journey into the world of talking animals in which Francis fed his master Best Bets, straight from the horse's mouth. Ten minutes in he was already squirming, having foreseen the ending by an hour or so, consoling himself with coconut ice which rained down like rampant dandruff. As the film continued, he couldn't find anything funny. Without the children there was nothing. Just coconut forming a snowfield on his shirt as life passed him by – Donald O'Connor as the payer of bills, the bringer of discipline and the sorter of mail.

Gags and showtunes were no substitute for family. Things had changed a lot in the last twelve months. The sequel could never match the original, Mickey Rooney would never be as good as O'Connor. This time last summer he'd hardly heard of William

Miller, Ellen was still his wife and his children his children. Now they always seemed to be elsewhere, in spirit as much as body.

Fans clicked away high on the ceiling. The ticket and candy bar girls sat along the back wall sipping lemonade and barley water, wiping themselves with flannels they kept cold in ice-water. Joseph saw the door opening and watched as one of the girls went out, returning with Ellen and the children, Ellen standing in the aisle, searching for him in light that was still too bright by half. Must have picked out my bald spot, he thought, as she ushered the children past knees and handbags, settling them in beside him and sitting at the opposite end. He sent the four bags, minus the coconut ice, back towards her, putting his arm around Chas and concentrating on the donkey's lines.

During intermission the children helped some of the men open high windows with a long, wooden pole. The first smell and light breezes of a southerly change blew in the front doors and fire exits they'd left open. Everyone could sense its approach. In the hall the mood changed from El Alamein to VE Day. Families gathered in clusters and laughter echoed between the Bessa brick walls. Flies retreated to distant barbecues and as the temperature started to drop, top buttons of frocks were done up in a frenzy of shame.

Joseph stood in the foyer biting the edges off a chocolate ice-cream, listening to Ellen explain how they'd only dropped in to pick up some wine. 'You said we weren't going till seven,' she said, putting part of the blame back onto him. What would O'Connor say? What could *he* say? Next it would be, Stop feeling sorry for yourself, making mountains out of molehills. Instead he tried a different approach. 'I spoke to Jim Fairlie today.'

'Fairlie?'

'He's acting manager.'

The shutters were pulled down on the candy bar and the girl pushed the buzzer. Empty paper cups blew in the front door from Murray Street, scraping across the floorboards and coming to rest against the door of the ladies powder room. 'He said I can transfer,' Joseph continued. 'To the GPO.'

She looked confused. 'So . . .?'

'So, we can set up in town. More opportunities in the city.'

'But where do we live?'

'I'll find a place.'

Ellen, caught between a buzzer, Alastair Sim and Chas pulling on her sleeve, could only manage: 'It's starting.'

'They don't show no ads,' the candy bar girl added.

'When?' Ellen asked.

'Whenever we decide to go.'

Ellen knew that there was no use trying to make sense of it now. Within minutes the five of them sat lined up on their pew, licking Choc-Tops which tasted sweeter to the accompaniment of high violins and the credits for *The Happiest Days of Your Life*. Strange, Joseph thought, smiling at Ellen with her face changing through various shades of confusion. Even Margaret Rutherford wasn't enough to cheer her up, eighty-one minutes of wicked school-girl comedy passing like so much Mahler on her father's radio.

The sky finally darkened, thunder crashed in the distance of the Barossa ranges and the audience let out a collective sigh. The wind picked up, blowing dust out of lifeless curtains and triggering an epidemic of sneezing. Moments later the rain started, lightly, and then before anyone realised, blanketing the town torrentially, drowning out Rutherford doing battle with impish school-boys, eliciting a small, miraculous round of applause from an audience in a fantasy of summer-ended, although later they'd realise it hadn't. For the next twenty minutes no one could hear what the actors were saying, but didn't care too much, realising their hibiscus and hydrangeas were getting the soaking they needed. With subsistence came reality and the realisation that the good bits, like film night, were few and far between. It didn't take much to catch up with the plot and when the rain returned in fits and starts no one made too much of it.

At eleven o'clock the lights came back on and people sat stunned in their pews. Standing up they made their way out through the locked up foyer, back onto the street. Walking home down Murray

Street, already dry again, Ellen didn't say a word until Joseph said, 'I have a paid day off on Wednesday.'

'We can all go somewhere,' she offered.

Joseph nodded his head. 'I'm going to Adelaide. Jim's lent me his car.'

'Why?'

'To look for a rental, for us.'

The children ran about on the grass of a small reserve, attempting to stand on each other's elongated shadows from a newly emerged moon. The grass was clipped short and all Ellen could think to say was how much it looked like the Streims' new wool-blend carpet.

'So?' Joseph said, at last.

'This is your ... ultimatum?'

'Ellen, I'm not getting back into that.' Next it'd be how they hadn't planned, or saved enough, or thought through the options. How he didn't realise how good they had it, how happy the kids were, how much they all loved the valley. It was an endless script. 'I've decided,' he said.

'And what about me?'

'Always you. You've never seen my side.'

'I've always defended you, when ...'

He smiled at her. 'I've had enough of talking. I've decided. Next Wednesday I'll find a rental. They'll even pay my relocation. I can start in the city the following Monday.'

Not I can. I will.

'Now you decide. I'm not hanging around waiting for Miller. If you stay, I'll do everything I can to get the kids. I support them, I decide. Okay?'

Ellen had stopped walking. He turned and looked back at her – 'Are you coming?' – and felt her presence a few steps behind him, head down, heard her cursing the rain which had turned their town into a giant pressure-cooker.

The following Friday, just before lunch, Joseph unlocked the door to the Tabrar family's new three-bedroom flat. It wasn't

Elizabeth, but it would do, for now. He opened the windows and walked out onto the back balcony, overlooking the Klemzig Tennis Club and a pair of trotters pacing the track around the GAZA football oval. A group of hausfraus in tennis skirts attempted jumping jacks on the grass, collapsing one by one in Klemzig's version of the League of Health and Beauty.

Joseph came back in and sat on the lounge, hitting it and filling the room with dust. Semi-furnished, the ad had promised. Fully appointed. Just off North East Road. Ten minutes from the city. Serviced by four bus routes.

One of which he'd caught from the city, taking up most of the back seat with his duffle bag as Klemzig Germans chatted in broken English. He was aware of the connection, but time had been against him on Wednesday, and after four or five flats they all started looking the same. This was the area where Pastor Kavel had first settled his boatload of Prussian crackpots, setting them up in the bush beside the Torrens, miles away from the English settlers. Naming the area after his old home-town, he soon had them building wattle and daub huts, thatching roofs and white-washing walls in a down-market fachwerk. Trees were felled and vegetables grown, carried into Adelaide and sold at the markets.

Within a few years, settlement had spread out from Adelaide, along a new road which passed within a mile of them. Kavel took it as a bad sign. Soon his followers would be building pubs and trading all manner of horse flesh on street corners. Maps were consulted and a distant paradise decided upon. Beside the banks of the North Para River he would found a town called Langmeil, with its suburbs of Tanunda and Dorien. Streets would be given names like Sobels and Traeger, honouring other pioneers in a gesture which would last until the Great War, when the trucks arrived with their Anglicised street signs.

Many decided to stay on at Klemzig, having grown tired of Kavel with his endless rantings about the imminent Apocalypse and Saxons and Celts being thrown into a hell of untamed Aborigines and cholera. They grew their vegetables and smoked wurst until they were overcome by the promised pubs and boarding houses which soon ran the length of Osmond Gilles Road.

A hundred years later there were still pockets of Prussia: a few bakeries, a pioneer cemetery with a few headstones of anchors and grapes never grown. Fruit shops and early stone cottages surrounded by fibro monstrosities already cracked down the spine. No one came looking for the Germans because they were too hard to find. If the locals wanted a touch of the Kraut they'd go to the Barossa.

Joseph had caught the bus in front of the Tanunda Institute at eight o'clock that morning, after having dressed and shaved as Ellen lay in bed, refusing to say goodbye or good luck. Eventually he took his bag and whispered, 'Bye.' Waiting and then closing the door behind him. Going into the children's room and waking them up, explaining how they'd join him soon, when everything could be organised. How things would be better in the city, dozens of movies screening day and night, trolley buses and trams, gelati and, best of all, a world without end, where they could study hard and become journalists, teachers, pianists, anything – having their own children and growing old beside a sea of inexhaustible tides. No one in their ears, day and night, telling them how rotten humans were and how the drinkers and laughers and watchers of Francis the mule would all end up in Hell.

He travelled down the road Arthur had walked, past the earth-works of Elizabeth and Parafield Airport with its Viscounts and Constellations, past the abattoirs, the outer suburbs and into the city itself. Getting off in Franklin Street, he asked where he'd catch the 273, and trudged with his bag four blocks to Grenfell Street. Getting on the bus, he realised he didn't have anything smaller than a ten-pound note, running into a deli for change as the driver and a busload of hot passengers waited. They drove past the Botanic Gardens, Collinswood and seventeen stops worth of well-clipped suburbs with their pittosporums and agapanthus, oleanders and multi-coloured gnomes. Getting off at O.G. Road, he headed off towards Klemzig, every bit as much a pioneer as Kavel.

Now, as he nodded off on his lounge, the smell of fresh yeast blew in on a light, warm, northerly breeze. He smiled. That was the hard part done, the rest would be simple. Before Christmas there'd be a car, and next year a house. None of the ironstones and black kitchens of Tanunda. Something modern. Cream brick with a galvanised iron roof, acres of kentucky bluegrass and a concrete footpath. Kids on Malvern Star bikes and church on Sunday, perhaps, if there was nothing better to do.

Wednesday night – two nights ago – flashed back at him. Arriving back from the city he'd taken Ellen into the garden and told her what he'd found. 'It's close to everything, a butcher and a laundry.'

'It doesn't have one?'

'You can sit on the balcony and watch the footy.'

'But it doesn't have a laundry?'

Just as he'd expected. 'The money will still be in our account, every Thursday,' he consoled her. 'Until you're ready.'

'For what?' she'd asked.

'To join me. What else?'

'It's that simple?'

'Yes.'

At which point Mary came out and smiled at them. 'Tea's ready.'

'Coming, Mum.'

'Enjoy your day in Adelaide, Joe?'

'Thanks ... Mum.'

Stirring himself in the half-light of the flat, the smell of yeast gone, staring up at a ceiling of vintage cobwebs, he wondered who would have the most patience. If she'd write him off and refuse to touch his money, asking her father or applying for the Deserted Wives Pension, accepting Sunday collections taken on her behalf.

No. Ellen was more than reasonable. It was just a matter of time. Patience. Patience and the dull thud of the harness racers training in the distance.

Nathan had spent the afternoon diagnosing sick fridges, testing the pressure inside evaporators to see if sulphur dioxide was evaporating in the coils, absorbing heat and cooling the cooling box. Other times the problem was in the motor, or the pump, or maybe just a faulty seal on the door. Like a doctor he had to recognise the problem instantly, taking in the symptoms with a look of confidence, shaking his head and reaching for his tools.

He knocked off at three o'clock and walked towards the main gates with a hundred others: grease smeared through hair and over work clothes wives wouldn't let them wear inside, dropping them on back porches and throwing them into laundry troughs. Men snapped satchels onto the back of old bikes and rode off down Churchill Road, fresh air in their lungs and light in their eyes, stopping to buy stamps and ciggie papers at the deli. Men who'd left brushes soaking in turps until tomorrow, until the continuation of the endless cycle of broad-gauge axles and boiled cabbage.

Nathan felt one of them now. A work-experience student and a veteran all at the same time. He knew what they meant when they talked about the Garratt 409 or an eight-wheeled compo brake, knew the smell of ammonia better than a wash-house full of freshly pressed shiraz, the taste of cafeteria stew better than bratwurst.

As he walked through the gates he heard a familiar voice. 'Nathan.'

Looking around there were just overalls and lunch-pails, the sweet ether of body odour and the din of men moaning.

'Nathan.'

Lilli fought her way through the slow tide of bodies and stood before him. 'Guess who?'

'Christ.' He grabbed her arm and pulled her towards a bus stop of waiting men. 'What are you doing here?'

'I live here,' she replied.

'Where?'

'Prospect. Just up the hill.'

He stopped to let it sink in. 'Since when?'

'Two weeks, just over.'

The first thing he thought of was the night in the ruined farmhouse, but then the threat she would pose to his new life – uncomplicated relationships with uncomplicated people, resurrected wheelchairs, the smell of antiseptic on Rose's tunic and sleepouts in the Church Avenue reserve. A few men at the bus stop looked at him. So what, she could be his sister. He turned away and faced a peppercorn tree. 'How did you know where I'd be?'

'I rang.'

She turned back and fixed the men. 'Five quid, the full hour.'

'Christ.' He took her arm and dragged her along as she laughed. 'How about a simple hello, how y' been?'

She re-claimed her arm and stopped in the middle of the footpath. 'I've come to apologise.'

'For what?'

'Which way?'

He pointed up the hill and they crossed the road, Lilli stopping to smell unfamiliar plants. 'It's obvious, what happened in Krautland,' she said. 'It wasn't me at my best.'

He thought of their final meeting at the railway station. 'You'd rather impress, what's her name?'

'As I said, not me at my best.' With an I-shan't-say-it-endlessly tone of voice.

'And that's it?'

'Now I'm a city girl. I'm not out to impress anyone.'

He looked at her out of the corner of his eye: head down, thoughtful, dragging her feet as usual. If it took six years to prove yourself to the Railways, perhaps he could try again. Faith. Maybe even a little of William's grace. It would end disastrously, of course. Lilli couldn't stop being Lilli, there'd be someone else, a time she could get a laugh at his expense. Then again, maybe one day she'd be an asset, a good mother, feeding him through an old age of dementia and wet nappies. Faith: like God promising to reveal the scheme of things to William, but only if he worked at it, studied, invested time and love in the satellites which orbited him.

'So where are you living?' he asked.

She stopped to study a stobie pole. 'My cousin Nerida, the forty-one-year-old teenager. She wants us to go out together. Apparently this will enhance our chances of finding a man.'

'How's that?'

She walked on, avoiding dog shit. 'Maybe she thinks I'll make her look younger.'

'Unlikely.'

They sat in the reserve and she took out a pack of Craven A. Lighting up she stretched out on the bench and blew smoke into the air, talking like Bette Davis. 'Yes, quite frankly, the Fechners were sad to see me go. Like you, I'll be sorely missed in Tanunda. An artist has been commissioned to render a likeness which will be placed in the Town Hall foyer.'

They laughed about Goat Square – and council workers pruning carob trees to within an inch of their lives, Mrs Fox and her flying fingers, Edna and her rheumatic Bach. Nathan detected a slight fondness in her voice, but certainly not a longing to return. 'You should hear how people talk about your dad,' she said.

'Yeah?'

'What do you think will happen, afterwards?' she asked.

He shrugged. 'Who cares?'

'You do.'

'He'll find some way of explaining it. The dates were off, or maybe because people didn't believe him.' He raised a fist in the air, William's fist, shaking with the knowledge of every verse from Hebrews. 'But it won't be his fault. That's why everyone thinks he's a nut. My dad the nutcase.'

She smiled. 'Do you think this could be inherited?'

He stood and walked towards number seventeen. His new home. 'Come on, I'll introduce you.'

Rose's note explained that she'd be back late from the hospital. There were chops ready to go, if they knew how to turn on the grill. Lilli sat at the kitchen table and he made her a milky coffee. 'This kitchen is very ... chrome,' she observed.

'Courtesy the Islington Depot. You'd never guess, eh? Better than Wohler's. Anything you want, they've got someone who'll make it. Carpenters, electricians, plumbers. Sometimes they make trains.'

'And what about fridges, you like fixin' fridges?'

'It's like selling bread.'

'Really?' She lifted her eyebrows, but then backed off, and Nathan could sense small victories.

'You working yet?' he asked.

'No.'

'What y' gonna do?'

She shrugged. 'Next year I'm going to study. Till then, I'll find another Apex somewhere.'

Nathan smiled. 'What you gonna study?'

'What do you mean, what am I gonna study? Something smarter than you, dumbo.'

'I got to Matric.'

She laughed, gagging on her coffee. 'Almost.'

'Very funny. And look how things have worked out.'

Again she retreated into her corner. 'True . . . and d' you know, *you* put the thought in my head.'

'What?'

'That y' gotta get out of that place. Five years too late. But . . .' She picked a pile of papers from the table and started reading.

The Revelation of Phil Drummond. Chapter 1. B. Grable was in the form of God, and God was good. Grable sat in a cubicle in the law library toilets and scribbled, Beware the Prophet Muller, for Muller is the devil incarnate. Muller rises from the earth with scrotums hanging heavy like watermelons.

'Is this yours?' she asked.

'It's Phil's.'

'It's fantastic.'

He shrugged, sipping his coffee. 'He reckoned he could do his own Revelations, better. One that made sense.'

Chapter 2. There were seven singers singing and one of them was Nat King Cole. Unforgettable, he promised, spreading the prophecy of the End of Days as related by Muller-Satan. Perry Como and The Chordettes sung for Grable-God. Let's get back, to the track where it all began ... The forces of good and evil battled until they became a cacophony, filling the sky with white noise which sent people scurrying to their closest League of Health and Beauty meeting.

She looked up at Nathan. 'What an imagination.'

And then he knew he'd got it wrong, introducing Phil to Lilli. Now there was no turning back. Still, he thought, Phil would probably see right through her. Or more likely it would be a case of nitro and glycerine, exploding, spreading human debris the length and breadth of Kilburn.

She continued reading aloud. '"Chapter three. Two angels came out of the sky. One was called Lewis, and one Martin. One fed lines and the other got laughs. They hovered above Grable's cubicle and Lewis asked, What message shall we give the people? Martin clunked him on the head: You don't talk to God like that. How then? Lewis asked. You say, Mrs Grable, your Holiness ... Eventually God got them to shut up and said, Spread the word, the world won't end, and all those who believe it will are klutzes. Furthermore, the Bible itself is a second-rate story, B-grade every word of it. Where in the Bible do you get a decent kiss? God was cut short by Phil Drummond entering her cubicle and dropping his pants."'

The story continued over four pages, describing a heaven carpeted in Axminster. Hell, meanwhile, was brimming with evangelical preachers who nightly burned large piles of Golden Voice radios on bonfires. Through all of this the angels Lewis and Martin travelled, pleading with the fallen to see their latest movie. The saved were warned not to get smug, sharing their Bush biscuits around a fire of sing-alongs.

'"Chapter twenty-eight,"' Lilli continued. '"The seven seals were cryptic toilet graffiti. As Grable explained them to her prophet Drummond, he wrote them down in a big, black book. Later he planned to spread this message far and wide. When she got to the seventh seal she trembled and refused to speak.'"

She looked at Nathan. 'Have you read this?'

'Yes.'

'And it doesn't bother you?'

Nathan shrugged, reaching over to the valve radio and switching it on. 'You'd have to know Phil to understand.'

She read again as Mick Harrison's *Music from the Archives* emerged from the static, Karajan wrestling with Orff's *O Fortuna*, filling the lounges and sitting-rooms of the suburbs with thunder. '"Chapter twenty-nine. What is it? Phil Drummond asked. Grable looked at him. I was wrong, she said. With the seal cracked, the heavens opened up. Agnostics and atheists levitated, becoming caught in a vortex which sucked them into a heaven of bookshops and jazz clubs. When only the pious were left, a giant monkey appeared with its own box organ, turning the handle and grinding out choruses from *The Whitehorse Inn*. The voice of August Kavel thundered across the sky, saying, The seventh seal explains how we will all be punished, for being so gullible.'"

As the last chord of Orff's music thundered and finally crashed to earth, she flung her head back and her arms out in a perfectly timed gesture. 'Nearly as good as being there.'

They sat listening to Mick Harrison's well-oiled voice introducing Dame Nellie Melba singing Puccini's *Donde lieta usci*. Violins, muted through time and static more than anything else, cut through the emptiness of the airwaves to tempt Melba to life – a sweet, single note, then others, unfolding into a tapestry of increasing orchestral density. A cough in the background, a bassoonist turning the page, and then Nathan and Lilli were both involved, the key suddenly modulating to indicate some drama they couldn't see. And then a single note hanging, and another, another unexpected change of key as the flutes and piccolos jumped about pizzicato. Silence. Melba musing, the low strings finishing her sentences with a single, dotted note. A clarinet following her voice, renewed and optimistic, into another sprawling verse of musical dementia.

Lilli stood up, faking the words, her left arm floating in front of her. She was a Lady Macbeth in polyester, caught up in other worlds, a little of the B-grade romantic lead laced with a dimly remembered high school understudy opportunity which never came off. But that was the power of music, to make her Mimi, or at least stop her from being Lilli.

As the flutes and clarinets joined forces to rehash motifs from the opening arias, Lilli approached Nathan and knelt at his feet. He smiled, and as the violins rose chromatically, she put her arm around his belly, resting her head above the gurgle of a near-empty duodenum. The music stopped and started again in another key, and Lilli stage-coughed her way down centre towards a hall table of Rose's Aboriginal artefacts. The violins threw her back towards Nathan with such force that they both went flying across the Drummond rug, settling beside a carpet python made real in late afternoon shadows. She kept mouthing the words, stopping to kiss him and move her hand down over his chest, pulling at his Railways shirt and seeking access to his grey, cotton-blend work pants.

There was little of the operatic to what followed. Shirts torn off, pants down around their knees. Mick Harrison, recovering from his own swoon, returned to the airwaves dispensing endless praise, corny but at the same time heart-felt. Mick said he'd only ever felt this way about one other woman, Callas, in whom he'd come to see utter perfection. He moved them onto Mozart's *Marriage of Figaro* overture, violins buzzing like frenetic termites before a series of drum-beating climaxes, settling in for another go, and another, louder and faster in the hands of Karajan.

This time there was no rubble to contend with, only a few disinterested flies settling on the rims of coffee cups. Apart from that the choreography was the same, Lilli clawing at chair legs in anticipation of kettle drums and cymbals, unsettling one chair, oblivious to it crashing across her legs; Nathan returning to a warmth and wetness which seemed simpler the second time around. He felt proud of his ability to keep going, to play out a whole scene where he had most of the lines but few of the laughs. After he'd finished he rolled off of her to the tune of Chopin's *Waltz in C sharp minor*, more cerebral than anything they'd heard that day, but not enough to stop her climbing back on top of him.

Timing. Nathan heard the letterbox clatter and sat up. 'Shit.' Grabbing their clothes and switching off the radio, he led Lilli to his bedroom and closed the door. They waited in silence, pulling on their clothes as quietly as possible, listening as Rose pushed the front door open, entered cautiously and called, 'Hello, Phillip?'

Lilli started laughing. Nathan covered her mouth with his shirt. 'It's me, Rose,' he called, 'I'm just getting changed.'

'Good-o.' A clatter as she picked up the chairs. 'You alright, Nathan?'

'Fine . . . thanks.'

Lilli laughed harder, muffling her face in Nathan's pillow as she stretched out on his bed. He walked across the room and opened the window, checking outside and whispering, 'C'mon.'

'What would you rather for tea, Nathan, chops or veal cutlets?' Rose called, looking at the two cups of warm, half drunk coffee on the table as a pair of flies fucked.

'Chops,' Nathan said calmly, as he crawled out of the window, imagining Rose with her ear to the door. As Lilli passed her body out of the window without a word, he stuck his head back in and called, 'Might have a quick snooze, if that's okay?'

'Fine, I'll call you when tea's ready.'

Rose stood listening to the window close, and then silence. She returned to the kitchen, clearing the cups and thinking, Stupid woman, too much time with my nose in other people's business. Smelling the antiseptic on herself she pulled eight potatoes from a box and started peeling them.

A few minutes later Phil came home, carrying a bag of books, trying the door to his room. Rose looked up from laying out chops on the grill. 'He's asleep.'

Phil smiled, 'Yeah?' and went in anyway. Looking out of the window he could see movement behind the pittosporum hedge behind Bob's shed. He could see a pair of ankles highlighted in front of the compost heap. Smiling, he settled in to watch, whispering, 'You dirty little bastard,' filling in the blanks he'd learnt from a gallery of Barr Smith graffiti.

Chapter Seventeen

Warm, but with breezes off the Southern Ocean, laying waves across tall, dead grasses, stirring dry leaves on carob and plane trees the length of Murray Street, sounding like sea shells strung on fishing line, bouncing off of each other like atoms in a piece of hot copper.

Early February, momentary relief as people opened windows and stretched out on parched Buffalo, sprinklers hissing valiantly in the early afternoon sun. The scent of freesias and jasmine sustaining parched gardens. William walking along, carrying a pile of hand-written handbills, stopping to clear lavender from the mouths of letter-boxes, folding and depositing them. Passing on with satisfaction, with the knowledge that it was the only way they'd listen.

Word had got around. Door-knocking had become a comedy of slammed flyscreens and hidden resentments, people fleeing half-pruned hedges as he approached. And even if they did listen, they were just being polite, excusing themselves to save burning sausages he couldn't smell. Eventually he started keeping a tally in a notebook: over three days he averaged a five per cent strike rate (people who had actually listened) – zero if he counted follow-ups. Still, when the Lord asked what *he'd* done to prepare for the thousand years, he'd be able to say more than just stockpile groceries and plant vines.

On the corner of Homburg and Cochen Court he folded his last handbill and deposited it. That was the last of last night's batch of fifty, hand-copied at his desk as Bluma kept him in coffee, eventually settling in beside him, taking a piece of roughly torn A4 and copying.

I, Wilhelm Muller, have lost several followers. People no longer able to hear the Word. The only one who stays with me is Seymour Hicks. The flower man has gone, the insurance seller. The mail-sorter, who I'd never seen pick up a Bible. None of this deters me, for the time is close at hand. I have proof if you'll only come see me, talk to me. At the End I won't be able to help you. Can't close the gates after the horse goes.

Re-read Revelations. This is your insurance. It's free. You will need it. I am not the loopy-loo my enemies suggest. I am a simple farmer with not much land. I have never made much money or held much influence.

Please. It will be as sudden as a flash of lightning.

To one lady who'd listened he'd conjured up a scene of Monday wash-day, reaching up to peg one of her husband's shirts when bang, like a shot from a .303, looking around but feeling herself dissolving between the cracks in the concrete path beneath her Hills Hoist. No, he said, Jesus won't have time to form tribunals, trying individuals in the manner of Nuremberg. That would already be worked out, people marked with invisible crosses on their foreheads, crosses that he, Wilhelm Muller, had the ability to see and wipe off with a rag and a bottle of God's own metho.

That night they copied another fifty and the next day, as the southerly dropped and the temperature jumped another ten degrees, he set off again. Birds retreated into the deepest parts of trees, managing the occasional note which split the silence of empty streets. People stayed in their stone homes, hibernating, shutters drawn and knocks ignored over the hum of fans. William wondered whether he should be catching the train to Adelaide, blitzing suburbs full of folks who hadn't yet heard of him and weren't yet familiar with his knock: four hard raps, like Death in a mask, scratching his chin whiskers in a frenzy. But like the

Watkins and Rawleigh man, you had to work your own turf, the day was only so long.

Out along Para Road the footpaths turned to dolomite and the houses became sparser. William kept trudging, reading his own pamphlet, *The flower man has gone, the insurance seller.*

Joshua, too gutless to tell William himself. Instead, as William had been told by Seymour, turning up on the Hicks' doorstep and asking Seymour for a walk.

A slow walk, during which they kept stopping and starting, picking daisies from hedges and admiring impatiens flourishing in full sun. Joshua started by saying, 'I can't tell William. I was hoping you'd understand.' Seymour by-passed the whole conversation Joshua had planned and asked, 'You had a visit too?'

'Ron and Gunther? Yes, but it wasn't just that.'

'So?'

Joshua tripped on the root of a bottlebrush. 'He's probably right ... but I don't feel like it's going to happen, now. I mean, look around you, all of this has been here forever. Why now?'

'Why not?'

'And then they told me about this other fella in America.'

Seymour walked on with his hands in his pockets. 'Exactly the same speech they gave me. They'd spent a bit of time cooking it up, but so what? They don't believe, we do.'

'I dunno, Seymour.'

'There's probably been a hundred people said the same thing in the last two thousand years. Difference is, they didn't know the things we do. See, it's like Hercule Poirot. Book starts with a murder. Who knows who did it? No one. Then we get the clues, everyone starts to have an idea, but only the clever ones work it out. Most people only know at the end ... few people work it out just before, that's William.' He looked at Joshua. 'I'm not going to convince you, am I?'

'No, I don't think so ... no you're not.'

'Well, that's that then. It's a pity – you might doubt William, but there were never times like this, Joshua.'

Joshua looked perplexed. 'Maybe there were.'

'There were rotten bits here and there, but never the whole planet. Just about to go up in a mess of bombs. If you ask me, that's how it's gonna happen ... bang!' They walked on quietly for a few moments, and then Seymour said, 'The thing I don't understand, is how you could believe in something so important and then ... not believe.'

Joshua shrugged. 'It's just how I feel. Maybe I was swept along a bit. Either way ...'

Seymour thought of the implications of this for him: the most gullible would stay the longest, caught up in the gravity of the Supernova Miller. Maybe he too would eventually succumb to the stronger gravities of common sense and the minor stars Hoffmann, Streim and Doms.

Joshua left Seymour at his front gate. Waiting until he'd turned the corner, Seymour got into his hearse and drove to William's, knocking, entering and finding him asleep on the back porch. Waking him up, he told him how he'd come on behalf of Joshua. William knew straight away what he meant, containing his anger, offering him a lemonade and asking for the details.

Seymour left as the sun set, explaining how he'd never trusted Joshua anyway, and how in *him* he had a faithful disciple right up to, and including, the final moments. After he'd gone, William went into his study and started tearing paper into pamphlet size pieces, taking his pen and writing, *I, Wilhelm Muller, have lost several followers* ... Explaining to Bluma how they would hit the letter boxes again, tomorrow morning, and would she mind fixing some coffee.

William sat on a fallen log at the far end of Para Road. He took off his shoes and socks and rubbed his bare feet on the stubble of last winter's vetch and barley. He was surrounded by empty, weedy paddocks, rusted car bodies overgrown beside tractor spares and piles of tyres no one would ever use. People still hoarding, when they should have been giving everything away.

People unwilling to be convinced. Waiting around for a hell of barbecue forks stuck eternally up their arses.

Blood rushed to his head and he steadied himself. He lost his balance and almost fell back over the log. Wouldn't that be funny, he thought, beaten to the prize. But pleasant in its own way, not having to stick around to suffer the politics and personalities, martyrdom narrowly avoided, death by slammed doors and shiraz returned to his doorstep. A dozen bottles in total, appearing in the mornings like rolled-up *Oracle*'s, protests from people whose disgust he couldn't begin to comprehend.

He fell forward, clutching the log and listening to his racing heart and uncontrolled breathing, spreading his hands out on the earth and steadying himself. And then whispered, '"It is also taught among us that out Lord Jesus Christ will return on the last day for judgement."' Becoming louder as he became more aware that he wasn't going to die, ever. '"To give eternal life and ever-lasting joy to believers and the elect but to condemn ungodly men."' Stopping, like Melba herself, on a high, loud note. Spitting into the dust and catching his breath.

He walked home slowly, deciding he'd try again tomorrow. Hoffman and Weinstock Streets, Second, Bridge and Bilyara. Then he noticed a figure walking behind him, calling, 'William.' William walked faster but the figure responded, breaking into a trot as he turned into Langmeil Road. The figure was closing, 'William, I just want to talk to you.'

Maths was on his side. Unless Joshua sprinted he wouldn't catch him. William walked through his front gate, up the path and in the front door, locking it behind him and collapsing on the floorboards he'd watched his father replace when they were eaten out by termites.

Bluma came up to him, kneeling down. 'What's the matter?'

'Ssh!'

They sat silently as Joshua came up their steps and knocked on the door. 'William, I want to talk to you.'

Nothing, only the smell of disinfectant from Bluma's freshly mopped lino. William moved his lips close to Bluma's ear and whispered, 'He chased me halfway across Tanunda.'

'If you don't stop delivering those pamphlets I'll take legal action. This could affect my business.'

William couldn't help it, calling out at the top of his voice, 'It's the truth.'

'I could say things about you, William, but I don't. I could go to the newspapers.'

'Feel free.'

Indeed, William thought, they'd soon be coming to him, asking for a quote or two, waving a few pounds in his face or maybe a year's free subscription.

'William, listen,' Joshua continued, 'think how you'll feel after March. You're making it hard for yourself.' As he had for others, testing and rejecting them like sardines in a cannery. 'Think of Bluma . . .'

William didn't reply.

'What if you kept it to yourself and came back to Langmeil? People would forget. You've gotta have a bit of faith, no one's set out to make it hard for you.'

Nothing. After a few more seconds of mutual silence, Joshua walked off. William opened the door and let some air in, returning to his study to continue transcribing like a monk.

William's father, Robert, had once told him that no piece of paper could be folded more than seven times. By this, William took it to mean that once something had got so bad it couldn't get any worse. From then on, any time either of them were in a spot (such as the time Robert was caught baiting the local tabbies) his father would look at him and say, 'Seven times'.

William could count more than seven, probably more than seven hundred, this time around. As a result of his betrayal at the hands of Joshua-Judas, he started to believe that things were about to turn a corner.

Arthur Blessitt had also started thinking this way. With his reintegration into the Langmeil community, his brush with minor stardom, his feeling of renewed vigour and energy and purpose, he'd come to believe he'd won the lotto of personal happiness. Nothing could stop him now, barring a heart attack or runaway truck, and even these could be seen as part of God's grand design.

But for both men there was more to come. For Arthur this realisation began the day after Joshua turned up at William's front door. He'd just completed his walk to Clare, stopping in at the Tanunda Club on the way home for a celebratory Southwark beer. He soon had a small group listening as he described the high-lights of his journey: a night spent with the Brothers at evenhill, tasting sweet altar wine into the wee hours, a photo opportunity with the mayor, a complementary meal at the Miner's Hotel and three blissful nights spent sleeping under the monkey-bars in the Rotary playground.

Then there were the bits he didn't mention. The swaggie he'd approached on the road between Auburn and Riverton, asking him, in an uncharacteristically evangelical tone, if he'd accepted Jesus as Lord and Saviour. The swaggie dropped to his knees and asked to be prayed over. Arthur put down his cross and obliged, putting one hand on his matted hair and lifting the other in a sort of slow-motion seig heil. Minutes later the swaggie stood up, took out a thick wad of bank notes and stuffed five hundred pounds into Arthur's pocket. Arthur gave it back and they sat down to discuss everything from Genesis to sago pudding. In time it got dark. They lit a fire and brewed tea which they drank sweet until three the next morning, blocking their ears every time a truck rushed past. The next morning when Arthur got up the swaggie was gone and the money back in his top pocket. Arthur wondered whether it wasn't the swaggie's way of unburdening himself. Either way, he used the money to shout drinks at the club on his way home. Surely he'd won the lotto, he thought, and others thought. Or the Bingo at the Nuri RSL.

He came out of the club half-pickled, the night still warm and light. As the door closed behind him, muffling the din of laughter he was responsible for, he walked over to the bench where he'd left his cross, breathed deeply to clear his head and stood motionless.

Gone. There was no doubt. That's where he'd left it.

Logic. Someone had moved it, to keep it out of harm's way. He looked down a side-alley, behind the club (where the Apex girls got their free grog), back up along Murray Street and over into the reserve. He sat on the bench to think. Other explanations. He popped across the road to a shop to ask if they'd seen anything. He returned to his bench. His next thought was the local kids, playing a prank. If that was the case it would turn up again somewhere, sometime, perhaps. Then there were the farmer's sons with their utes or fellow parishioners from Langmeil having a joke. The fellas from the pub keeping him busy inside while some of them popped out to move it.

Or William. Surely not. He didn't have the cunning, or the agility, to whisk it away unseen. But then again, he could've arranged for it: Seymour, Ellen's kids . . .

Either way, there he was, without his cross. If it was gone it was gone. The worst thing was the suspicion the theft would leave. Tanunda becoming like some parts of the city he'd passed through, where people had warned him to sleep with his cross tied to his leg.

He went back to the front bar of the club and screamed out, 'My cross is gone.' A hush, just in case another round was involved. 'It's been stolen,' he whispered, and everyone heard him. One man said, 'It'll turn up,' and in these words Arthur heard the promise that it wouldn't.

He asked for a pen and paper, writing a note and pinning it to the hotel notice-board, complete with a sketch of the cross and an approximation of the tyre tread. He returned to his bench outside, asking people who walked past, 'Have you seen my cross?'

The tourists had him figured as the village idiot and Ellen Tabrar, returning home with Chas and a string bag full of groceries, stopped to ask what was wrong. Eventually he said, 'You don't think it was William, eh?'

She leaned back and almost laughed. 'Arthur, he doesn't have to try that hard to make enemies.'

'No, I didn't think so.' But the thought persisted, as he walked home with his head bowed, as though he might stumble across a clue: a tyre tread, an unwashed sock. Arriving home he took off his shoes, climbed into bed and fell asleep without so much as switching on a light.

But there was worse to come for Arthur. His nose tingling as he woke the next morning to the sound of rustling pampas grass outside his window. He pulled the window closed, blew his nose and stepped out onto the back porch.

Dead. Half a paddock of lisianthus Bruno had promised to water. He ran out in bare feet and flannelette pyjamas, kneeling beside the white, purple and mauve flowers. Whole rows, with a few valiant plants surviving here and there, others already brown and broken, lying flat in the dust. He ran back and turned on the irrigation tap but nothing happened. Fighting through an outgrowth of wild, dense lantana, he eventually found the isolator and turned it back on. Water slowly started flowing between the rows, gathering dust and turning it into a stream of mud.

He stood up and turned towards William's house. Various thoughts passed through his head and he nearly called them out. Instead, he walked over to Bruno's house, knocking on his front door and reminding himself not to become emotional. 'Bruno.'

'Arthur, you're back. How was Clare?'

Arthur put his hands on his hips. 'Fine, until I had my cross stolen.'

'No, where?'

'Bruno, my flowers.'

'I couldn't get any water. I looked everywhere for the stopcock. I was going to call the water people but the flowers looked okay. And Edna said you'd be along directly.'

Arthur sighed. 'Someone turned it off.'

They both looked over at William's place. 'You don't reckon?' Bruno asked.

Without a reply, Arthur walked out of Bruno's yard and followed the path up to William's front door. Knocking, he called out, 'William, do you know anything about my water supply?' There was no reply and he knocked harder. 'William!' He looked over at Bruno, watching from his front porch. 'Thanks anyway, Bruno,' he called, 'at least some of us still try to live as neighbours.'

Bruno waved and went back inside, unwilling to become more involved, lest William become more irrational. He'd read about such things in the city: neighbours building high brick fences or filling their yards with barking dogs, playing Beethoven until four in the morning or burying broken glass in vegetable patches.

Arthur went home to check his carnations, which had fared better. He pumped the soil with water until it would take no more, emerging from his house every hour or so to check his lisianthus, looking over to William's vegetables and well-watered vines and trying to remind himself that he was still a Christian.

There were other possibilities: kids again, or locals playing a joke, maybe someone responding to the publicity he'd brought to the town. But Arthur had never had a single enemy, let alone such an organised one. If he accepted that it was malice then he'd have to start installing locks on his doors, fencing his flowers with wire and buying a guard dog.

The next morning, when William came out into his back-yard, he found Arthur's cross lying on the ground, cut neatly with a saw at ground level. He walked over to his fence on Arthur's side and called out, 'I didn't touch your water.'

Arthur lay in bed smiling, wondering what would come next. In time William went in for breakfast, calming himself with a devotion from Hebrews, hearing his father's voice whisper, 'Seven times,' and wondering what he'd done to deserve all of this hate.

That afternoon Arthur rang Lawry's and had two lengths of Tasmanian oak delivered. Setting up trestles in his back-yard he started sawing and planing in full view of William's back porch and side window.

Bluma emerged with a basket of washing and called, 'Hello, Arthur, what you doing?'

'It's my new cross. To replace the one that got stolen.'

'That's terrible. What's the world coming to?' she said, before passing into the wash-house as Arthur started cutting tenon joins and fitting the pieces together. When his cross was glued and screwed and a new wheel fitted, he warmed his iron poker and branded the words again: *What shall I render to the Lord, For all his bounty to me?* Just before sunset he put on the first coat of varnish and settled into a chair beside his creation, drinking unlabelled wine and listening to the last chorus of birds.

Just after dark he turned off the tap to his flowers and walked among the garden beds, looking at a hundred-plus lissies drooping face first into the mud.

William was watching him from a crack in his back window. Bluma came up behind him and said, 'For goodness sake, get out there and talk to him.'

William didn't reply, making a beeline to his study and his pamphlets.

Next morning William was up early. He didn't want to miss seeing Arthur's reaction when he found the table and cross he'd made for the Millerites sitting in his backyard. William had opened the cocky's gate between their two homes and pushed them through.

Later he watched from his window as Arthur made up the table with a table cloth and rested the cross up against his rainwater tank. That afternoon he picked out the dead flowers and replanted the ground with calendulas, returning to his cross and the varnish William could smell from his study.

Chapter Eighteen

Four times daily: 10.00, 2.00, 4.00 and 8.00, regardless of the weather. Lately there'd been problems with Yolanda, the Sexsational Dancer, who bluntly refused to work if the mercury hit a hundred. Joe Hobson, MC, would go behind the Easter Wondershow tent and say to her, 'I'm not asking you to cure the cancer, just wiggle your arse.' One day, when she was being particularly obstinate, he said, 'We need to get your banner repainted, you're not looking much like *that* Yolanda anymore.' The Yolanda of suspenders and waif-like waistline, glowing white teeth and nibble-me shoulders dripping baby oil and hiding a cleavage (it was said) which moved with the slightest breath off the Semaphore sea.

Nathan and Lilli stood at the back of the crowd outside the tent, still dripping from their swim in the Semaphore baths, balancing on a gutter to see over a sea of towelling hats. Phil, in one of Bob's old work shirts, sat down on a bench and started peeling a banana. 'Yolanda's seen better days,' he said, as Joe Hobson paraded her around stage in sequined leotards. Lilli looked at him. 'You've seen her sexsational dance?'

'That I'm not ready for. Apparently people pay, though.'

A line of them, at a small booth beside the stage, buying tickets and entering the tent in anticipation of Moulin Rouge with cellulite. On cue Yolanda waved goodbye to the crowd and followed them in. Nathan was holding Lilli's hand but his mind was elsewhere: front row centre in the Wondershow tent, as underwear was tossed from the stage, landing across his face in a wheeze of stale farts.

Yolanda with Bible, ripping pages from Hebrews, dipping them in glue and pasting them across her naked body. Yolanda suddenly become his mother, hanging her privates across a washing line on the main stage.

Phil stretched back and munched on his banana. 'They never found their giant python.'

Lilli looked at him again. 'Who?'

'This lot.'

She sat down beside him as he continued talking. 'Vanessa Lee from Tennessee, she was Yolanda's predecessor. Draped a giant python across her shoulders. One year it disappeared. Since it was worth a lot of money, Joe Hobson contacted the paper.'

Nathan looked back at him, grinning. 'Bullshit.'

'Without a word of a lie.'

Nathan noticed how Lilli had angled her body towards Phil, who bit off more banana than his mouth could hold, apparently disinterested and disconnected from both of them. 'The story appears and of course everyone's too scared to come. Semaphore's deserted. Then they run a story that it's found. But no one ever saw Mrs Lee from Tennessee, or her snake, again.'

Nathan watched Lilli lean towards Phil and remembered her words, *Not me at my best.* His one consolation was that his ability to read people's characters was still improving. With every smile and grin he saw his notion of eternal togetherness – he and Lilli, a child or two – dissipate a little more, like a sax solo from the Joe Aronson Synco Symphonists fading as it broke over the Torrens. Or were these doubts more of his father, he wondered, the purist, the tester and rejecter of people, the all-or-nothin', one-winner-takes-all puritan. He knew Lilli's behaviour wasn't Phil's fault, although Phil wasn't helping. Lilli lacked what William called constancy. But then again, what did William know?

Joe Hobson was the Aronson of the foreshore, replacing T-bones with Dixies and jazz with tinny, prerecorded Glenn Miller. He straightened his bowtie and introduced Vanessa the Undresser, a grain-fed Betty Grable who made Yolanda look like Stan Laurel.

'What she doesn't show isn't worth seeing,' Hobson promised, asking the audience to look out for plain-clothed detectives. Vanessa descended into the dim, smoky tent, followed by a string of gents removing their hats in the manner of St Michaels, Sunday morning, nine a.m.

Nathan looked back at Lilli and Phil and this time Lilli seemed to notice him. 'Nathan, I was telling Phil about our shot at Sunday School. Remember, pin the tail on the martyr?' She started laughing, turning back to Phil and elaborating. Phil looked at Nathan and raised his eyebrows, as if to say, What am I meant to do? Nathan smiled, realising that Lilli was completely misreading Phil.

There were other choices. Zoltan the Fire Eater, there to give the Eastern Wondershow some dimension, bringing skill and artistry to the tent of otherwise smut. Lighting a pair of gruesome-looking sticks and plunging them in his mouth. Throwing a petrol flare over the audience of hatless men with flagging erections. This was Lilli's choice: to light up the darkness with something remarkable or, as Nathan guessed she would, continue with more of the same.

As the show continued, against a backdrop of human sacrifices and flying carpets, those who were willing to suspend belief had the best time. Darkness allowed them to believe that the severed heads were real, that Vanessa really got it all off. This was Semaphore's version of Langmeil, the miracles of Sinbad the Sword Swallower every bit as real as Christ's, an audience praying in the form of mouths hung open in disbelief. And somewhere amongst them there was a William Miller, convinced that all the trickery was real.

Lilli, Phil and Nathan walked up to the Esplanade and caught a trolleybus, its two arms reaching up to a latticework of overhead wires suspended from poles. The arms would spark and sometimes slip off the wires, jumping frenetically about until the driver got out to reattach them. Largs Bay grandmothers would moan, 'Not again,' as the sun beat in through tempered glass. When an old Scot, sitting three seats in front of them, muttered, 'Jesus fuckin' Christ,' Lilli looked at Phil and laughed under her breath. Phil looked at Nathan and raised his eyebrows the same way as earlier, deferring to Lilli's hand on his arm and giving her an explanation of his Biblical narrative.

That night, as the two boys lay awake in their beds, waiting for sleep and something that resembled a breeze through their window, Phil said, 'I didn't know what to do.'

Nathan smiled. 'I felt sorry for you.'

'How?'

'I dunno. The thing is . . .'

Phil turned over. 'I felt sorry for you.'

There was quiet for a while, crickets at various pitches and tempos filling the emptiness with an electricity every bit as musical as the Sunbeam trolleybus. Out of this silence Phil said, 'Vanessa the Undresser,' and they both cracked up.

'Night fellas,' Bob said, walking past their door.

Two replies and then Phil in analytical mode. 'Maybe it's the novelty of a new face, in which case she'll get over it. On the other hand . . .'

Nathan jettisoned a pillow and farted. 'Let's put it this way, do you think she'd ever try to crack onto you?'

'That's the question. And more importantly, how would I react?'

'Well?'

'How would you like me to react?'

'That's not the point.'

Phil sighed. 'Sex, yes. Especially in a rugged outdoor location. Relationship, no. Nothing personal, but I'd end up smothering her with a pillow within a month. Therefore, the question is, would it be worth ruining our friendship for approximately thirty seconds of intense nervous stimulation . . . especially when you consider there are simpler, no fuss alternatives. Therefore, to answer your question, no.'

Nathan detected a breeze across his forehead. 'I don't know if that makes me feel any better.'

'To paraphrase Darwin, eat, root, and root some more . . . we may only have six weeks left.'

305

They laughed. Rose stuck her head in the door. 'What you two laughing about?'

'March twenty-one,' Phil replied, 'put it in your diary.'

'Why?'

'The Second Coming.'

As outlined in the verses Rose had found on the dining-room table, sitting down with a coffee and a dose of Perry Como, reading and laughing as Kavel was upstaged by the gags of Martin and Lewis.

Rose closed the door, went into her bedroom, dropped her dressing-gown on the floor and climbed into bed. Single sheet, cotton blend tropicana. Fluffing up her pillow she searched for *A Man Called Peter* and settled in for an agreeable dose of the Messiah via the Reverend Peter Marshall. Every night she got to know him a little better, imagining his thirty-something good looks and brandy-warmed breath, preaching from pulpits the length and breadth of the Americas, animating Jesus in the same way Chips Rafferty had reinvented the Aussie battler. Belief suspended, the reality of Miller and his Revelations lost in a bed-spread of woven marsupials.

Her husband, meanwhile, sat in the darkness on a stone wall in the backyard. Wiping Ballarat Bitter from his mouth he wondered if the fellas at work had started to notice his changing condition, if they were becoming tired of his weary body dragged from one end of the day to the next.

'It's not like Bob,' he could hear them saying.

Although no one had said anything to him: the ever reliable Bob Drummond, pulling on his jacket and clocking off, crossing tracks without so much as hearing the eight-wheeled cafeteria being towed past. On his way back home, dogs barking at him through rickety picket fences, the lady in the cottage next to the deli saying hello. Replying, but sighing at the same time.

It was just how he felt. They must have started noticing. Maybe they were just waiting for him to get over it, as he usually did. Arriving at work one morning with a bag of sly grog and his Menzies impression.

He stubbed out his Garrick filter-tip and blew the smoke into the empty night sky. Rose's God could sniff it out and apportion blame. No. No God. Just emptiness, and the smell of deep-fried flake from the Kilburn fish and chippery.

He left his bottle half empty and went in, locking the door behind him, going into the bedroom and laying on the bed fully clothed, his hands behind his head.

'Get them things off,' Rose said, keeping her eyes on her book. 'You don't know what it takes to get grease out.'

He still didn't move, so she looked at him. He met her eyes like a child and said, 'I got the cancer, Rose.'

She lay down the book and stared at him. 'What d' you mean?'

'In me throat.'

'Jesus . . .'

The night was broken by a group of children squealing somewhere, growing into laughter. Rose stared ahead at a Hans Heysen on the wall, but couldn't think what to say.

'This doctor reckons it's the fags,' he continued. 'I told him my dad smoked till he was eighty-six, then had a stroke. He says, "Yes, well, it's like a lottery, isn't it?" Just like that . . . it's like a lottery, you win the cancer.'

Rose couldn't help being Rose. 'It's just his job.' She cast her mind back over her book and searched for something to say, something Peter would say (*Bob, every man is given a time, and has to make the most of it*). But it was just a book. Even Phil could, and would, find better words – sincere and heartfelt things. Although when Phil did find out, the thought that would haunt him most was how science, and his books, had let him down, how there wasn't a thing in a thousand volumes of pharmaceuticals to help them.

'What are they gonna do?' Rose asked.

'Nothing.'

'Why?'

He looked up at her. 'It's right through.'

The coughing was something that dated back twenty years. Things hadn't turned nasty until about a month before. 'I was walkin' to work and there it was in me hands, blood. Nathan looks and says, "Jesus,"' as Bob had pretended it was a blood nose. The following day he had gone to see the work's doctor, taking time off for tests and a visit to the Royal Adelaide, watching out for Lavender Ladies who might give him away to Rose. Then back to the doctor, on the second floor of the Webb administration building, surrounded by wood panelling and antiseptic familiar from Rose's tunics.

'Throat cancer,' the doctor said, as detached as a train conductor. Bob sat back. 'That's what I thought you'd say. What do they do for cancer?'

'You want the truth?'

Bob sighed. In those few words he saw his future. He'd had the feeling before, one night on the end of Largs jetty, years before Rose or Phil or the house or anything. Just him and a fella in a six-way coat, saying, 'You got any money?' And before he could even check, the stranger pulling a knife. All he could remember was looking out to sea, to a cloudy, moon-lit horizon, and thinking, Well, if that's it. Saying, 'Would you use that thing, if I didn't give you money?'

'Of course I'd bloody use it. What are you, simple? Give me yer fuckin' money.'

Fishing in his pocket for change and handing over a wallet empty except for a holy card of Our Mother of Perpetual Help he'd been given by his mum. Who'd promised him the glowing figure would watch over him: at home and work, even at the end of Largs jetty, sprinkling a glitter of arc lights like so much burly into the water, uttering blessings and promising to walk with him all the (remaining) days of his life, watching for locos as he crossed tracks, trucks as he crossed Churchill Road but promising nothing, when his number came up.

'It's not me I care about,' he whispered, still stretched out on the bed. 'It's you and Phil ... and Nathan.'

'Don't talk like that. We'll get you to a proper doctor, not that Railways idiot. Cancer's just like, like a cold. Plenty of people – '

'Rose.'

In the next room, Phil was telling Nathan about his deep-sea diving at the Semaphore baths; swimming dolphin-like between bodies bulging from Jantzen monochromes, wooden Dixie sticks stirred up in the swell of high divers as somewhere from the surface a voice sang, '"Animals crackers in my soup . . ."'

Nathan looked at his friend. 'You go to all that trouble, and yet you didn't even say hello to anyone?'

'Miller, there's more to life than a root.' Loudly. 'A root.'

'Phil!' Bob called from next door.

'It's Miller-slash-Muller,' Phil shouted. 'You oughta hear what he's saying.'

Phil, quietening, whispered across the room, 'I go to the Art Gallery to look at nudes. Doesn't mean I get up and try to root them.'

Rose had worked out what to do. 'Lorna, at the League of Health and Beauty, her brother's a doctor.'

'Rose,' he replied, half singing her name.

She sat up. 'First thing is –'

'Rose, the world is full of doctors, doesn't mean that people don't die.'

Silence. She looked at him. 'So that's it?'

'No, it's not like that.'

'What, twelve months and then – '

'More like six.'

Rose was confused. What could you do in six months? Plant a few marigolds, go see the Blue Lake again? If he was right it would all be over before spring. The bulbs would still be cold in the ground, the wading pool and barby packed away for winter, and who'd get them out again, Phil? And what about next Christmas, when she needed someone to steal a pine tree from Kuitpo forest? Still, she couldn't give voice to these thoughts. Things would have to go on, business as usual. Over the next few months, as Bob became sicker and finished work, Phil would accuse her of being in denial. Nonsense, she'd reply, have you put your socks away?

'Why didn't you tell me earlier?' she asked, whispering.

'I had to be sure.'

He'd thought about the open confession around the table, or notes full of inadequate, stumbling prose, but in the end there was none of the drama of *A Man Called Peter*. He knew that she'd find a way of telling others, of sustaining them, and in the end, after he was gone, cooking the food and washing the oil stains from the drive that used to be his job. She was practical like that, strapping on her lavender apron and pushing the lolly-trolley through the coronary ward of life. And as if to prove this, she called out, 'Nathan, Phil,' and pulled the sheet up over her nightie as she waited for them to come in.

It was late when Bob opened his shed and switched on the light. He finished his Ballarat Bitter in a better frame of mind and eventually forgot everything as he got caught up in a confusion of spokes like broken, uncooked spaghetti.

Nathan, falling asleep, wondered if there really was a God after all, if Phil and Lilli weren't right. A God that sustained the worst and crushed the best under his size nine heel. A God caught up in the end of everything as the dutifully lapsed and agnostic worked at sustaining life, feeding families, battling soursobs and succumbing to the cancer. There was no way to look at it that made sense. Maybe God just looked after his own, in which case everything he'd been brought up to believe was bullshit. Suffer the little children. Bullshit. Pray for the aged and infirm, the fallen and diseased. Bullshit. Just let them die and go to Hell.

All at once he felt utterly pessimistic. If the End did come, it wouldn't be soon enough. Talk about people disappointing Jesus. Jesus was the great disappointment.

Phil, meanwhile, sitting opposite Nathan in silence, had never felt more helpless. Words, analysis, sarcasm – even the complete and utter honesty he saved for special occasions. There was nothing you could say. The world was just a giant lump of shit hurtling through space. You just had to get used to it.

310

The following Friday Bluma dragged a reluctant William to Adelaide, persuading him with an all-Wagner concert by the South Australian Symphony Orchestra, the highlight of which was the Prelude and *Liebestod* from *Tristan and Isolde*. William had heard it a thousand times, maybe more, on Robert's old gramophone, which had since sat unrepaired in the cold cellar for the last twenty years, absorbing the smell of pickled pig and sauerkraut. Every week or so Robert used to fetch it from his study, wind a little handle and put the arm on the Wagner record. When it finished he'd play it again, and again, sometimes describing Isolde's demise as they all listened, imagining the boat tossed on the waves, the fake beards and creaky scenery. All made real around a Tanunda black kitchen.

To William it was the soundtrack of the stories they read in the kitchen, distant and epic, populated by seven-foot Teutons with swords, early Lutherans in search of the infidel. Until one day his mother brushed past and knocked the gramophone off the table, damaging the mechanism and breaking the record in two. Robert had meant to get it repaired, but then died his own love-death, leaving the melody wafting around in William's head. In search of rediscovery at the hands of a *real* orchestra.

They crossed North Terrace from the railway station, carrying overnight bags packed tighter than the Glenelg tram. William stopped the traffic with his hand, motioning for Bluma to cross as he waited. Mercedes and near-new Holdens revved impatiently and he smiled at them, thinking, Your time's coming. Adelaide would be a different place soon: cars driven at safe speeds by drivers who were more than happy to give way; politicians cast out from nearby Parliament House as surplus, attempting to return to jobs in insurance and stockbroking; families stopping to pray on median strips; coppers on point conducting traffic as harmonious as *Tristan*; whitegoods traders punished eternally for obscenely high mark-ups.

They climbed the steps of the South Australian Hotel, William feeling out of his depth, as if he might be walking into the very mouth of Hell. Greeted by Satan in the form of Lewy, the maitre d'hotel, impeccably dressed in suit, spats and polished shoes, his shirt and bowtie as crisp as the day he'd bought them. 'Good afternoon, Sir, Madam,' he greeted, opening the door and showing them to the front desk, ringing a bell and shouting, 'Barry,' in a voice which filled the lobby. 'Hope you enjoy your stay, if there's anything I can do for you, let me know.'

Lewy was far too greasy for William. He could see past the act. This was exactly the sort of thing Jesus would sniff out. No doubt Lewy had a cross around his neck, but he was as much a part of Babylon as the publicans and bookies. Like the lino, the hotel was another compromise, for Bluma, who'd stood by him through the thousand shattered records of his own existence, of marriage and children and powdery mildew on their vines. Unfortunately it was the only reward she understood. Other wives in other times would've expected nothing more than Jesus. 'Can't we just go up?' he whispered, as they stood in the lobby.

'Someone'll take our bags,' she smiled, lapping it up like a saucer of milk.

'I can carry them.'

'That's putting someone out of a job.'

It had been six years since they'd stayed at a hotel, a trip to town to watch the Pacific Victory celebrations, to show Nathan the stuffed mammoth and mummy at the Museum and Roberts and McCubbin at the Art Gallery, William drifting off into an ecstasy of Titian and Giotto, endless Christs and weeping Marys in photographically perfect oils; Nathan standing beneath a Bruegel, craning his neck to make out the detail in a market-day painting – hundreds of peasants caught up in their own realities as if it were Goat Square. Ale and pigs replacing snow domes and key-holders, travelling players replacing the *Play for the Apocalypse*.

They'd stayed at the Castle Hotel in Edwardstown. William's choice. When Bluma remembered it she shuddered. Gargoyles, monkeys and a life-size St Patrick watching them in the dining room as they ate Shaslik Mexicaine and Entrecote a la Esterhazy and listened to a troupe of Hungarian refugees sing folk songs under an abstract mural by a Japanese artist who'd committed ritual suicide in Tokyo only a few weeks earlier.

This time it was Bluma's choice. Only the best. The South Australian. Settling into their room she eyed the complementary spumante but sighed when William opened it and poured it down the sink. Still, she knew she had to make her own compromises, especially if she wanted her plan to work.

In the form of a meeting with Nathan she'd planned the previous night, sneaking into Arthur's after William was locked away in his study. Ringing the Drummonds and talking to Rose for almost an hour, reassuring her in the best way she could, promising she'd pray for Bob, wishing there was more she could do. Explaining how she'd had aunts and cousins with the same thing, and how you just couldn't work out the whys and wherefores. Rose was cheered, having talked to someone who understood her in the same way she understood others. 'You'd be perfect for the hospital,' Rose had said. 'Both of us in lavender, roaming the wards, enjoying a chin-wag.'

Eventually Nathan had come on. 'I'm getting him to town,' Bluma said. 'We're coming down tomorrow to see a concert at the Town Hall.'

'How did you persuade him?'

'It's that record he broke.'

Nathan shook his head. 'He only does things if he wants to.'

Bluma looked at Arthur, sitting knitting in a threadbare lounge, and smiled. 'Let's not start. Now, when should we meet?'

'He won't want to –'

'Leave that to me.'

'You gotta tell him.'

'I'll tell him.'

Arthur listened intently, anticipating every twist and turn of the conversation, knowing how Bluma worked and what she was planning. When she got off the phone Arthur said, 'You sure you want to do it that way?'

'Don't worry, I know what I'm doing.'

'It's just, when William sticks his heels in.'

'Trust me.'

Nathan had returned to the Drummonds, busy playing Monopoly on the lounge-room floor. He'd stood in the hallway and watched them, distantly, and wondered how much longer he could remain a part of their family. He wondered if they ever talked about him, working out ways to tell him it was time to move on. No, unlikely, he thought. They'd given him a new start. Watching them laugh together he wondered how he'd ever repay them, how he'd ever explain his gratitude to Bob. He would have to say it. There was a lot he was unsure of in life, but this was one of those things you could just sense. One of those things that defined you and built you up and did away with the risk of eternal regret.

'Bluma says she's thinking of you,' Rose said to Bob.

Bob had smiled, speaking slowly. 'Good-o.'

Now, back at the South Australian Hotel, Bluma and William went down for tea, settling in on the balcony overlooking Parliament House. A large blackboard, sitting under a portrait of the King, promised a *Dance Orchestra Every Night*, although someone had scribbled on the bottom, *Not Tonite, Sick*.

They ate so early they were almost alone. Bluma guessed it was for the best, sparing her the usual tirade of William's amateur psychoanalysis. She persuaded him to try the chef's special, Iced Heart of Palm Brazilian, as she devoured a poached rainbow trout in fennel and lemon. A preoccupied waiter kept appearing to ask them if they were happy and explain that there were plenty of Americans staying at the hotel. Eventually William agreed that the place wasn't so bad, losing himself in a fantasy of overgrown palms and fans clicking gently in the manner of a budget Raffles.

They bypassed coffee and Swiss pastries in the Carioca lounge and set off down King William Street. By now William had adjusted to the city, walking slowly with his hands behind his back and taking it all in: a double-deck trolleybus broken down on the corner of Rundle Street, commuters staring down with

314

helpless expressions. A few policemen outside the Imperial, waiting for six o'clock closing, warning jay-walking reffos and grandmothers in hats with terylene netting of the dangers of crossing against the lights.

The crowd spilt out to the footpath in front of the Town Hall. Voices buzzed all around him, and all at once William was William again, folding his arms and saying to Bluma, 'An audience of stock-brokers. This music should be for the common people.' And as if to prove his thesis, he listened in on conversations, pointing out accountants and headmasters in tuxedos as they pronounced Wagner with a 'W' and compared their children's schools.

Naphthalene hung heavy in the air, mixing with California poppy and the smell of inter-married perfumes. Bluma felt like a slice of plain bread in a sea of croissants. Her brown frock stood out among the fitted gowns. William was aware that his father's shirt and tie had seen better days, but didn't care, strutting around with a touch of the Trotsky, deciding he'd come to represent the workers denied their culture. He guessed they were probably all closet-Christians, dragging themselves to some C. of E. circus every Sunday morning in search of spirit which had long since deserted them. Still, they had the King and P.G. Wodehouse sitting beside them on the Monday morning tram.

William went to the toilet, choosing to wait for a cubicle rather than line up with the soon-to-be-judged. Returning to the foyer, he stood beneath a poster which read *Bhaskar and Company, Dances of India*, with the date, March 2, Adelaide Town Hall. A stylised sketch showed Bhaskar (who'd studied under Master Ellappa) involved in the 'Naga Nirtham', the Dance of the King Cobra.

March 2. Friday March 2. Today. He turned to an older couple and asked, 'Is this what you've come to see?'

They both nodded enthusiastically. 'The Temple Dance, especially,' the woman smiled. 'Anjali and Bhaskar, are you familiar with classical Hindi dance?'

'But what about Wagner?'

'Wagner was last week. We have Beecham's recording of the *Venusberg* music, you know it?'

William found Bluma and whispered loudly in her ear, 'You got the dates wrong.'

'No.'

But there was no point blowing his top, at least not here. With no chance of a refund he'd have to make do. Moving into the auditorium and taking his seat he tried to talk himself into it. In the brightly woven tapestries he tried to see images of mountain ranges, like the ones described in the travel brochures he found in Dr Scholz's waiting room. In the tuning-up of the untunable sitar he tried to hear one of the Mrs Fox's melodies. But in the end it was just so much inedible curry, hot beyond the limits of the average palette.

He made it past the *Eclipse of the Moon* and the *Dance of the Golden Plates*, but when *Puja, the Prayer to the Creator* was begun, he looked at Bluma and nodded.

'Sorry,' she whispered, shaking her head and guessing she'd never hear the end of it.

The following day they checked out and walked to Rymill Park, where Bluma persuaded him to hire a rowboat. As they drifted gently across the shallow lake he said, 'I'll never come again,' convinced more than ever of the futility of compromise. 'Maybe we can buy the recording,' Bluma offered, but he didn't reply, remembering the row of knees and handbags he'd had to climb over to get out of the auditorium, falling across the lap of some old girl, his hands ending up across the top of her legs, pushed off disgustedly as he tried to regain his footing. Walking out of the auditorium, calling as he left: 'God is our creator, Christ our Saviour.'

He reached over the side and touched the concrete base of the lake. 'Nothing is real,' he mumbled.

Bluma took the oars. 'Life's what you make it.'

'No, it's what God makes it. This isn't a lake, it's a big gutter. How could anyone enjoy boating in a big gutter?'

'People do.'

'No doubt.'

They returned to the kiosk, bought ice-cream Dandies and sat down at a wire-framed table. Just before eleven William said, 'If we go now we could get the early train.'

'No,' she replied, holding his hand, 'you promised.'

'Well, what shall we do?'

'There's plenty.'

She kept checking her watch, scanning the walking paths and cafeteria.

Nathan stood behind an oleander, a hundred yards east, watching his parents and wondering what to do. He could read his father's mood – tired, frustrated and out of his depth. It didn't augur well for their reunion. He thought of turning and leaving, explaining to his mum later how he could sense it wasn't the right time. But in the end it was Bluma who persuaded him, sitting without conversation, head drooped, looking more alone than he'd ever seen her.

He started walking down the hill towards them. Bluma saw him straight away and smiled. Then William, following Bluma's eyes, looked at his son. Nathan shuddered as his father stood and faced him with a blank, cold stare. Nathan stopped in the middle of a rose garden, sustained by the smell of crimson-red roses. William looked at Bluma, picked up his overnight bag and set off around the lake, almost breaking into a trot as he departed towards East Terrace. Eventually he made it to the railway station, settling in beneath the departures board and staring at an over-size clock the Railways checked against Greenwich Mean Time once a week.

Nathan and Bluma talked until after two, and then he walked her to the station, leaving her at the top of the ramp with a hug and a kiss as she stuffed a twenty quid note in his back pocket. 'Soon,' he consoled, 'then he'll see sense.'

Bluma walked down the ramp and found William sitting stony-faced under the departures board. 'He was looking forward to it,' she said.

317

No reply.

'I had to try something, William.'

He turned and looked at her, 'It wasn't what you did, it was how ...' He offered her a peppermint. 'C'mon, if we miss this one we'll have to stay over.'

He stood up and walked past the man in the blue, greeting him with a single finger waved in the air.

Chapter Nineteen

No one could remember so much heat, so late in summer. Mrs Lynch, Rose's neighbour to the left, seemed to recall a time in 1905 when it cracked the century for well over a week, ending (strangely enough, she observed) when General William Booth, the Salvationist leader, climbed a ladder in front of Adelaide Station, shouted a final message of support to his loyal followers, dawdled down the ramp and boarded a train never to return. A small army of peaked caps and bonnets lined the platform and sang 'For he's a jolly good fellow' before the wind changed direction and clouds drifted in from the east. 'Make of it what you will,' Mrs Lynch observed, 'but he was forced off at Riverton when the change buckled the rails.'

'Nothing like this,' Rose observed and asked, all at the same time.

'No, this is bloody cruel.'

Rose said how it was like God turning on an oven, fan-forced like the new Kelvinator ones. She thought of William Miller's prediction and wondered if he mightn't be right, if this wasn't God's way of getting them acclimatised. Still, it'd been hot before and it would be hot again. You just had to cope and wait for the change, the wind from the south, laden with more salvation than William Booth's tambourine.

It had started on Friday. The works at Islington were closed when it reached 106. The men were told not to return until the day of a change. Saturday, 107, Sunday, 103, Monday, 113 and today, Tuesday, the all-time record, 116 – proudly announced by

Mr Bromley, the government meteorologist who, having presided over Adelaide's coldest day and heaviest rainfall, had refused to retire until the hat-trick.

The residents of Church Avenue, Kilburn, set up a sort of humpy town in the reserve. Other streets claimed other areas and soon it was a village of sorts. Different clans took turns mopping out the public lavs and looking after the kids when the schools closed. Sprinklers were lined up like batteries of ack-ack guns and left running for hours on end, turning the grass in the centre of the park green and burning leaves on the hydrangeas.

Bob Drummond was glad to be out of doors and off work. Although the place gave him the shits at times, he had no intention of finishing up. Almost as bad as a pre-paid funeral. He could still remember Winston Churchill on the radio during the war, talking about success and how it was the ability to go from one failure to another without giving up. Anyway, the thought of them giving him a watch and cutting cake and signing a card was too much. Former best mates staring at him out the corner of their eyes with pity, poor ol' Bob getting ready to go off and die somewhere. Stuff 'em. He'd hang around as long as he could, haunting them, like a living ghost they wouldn't soon forget.

Rose lay beside him as their two boys held Lilli's head over a sprinkler. 'What you thinkin'?' she asked. But he wouldn't tell her the truth, about how he was remembering six-year-old Phil building a dirt-floor cubby beside their old diosma hedge, burying Juicy Fruits in a hole he'd dug with one of Rose's best spoons. Of how Phil said, formally, 'Don't tell Mum, it's for the daddy-long-legs.' Hiding from the world behind a piece of plywood he'd salvaged from the shed.

'They won't fit them in their mouths,' Bob had replied.

'You'd be surprised,' Phil whispered.

Instead of telling Rose this, he looked at her and said, 'I wonder where them gum trees get their water from?' Using science as a cold blanket for all things emotional, things which couldn't, and in the end, needn't be said.

From her house Mrs Lynch opened her venetians and looked out across the park, smiling. She went into her kitchen and lit the stove, taking out flour to make scones. Just after dark she slipped on a frock and crossed the road with her basket. Soon the Church Avenue clan was gathered around dishes of jam and whipped cream melting into milk. Then she went and sat against the trunk of a big old sugar gum, closing her eyes and waiting for sleep. Bob watched her, contented. In time he fell asleep himself, still listening to Phil explain Tchaikovsky's suicide to an indifferent Lilli.

The next day Joseph Tabrar woke early, seagulls flying low over his flat, spreading themselves over the football oval. He sat up and rubbed his eyes, reaching for his shirt and pulling it on. It seemed like most of Adelaide was off work, but the mail still had to get through. A letter he'd been writing fell to the ground and he picked it up.

> Dear Ellen,
>
> I can't guess what you're thinking or feeling at this time, with only a few days till the great disappointment. For me, I'm happy, cos I know it means you and the children are a step closer to moving here. I have faith in your good sense. Also, in our love, which in the end will be greater than other things.
>
> Hot here. But Tanunda too I guess. Some nights I don't sleep so well. This is me lonely maybe, and the flat, which is hot but only very temporary, as I have already explained.

The following pages were letters to the children, describing, as he already had in a dozen others, the city and its many wonders. Careful to avoid any criticism of Seymour, or even William. Creating, in every word, an alternative existence they wouldn't be able to resist for too much longer.

Thursday, March 19, two days to go. William woke early, tasting bacon in his mouth, smelling summer through every uncut hair in his nostrils. Without waking Bluma or eating breakfast he pulled on work pants and a shirt and headed off for Murray Street, past stores whose every detail had become as familiar as the freckles on Bluma's arms. Paddon's Garage, mortar crumbling between weathered ironstone, Mr Paddon himself out with his trowel, pitting himself against the rising damp of a thousand cleared paddocks. Tanunda Motors, its bitumen cracked in a spider-web William could draw from memory, starting at the footpath and finishing at a peppercorn tree consuming the walls of Davis' Tank and Silo Makers. John Horsburgh's papers and tobacco, breathing Port Royal onto a footpath which led around the corner to the Salvation Army hall, recently given over to Heron's the draper with his Methodist church bell hung over the doorway, used and abused in the early afternoon as school kids climbed on each other's shoulders, ringing the bell and running for their very lives as though they were the first that had ever thought of it.

William knew that the township of Tanunda would be safe, mostly. Unaltered in its composition of small details forming a whole. That's why he couldn't understand why people had been so hard to convince. Like Miels the barber, wielding his clippers under a crucifix of polished oak, Jesus weeping for the same haircut a dozen times a day, five days a week for eternity and beyond. Miels was a sensible Catholic but like most, too eager to accept Rome's version of events. Apparently the Pope hadn't read Revelations. 'You've made yourself a name, William,' Miels said, as he trimmed William's hair to within a micron of his scalp.

William ran his hands over the stubble. 'I haven't made it, I was given it. Speak your mind you make enemies, Barry.'

'Dunno. I speak my mind all day, don't have no enemies. None that I know of anyway. Though I had this dream last night that me house was robbed.'

A man so involved in small talk, busy bending over balding heads, William thought, that he doesn't see his roof slowly cracking and caving in. Barry Miels – in his white, short-sleeved, cotton-blend uniform – made of more veneer than the lino which ran up his shop walls in a splatter pattern his wife had picked out. Barry, with the races on the radio, refusing to change stations for the William Millers of the world.

William felt ready. He stopped at Eudunda Farmers and bought a bag of oranges, finishing two before he arrived at Seymour's, sitting on the front porch with Bluma and the Hickses, up to their wrists in juice and pulp as sweet as it was sticky. The smell of near-perfect pot cake drifted out of the windows, tumbling towards the footpath like Horsburgh's tobacco, carrying (in a vision, a landscape of food thrown up in the final moments) the smell of pickled cucumbers and Bruno's best blutwurst.

There was work to be done. Things to be made ready. As Bluma and Mary kept cooking, William and Seymour set to the yard, weeding, pruning and watering parched shrubs, cleaning up piles of rubbish and putting out bins for trucks that might or might not come. And when they'd finished they went to William's and did the same, labouring in singlets in the full sun as Bruno and Edna watched in amusement from their refrigerated kitchen.

Friday was more of the same. Arthur Blessitt followed the progress of the mercury on his radio, regularly retreating to his backyard and his water tank, lifting the access and immersing himself in a dark, murky world of sediment and kerosene. If the world did end they'd never find him here, floating like a baby in a pool of stale amnion.

Saturday, March 21, 1952. William was up early, setting up a trestle under the myrtle his grandfather Anthelm had planted in anticipation of this very day, setting out seats and wiping off cobwebs. Arthur watched, through a small rust hole in the top of the tank, as he floated. Eventually he saw Mary Hicks and Bluma emerge from the house, laying a setting and arranging dishes covered with foil.

Edna Hermann peered from her venetians as her husband read from the *Oracle*: 'Tomorrow, March 21, is the day of reckoning.

Have you packed your bags and said your prayers? Mr Miller has ...' The newspaper naming names: Seymour, Mary, Ellen and the children. Continuing the shaming the Elders had tried to help them avoid. Anticipating the conclusion of the drama which had started with the handbills, continuing via doorknocks and washed-out rallies.

Just before lunch, William, Bluma, the Hickses, Ellen and her children gathered in the shade of the myrtle, praying and eating. Chas Tabrar pulled his mother's sleeve and asked, 'When's it gonna happen?'

William overheard and said, 'When He's ready,' starting to become a little unsure himself. Not that he could complain. If he'd wanted a sign, what better than nine straight days of heat? When the story of the last days was written, this would be a chapter unto itself, requiring no dressing up or exaggeration to make itself mythical. People would read about his backyard devotion and say, 'Wow, what sort of man was this Miller?'

Back in Adelaide, Nathan and Phil had returned to the Semaphore baths. Nathan was full of anticipation, contemplating new beginnings after a year of changes more dramatic than *Blue Hills*. All of it necessary in the end, he supposed. Like Phil said, you had to crack an egg to make an omelette. Changes that might require forgiveness on his part, although God knows it'd be hard. Watching Phil on a bench, sucking in his guts as he talked to a girl twice his age, he guessed you had to let people go on making their own disasters.

Meanwhile, Joseph Tabrar lay in the Parklands, his shirt flapping open in a hot northerly. Like Nathan, he was full of anticipation, four pages of rentals sitting beneath his lunchbox, circled, crossed out and recircled in red. He smiled, and sighed, listening to the crows crazy with heat and a jackhammer sounding distantly from the city.

The Millerites were barely into their dessert when Arthur emerged from his water tank, completely naked, smiling at his audience and trying to cover himself. William cleared his throat, picked up his Bible and turned to Luke, reading as Seymour redirected his grandchildren's stares.

Arthur went inside and dried himself off. He answered a knock at his front door and found Trevor Streim and Ron Rohwer standing with broad, happy smiles and bottles of Woodroofe's lemonade. 'This is unusual,' he managed.

'Aren't you going to invite us in?' Trevor asked.

'Of course.'

Arthur tried to settle the Elders on his lounge but they insisted on going outside, settling in on his ark beneath the lopped cross still resting against the rainwater tank. Soon they were joined by Gunther Fritschle and Ian Doms, and after lunch, Bruno Hermann, who brought along a string of sausages. Arthur played the uneasy host, setting out cups and opening a few bottles of wine William had given him the vintage before last.

William refused to look at them, blocking out their voices as he moved through the Gospels, realising that this was the final test. He could hear them raise their voices, laughing at jokes that probably weren't funny, patting each other on the shoulders and messing each others hair in a way they'd never generally do.

Arthur just sat quietly, watching the Millerites and feeling guilty, trying to think of a way of telling them that this wasn't his idea.

Chas pulled Ellen's sleeve again and said, 'Can we go over there?' But before she had a chance to reply, Seymour slammed his fist down on the table, staring at the children and saying, 'They should know better . . . now listen.'

William, Bluma and Seymour eventually fell asleep in their chairs, Mary stretched out on the grass beside them. The children started a game of cricket, and when the ball went over Arthur's fence David went to fetch it.

'Having fun?' Trevor Streim asked.

'Not as much as you,' he replied.

The laugh woke Seymour. 'David!' he called, scowling, waiting until his grandson had returned to the fielding before closing his eyes and snoozing.

At eight o'clock the Millerites made a meal of leftovers. 'Pathetic,' William whispered to Seymour. 'It's like the Keystone Cops. Is that the best they could do?'

On Arthur's side, Gunther built a fire and Ron cooked pancakes beside Arthur's wilting carnations. After dark the fire grew larger and the party louder. They stood around the flames with bottles in their hands, occasionally hushing into a discussion which was followed by a half dozen flame-lit faces turning to look at the Millerites.

The Miller party had returned to the Bible, read by the light of a gas-lamp. The children had fallen asleep and Ellen had covered them with rugs. As William droned in their ears, their minds drifted into their own personal realms. Ellen's to Joseph, sitting alone somewhere, waiting; Mary's to Seymour, and how she'd soon have her old husband back again, bruised and damaged but wiser for the experience. And Bluma's to Nathan, sitting in his loft (which William had since converted to storage) reading a text on the mechanics of temperature. Calling down to them as he used to, 'Goodnight, Mum, Dad . . .'

By eleven things had grown quiet on both sides of the fence. The odd, occasional slapping of a mozzie, a bottle dropped and smashed in Arthur's yard. Just before midnight William started reading from Revelations, mumbling in a rushed monotone that hid his anxiety.

As midnight came and went the Elders and the others fell silent and looked over at the Millerites. William kept reading until ten past twelve. At the end of chapter three he looked up at his friends and said, slowly, 'Maybe I've miscalculated.'

Seymour looked at him. 'But you were so sure.'

He kept reading the Bible, as if there was something he'd missed.

'William,' Trevor called, across the fence, 'how's about you come over and join us?' But William just kept reading, silently, following passages with his finger as if he'd already found where

326

he'd gone wrong. Mary and Ellen started clearing the dishes and Seymour sat motionless, his head bowed.

Soon after both parties broke up. Arthur emptied the last of the wine onto the fire and it fizzed and smoked and eventually died, leaving his yard in darkness. He stripped and climbed back into his rainwater tank, watching Seymour stretch out his hand and cover William's, squeezing it and then standing to go inside, taking the first of his grandchildren with him.

It was just after one in the morning. Seymour's grandchildren were asleep in William's bed. Mary, Ellen and Bluma were in the kitchen drinking coffee. Seymour and William walked back to the privacy of William's vines, knelt and started praying. The plan was to create and continue a dialogue with God until they were given, or came to understand, some explanation. By two o'clock the women were calling from the house. Seymour stopped praying: 'William, I'm not getting anything but sore knees . . .' They stood up, shook hands, and Seymour returned to the women on the porch. William walked through the vines towards the track at the bottom of his property. Sitting on a fallen log he resorted to logic.

By three o'clock he had the glimmer of an idea.

Trying not to wake Bluma, he went into his study and turned on the light, sitting and opening Anthelm's old Bible, writing inside the back cover, *Tonight I saw distinctly and clearly that instead of our Saviour coming out of the Most Holy of the Heavenly sanctuary to come to this earth, He has in fact entered the second apartment of that sanctuary, and that He has work to perform there before coming to earth.*

His revelation was that just as the Old Testament had explained, there were two phases in the ministry of the old priests: one known as the Heavenly sanctuary, the other as the Heavenly holy of holies. He was right after all, only instead of Jesus moving from the Heavenly sanctuary to earth, he'd detoured via this other realm to see out the second stage of his ministry before returning to gather his followers.

Bluma, waking up in an empty bed, got up and opened the study door. 'What are you writing now?'

'Nothing, I can't sleep . . . go back to bed.'

That night the wind changed and dark clouds moved in, opening up as Bluma drifted off.

The rain was gone by morning and the next day was balmy. Like William's mood. Locking himself in his study and refusing to emerge. Returning to Anthelm's Bible and writing, *Were I to live my life over again, with the same evidence that I had, to be honest with God and man, I'd do the same again. I confess my error and acknowledge my disappointment. Yet I still believe that the day of the Lord is near, even at the door . . .*

Like Bluma, standing, listening, trying to tempt him out with fried sausage and fresh bread. At one point he stopped answering her completely.

But just after six p.m. things changed. William emerged from his room, throwing his hands in the air, picking Bluma up by the hips and trying to lift her. 'Praise Jesus!' he cried, dancing about in circles and kissing her on the cheek.

'What?' she asked. 'What is it?' Thinking he'd finally admitted the truth to himself.

But he looked her squarely in the eyes and said, 'I was reading my *Concordance*, and here in the chronology, a simple note: "In figuring the *terminus ad quem*, we need to make allowance for the fact that the Christian era is dated from Year one, not Year zero . . ."'

She looked at him. 'So?'

'I was a year off. There was no 0 BC. Therefore, in a sense, this year doesn't happen till next year.'

She dropped into a chair. 'William . . .'

'What?'

'Not again . . .'

He looked at her sternly. 'This time we tell no one, except Seymour.'

Bluma shook her head, quickly at first and then in slow, wide arcs. 'No . . . no no no.'

'This time –'

'No!' She stood up, both fists clenched, and held them against her body. 'Not again, William. I won't go through it again.'

'Bluma.'

She took a deep breath and her body stiffened. 'I don't have the strength, William.'

'Let me explain.'

'No!' She walked towards their bedroom and closed the door, but he followed her in anyway.

'I admit,' he explained, 'I should've thought it through more. It was such a simple thing.'

She took a suitcase from under their bed and unzipped it.

'What are you doing?' he asked.

'I want to see my son,' she replied.

He took the case from her and started zipping it up. 'You will.'

She tried to take the case back but he wouldn't let it go. 'William,' she said, fighting to take it with all her energy. Then she let go, and screamed at the top of her voice, '*Give me the case.*'

William let go and took a step back. Instead of reclaiming the case, she turned and walked out of their bedroom, out the front door and into the darkness. She walked the streets of Tanunda for an hour, deep in thought. Eventually she asked for a room at the Tanunda Hotel, telling the manager, a friend of Seymour, that William thought it best while he painted.

William searched town for two hours, blinded to everyone and everything passing by, trying to work out where Bluma might go to get away from him. Not that she'd ever done anything like this before. Except for the time, just after their engagement, when Bluma's mother wouldn't let him past their front door for a week. In the end it turned out to be something she'd heard via a friend via a friend. Something about his father, and the coming of the Lord. Completely untrue, or so William explained to Bluma, standing beneath her window one dark night when her parents were asleep.

But this was different. Bluma was his wife now. Valley wives,

Lutheran wives, didn't do this sort of thing. This smacked of a romance novel. The American way. The had-it-too-good-for-too-long way. Soft. Not the Bluma he knew.

And he knew her well. Like the seasons, or the taste of a ripe grape. He knew every thought she had before she had it (or so he believed). Which made his search even more frustrating. Where was she? A bench, the grandstand, on a train to town? He knocked on Seymour's door (claiming she'd said she was off visiting somewhere) but couldn't bring himself to check Joshua's or Arthur's place. He could just imagine her in Arthur's living-room, sipping on watery coffee, portraying him as some sort of ogre.

Oh well, what's it matter, he thought, in the end. If that's the way she wants it. Returning home he was expecting to see her there in their living-room. But their house was dark and cold and empty.

The next morning when William went to buy milk and bread (the first time he'd had the shop stuff in years) Seymour stopped him outside the Lutheran school and asked, 'You didn't need any help?'

'Doing what?' William replied.

'Painting.'

William was careful with his words. 'Who told you this?'

'Paint triggers Bluma's asthma?'

'Yes ... yes.'

'How long will she be at the hotel?'

Ten minutes later William was at the front desk, and a few seconds after that, up the stairs and outside Bluma's first floor room. 'Bluma,' he called, knocking loudly.

Sitting in bed eating her breakfast, listening to the radio, Bluma took a moment to think. Whether to answer him or pretend to be out. Whether she should call down to have him removed, or open the door and have it out in the hallway.

'Bluma,' she heard him call, 'don't be so melodramatic.'

She sat, tight-lipped, pulling the sheet up over her legs, wondering if this man was really her husband.

'Bluma, open the door and we'll talk.'

She didn't answer him.

'Bluma!'

He continued knocking and pleading for another ten minutes before he gave up. Bluma sat silently in bed for another half hour before she dared pick up the phone and ask the front desk if he'd gone. 'Yes he's gone, but he wasn't happy,' a voice explained. Then she got up and showered and sat in a chair overlooking Murray Street, unsure of what to do. She saw William emerging from a shop and looking up at her room. She shot back, falling to the ground and crawling to a distant corner. She sat there for another hour, scared, cold, shivering, before a pass key opened the door and a maid entered.

'Just leaving,' Bluma said, standing, turning away from the maid as she pretended to fix her hair.

'Shall I fix your bed?'

'Yes, that would be fine.'

She passed quickly out into the hallway and William was waiting there, standing with his arms crossed, leaning against a wall of crimson-red wallpaper. 'Can I buy you a coffee?' he asked.

She was nowhere near as confident, standing slumped, red-faced and fighting for breath. After a few moments she said, 'I suppose so.'

Over the next hour, drinking coffee and eating stale torte at the Zinfandel tea rooms, William did what he did best: talk her around to seeing things his way. The old William Miller, the crackpot, the zealot, was gone, he promised. From now on their life would be like it used to be: everyone happy and sociable. His dates would be *his* dates, he promised. Kept as secret as their bank balance.

Bluma knew she should have stayed angry, but she couldn't. In the end it was much easier to believe what he said, like Joshua and Seymour had. William was good on the attack, but weak on the retreat. He could convince some people of anything, she guessed. He'd even made an artform of avoiding saying he was wrong, or sorry. And still people believed him. Or at least humoured him.

Bluma sat staring into her coffee, retreating into a silence of words thought but not said. Although she'd think, later, that this episode was the closest she'd come to saying, William, you're a drongo. I really don't know how I ended up . . .

But then censoring even her thoughts.

From now on, she thought, as they walked home together, as William barked incessantly in her ear, she'd leave her disagreements to lino and mud on boots and a million inconsequential things she knew he'd give in to.

A few days later the weather broke. William told Bluma it was time to face the sly looks and bemused grins he knew awaited them. And so, on March 26, with his clothes freshly pressed, his head held high and a smile stretching from one ear to the other, he took his string bag, put his arm in Bluma's and closed the door behind them. He covered the length of Langmeil Road and Elizabeth Streets, greeting old neighbours (who no longer bothered rushing inside to avoid him) and stopping at the Eclipse deli to arrange for his newspaper and milk deliveries.

'For how long?' the shop-keeper asked, smiling.

'I'll give you notice,' William replied, refusing to be baited. No handbills or rallies this time, as promised. No rush to convert or save souls; in fact, no use trying to persuade anyone.

The sun was receding from the earth, allowing the grapes to finish to perfection. There were bottles to wash and then the harvest, again, reminding them that the cycle came full circle, compensating simple mortals for the bruising and losses of another year. A breeze from the south-west rattled carob leaves in a painfully familiar synthesis of smell and sound, of things seen, remembered, forgotten, someone's uncle dead in the ground five years now, no, it couldn't be that long, or could it . . .

William and Bluma sat on the bench in front of the Tanunda Club and watched the world pass by. William looked in his jacket pocket for a musk but found a bunch of stapled papers. Opening them out he smiled and showed Bluma his name-change application. 'Look, I never got around to posting it.'

She shook her head. 'You were never serious, Wilhelm.'

'I was.'

She looked into his eyes and smiled. It was his way of buying lino. She ripped the application into tiny pieces and let them blow away in the breeze.

'I was serious,' he repeated, stretching out his legs and putting his hands behind his head. 'Like other things, people make it too difficult. You give in, you compromise.'

Bluma looked up to see Ellen Tabrar standing before them, hands on hips, her face as cold as the granite soldier they all avoided on Anzac Day. 'Bob Hope double-bill, next week,' she began. 'You like Bob Hope, William?'

'Can't say I do.'

Ellen stared at him. 'And Amgoorie tea. They're just about giving it away at Mackenzie's. You shop at Mackenzie's, William?'

'No.'

'Mackenzie's is best. Cheap.'

Why won't she look at me? Bluma thought. 'Where you off to?' she asked.

'Home,' Ellen replied, glancing at Bluma but then returning her stare to William. 'Joe wrote. He said it would be a great disappointment. That's what he called it: the Great Disappointment. Wasn't much great about it.'

'In what sense?' William asked.

'In any sense.'

'It was a big disappointment. But I've moved on. I've worked out where I went wrong.'

She smiled. 'Where's that?'

He explained his refiguring, and how it meant they should have been waiting for March next year, but how there'd be no point trying to convince people now. Except for the few. 'Like your dad. You gotta tell him I want to talk to him.'

But Ellen just looked at Bluma and said, 'They've got chenille dressing gowns, blue and pink.'

Bluma smiled and bowed her head as, without revealing any

of her own plans, Ellen smiled a sort of goodbye and walked off. Bluma looked at William and said, 'She's got Joseph on her mind,' but he didn't reply.

They stood up and kept walking. Passing the Apex, Ron Rohwer emerged with an armful of pasties, realising too late but deciding to make the most of it. 'William, Bluma . . . must be time to crush again, William. You need a hand, you call out, eh?'

William made an effort, if only for Bluma's sake. 'Thanks, but I've got Seymour gonna help me.'

'Expecting a good harvest?'

'Never know till it's done.'

'Of course. Still, you need a hand, you call.'

And then Bluma saved the day. 'I'll see you on Sunday, Ron.'

'Good.' Ron looked at William. 'That'd be fine, eh? I'll tell Pastor Henry.'

William didn't want to tell him about his new dates, shaking his hand, upsetting his pasties and passing on. 'Two-faced bastard,' he said, as they walked.

'As hard for him as it is for you,' Bluma replied.

'Garbage. As long as I go back to church. See the error of my ways.'

Compromise, more and more, dragging him down into the gutter. Maybe he'd have to become a recluse after all, avoiding the misunderstanding which loomed above his head. And then he saw Joshua Heinz, a hundred yards away, heading towards him. He stopped, thought, grabbed Bluma's arm and said, 'I'll see you back there.'

William walked home as quickly as his legs could carry him, locking himself in his study, taking his pen and writing, again and again, in his grandfather's Bible, The Great Disappointment, The Great Disappointment.

Chapter Twenty

Ellen helped Vicky load the last of their four suitcases into Seymour's hearse. They piled in and Mary turned the key in the ignition, sparking a clang of metal, a car full of laughter and the grin of Michael Haddad, their Lebanese postie. Mary fought with the column-shift, looked at Ellen, crossed her fingers and tried again. The hearse chugged to life and everyone smiled, except Vicky, who flung open the back door and ran towards the house. 'Hold on.'

'Hurry up,' Ellen called, trying to wind down the window, eventually giving up and pushing it down with her hands. Vicky jumped down the steps and flew along the garden path, smiling and hugging her *Hollywood Annual*, Stewart Grainger grinning on the cover as he made up for another scene.

They drove past the Bowls Club, refugee Anglicans in white standing in full sun, adjusting the tops of wool-blend socks which wouldn't stay up, retreating to the shade of the Fargus Barker Memorial Lean-to, unscrewing thermoses full of hot tea and pouring it into chipped mugs. In the back-blocks, beyond the club, Moy's chaff-mill worked at full steam, loading wheat bags into carts pulled by teams of four horses, drivers sitting twelve feet high on top of the loads, holding reins so long they had to be made especially. Past the Anglican church and Wohler's, the Apex and Tanunda Motors, Doph Gordon standing beside a Humber with a look of satisfaction. Nothing I'll miss, Ellen guessed. Just things I'm familiar with. Like where they kept the Rice Bubbles at Mackenzie's, or which doctors you could trust to keep quiet.

Both of the boys were full of excitement and anticipation, ready to reclaim their father and hold him to his promises of endless cinemas with endless choices, Francis the mule stretching into a future of popcorn and choc-tops, marking the years with stories infinitely more enjoyable and believable than Mr Miller's. Flying carpets and bearded women and milkshakes the flavour of chewing gum, classrooms minus crucifixes on every wall, homes minus rising damp and bakeries minus endless slabs of custard cake. Butchers stocked with fritz and lamb roasts and newsagents risking the wrath of God to stock *Superman*.

Vicky had mixed feelings, unhappy to be leaving so many friends behind. 'We'll come for visits all the time,' Ellen had consoled, but that wasn't the same. She'd even miss Mr Rechner, who'd always had plenty of time for her, considering her connection with William and her father's move to Adelaide. But in the end Ellen had convinced her, brought her to the understanding that family was more important than anything, which is why Joseph had had to do what he'd done. To keep them together for an eternity of small things.

As they pulled into the station carpark the train was already waiting. Mary dented Seymour's bumper-bar on a date palm, wrestled the shift to select 'park' and killed the motor. She watched as her daughter and grandchildren each carried their own suitcase, full of only a fraction of what they owned. The rest would follow in a month or so, after Joseph finally got the keys to the house he'd selected.

Mary was dreading the arrival of the moving van; not only because of its finality, but because of the emptiness it would leave behind, the dilemma of what to fill the spaces with once she'd cleaned up the dust and mopped away the sauce stains. As she wandered like a ghost, Seymour telling her to get a hold of herself.

Mary watched through the window as Ellen settled her children in economy class and returned to the platform. As the whistle blew, Ellen took her mother's hand and said, 'We won't be far.' Mary smiled. Although it should have been a special moment, it just seemed bleak, full of unreconciled endings and worse, William's voice in her ear, reading from the Bible on the night of the not-so-great disappointment. Mary kissed her daughter on the cheek and hugged her, holding her tight and waving to the children with her one spare hand, then turning and walking down the ramp, already planning her first visit.

The highlight of the journey down was curried-egg sandwiches and a lay-over in Gawler to take on water. Close to the city the train stopped a hundred yards south of North Adelaide station, heat radiating up through the floorboards from gravel warmed by an April sun that couldn't shake summer. They waited for almost half an hour, as voices shouted to each other from the front of the train, as cylinders cooled and coal lost its glow in the boilers.

And then, climbing into their carriage, appearing in the door-way, a postal worker in a sweat-soaked shirt. Joseph kneeling down as his children ran to him. They took him back to Ellen and he sat next to her, holding her hand. 'It came over the speakers at Adelaide . . .'

Over-hearing, other passengers moaned and stood up, making for the carriage door and a long walk home, calling for the con-ductor and asking if there'd be a bus. 'Soon,' he promised, looking towards the city in the near distance, its sandstone and granite polished in the heat haze, dressed with billboards and plane trees with burnt leaves.

'Welcome to Adelaide,' Joseph grinned, carrying two of the four suitcases across the tracks, giving way to a C.R. shunt in search of its load. The two boys, unable to imagine a better way of starting their new lives, half-dragged, half-carried the other two cases behind their father. Mother and daughter followed, tripping and supporting each other, lost in fits of laughter they couldn't explain.

Although Joseph could, delivering his family out of the mouth of disaster. A lonely figure, a little excited, carrying his sense of duty lightly, leading them towards the green of the North Adelaide links, wondering how he was going to fit so many people and so many bags into the clapped out Morris he'd just bought on hire purchase.

Just as he'd expected.

William watched from his back window as Bluma nattered to Edna over the fence. He made a coffee and she was still there, cut up the potatoes for tea, put them in a pot and checked again. By now Bruno had joined them, waving a stick of wurst about in the air as some sort of peace offering. William watched, but refused to go out. It seemed there was only one path. Solitude. Like Jesus in the desert, doing his best to avoid the Hermanns of the world.

She came in and presented him with the sausage, but before she could speak he said, 'I know, I saw,' slicing up carrots and dropping them into the water.

'I'll do that,' she said.

'No, it's alright.'

She put her hands on her hips, staring at him coldly. 'Come out and say hello.'

He took his time to answer. 'No. Not that I wouldn't be civil.' Thinking, they don't mean to gloat, but they do.

Bluma shrugged. 'You underestimate people. They're happy to let you be.'

He nodded his head. 'No ...'

She took out pork chops, and flour, and started to dust them. They worked on in silence, anticipating each other's next move, adding wood to the stove, descending into the cellar for pickled beans.

That night, as rain pounded down on their roof, William left Bluma alone and walked down the hall towards his study. He noticed an envelope under the front door, minus name or explanation. (Delivered by a young boy who happened to be walking past the Langmeil gates as Henry emerged. 'You Doph Gordon's boy?'

'Yes sir.'

'Do an old fella a favour, will yer?')

William closed his study door and opened the envelope, flattening out an article hastily torn from a magazine, a few passages

338

underlined in red, the author careful to avoid any handwriting which might give him away.

The article was a criticism of the Millenialists, comparing their 'creaky chiliastic ideas' with every Christian folly from the Crusades through to the Salem witch trials. The author, an American professor of theology, used strings of four and five syllable words to bring down the zealots who were harming Christianity – the Christianity of tolerance and understanding, healing and serving the poor.

Eventually the professor got onto dates, and how they could never be trusted. The Millenialists make assumptions which don't hold true, he claimed. A two-page list outlined and demolished them all. William didn't have to look for the ones which applied to him. Someone had already underlined them. For instance, the author argued, the fallacy of the 'cleansing of the sanctuary', outlined in Daniel 8: 14, which *apparently* stood for Christ's return to earth, although this was never actually said. Or the decree of Artaxerxes, *apparently* issued in 457 BC, but if anyone actually bothered to read Daniel ... Oh yes, *Cruden's* had it right, but where in *Cruden's* did it explain how an ancient year equalled 365 days? Who was to say a day in prophetic writing represented a modern year? And even if the maths *was* right, didn't the Bible contradict itself when the Gospel of Mark claimed no man knoweth the time, or when Matthew explained that even the angels in heaven were kept in the dark.

The list went on, scrawls of red down the page, and over onto the next. William stopped reading. This time a year ago he would have got out his matches and burnt the pages. This time he just folded them, replaced them in the envelope and locked them in his desk drawer. It was obvious he'd have to set aside a lot of time to dispute it, through research and reading, commentaries on the Bible and a fair dose of faith. He *could* do it. And maybe he'd make an argument. But who'd believe him, who'd even listen to him anymore? He turned off the light and went into bed, trying to keep this thought out of his head. Over the next few days it would return, and he would feel the ground shifting beneath his feet like never before.

It was a Sunday. The rain cleared and Seymour arrived early to help William with the harvest. Bluma kept them in coffee and cake and towards the end of the first row Seymour said, 'Ellen mentioned you'd come up with another idea?'

Come up with? William emerged from behind vine leaves to explain. By the time he'd finished he knew Seymour wasn't convinced. 'It could be, William . . .' Working on in silence, like Bluma, unable to find words for what he was thinking. William, meanwhile, retreated into his final consolation, the voice on the Hill of Grace, speaking to him and him alone, telling him things that were as true then as they were now. A voice without specifics, challenging him to seek the truth and tell it to others. And what if it took twenty attempts, or three consecutive lifetimes? Stiff. This is what he'd been asked to do.

He sat down, took a small Bible from his pocket and started reading. Seymour sat beside him and listened, hearing words that didn't add up to anything anymore.

'"There be some that stand here which shall not taste of death till they have seen the Kingdom of God come with power . . ."' William looked at Seymour. 'Are you with me?'

Seymour sighed and bowed his head. A pair of crows started up in a distant sugar gum. The sun broke through cloud and the last of the rain on the vine leaves glistened, with every colour all at once. William knew he shouldn't expect a reply, knew that Seymour would never be against him, but would never be with him again. He put the Bible back in his pocket and stood up, taking a heavy bunch of grapes and cutting them from the vine. After a few seconds Seymour followed suit and they worked on together.

Lunch came and went but Bluma was nowhere to be seen, busy next door sewing Arthur's pants.

William Miller believed in the end of the world.

When Bluma came home late from church the next morning,

William was still thinking about it. As she told him about how she'd been publicly welcomed back, he couldn't help but feel, still, that they were all wrong. Standing beside him as he continued harvesting, she said, 'Come in for lunch, I have a surprise.'

'What's that?'

'Come on.'

'Later.'

As she walked back to the house he watched her go and realised he was all alone. No one was with him on the Hill of Grace and no one was with him now. His choices were simple, as simple as snow falling, landing on your arm but melting before you could touch it. He heard Bluma behind him again.

He turned to see his son standing beside a freshly picked vine. Nathan smiled and said, 'G'day, Dad.'

William saw a new man before him, fatter and wind-blown, whiskers growing where they hadn't before, a grin full of optimism and a confident new tone. He looked at Bluma, and then back at Nathan, grasping secateurs as sharp as the day Anthelm had bought them. In the distance someone started hammering, and a woman's voice called out for firewood. A honey-eater flapped its wings as a twig broke beneath its weight and Edna came outside with a wash-basket of Bruno's singlets.

Author's Note

I would like to thank my wife, Catherine, for helping give me time to write. Also, my sons Eamon and Henry, who help keep me in touch with reality. Thanks to Michael Bollen, Gina Inverarity and Ryan Paine for their thoughtful and detailed editing, and to the rest of the team at Wakefield Press. Thanks to my agents Rose Creswell and Annette Hughes who have promoted my work here and overseas. Also, Stephanie, Barbara and many others at the SA Writers' Centre who continue to help and encourage writing in South Australia.

Finally, I would like to acknowledge Noris Ioannou's book, *Barossa Journeys: Into a Valley of Tradition* (Paringa Press, 1997).

Ash Rain

Corrie Hosking

A bushfire in Dell's childhood still haunts her. She dreams up new starts, but her spilling stories cannot over-write the past.

Evvie dances into Dell's life. She has run as far as she can from her family, but her country keeps calling her back.

Evvie's daughter, Luce, is most at home in the company of creatures. All she wants is her collection of bugs and a guinea pig for Christmas.

Dell meets Patrick in the pub, but he's going back to Scotland. Her life finally rupturing, Dell follows. She leaves a hole that Evvie and Luce struggle to fill. They must find each other again, without Dell. And Dell must discover how love works half a world away.

Ash Rain explores the corners and crevices where love can grow in unexpected ways.

Winner of the Adelaide Festival Award
for an Unpublished Manuscript

ISBN 1 86254 634 7

For more information visit www.wakefieldpress.com.au

Spirit Wrestlers

Thomas Shapcott

Spirit Wrestlers is a haunting, poetic novel by one of Australia's finest writers.

It tells of the arrival in rural Australia of a strange religious sect, an ancient Russian primitive group who believe in hard work, pacifism, vegetarianism – and the power of fire.

The group maintains a mysterious, closed existence that nevertheless begins to affect surrounding communities and individual lives. Two teenagers, Johann and Ivan, the local and the newcomer, discover similarities, and differences.

Spirit Wrestlers is a novel about faith, and competing faiths, acts of terror and acts of peace. In language of considerable beauty it speaks straight to the heart about our unsettled, dangerous world.

Follow Johann, Ivan and Olga in a saga of passion, surprise and discovery that you'll never forget.

ISBN 1 86254 645 2

For more information visit www.wakefieldpress.com.au

Wakefield Press is an independent publishing and
distribution company based in Adelaide, South Australia.
We love good stories and publish beautiful books.
To see our full range of titles, please visit our website
at www.wakefieldpress.com.au.

Wakefield Press thanks Fox Creek Wines
and Arts South Australia for their support.